LIES
I
LIVE
BY

ALSO BY LAUREN SABEL

Vivian Divine Is Dead

LIES I LIVE BY

LAUREN SABEL

KATHERINE TEGEN BOOKS
An Imprint of HarperCollins Publishers

Katherine Tegen Books is an imprint of HarperCollins Publishers.

Lies I Live By

www.epicreads.com

Library of Congress Control Number: 2015954394
ISBN 978-0-06-223198-7

Typography by Ellice M. Lee
16 17 18 19 20   PC/RRDH   10 9 8 7 6 5 4 3 2 1
❖
First Edition

To Alex, my baby girl. You make it all worth it every time you smile.

PROLOGUE

It all started when the spoon bent.

I didn't mean to do it. It just happened, completely out of the blue at Stanford University's Christmas party, among Mom's nerdy colleagues and their families. One second I was staring at my reflection in my coffee spoon, waiting for Charlie to stop talking to my mom about college, and the next moment the spoon was bent at a ninety-degree angle in my hand.

"What were you thinking just then?" a voice asked inches from my ear. It was a washed-up looking hippie, with stringy blond hair and the stubble of a beard.

I tucked the spoon into my purse before anyone else could see it. "I was thinking how stirring coffee has just become problematic?"

I glanced over at Charlie and Mom to make sure they hadn't noticed the bent spoon. They hadn't. Not that they would, with Mom trying to convince Charlie of the hundred reasons he should stay in San Francisco forever, rather than taking her only child away from her. It struck me that the problem with being an only child is the word *only*.

"Can you do that again?" the hippie asked, and reached for the spoon in my purse.

I put my hand over my purse. "You do realize that I don't know you, right?"

He sighed and withdrew his hand. "You're right. I should spend the next hour explaining how I know about the migraines that paralyze you several times a week, and how, when you're falling asleep sometimes, you suddenly know things that you shouldn't know, things that are in other people's minds."

I felt my mouth fall open in surprise.

"And then I should explain how you sometimes guess what's going to happen long before it does," he continued, "and you see really terrifying things happening to people, and how you've tried to hide these things from the people you love, scared they'll call you a—"

"Freak," I whispered.

"And after we've gone through all that, assuming we won't have been interrupted by your mom or boyfriend, I'll ask you to bend the spoon again, and you'll do it because you'll know that someone finally understands you, and that your future is going to be very different from now on than how you had ever imagined it to be."

I took the spoon out and handed it to him. He straightened it between both hands, and handed it back to me. "Name's Indigo," he said.

"Mine's Callie," I said, and then, when he smiled in response, I added, "but you probably already know that."

He nodded, and I quickly glanced over at Charlie and Mom, who were still in a passionate discussion about college.

"The things you see in your mind—they're real," Indigo said. "The fact that you can see them makes you a target, and if the people you love know the truth about what you can do"—he nodded toward Mom and Charlie—"they become targets too."

I swallowed hard. "Targets?"

Indigo nodded. "You know what I'm talking about."

That was just it: I did know what he was talking about. I had seen people in my mind dying in the most horrible ways. Somehow I knew that those people were targets, but of whom or why, I had no idea.

Around us, the room buzzed with activity. Kids ran around, spilling sodas out of their plastic Stanford cups, and parents yelled vague instructions to them while carrying on conversations about left-wing politics. In the midst of it all, we were completely unnoticed by the partygoers.

I first checked to make sure Charlie and Mom weren't watching, and then I held the spoon out in front of me. In the curved metal surface, I could see two faces side by side: my confused face and Indigo's smile. When the spoon bent again, his smile got bigger.

"Focus that same energy somewhere else," he said. "Test it."

At the time, I didn't know exactly why I was doing what he told me to do, but it was as if I couldn't do anything else—like this moment had been waiting for me all these years, and I just had to live it. When I focused on a metal light switch across the room, I felt this intense confidence, this feeling that my life was mine alone, and that I could go anywhere and do anything with it. As this feeling surged through me, I felt heat sliding down my arm into my fingertips.

"Test your power," Indigo said.

It was like the word "power" flipped some switch inside me. I lost focus, and my gaze slid a few inches over, to a small metal box.

The fire alarm went off.

Everyone screamed and ran for the exits, grabbing their kids along the way. Across the room, I saw Charlie and Mom headed toward me, and when I looked over, Indigo was gone. Ice-cold drops of sprinkler water pelted my skin and I tensed from the cold. In my fist, where the spoon had been, there was now a card with a phone number on it. Right then, I knew that everything had changed.

I would never be normal again.

CHAPTER ONE

"Callie?" Indigo says from across the darkened room. I open my eyes, suddenly realizing that I've written the word *normal*, and I'm drawing a dark box around it. "What are you seeing now?" he asks. Indigo's voice is so familiar by now it amazes me that I've only known him for a little over a year. So many things have happened since the Christmas party, things I can never say aloud to protect the safety of our nation, and the people I love.

I look at the word *normal* stretched across the white copy paper, mingling with the drawings of cargo ships and parts of radioactive bombs. "Sorry," I whisper, wishing it wasn't too late to hide the paper. I focus again, this time on what I'm supposed to be looking at. *The aircraft carrier.*

I let myself sink into a trance again, and my mind feels like it is twisting, stretching. The world slips past me, faster and faster, until the blur makes me dizzy. I fall into the shattering of it, the rough pieces of images real and imagined merging into a kaleidoscope of colors. As the dizzying colors get brighter, my mind wanders to places thousands of miles away, to an ocean I've seen a hundred times, but never with my own eyes.

"Callie? Are you okay?" The voice comes from far away, as distant as a dying star, and I'm suddenly remembering the day Mom told me Dad was never coming back, and the way the truth crushed me under its unbearable weight. That was back when I valued truth, and finding out I had been lied to meant something—back before I knew everything was a lie.

"Callie?" the voice says, and now faster, dizzier, into a white space, a space without anything, no walls, no boundaries, just the deep blue ocean, and the reflection of something (me? a bird?) skipping across the water. "She's not responding," the voice says, and the backward count begins. "Ten . . . nine . . . eight . . ."

I feel myself being sucked out of this world, and I'm grasping onto nothing, my arms flailing out like a bird.

"Seven . . . six . . . five . . ."

And then I see it.

Weaving in and out of reflections, the aircraft carrier coasts almost motionlessly across the waves. I swoop closer, constricting myself until I fit through the carrier tower's solid steel roof.

I taste metal. I am vapor. I am moving and not moving, all at once.

When I emerge into the control room, I see the Russian captain directing aircraft activity from his stately leather chair. "He's still there," I say aloud.

The counting stops abruptly. "Where's the target?" Indigo asks.

I am aware of the pen in my hand, and the sheets of paper I'm pressing the pen against, but I don't watch as my hand moves in jagged lines across the paper. I just feel my way through the sketch, slowly developing what I see in my mind until it's a clear picture on the paper, a picture of a control room with the captain in his chair and the helmsman steering the ship and, on the deck directly below them, wispy red smoke.

"I see the target," I say.

The red smoke is why I'm here. Unlike the other psychic viewers, I can see a rare type of electromagnetic radiation.

This type of radiation is found in several different metals, many of which power your standard X-ray machine, TV set, or computer chip. Or your deadly, military-grade laser on a Russian aircraft carrier thousands of miles across the ocean.

The radiation is the reason only I can work this case: I'm the only psychic at Branch 13 who can see it. We all have our own specific talents, and this very one just happens to be mine. This is why Indigo calls me his secret weapon. But I don't like thinking of myself, of my mind, as a weapon. Something created to hurt people.

"What's the target's location?" Indigo asks. "And which direction is it facing?"

"It's on the fantail," I respond. "Facing the bow."

"Good," Indigo says, writing down the location on an index card and clipping it onto a sealed manila envelope. "We're done for the day."

There are some clichés that are true.

One of them is that people are like books, full of adventure and romance and dark moments. But if we are all books, my book is more fiction than nonfiction. Even the index is all lies; each chapter is invented to make me look like a normal girl.

The truth is that I'm the kind of book most people

never open. I don't blame them, not really. According to my boyfriend, Charlie, I don't allow anyone to get close enough to me to let them peek inside. Unlike him. Charlie is one of those people with nothing to hide. He assumes the world is an open book, a place where all is revealed if we just read it. That's one of the things I love about him.

He's easy to lie to.

These are the basic facts about me:

I am seventeen.

I live in San Francisco.

I work for a secret government agency.

I am a psychic spy.

CHAPTER TWO

Right now, all over the world, there are psychics searching for dangerous weapons, biological hazards, serial killers. But you'll never know about it. The government will deny it. "That is not reliable information," they will say, not mentioning the hundreds of psychics behind closed doors, accurately finding kidnapped people and murder victims. They won't tell you about how some minds can see below the ground, above the earth, backward and forward in time. And they won't tell you that some of them are housed in mental institutions, or that one of them is your neighbor, or that one of them is below the legal voting age. Or that, for those people, life is a secret they can't share, so they are always alone, except for one place: in their own minds.

Indigo and I may be done viewing for the day, but that doesn't mean I can go home. Our monthly training, as short as it may be, comes way too often for my taste. I sigh and lean back against the couch cushions, my body stiff from hours of viewing.

While Indigo leaves the viewing room to drop the sealed manila envelope into the Completed Sessions file, I crumple up the paper with the word NORMAL on it. He's always saying how lucky I am to have such a gift at my age, and I don't want him to know the truth: that sometimes my ability feels less like a blessing, and more like a curse, pain reserved only for me. I mean, what if I don't want to see the future? What if I just want a normal life? I toss the crumpled-up paper at the trash can, but it bounces off the edge and rolls across the floor. I pick it up, back up a few feet, and throw it again, but I'm an inch too far to the left.

"So much for practice making perfect," I mutter under my breath.

"Don't forget about training this afternoon," Indigo says, coming back into the viewing room. He picks up the crumpled paper and pauses by the trashcan to unfold it. "Normal?" he asks, raising his eyebrows.

I shrug. "I obviously wasn't writing about you."

He grins. "Obviously."

"Let's just do this training thing," I say, planting my scuffed combat boots on the floor. I'm never excited to stay late after work, as much as I love what I do. By the time I've viewed a full session, and then written an extensive deposition of the day's session, I'm exhausted. But I admit I'm lucky: unlike Martina and Pat, I don't emerge with mental bruises from my training with Indigo. He tries to break into my mind, of course, and I try to defend my mind in return, a sort of mental sparring, but when he gets in, he doesn't yell "Yahtzee!" the way he does with the adult viewers—he just irritates me exceptionally well.

"Still hiding that acceptance letter from your mom?" Indigo asks calmly, sitting down in the chair across from me.

"Read my mind much?" I joke, although I know our gifts don't work like that. Using psychic powers is like finding a single grain of sand in a desert: you have to focus deeply on what you're looking for, and after sifting through the desert, one grain shines a little more brightly than the others, and that's what you focus on. It's not something we can just do, like flipping a light switch. It often takes hours to do one session, and since the process is so brain-draining, one session is all Indigo allows us to do per day.

"Nope, no mind reading going on here," Indigo says.

"You're just predictable." He balls up the paper again and throws it at the trash can. "And the crowd goes wild!" He grins.

"Yay," I say without enthusiasm.

Indigo looks at me closely. "For this training, try to close down the emotion."

"You do know you're saying that to a teenage girl, right?" I ask, kicking my combat boots impatiently into the floor. "Almost ready," I say. I pull out my Chapstick and run it over my lips, and then flick some of my hair out of my eyes. "Okay, I'm ready."

"You don't need to do your nails or anything?" Indigo jokes.

I look down at my unpainted fingernails, made worse by my chewed-to-hell cuticles. When I'm stressed, they're the first to go. "Going à la nude," I say. "Watch out."

Indigo picks up a file folder on the table and flips through the worksheets we've already completed in the past dozen training sessions. "Here we are," he says, stopping at a file. "Reading body language."

"Not again," I groan.

Indigo nods, and I can tell that there's no negotiating on this even though we've been over it at least five times. I know that reading body language is important since the people I'm watching in my sessions are often lying, and for the sake of national security, I need to know exactly what they're saying and what it really means. If I was able to reach the second level of psychic power—*influencing* through either mind control or altering physical matter, like bending metal, I would be able to not only read minds, but change people's decisions and environments. Indigo tries to push me to get there, but ever since my first and only time metal bending, I haven't come close. So far I can only watch things happen, hand over the information I see, and hope the CIA does something about it.

"Ask me a question," Indigo says, officially starting the session. He settles his face into a perfectly blank stare.

"Am I your favorite viewer at the agency?"

"No." Indigo's face stays as blank as a sheet of paper, but I notice that his eyebrows draw slightly upward, making soft lines appear across his forehead, and he purses his lips minutely. Barely noticeable, but telltale micro-expressions of someone who's lying.

"Easy peasy," I say, rubbing my hands together to let him know I'm just getting started.

"You can't ask questions you already know the answer to," Indigo complains.

"It's possible you could have another favorite here," I respond.

"Like who?"

I shrug. "Not satisfied with my question? Fine. You ask one, then."

"How about this one?" Indigo says. "Tell me which one of these things is a lie: I was born in Indiana under a different name. My father's name was Joe and he had three cows and a goat named Chicken Little. I got As in school but decided college wasn't for me."

I watch Indigo carefully throughout the entire story, noticing every time his eyes shift to the right or he shuffles his feet or touches his mouth. "You were a C student," I finally say, and he nods. "Real name?" I ask.

"Gary," he says. "Changed it when I moved here." Indigo glances at his watch, and a concerned look flickers over his face. He abruptly stands up and smooths out the wrinkles in his royal blue pants with glow-in-the-dark stars. Sometimes I can't believe I work for a dude who looks like his own constellation. "Let's cut this one short," Indigo says. "Say hi to your mom for me."

"You know how she feels about this whole thing." I sigh.

Indigo's still under the illusion that my mom signed the legal form for me to work at Branch 13 as a minor. Even though the form said my position was a "governmental internship," if Mom found out even one hint of what I was doing, she would dig until she found the truth. And as Indigo warned me in the beginning—if people know what I do, they could end up being targets of the criminals we are searching for—I knew I couldn't take the chance. So I threw the legal form in front of Mom as she ran out of the house, late for a lecture on astrophysics. She didn't even ask what she was signing, and "field trip" more than sufficed. To this day, I just maintain that Mom's uncomfortable with the whole thing, and Indigo never brings it up or asks to meet her.

"She'll come around eventually," Indigo says.

I stand up and shrug into my faded hoodie. "Tomorrow, then?"

Indigo salutes me. "*Mañana, chica*. The good fight continues."

CHAPTER THREE

I'm not surprised that my house is empty when I get home. It's more like a show home, a modern series of glass boxes placed together, never intended for "family use." Of course, my mom didn't ever expect to have a child. Because of something to do with Mom's uterus, she lived childless until she was forty. And then—surprise! I was born with a full head of jet black hair and eyes gray as steel, and "small as a baby kitten," she always says. I'm still on the short side, but that's the only thing small about me, at least according to Mom. She always describes the day of my birth as both "amazing" and "quite painful," like she accidentally shoved a metal spear into her foot, and had to leave work early to get it out. But Mom's like that; she doesn't sugarcoat things. That's why she refuses to have a television in our house. "It's the opiate of the masses," she told me when I was little. "Invented to keep us dumb."

I take off my shoes by the door and cross the stark white living room into our gleaming black marble kitchen. Like every Tuesday night during the school year, there's a note on the counter.

I'll be home after class. Make yourself some dinner, xo Mom, it says.

The XO makes me laugh. Mom is kind and loving, but she's not a hugger, not by a long shot. I wrench open the fridge, reach past a bottle of white wine and a carton of skim milk, and grab the box of leftover pizza.

"Pineapples and ham," I mutter. "What a combo. Who would've thunk it?" I pick off the juiciest piece of pineapple and pop it into my mouth, and then grab a *National Geographic* out of the pile of magazines on the kitchen counter. It flops open it to a picture of white shuttered houses climbing a hillside. Now that's the life. Peaceful. Innocent. Most likely radioactive-metal free.

I finish my pizza, and then I take a spoon out of the silverware drawer and try to bend it with my mind. It doesn't work. Indigo says that many psychics can bend spoons occasionally—it's a recognized sign that you might have extrasensory powers—but it doesn't mean you can bend metal with your mind on a regular basis. It's more like a one-time entrance fee to a very exclusive club—a club I will never fit in to, because after that night, to my endless frustration, I've never been able to bend metal again.

I hear a knock on the front door. I drop the spoon and flip around to see Charlie leaning slightly into the doorway, his black hair falling into his copper eyes. "Sand piles," he says, and grins. His easy smile wraps around me, makes me feel warm inside.

"Hoover Tower," I respond, coming into the living room to meet him. Charlie and I have this secret game: we say what reminded us of each other during the day. We've been playing it for almost six months, and we've never missed a day. Sometimes it's a bird fleeting across the sky, or a poster of a cat hanging from a tree. But today, it's absurdly phallic.

"I thought you might be home," he says, coming in and closing the door lightly behind him. "And alone." As soon as the door is closed, he cups his hands around my face and kisses me. His lips are soft, and he smells like salty earth. "Oh, and as rockin' hot as ever."

Charlie can always make me blush. He's the only one who can, though. No matter how many guys compliment my gray eyes (read: boobs) or shiny black hair (read: butt), he's the only guy whose words really mean something to me.

"Hmmm . . ." I fade into his arms, grateful that out of

all the people at Bleeding Heart Catholic School—or as we called it, Bloody Hell—we found each other. And when I graduated high school last December—a semester earlier than Charlie and everyone else in my grade, thanks to Indigo's need for me to start viewing immediately, and full time—he was the one person I missed seeing in the halls every day.

Charlie bites my lip, and I shove him playfully, and we get into an all-out wrestling match, right there in the living room. When we're finished, and I'm pinned beneath him on the couch, sweating, he asks, "Hoover Tower?"

"Unusual choice," I admit. Two hundred eighty-five feet tall, topped with forty-eight bells that President Hoover declared should only be rung for peace, it is not exactly sexy. But sturdy, and strong, and always there. "Sand piles?"

"Ah, not so much the object, but the shape," he says, eyeing my chest.

I slap his fingers away from my boobs, and he grins and kisses me again, his strong fingers wrapping in my hair. "I missed you," he says. "Miss me?"

"Occasionally," I say, although my heart is pounding, *yes, always.*

"Work okay?" he asks, and I nod. "And baby Emma?"

"She's fine," I say, kissing him again to stop him from talking. Emma is the imaginary child at my imaginary nanny job. She has a bedwetting problem, and will only eat macaroni and cheese, and her stuffed turtle is named Turtle, mostly because the people at the CIA have absolutely no imagination.

His lips brush my cheeks, my ears, my neck, and I feel my body unconsciously lift up to meet him. "Bronze ring," he says. "In a store window."

"What?" I mumble against his shirt.

"It reminded me of you," he says, "of us."

Us. I still find it amazing that two letters can spell out a whole life.

Still hovering over me, he whispers, "Come with me."

I sit up, biting my lip, and he slides off me onto the couch. I am sure he's going to ask me about it again, and I'll have to say no again. I hate saying no to Charlie. "Where?" I sigh. *Don't say New York.*

"Upstairs?" He whispers, picking up on my hesitation to get into the New York argument. I'm relieved that I won't have to lie again, although one is already forming on my lips. But right now, I just want to forget that I ever got accepted into NYU, forget that, as much as I would love to go to college in New York with Charlie, my job here, as secret as it is, is the most meaningful, most important thing in my life. I mean, if you could save people's lives from radioactive weapons and actively chose not to, would you feel good about that?

I run my hands down Charlie's chest until I can feel the sharp curve of his waist. "Why not right here?" I respond. "We're alone."

"Sure," he breathes against my cheek, then finds my lips.

"Callie?" A voice calls through the living room window, and Charlie nips at my lip hard enough to make me squeal, half in pleasure, half in pain. "Calliope?" Mom calls again. Calliope—the muse of eloquence, daughter of the god Zeus.

I push Charlie off me and jump to a standing position beside the couch. "In the living room."

"Home already?" Mom asks through the window.

I get up and unlock the front door. "It's seven o'clock," I remind her. "Most normal people have eaten by now."

"Oh, Cal, you and this normal thing." Mom steps into the living room, stopping short when she sees that I'm not alone. "Charlie, what a pleasure to see you."

"The pleasure's mine, ma'am," Charlie says, getting to his feet.

She waves her hand for him to sit down, and he settles back on the couch. "How's your mom?" Mom asks, as if she and Grace have anything in common. Mom's an academic; at fifty-seven, she runs the science department at Stanford, does occasional work for NASA, and uses words like *existential disorientation* in a regular sentence. Charlie's mom is a masseuse, is obsessed with healthy things like brown rice and seaweed, and doesn't call parties "necessary social intervention." I love Grace.

"Mom's fine, thanks for asking," Charlie says.

"Glad to hear it," Mom says, and then she blushes, so I know she's lost something even more important than her house keys this time. "Has either of you seen my phone?"

Mom says she doesn't save room in her brain for the small things, and with her genius intellect, I believe it. But sometimes I feel like the parent, following her around and picking up her misplaced books and wire-rimmed glasses.

I scan my memory. "Um . . . kitchen. Third drawer on the left, second row, two items back," I say.

Mom pops into the kitchen and I hear her banging drawers open. "Found it!" She steps back into the living room, her house keys jingling from one hand and cell phone from the other. "They were both in there," she says. "But I've definitely lost my knitting needles."

"And your yarn," I remind her.

She smiles. "I'll order Chinese. What do you want? Tofu with vegetables for you and ginger shrimp for Charlie?"

"Actually—"

"That sounds good," she continues, dialing the number to the Happy Fun Restaurant and switching to Mandarin. *"Nín hao."* Mom speaks three different languages fluently, and talks about string theory like it's an item on her grocery store list. She's a lifelong MENSA member and always invites me to the meetings. She says that with my IQ, I can get in, but what would we talk about? Math equations? No, thank you. "I'll leave you two lovebirds alone," Mom says, getting off the phone. She presses a fifty-dollar bill into my hand, but I shake my head and hand it back.

"I've got it," I say, pulling my wallet out of my back pocket. Ever since I started working for Branch 13, I've noticed how Mom looks at me like I'm an adult whenever I offer to pay for things. Mom even brags that she's never seen anyone more dedicated to a nannying job than I am, and raves to her boyfriend, Richard, about how I contribute to the household expenses. I take a couple of twenties out of my wallet, not missing the look of respect I see on Mom's face for paying my own way.

Of course, I'd work at Branch 13 even if I didn't make any money.

The disappearance of my almost daily migraines would be reason enough on its own. Indigo says that psychic viewing helps because the part of my mind that I view with gets tired by the end of each session, and so a headache doesn't build in the unused tension in my brain. When it comes down to it, I'll take mental pain over physical pain any day.

"The food will be here in forty-five minutes," Mom says. "Call me when dinner arrives." She bounds up the stairs, checking her phone as she goes, and I sink back down on the couch and cross my legs. Charlie does the same, and I am relieved to feel his knees pressing against mine.

"What do you want to do?" he asks. "We've got half an hour."

"Let's go to the Panhandle," I say. "I don't want to miss the sunset."

Charlie and I have a tradition: we watch the sunset together several times a week. Even if we can only meet for fifteen minutes, we watch it lower its big blinking eye over the ocean. We watch night come rolling in, making us invisible to everyone but each other.

The Panhandle is that narrow stretch of grass leading up to Golden Gate Park, and eventually, Ocean Beach and the cold, growling Pacific. It isn't wide enough for anyone to do anything with it, which is why we like it. Its uselessness, mixed with its stubborn insistence to exist, is heartwarming. And it's just at the end of the block.

When we get there, the sun is fainting on the horizon, painting the park and the houses that line it a creamy orange. As the sunlight rolls in over the hills, consuming houses in its steady push inland, it reminds me of the red smoke from my session with Indigo, and I shiver at the thought of the Russian laser somewhere out at sea, maybe headed for our shores.

"So, when do you wanna meet up next Saturday?"

Charlie asks, breaking into my thoughts.

I stare at him blankly. "Next Saturday?"

"My show?" Charlie looks at me with a mix of confusion and hurt.

Of course—Charlie's photography show! It's only the biggest thing that's ever happened to him. Charlie takes these amazing photographs of the insides of vacant buildings. He's already gotten into one of the best art schools in the country, starting this fall. *In New York.*

I turn to him, suddenly noticing how the air is packed tight with the smell of eucalyptus. "Starts at six?" I ask quickly, hoping he didn't notice that I'd forgotten.

Charlie nods. He's chewing on his bottom lip, something he does only when he's extremely nervous, and I know that he needs me there. "Can you meet me at two at our favorite noodle place?" he asks. "And then we can hang the photos for the show."

"Two o'clock sharp," I promise.

A look of relief spreads over his face. "Thanks, Cal. Because the other photographer backed out at the last minute, so it's just me. My first *solo* show."

"Congratulations," I exclaim, tears popping into my eyes. I blink them back and look up at the trees raising their thick trunks into the sky, their waxy leaves tinted buttery yellow by the sunset. *Be happy for Charlie*, I tell myself, but *he's moving on* is what I hear instead.

"There are sunsets in New York," Charlie reminds me. "You could get a nannying job there. Or take some college classes."

"I'm going to San Francisco State, remember?"

"But you could—"

"No. It would break Mom's heart," I respond.

"But your mom's got Richard now. It's not like she's dating some jerk academic, or wasting away at home, waiting for the man who will never return," Charlie says.

I'm stunned that he brought it up. I don't think we've talked about my father since the day Charlie's dad passed away last year. At the time, I'd never talked about my father before, not to anyone; but I'd never seen anyone so sad, like all of the life had been sucked out of him, so I told Charlie everything I knew. It wasn't much, just some snippets I've picked up from my mom over the years, and the entire knowledge of my father took less than half a minute.

"As far as I know, the story was completely made up," I admitted to Charlie at the time, and then told him the story about Mom getting her PhD at Stanford, and her affair with her professor. Supposedly, while Mom was getting her degree in some obscure branch of nuclear physics, they fell in love, made me, and spent two years shacking up in faculty housing. Then one day, when I was about two years old, he resigned his position at Stanford and disappeared. She could never find him again.

Like I said, probably bullshit. My father was probably a truck driver.

"My so-called dad has nothing to do with it," I say, and I wonder if that's true.

"But . . . do you ever . . ." Charlie pauses, "wonder about him?"

"All the time." I kick the leaves with my combat boots. "Like why he left us. And why he didn't care enough to stick around and watch me grow up. And if I'm like him at all." I watch the leaves floating through the air. "But maybe it's better not to know."

Charlie shrugs. "You're probably right," he says. "Maybe it's better that way."

"What do you mean by that?"

"I just mean that he could be anybody, you know? Maybe he's a billionaire sailing the Caribbean on his yacht," Charlie says. "Or maybe he's a bum smoking pot in Haight-Ashbury."

"Sometimes I think that Mom lost him under all her paperwork."

"That's entirely possible," Charlie responds.

"But what would I say even if I did find him? I'm the daughter you abandoned fifteen years ago?" I shake my head in disgust. I'm expecting Charlie to agree with me, but instead, he turns his head away, and I see that he's barely managing to hold back tears. "Why do you ask?" I continue, more gently now.

"I just thought about how much I miss my dad, and how I'd trade anything . . ." Charlie trails off. He spreads his fingers in the sky so they cover all six of the visible stars, and then moves each finger like he's pushing the buttons of stars one by one. "My dad will never see my show," he says, choking up.

Charlie's photography show next week. That is what this is about.

"He'll never know that what he taught me paid off, all those hours we spent," he continues. "I wish he could be there."

"He will be," I say quietly, which I know is cheesy, but it's the only thing I can think of, especially since my mind is screaming at me, *At least you got to know him.* I blink the tears back from my own eyes. "And I'll be there, and your mom, and Colin. We'll all be there to support you."

Charlie mumbles a response, but I'm not listening. I'm thinking about how much I wish I could go with him to New York next fall, and how as much as I'd have trouble leaving Mom, I can't tell him the real reason I can't go: the government is depending on me. If I'm not around to find deadly radioactive weapons, no one will be.

CHAPTER FOUR

I linger in front of the door to my building the next morning, enjoying the appearance of being a normal college freshman. Since my office looks like any other redbrick building on the Berkeley campus, sometimes I pretend I'm a student here. For a moment, I imagine that my worst fear is failing my English exam instead of being unable to stop a dirty bomb from hitting US soil.

But as soon as I pull the building's front door open, I sink back into this reality, the one that stars me as the youngest psychic viewer ever to work at Branch 13, a private agency that contracts exclusively with the CIA. When Indigo found me over a year ago, he explained to me why it was essential that no one knew about my job as a psychic viewer.

"If the criminals we are chasing think someone we love could have some information about our missions, they'll stop at nothing to extract the information from them." Hence that whole field trip thing with my mom.

The front door closes behind me, sealing me into the small space in front of the X-ray machine. Other than the whirring sound of the conveyer belt and the ever-present sound of National Public Radio, the lobby is silent.

"Hello?" I call, knowing that Anthony won't be able to hear me on his hourly smoke break. Anthony's our security guard, but he's about as protective as a three-toed sloth, and just as fast. His beer belly is as round as his balding head, and he couldn't run if his feet were on fire; but worse than all that is his insistence on talking about himself in third person.

While I wait for Anthony to return from wherever it is he's disappeared to, I listen to the radio. The reporter is talking about a satellite that was just shot into space.

"It will enter a ring of satellites twenty-three thousand miles above the earth's surface," the reporter says. "Regarding the recent solar activity, NASA says—"

"Anthony's back from the dead," Anthony announces, returning to the front desk. He whistles under his breath. "And no one better to bring me back to life than you."

"Good morning," I respond, ignoring his flirtatious

tone like Indigo has advised me to do. I drop my bag onto the X-ray machine's rubber tongue and walk through the metal detector, wondering what I look like with just my bones exposed.

"It'd be a better morning on the back of a Harley, out on the open road with you," Anthony says from behind the front desk. He flips off the radio without taking his eyes off my naked, bony body on the screen. "Still fighting the good fight?" he asks, clearly copying Indigo's famous phrase.

I nod, wondering which fight Anthony's talking about. Of course, I'll never know. Branch 13's number one rule of psychic viewing is never to psychically spy on anyone outside of work. "You can lose your mind doing it," Indigo says. "Without the proper controls, you can enter a session, and never come out."

It's still tempting to sneak a peek inside someone's mind, especially when I can't tell what Charlie's thinking, but I always remind myself how Indigo said that human minds are made up of millions of little parts, all of them working together like gears of a clock. If even one of those parts gets pushed too far and cracks, the whole thing falls apart.

"Fighting the good fight?" I repeat, answering Anthony's question. "Until hell freezes over."

"Anthony feels the same way," Anthony jokes, "but he's on the side of evil."

"Me too," I respond, making devil horns with my index fingers. "Evil all the way."

Even though I'm kidding, I can't help but think about Indigo's initial warning about letting the evil in this job affect me too deeply. Back then, I didn't really understand what he was saying. It was only later that I realized how evil the world really could be. But by then, I'd helped Branch 13 stop an armed terrorist from boarding a plane to Newark, and I knew I could save lives with my gift. I knew then that I'd never walk away from this job, no matter what it cost me.

"Keep up the fight," I say to Anthony. I pick up my backpack and hurry upstairs to the staff room before the last of the coffee runs out.

The staff room is a tiny windowless box with a candy machine, a table with four chairs, and a cheap coffee pot. Indigo claims our entire staff room fits into one stall of the CIA headquarters bathroom, that's how low on the totem pole we are. Since Branch 13 is funded by the CIA, and we get all of our orders from them, we consider ourselves part of the government. But since they don't want to be publicly responsible for a band of freaks we have a contractual agreement: we don't frighten the taxpayers by being openly on the government payroll, and in exchange, we are allowed to take on extra clients if we want. Not that I've ever seen any extra clients.

In fact, I've never seen *anybody* I don't know come into the office, I think as I wander into the recovery room, where we hang out and "de-stress" after our sessions. I pause for a moment, taking in pale blue walls, which Indigo painted specifically because blue is supposed to be a calming color. He's also placed soft couches haphazardly around the room, and as always, the lights are kept dim.

I bypass the recovery room's empty couches and pull open the staff room door, happy to see there's a bit of coffee left at the bottom of the pot. I pour myself the watery coffee, add lots of sugar and creamer, and am heading out to the recovery room when a young guy I've never seen before struts into the office, his arm around Indigo.

"Turbulence, the whole way here," he's saying, but he stops when he sees me, his lips slightly apart, his electric blue eyes tingling across my skin.

"Callie, meet Jasper. Jasper, Callie," Indigo says. He looks back and forth between us. "You'll be working together."

I have a boyfriend, I remind myself, but those thoughts break apart in the force of Jasper's eyes. He crooks a smile at me, this kind of lopsided, joyful smile, more like a mischievous child than a teenage guy. His eyelashes are long, curling up at the ends, and his lips look full and soft. *Why am I looking at his lips?*

"Cal-lie," he says, splitting my name into two distinctly separate words. "What's going on, Cal-lie?"

I find it charming; I can't help it. Indigo obviously does too: he's glowing with pride like he found a shiny penny at the bottom of a mossy fountain.

"Looks like work, smells like work," I force myself to answer. "Must be work."

The grin gets wider. Jasper rubs his closely shaved head with the palm of his hand. He has on a silver ring, thick and choppy, and a bracelet made of wooden beads. "I see that." His mouth turns up at the corner, making him cuter than before. My stomach clenches.

Seriously, Callie? Get it together. He's not as good-looking as Charlie—not nearly. Charlie's magazine-cover material, and this guy, well, he's almost as short as me, and the hairs on his hands are coarse; he's no beauty queen. But there's something about him, something magnetic, something mesmerizing.

"Callie's the one I was telling you about," Indigo says.

"Saving the world from radiation," Jasper says.

"All in a day's work," I respond.

"Jasper just transferred here from our New York office," Indigo says.

I've never met anyone from that office. It's the office I'd like to work in someday, but it's only for psychics who can influence events, not just watch them happen.

"Welcome to the happier coast," I say. "You planning on staying long?"

"Long as I can," he says.

"Just leave before you start saying *groovy*."

"Good advice."

"I've got lots," I say, trying to look away. "Ask anytime."

"I will," he says. His blue eyes are drinking me in, making me dizzy, like I'm swirling around and around in a whirlpool. "And really, the pleasure is mine."

My hand tucks a strand of my hair behind my ear, and I grimace at my own awkward preening, but he doesn't seem to notice. "I didn't say it was a pleasure."

Caught in the magnetism of his stare, I nod my head quickly and walk past him into the recovery room. I've only gotten a few steps when I feel his hand on my arm, and a warm tingling feeling goes through my body. "Good to meet you, too," he says.

I'm still shaky from my encounter with Jasper, but I quickly pull myself together and join Indigo in the viewing room. It's nothing much, just a small beige room with no windows, the only decoration a red-and-white Mickey Mouse balloon hovering near the ceiling. There are psychic spies all over the world, and nothing is more valuable to them than seeing into the secrets now lodged in my mind. That's where the balloon comes in. If those psychics picture me in this room, and they see a Mickey Mouse balloon, they won't believe they are seeing the truth, because what self-respecting government program would keep a floating Mickey Mouse balloon in their top-secret headquarters?

I lie down on the couch in the dim room and stare at the ceiling. I'm shaking to my core, trembling in a way I never have before, not even with Charlie. *Why does Jasper have such an effect on me?* Crossing my arms over my chest, I breathe deeply, and make myself focus on my work.

Indigo sits down in the chair across from me, a sealed manila envelope containing my target in one hand. It wouldn't be helpful to open it—inside, there's just a set of numbers that don't mean anything to me, or at least not to my conscious mind; they are just there to trigger the viewer's vision. It's also double blind—not only do I not know what the numbers are or what they represent, neither does Indigo. The only person who does know is hidden behind a desk somewhere at the CIA, and will forever remain anonymous.

"Was it just me, or was there some serious energy going on there?" Indigo asks me.

I cross my arms over my chest and smile. "Shut up."

"Don't freak out," he says, and holds his hands in the air. "I'm just saying Anthony's gonna have some competition."

"Anthony?"

"And every other man who looks at you like you hung the moon," Indigo says.

I roll my eyes. "Don't flatter me. I know what you're doing."

"What am I doing?" Indigo asks innocently.

"You need a favor."

"That's not true!" Indigo protests, but then pauses. "Well yes, it is. You up for doing me a favor?"

"As if I'd say no."

He grins. "Can you make Jasper feel at home here? He's a talented guy, but a bit rough around the edges."

"Of course," I say proudly, but inside, I feel a surge of anxiety. "Will we be monitoring each other?"

"From time to time," Indigo says, which surprises me. Indigo usually insists on monitoring me himself. Since Branch 13's west coast office is so small, with Indigo in charge and only a handful of psychics beneath him, I've only been monitored by other viewers a few times, and since we all have different schedules, I rarely see anyone other than Indigo anyway. It doesn't bother me too much, but it does make it hard to get any monitoring experience. Over the past year, I've only been a monitor a couple of times, and only when Indigo asked me to.

"Consider it done," I say.

"Thanks," Indigo says, and I nod. "Now let's get to work." He puts the sealed envelope on the table in front of me, and then presses Record on the remote control, which starts up a video camera in the upper right corner of the room. *Click.*

Every psychic has their own method, their personal way to get into the zone. Some people can go straight in, bypassing the voices yelling about the forgotten house keys and the undone errands. But not me. I start by imagining a brown leather suitcase. I open it, and one by one, stuff each anxiety and distraction into it, which, sad to say, takes a while. Then I close and lock it. I'll get it on the way out. It's always there, waiting.

Jasper flashes through my mind again, but I push him away. Instead, I imagine myself on a boat in the ocean, putting on scuba gear, and getting off the boat into the warm water. I drift toward the ocean floor, slowly adding small weights until I'm ten feet from the bottom, from full sleep. I glance up at the surface of the water. It is mirrored, reflecting the gray-blue sky that doesn't really exist. That is awake. So I stay here, hovering between awake and asleep, living and dream, for several hours, until the visions start to come.

At first they trickle in, just dim sights and sounds, but then red smoke blinds my eyes. An explosion rocks through my body, and the images come fast and furious, images I can feel but can't quite see: a door flying open, a window shattering, red smoke surging and leaping across the horizon. My breath catches in my throat as the smell of burning hair prickles up my nose, and roaring pounds through my ears, eating up all other sounds.

Through the darkness, the red smoke clears, and for a brief second, I see a logo painted onto the side of a building, and then it's gone. At that moment, something washes over me—a feeling of falling fast, like when you go over a hill on a roller coaster and your body drops while your stomach hovers there, in midair.

I hear Indigo's voice, bringing me back to the moment: "Where's the target?" he asks. I suck on the word *target*, a hot stone in my throat.

I spin around, trying to locate the source of the radioactive red smoke, but I can't find it. My nostrils burn, and I sputter out a cough. When I look down at the ground, my thumbnail automatically presses into the thin skin of my index finger, jolting a sharp pain through me.

Beneath the layers of red smoke is a body, plastered facedown on the sidewalk, covered in glass shards and blood.

After our session, I can still picture the body trapped under the red smoke, and how the smell of blood mixed with the odor of burning hair.

From the chair across from me, Indigo is watching me

finish writing my observations on a post-session file. I glance up at him, and although he doesn't say anything, I know he wants to.

"Silence doesn't fit you," I say.

Indigo leans forward in his leather chair. He props his elbows on his knees, and rests his chin on his upturned palms, like he's holding up the weight of his face. "What happened in there? You were kind of . . . mumbling."

Although I know better by now, I touch my ankles to make sure blisters haven't bubbled up on my skin. Even though I couldn't actually feel the radiation pour over me, my mind imagined the pain, which can sometimes feel just as real.

I draw jagged flames around the word *RADIATION* on my long post-session file, and then I push the paper across the table toward him.

He glances down at the paper and then back up at me. "Any hint of a location?"

I shake my head. "It was dark. But Indigo, there was a person caught in it." I shiver at the memory.

Indigo takes a note on his notepad. "Did you see anything else?" he asks.

"I saw a logo on a building, but it was only for a second." I pause, trying to remember exactly what it looked like. "It looked like an infinity sign, but each side was an oval-shaped earth. Like two earths glued together." I wipe my sweaty hands on my jeans, and the denim catches at my dry skin.

"Do you know *when* it happens?" Indigo asks.

"I must have missed the subtitles," I joke. Since psychic viewers never know the exact time we see something, we can never assume it's happening at that moment. Sometimes we'll be viewing a weapons manufacturing warehouse, for instance, and see people building a cannon, and that will be a dead giveaway that we've gone back to a time when people actually used cannons. But that's our only clue. There's no flashing year at the bottom of the screen. Then, after we emerge from the past, present, or future, we report what we see, try to wipe our hands of it, and go home for the day.

Home. I rub my fists in my eyes. Even though it seems like one session per day wouldn't take a long time, it always does. Between preparing to view, viewing, and writing about it afterward, it takes several hours of concentrated mind work every day. And after a session this intense, I really want to go home and get in bed, curl up with a cup of coffee, but I promised Charlie I'd meet him after work.

"Something about the place felt familiar," I say, standing up from the couch.

"Like you'd been there before?" Indigo asks. "Off the record, of course."

"Off the record? Maybe." I get to my feet and head

toward the door. "You homeward bound?"

Indigo shakes his head. He never stops working. "But you should be," he says, bringing his hand to his forehead in a fake salute. "Good work today."

Thinking of how my mom would wince at my terrible faux Spanish accent, I say, "*Hasta mañana, compadre.*"

That makes Indigo smile. And since I'm the only person around the office who can make him smile, that's worth any price.

CHAPTER FIVE

Even at four o'clock on a Wednesday, Pier 45 is humming with activity.
There's a merry-go-round playing circus music, a bunch
of booths catering to tourists (really, who else buys sand
paintings?), and a cluster of food stalls. As I walk past
the booths, glancing at the sea lions barking from their
floating wooden docks at the end of the pier, I'm so lost
in thought I almost run into the homeless man shouting, "Beware, earthlings! A great flood is coming!" but I
manage to avoid him just in time and duck into the Musée
Méchanique.

In the entrance, the creepy chuckle of Laughing Sal
scratches like steel wool against my nerves. "Har, har, har,"

the giant doll laughs, her mechanical body jerking back and forth, like someone having a seizure in slow motion.

"Charlie?" I move down the aisle as quickly as I can and maneuver through hundreds of old machines. Charlie usually works in the back, near the plaster model of a two-headed baby.

"Charlie?" I call again, and hear a snort of laughter coming from Death Row.

Death Row is a row of machines that Charlie and I are obsessed with. My favorite is an old machine called Execution. When you put a penny in, a little wooden character comes out of the tiny brick building, puts a noose around his own neck, and gets hanged. *Can't find more fun for a penny anywhere,* Charlie always says.

I hear Charlie's sturdy laugh again, and then, behind the animatron that continually vomits onto a pile of old bottles, I suddenly see who Charlie is talking to.

She's the kind of blonde that makes you think she really has more fun. She has on these skinny jeans—I mean blood-clot-inducing tight—and a T-shirt that says *New York City* in cursive over the Statue of Liberty. *How original.* But it's low cut and high on her tummy, and only a blind man wouldn't notice the glistening of her tanned skin.

I quickly turn away, and pretend to be interested in the animatron spewing puke until I feel Charlie come up behind me.

"Hey, Cal," Charlie says, hugging me around the waist from behind, and then turning me around to face him. "Sorry 'bout that. I was with a customer."

When he says customer, his eyes fleet over to the girl. She's putting a coin in the belly dancer machine, a machine no one but dirty old men pay for. *Right. She's here for the machines.* I raise my eyebrows, and I swear Charlie blushes.

"New in town," Charlie says, and then, turning away, "I'll get my stuff."

Charlie and I do what we always do when I meet him at work. We sit on the wall over the ocean, cracking soft-shell crabs open with our bare fingers and dipping their thick white flesh into tin cups of melted butter and garlic. I stuff a piece of crab in my mouth and lick the butter off my fingers as it dribbles down to my wrist.

Below us, the sea lions are barking at one another on their floating piers. They are slick and shiny, like tar-covered dogs. They have these ridiculous whiskers, and they flap their webbed feet at each other as they scramble to get onto the dock. I laugh aloud as a tiny sea lion pushes a giant one into the water. He swims around, looking for a place to climb up and sun himself in the last few rays of light.

"Freshwater pearl at sunrise," Charlie says. He points

across the pier at a wooden booth painted with cheesy ocean waves, advertising how, for $14.99, anyone can crack open an oyster and fish out a pearl. A couple of tourists are there, and a little boy is squealing in delight as he pries open an oyster.

"Belly dancer machine," I say, and I can tell he's disappointed that I didn't think of him until an hour ago. *When he was flirting with that girl.* I frown, tracing the girl's silhouette against the darkening window in my mind.

"Callie?" I feel Charlie's warm hand on my arm, and my heart slows down its frantic beat. He rubs his thumb above the blue veins in my inner wrist, and I take a deep breath. "What's wrong?"

I focus on the biggest sea lion, now finding a place on the dock between two glistening black bodies. I wish I could tell Charlie about my real job before these lies eat me alive, but it's all trapped in me, shrouded in secret, smothering me from the inside. "Who was that girl?" I ask him instead, looking at my heels bouncing inches off the sea wall with each swing of my legs.

"Which one?" he asks. I look up at him, briefly catching his eyes before he looks away. "She's going to Pratt next year."

She's going to Pratt? With Charlie? I don't want to look him in the eyes, so I watch two sea lions fighting for the center of the pier. Other sea lions are bailing, diving off the dock, leaving the two of them alone on the wooden slat. I picture the NYU acceptance letter in my desk, and an uncomfortable sensation grows in my chest, like I don't quite fit into my body.

"I asked about her New York T-shirt, and she mentioned she was going to study art at Pratt next year. I said we should hook up for coffee sometime and talk about the photography program," Charlie says.

Hook up for coffee? When does Charlie ever talk like that?

"She's from SoCal," Charlie continues.

The horrors of Hollywood, and deserts, and botoxed mindless blondes. "She looks like it."

"She's nice," Charlie says defensively, and I feel my skin prickle. "She said she's coming to my photography show. Anyway, she wanted to meet you."

"I bet she did." I wonder why I'm getting so jealous. I trust Charlie completely. But since I met Jasper this morning, I know what it can feel like with someone else. How my spine can tingle in a way it never has, how catching eyes, touching hands, is like a fever.

The office is rippling with tension this morning. It's rare to see Indigo in a bad mood, but today he's stewing around the staff room like he's wearing a big cartoon rain cloud above his head. In the candy machine behind him, a Kit

Kat is dangling defiantly above the slot.

Standing stiffly beside the staff table is Michael. He's a small, pale man with a lazy, wandering eye. Michael used to be a psychic viewer here, but after his mind snapped, he's only here occasionally, under Indigo's supervision.

"Hi, Callie," Indigo says, and then he stops pacing and glares at the candy machine. Michael flicks his finger to the right, and the Kit Kat appears in Indigo's hand.

"Thanks, Mike," Indigo says.

So it's not a rumor. I've heard Indigo say that Michael is an expert at telekinesis, which means he's able to move things just by thinking about them. Telekinesis is not that weird, when you think about it: we use invisible energy wavelengths every day. When we use the microwave, we use invisible rays to cook our food. When we listen to the radio, we use radio waves to connect us to different types of music. So is it that strange to use invisible thought waves to push or pull an object in space?

I wish I could do it, but few people can. I briefly wonder if Michael was offered a spot in the New York office before he lost his mind.

"Hey Mike, thanks," Indigo says again.

Michael doesn't respond; he just shifts from foot to foot, his hands loose at his sides like unused guns. He looks around, his eyes registering the lack of bars on the windows, the unpadded wall, and he sighs. *Here again,* I guess he's thinking. I felt that same way this morning, after staying up late last night thinking about Charlie and the girl with the crop top. Does Charlie somehow sense he could know every part of her, and that with me, he never will?

Indigo walks up beside me and places a hand on my shoulder, making me jump. "Real shame, that one. Used to be one of our best," Indigo says, as if I've never heard him rave about Michael's psychic powers before. Indigo spins his finger in a circle around his ear. "But when they get *in here* . . ."

I shiver. "What happens? I mean, exactly?"

"When people break into someone's mind, the brain instinctively fights to get the intruders out. Kind of like white blood cells attacking a flu virus," Indigo says. "This fight puts enormous stress on the brain. Eventually the brain gives out, like what happened to Michael." He shakes his head sadly. "Anyway, I had to do what was best for him, even if he didn't like it."

"Michael didn't want to go to Shady Hills?" I ask, referring to the mental institution that is now Michael's home.

"No. But when someone has their mind broken into, it's a quick downfall into madness. It's my job to retire those people."

The word *retire* makes me think of people shooting horses with broken legs to put them out of their misery. A chill runs down my spine.

"So what's the crisis this time?" I ask Indigo. I wonder if Michael's presence here has anything to do with the laser on the Russian aircraft carrier or the body I saw trapped under the red smoke of radiation.

"That's classified," Indigo says, which doesn't surprise me because Indigo only brings Michael in during emergencies. Besides all the red tape Indigo has to go through to get a clinically insane person a day pass to a classified facility, what if someone found out? The government might shut down our whole organization to avoid a news headline like, "America employs mental patients to find military secrets." But Michael is essential sometimes. His letter- and number-reading abilities in his sessions make him very, very dangerous—or very helpful, depending on whether you're the one hiding the classified military secrets, or trying to find them. "I'm working with Michael, so you'll be Jasper's monitor today," Indigo continues. "He's waiting for you in the viewing room."

"Psychic Welcoming Committee at your service," I say, saluting Indigo.

"Try not to overwhelm him with your . . . um . . ."

"Attitude?" I suggest.

He nods. "With your *you*."

"Consider my 'you' sealed." I zip my mouth shut and throw away the key.

Indigo grins at me before he turns back to Michael, and

I have no choice but to grab a cup of coffee and head into the viewing room.

Jasper is leaning back in the leather reclining chair, his eyes closed. I watch him for a moment, the way his eyelashes flutter and his chest rises and falls under his red zippered hoodie. Then his eyes snap open.

"Watching me?" he asks. He yanks the side lever, and the chair jolts to a sitting position.

"And I would be doing that *why?*"

"It's okay," he says. "I was watching you, too."

"Did you even hear me?" I ask.

"Not much else to do around here but watch you," Jasper says, "and play fortune-teller." He taps his finger to his temple, his wooden beads jangling from his wrist. "You are thinking about . . ." He pauses, tapping his temple again, his face getting really serious. "Why this office always has such horrible coffee."

I feel a smile crack across my face. "Better in New York, was it?" I say, taking a sip of my watery coffee and grimacing.

"Nothing's better in New York," he says, "this being the happiest coast and all that."

"And all that," I agree.

"You shouldn't drink that stuff," he says, nodding to my cup of coffee. "Stunts your growth."

"That's what happened."

Jasper picks up his coffee cup and takes a sip, making a pained face. "You ready?"

It's always nerve-racking to work with another psychic for the first time; how will I know he won't judge me when I lay my heart out pulsing on the page, or spit incomprehensible words in the air? It may be selfish, but I'm glad he has to go first.

"Always." I press Record on the remote control, and the red light on top of the video camera flips on. *Click.*

Jasper shuts his eyes, purses his lips, and then he's gone. With each minute that passes, I feel him pulling farther away from me, withdrawing to a deeper place, on the other side of the universe that I can't see. As he goes in deeper, I wonder what his method is for getting into his psychic zone. Does he put on scuba gear and release himself slowly into the ocean, or imagine a spinning golden orb, like Indigo does? Jasper's hand starts up first, moving across the paper, drawing something in exquisite detail.

"I'm outside," he says slowly. His hand is sketching faster, his voice sounding thicker now. "It's nighttime . . ."

As he trails off, I can tell it's getting painful for him because tears start to well up in his eyes. That's the tricky thing about viewing coordinates. You imagine the coordinates in the envelope, like N39°54.16W68°72.5, and at first, it means nothing. Then you start to see images, to lower yourself into a world flooded with sound, shapes emerging from shadows. Small solid shapes like *ball* and *tower*, objects you can feel with both hands. The feelings come next. It takes a while to get to emotions and physical sensations, but when they come, you can't flinch or look away. You have to take it all, be the receptacle. Right now, I can tell that he wants out. But you have to take that too.

"I'm not alone," Jasper says. "There's someone else out here, and he's injured." His eyes are now open, and filled with tears.

I'm surprised by his tears. He seems so tough on the surface, but underneath, is he just as scared and vulnerable as I am?

"There's glass all around me," he continues. "It looks like a broken window or something."

The comparison to a broken window is the problem, and at this point I have to say AOL, which stands for Analytic Overlay. That's our code word for scratch the session, because the analytical mind has moved in. When we psychically view, we only use the primitive mind, but once we start making relationships between something we know and something we don't, the analytical mind has stepped in. It's not reliable, because what if you say it looks *like* a nuclear weapons facility, but it's a just a steel factory, and we attack based on that info?

"AOL," I announce, louder than I need to. Having an AOL is always embarrassing because it means you've wasted the monitor's time; you've let your humanity get the best of you.

Jasper seems as surprised as I am that he's crying. "I've never done that before," he says, all traces of his cockiness gone. He wipes the tears off. "I really screwed that up, didn't I?"

This Jasper is even more likable, I want to say. *I hope he sticks around.* "You did," I say, "but this stuff still counts, off the record."

I nod at the small stack of papers in his hands, the ones he sketched while he was viewing. He shrugs and hands them to me, and I can tell from his flushed face that he's still a bit embarrassed. *How cute.*

I open a file folder and start to put the papers in, but as I turn them over so that they are right side up, I do a double take. It's a drawing of person lying face down in a pile of glass shards. He's wearing a hoodie with the hood pulled over his head, and one of his arms is flung out beside him. On the back of his hand is a large tattoo of a star.

There's something about the figure on the ground that's familiar, I just can't quite put my finger on what. *It's not your job to analyze, Callie*, I remind myself. Still, as I pack up and head home, I can't shake the feeling that I know that person. That person who is bleeding and possibly dying and who I can't help at all.

CHAPTER SIX

The house smells like fried food when I get home that evening. I follow the smell into the kitchen, where Mom is sitting at the table, a smattering of Chinese food boxes around her. "Hungry?" she asks.

I drop my backpack onto the floor. "Not really."

"Try a bite," she says. She pushes a box toward me. "Chow young with fried wheat gluten."

"Ooooh, worms," I say, grabbing the box and taking a bite anyway. The slimy gray noodles taste even worse than they look. "It's good," I lie.

"How was nannying?" Mom asks.

"Fine." I say, but as always, lying to Mom gives me a sick feeling in my stomach. *I'm lying to protect her,* I remind myself.

"Eat," she urges.

I take another bite, just to make Mom happy, though now that I've started, I realize that I'm starving.

"Did you eat today?" Mom is always worried about whether I ate or not. Like I'm going to starve to death in the wilds of San Francisco. The funny thing is that Mom rarely eats. In all the pictures I've seen of her from before Dad left, when I was just a toddler, her face was round and smiling, but now she usually looks thin and stressed. At least she did, until she met Richard.

"Yes," I lie, "I went to lunch with a new friend."

"Oh good. What's her name?"

"*His* name is Jasper."

Her eyebrows lift, and her face says, *What about Charlie?* But her voice says, "What's Jasper like?"

"He's um . . . different."

"Different good or bad?"

"Good different," I say, and I almost add, *like me.*

"Is he a friend of the Bernsteins'?" Mom asks.

Ah, the Bernsteins—a dentist and psychiatrist, parents of Emma, cutest child in the world. Big house, garage with twin BMWs, all the trimmings a fictional family can get.

"Yes," I say. "He's their . . ." I almost say son, but that's too much. Always maintain enough of a separation to make it believable, Indigo says. "Their nephew," I finish. "He's home from his first semester of college. They wanted him to meet someone around his own age."

"The Bernsteins have been so nice to you," Mom says. "Why don't you invite him over for dinner sometime?"

"Mom!" I protest. "We don't owe the Bernsteins anything. Besides, I've only had *lunch* with the guy. And you don't cook."

"So?" Mom lifts her chopsticks out of the box of gray noodles. "We could feed him this."

I grin at her, imagining Jasper sitting at our dinner table between Mom and me. "He's not the worm-eating type."

Mom smiles back, and then asks, "Are you going to see him often?"

Every day, I think. My mind races back to when I met Jasper: the sound of my name on his tongue, his magnetic blue eyes drinking me in, the searing heat racing up my arm when he touched me. *How am I going to work with him?*

"Where's Richard tonight?" I need to change the subject before I start blushing.

"You know him. Probably saving lives or something equally heroic." Richard is Mom's firefighter boyfriend, who has recently moved in with us. What she'll never know is that she met Richard because of me. That night I bent a spoon and set the fire alarm off, Richard showed up in his full fireman gear. Mom was temporarily rendered speechless—which is hard to do—and they were so caught up in each other, if there had been a fire, neither of them would have noticed.

"Definitely heroic," a voice says from the living room.

"Richard!" Mom squeals, jumping to her feet and dashing into the living room. "You're here!"

"Nowhere I'd rather be," I hear Richard say, and then I hear Mom squeal again.

"Put me down!"

Richard carries her into the kitchen in his arms. Compared to my petite mom, Richard looks like a giant. He smiles down at her, and she strokes the tidy gray mustache in his friendly, rounded face. "Made for laughing," he always tells me.

"Hey Cal," Richard says, placing Mom gently back in her chair.

"Save any lives today?" I ask.

"We got everyone out okay," he says gratefully. "Got another one for you," he adds, pulling a magazine out of his back pocket and tossing it to me.

I'm not what I think of as a collecting type of person, but ever since Richard found out that I love *National Geographic* magazines, he's brought them home from the fire station every month. The pictures are so beautiful that I can't bear to throw them out.

I study the cover. It's a picture of a black night sky full of stars, and right in the center, an old water ring is etched into the cover. Along the spine it says: *The Space Race Continues.*

"Heroic, just like I said," Mom says. She pushes a take-out box toward him with her chopstick. "Join us for dinner?"

Richard tips it over with one finger and peers inside. "Had dinner at the station."

"Lucky you," I say.

Richard pulls out a chair and sits in it, looking way too large for Mom's IKEA furniture. By the way he shifts subtly in his seat, I can always tell that he's uncomfortable too, although he'll never say so. "Getting excited for fall?" he asks me.

As far as they know, I'm going to San Francisco State, and I couldn't be happier about it. I haven't told them about the acceptance letter to NYU in my desk. Why tell them if I can't go anyway? Besides, if I told Mom, and she did encourage me to go, I'd have to make up a convincing lie about why I can't go to New York. Sounds exhausting. "Of course," I respond.

"Good," Richard says, and hands Mom her house keys. "Found these on the way in."

"I've been looking for those," Mom says.

"In the door," he says. "Again. You sure know how to leave things in easy places for me to find."

They grin at each other. Mom's joy is so pure and uncomplicated that it worries me. Over the past fifteen months, I've learned to care about Richard a lot. He's the first man I've ever been able to imagine myself, eventually, calling *Dad*. I want him to stay around. And even though I know Mom does too, she's usually as careless with her boyfriends as she is with her house keys. Over time, they get lost.

And this one I don't want to lose.

The quad is full of students this morning, most of them either racing to the science building for their Friday morning class, textbooks gripped tightly in hands, or sitting in groups chatting. I walk through the mass of Berkeley T-shirts and shaggy-haired students, not interested until I see Jasper across the quad. My heart leaps as I watch him take large steps across the grassy lawn, heading away from the redbrick buildings. He's swinging a black helmet absently from one hand, and his face is angry. He looks totally different from the boy I met two days ago, the one who split my name into two syllables. I watch him duck around the science building before I cross the quad and enter our building.

As usual, Anthony is sitting behind the front desk eating Cheetos. He's on the phone, so he holds up one orange index finger for me to wait.

The conveyer belt starts up with a whirring sound.

"Chicks love shooting stars," Anthony is saying. I tap my fingers impatiently. "Coming," Anthony mouths over the phone, and then focuses on his call again. "Big blanket this time, dude. Anthony doesn't wanna sit next to your ugly face. Out." He hangs up the phone.

"National emergency?" I ask as Anthony steps up to the metal detector. I take off my jacket and backpack and drop them on the conveyer belt. The house keys in my jacket pocket jingle as they hit the rubberized surface.

"Something like that," Anthony says. He holds out the bag of Cheetos toward me. "Cheeto?"

I shake my head. "Not really a breakfast food."

"Since when does food have rules?" Anthony protests.

"Since always."

Anthony looks at the black-and-white images of my jacket and backpack on the X-ray. "Cell phone, house keys, no ticking packages," he says, checking each off on his fingers.

"Oh good. So I'm not a terrorist."

"Apparently, no. But you'd be a lovely one."

"Thanks," I say, and then I step into the elevator and let the doors shut behind me.

Indigo is waiting for me in the viewing room, perched tensely on his leather chair. He's sipping coffee from a white Styrofoam cup, a scowl slashed across his face.

"You all right?" I ask, wondering if Indigo's scowl has anything to do with the angry look I saw on Jasper's face when he was leaving the building.

Indigo glances up at me, the cup almost to his lips. "People don't always see eye to eye," he says, "especially where money's concerned." He drinks half of his coffee in one gulp. "I mean, it's not like he has to keep this place running." Before I can ask anything else, Indigo mutters, "Terrible coffee."

"The worst," I agree.

A smile crosses Indigo's face as he motions for me to sit down across from him. "Let's get started."

I settle down on the couch, both dying of curiosity and equally glad that I'm not involved. What could Jasper possibly fight with Indigo about?

"Focus," Indigo says gently.

I lean back against the cushions and close my eyes. I hear Indigo shuffling paper across from me and open my eyes briefly, but he mouths *sorry* and stops moving. I close my eyes again, and let myself sink into the water.

At first, there is just light and color. Then shapes emerge, and basic feelings: cold creeping under my skin, the flickering of fish passing through me, an uncomfortable tickling sensation. Then, above me, I see the hull of the aircraft carrier. *That's where I need to be.*

Soon I am swimming and flying and rising, a bend

of light in a glass of water, and then I am on the aircraft carrier.

It's complete chaos.

People are running past me in a whir of movement and sound. The noise is deafening. An alarm is going off, a high-pitched squeal, and over the alarm, male voices are barking orders back and forth. I can feel the heart-racing panic, but I'm not sure what's going on.

Looking for the source of the panic, I float through the aircraft carrier, starting with the island, the six-floor tower in the middle of the deck. I see the island laid out as a blueprint, little boxes stacked neatly one on top of the other: first the Primary Flight Control, then Vulture's Row, and then the Control Room. This time, there's no Russian captain leaning back in his leather chair, just an empty room with papers scattered across the floor, like he jolted out of the room at a dead run.

"Focus on the target," I hear Indigo say above my vision.

I drop down the island until I'm floating above the flight deck, and directly below me is the laser. It's mounted on a square metal base, with tracks for it to rotate on, although I've never seen it move. "I see it," I say aloud.

A voice booms through the ship's intercom and people start rushing toward the fantail from all directions. As people move faster toward the laser, I realize that the laser is also moving. It has always pointed at the bow, the front of the boat. But now it's slowly rotating toward the stern, the back of the boat.

The Russian captain races out to the fantail. The laser is facing the stern now, and the captain's confused look tells me that this was not what he had planned.

"What do you see?" Indigo asks above the scene.

"The laser has turned in the opposite direction," I say, "and it seems like no one knows why."

CHAPTER SEVEN

As I walk to the diner near my house, my mind is still whirring with images of the laser, and the captain's shocked look when he saw it facing the stern. I almost trip over a crack in the pavement, and force myself not to think about it. After my exhausting session with Indigo, I need to get away and rest my mind.

Charlie's not here yet, but Sylvester is holding the door open from the inside, a smile beaming across his face.

"Hello, Callie," Sylvester says in a thick Ugandan accent. The owners are two brothers from Uganda. One is a doomsdayer, and he's been trying to convince me to stock up on end-of-the-world supplies for years (you know my answer), and the other one is Sylvester. He serves a good cup of coffee, and makes an okay tofu scramble. Better than mine, anyway.

"Hi, Sylvester," I take a seat on the cushy white love seat to the right of the kitchen. Dangling from the ceiling above me, there are billowy waves of white material, so it feels like I'm sitting in a cloud. "Waiting for Charlie," I add, and Sylvester nods and slips back into the kitchen.

I love the American Dream Diner. The brothers changed the name from the Ugandan Café to the American Dream Diner when they got their green cards a few years ago. "We are Americans now," Sylvester told me, and gave everyone free coffees for a week.

As I settle into the cloud, the laser on the aircraft carrier flashes through my mind again, and, as if a trigger has been pulled, I hear Indigo's voice in my head: "Analyzing information outside of the office can compromise the mission." As hard as it is not to think about what I see at work, Indigo's right, because if I analyze something I viewed in a session, and then I view it again, I may make judgments about it that result in incorrect information. It is precisely this lack of analysis—the ability to only see, not judge—for which I am hired. But still, sometimes I can't help but think about it, like now, when I can't stop wondering why the laser turned in a different direction, and why the captain didn't know it was going to do that.

Did somebody else have control of the ship's laser?

The kitchen door opens and Sylvester pops out with a cup of coffee, his phone pressed to his ear. Behind him, talk radio leaks out of the open doorway, and the monotone voice of a NASA scientist explains the meaning of meteorites and asteroids to the ancient Egyptians. Why don't adults ever listen to music?

Sylvester puts the coffee down in front of me and smiles briefly before going back to his phone conversation. "But Leroy," he says, and then pauses to listen. "You've said this before." Sylvester sounds irritated talking to his brother. Leroy's sure the earth is going to come to a violent and dramatic end, and soon. It's possible, I guess, but Leroy also has a mud-walled basement that he dug with his own hands, filled with a thousand bottles of water and an inflatable life raft for the next flood, or so he says. "Well, don't come, then," Sylvester adds, hanging up the phone as he walks back through the swinging doorway.

When the door closes behind him, I pick up my cloth napkin and unroll it. A knife, two forks, and a spoon fall out with a clang. I lift the spoon by the end, and, after checking the doorway to make sure Charlie's not coming in, I stare at the spoon. As usual, my lips form silently around the word *bend*, but nothing happens. *At least Mom met Richard because of that party*, I remind myself, smiling at the memory of Richard bursting into the drenched Stanford dining hall in his yellow fireman gear.

The bell dings from its rusting hook on the door, and I drop the spoon on the table. Charlie looks stunningly handsome, as usual, in his blue rugby shirt and a pair of faded jeans. His face breaks into a smile when he sees me. Behind him, Colin trudges in, wearing a Superman T-shirt, his hands deep in his pockets. At twelve, Colin has the social skills of a four-year old, but is the sweetest boy I've ever met. When he sees me, he barrels in, his big head of pale hair atop skinny shoulders.

"Sorry, I had to bring Colin," Charlie says as Colin scampers off into the corner booth, where there is a gigantic set of Legos in a red plastic box. Charlie perches on the white vinyl cushion beside me and throws a quick wave at Sylvester, who has popped his head out of the kitchen to greet him.

"One black coffee and a steamed milk," Sylvester says. "And one egg over easy with toast, one tofu scramble with fake bacon, one pancake with whipped cream." We nod our agreement. Charlie and I always have breakfast for dinner at the diner. It's kind of our thing.

"School's a total drag without you," Charlie says, scooting across our booth until his knee is pressed against mine. "I actually have to *learn* now."

"Is that all I am? A distraction?"

"Yes, definitely," Charlie says, kissing me on the nose. "But a good one."

My nostrils get itchy all of a sudden, and I wrinkle my nose. "I think I'm allergic to you."

"Not a surprise. Happens all the time," he says, hooking his arms over the back of booth. "I like meeting here. It has everything I like: Coffee, check. Pancakes, check. Legos for Colin, check."

"You missed something."

"Did I?" he says, and then adds, "Callie. *Big* check."

I grin. "Do you have anything left to do before your show?"

"Everything. I have to print the photographs, find semi-cheap frames, and frame the prints. Then I have to tell everyone I know to come, since if nobody shows up I will be so embarrassed I might just die right there."

"You haven't told anyone yet?"

"I've told everyone I know, and some I don't. But I have to *remind* them, that's all."

Sylvester pops out of the kitchen, deposits Charlie's coffee on the table, and crosses the room to give Colin his steamed milk. Colin takes it from his hand without looking up, so Sylvester adds a Lego to Colin's tower, which is now starting to look like a spaceship, and rubs his messy hair before ducking back into the kitchen. Alone again, Charlie and I sip the cups of rich Ugandan coffee gratefully. At least that's one thing Sylvester hasn't Americanized.

"A new one?" Charlie asks, pointing to my open backpack.

"Richard gave it to me," I say, pulling the *National Geographic* out of my backpack.

"Pretty cool," Charlie says. He takes it from my hands and flips through it, looking at each of the pictures. "How big's your collection now?"

"Almost a dozen," I say, leaning over to see the pictures.

"I'm so glad you're still getting along," Charlie says.

I know what he means. I've never really been into any of Mom's boyfriends. I think about the handful of men Mom's been through over the years, and how none of them ever made her happy for long. There was Saul, the Jewish Museum curator, Paulie, the Stanford librarian with the long ponytail, and Chris, the accountant with the monotone voice. And then, out of nowhere, Richard the fireman. I think she was as surprised as I was by her attraction to him. "It's nice just to see her happy," I say, warming my hands around the steaming mug.

"It is," Charlie comments, taking a sip of his coffee. "He's good for her."

"He is," I agree, and I already feel better. Five minutes with Charlie and I'm back to normal.

This time, when the door swings open to the kitchen, Sylvester steps out and hands us our giant plates of food.

Colin scampers over and climbs into the booth between us.

"Do you know how the dinosaurs died?" Colin asks me, and then answers his own question, "When an asteroid hit the earth. How fast does a satellite travel?" he asks immediately, and then answers himself again. "Eighteen thousand miles per hour."

Colin is playing his do-you-know game again. He shoots questions at you until you realize how little you actually know about science, and how much he does know. Charlie says it makes his ears bleed. But he says it with a half-smile, half-grimace. Charlie has a soft spot for Colin. That boy gets away with everything.

"Let her eat," Charlie says gently, and I grin over at him. *I don't mind.*

Colin ignores him, waving his hands in my face as though I'm across a football stadium, not a foot away. "Callie," he sings.

"Huh?"

He waves his hands in my face again, more violently this time. "How many gallons of water are there in the ocean? Three hundred twenty-six quintillion gallons." He giggles.

"Colin, sit down," Charlie says.

Colin jumps off the booth and runs around the room with his arms open wide, skipping along on his newfound wings. "Radioman says that's three hundred forty-three million trillion gallons," Colin yells. Radioman is what

Colin calls the reporter for *Science Friday*, a science radio show that plays on, well, Friday. Or every day for several hours, if you're Colin. I look at Charlie, and he shrugs.

"Colin, sit *down*," Charlie says more sternly this time.

Colin speeds back to us and plops down at the table in front of his food. He shovels his pancake in his mouth and keeps trying to say something, but Charlie shakes his head repeatedly, until I think it's going to make him dizzy.

"Callie Sandwich," Colin says, tugging on my sleeve. "Did you know—"

"Big kid time," Charlie finally says, and Colin lowers his eyes to the table and continues to shovel his food in, but silently this time. "Thought any more about the place-that-will-not-be-named?" Charlie asks me.

Charlie hasn't told Colin that he's leaving for college yet. Since Charlie isn't leaving for another four months, he says he has plenty of time. Of course, he's been saying that for two months now.

I shake my head. I love Charlie, I do, but my job has to come first, like Indigo says. And unless I manage to magically start bending metal and influencing minds in the next few months and get transferred to the New York office, I'm stuck here. "I'll let you know if anything changes," I say.

Charlie nods, and it tears me up how hard he's trying to be supportive of whatever decision I make. But we both know that four years is a long time. I just wish I could tell him the truth of why I can't go, and explain that this job as a psychic viewer—as inconvenient as it is right now—is the core of everything I am.

Of the person he loves, who he doesn't know at all.

CHAPTER EIGHT

Charlie and I hang around my house all weekend listening to music, scouring the internet for funny kitten videos, taking turns explaining our nonsense conversations to Colin. Basically doing what people do who don't have TVs. But sometimes having a boring weekend like that is a relief, especially since, when I walk in the office today, Indigo says we have to work in the Faraday cage.

"Orders from up high," Indigo says, which means that he can't tell me anything more, and maybe that he doesn't know either.

The Faraday cage is a circular cage, like a metal hamster ball, and the viewer sits inside of it. The cage is blocked by electromagnetic radiation, so that when I am watching other people's lives, they aren't watching mine. Because it's very difficult to psychically break into from the outside, it's the safest place to view classified information. The United States isn't the only country that has psychics working for its military, and we've all heard the rumors about the dangers of enemy psychics: if one tries to break into your mind, it can be dangerous, but if several break in at the same time, it can drive you out of your mind.

"Why don't we have more of these in the office?" I ask Indigo, thinking of the information that goes through our minds every day. Would the CIA headquarters just let people walk in and look through classified documents?

"They're expensive," he says. "And the government gives us less funding than the canine unit. But on the up side, we do have Mickey."

We have the Mickey Mouse balloon instead. Stellar security.

Once I'm seated inside the cage on the hard metal seat, Indigo closes me in and takes a seat outside the cage.

"I'm right here if you need me," he says.

"You and the ejection button."

We go through the same drill: Indigo shows me a sealed envelope; I pack my worries into a suitcase, drift deep into the ocean in my mind, and picture what is inside the envelope. As always, an image comes to me.

From what I'm able to see, which isn't much, I'm floating in darkness, hearing only the splashing of waves around me. For what could be an hour or several hours, I am floating there, just watching and listening.

Then, after what seems like forever, the face of a child floats into my mind. He has dark skin and brown eyes, and his clothes are ragged but clean. He has this mischievous look, and something about him tugs at my heart in an almost physical way. I feel myself smile just looking at him.

"What are you looking at?" Indigo asks over my vision.

"A boy," I say. "An adorable little—"

Then I see it, something that makes me shudder through every cell of my body. In the boy's pupils is the reflection of a giant wall of water. It must be taller than a house, and it's about to crash over him. The boy backs up, but there's nowhere to go. I can feel his terror, and there's nothing I can do to help him. Then the white crest of the wave breaks, and at the same time, the boy cries such a desperate sound that it shatters across my mind. The sound jolts me out of my vision, and when I look at Indigo, there are white spots floating in front of my eyes.

"Welcome back," he says, and glances at his watch. "That was a long one. See anything interesting?"

"There was this kid," I say slowly. "And a giant wave was crashing over him. But it was too dark to see where I was." I shift on the bench, wishing I could go in again and find out something that could help him. "Maybe just one more time—"

"You know the rules," Indigo reminds me.

I still remember the speech Indigo gave me when I first got here. You don't need someone to break into your mind for your brain to give up on you. "Rules were put into place to protect us," he told me. "Where we go in our sessions, they're deep places. If we live too often in that space—or if we put too much pressure on our minds when we're in there—we might lose the ability to live in this one. Understand?"

"I know, don't push my mind past its breaking point," I chant.

"That's right," he says. Indigo opens the Faraday cage and gestures for me to climb out. He holds out my post-session file, and I take it from him and sit down in a chair outside the cage. As I methodically write my report, I can't help wishing I could have done something to help the little boy. Not that anyone can stop a tidal wave, but if I know where and when it's going to happen, maybe I can make sure he's not there. *Could he have been on an island? Maybe in the Pacific?*

Not being able to analyze what I see during a session is like someone leaving a puzzle lying around and ordering you not to put it together: you may not with your hands, but you will with your mind.

My post-session report is usually at least five pages long, outlining everything I saw, heard, and felt during my hours of viewing. As Indigo says, nothing is unimportant, as we never know which detail could help the CIA find a potential terrorist or discover the location of a radioactive bomb. Sometimes just the fact that the boy had dark skin or the wave was facing a certain direction is enough to prevent a major disaster from happening. While I write my report, Indigo studies the notes he took on my session, pops out to go to the restroom and get a candy bar, and straightens up the room for the next viewer.

When I'm finally done, Indigo asks me if I want to go over my report before I leave. Sometimes I do; sometimes I need to decompress after a session before I go out into the real world, even if that real world is only the recovery room down the hall. The world of the mind and the physical world are two totally different things: and sometimes it takes hours to prepare one for the other.

But I shake my head and hand him the long, detailed report. He shuffles through the half-dozen pages, glancing up at me every now and then. "So no smells or tactile impressions?"

"No touchy, no smelly," I say. "And no clue when or where."

"Okay," Indigo says. "Good work." He gets up from his chair and holds out a hand to pull me up, but I stand up on my own.

"You're the old one," I tease. "I should be helping you up."

"Good point," Indigo says, pulling open the door and gesturing for me to leave first.

Indigo heads to his office, and I hear him drop the sealed envelope in the Completed Sessions box. Unless a target will be viewed again, Indigo puts them in the box, which he then delivers to the CIA headquarters, to the contact only he knows the identity of. Supposedly, once there, the files are destroyed to maintain secrecy, although nobody really knows.

I walk through the recovery room and push through the swinging door to the staff room. I'm still so preoccupied by the child's desperate wail that I almost walk straight into Jasper. He's leaning against the table, sipping coffee.

"That bad?" Jasper asks as I jerk to a stop in front of him. "Wanna talk about it?"

I shake my head. I've been holding this stuff inside of me for so long that I don't even know how to talk about it. It's like explaining a dream, but it's real.

"It's hard sometimes, isn't it?" Jasper asks, putting his coffee cup down on the table over the worn-in water ring. "We just watch, and there's nothing we can do."

I slump back against the candy machine, wondering if Jasper is reading my mind, or if he really feels this way, exactly the way I feel.

"But you can influence, can't you?" I ask.

Jasper shakes his head. "I can bend metal," he says, "but only within a hundred feet."

"Is that why you left the New York office?"

"Nope. Issues with the boss. I've got a problem with authority." Jasper's grin reminds me of how different he looked yesterday when he was storming across the quad, and of Indigo's angry look when I got in here.

"No kidding," I say.

Jasper sits at the table and pulls out a metal chair for me. It scrapes across the tile floor, and the screeching hurts my ears. I think about sitting down and telling him all about it, but then I remember the way it felt when he touched me. It was like my whole body unconsciously leaned toward his, and even though I tried to remind myself that I'm taken, something inside of me *wanted* him. There was nothing logical about it, and it was like nothing I've ever felt before, but it was real. It made me dizzy and shaky, and I just can't handle that right now.

I push myself off the candy machine. "I have to get home," I say, my words coming out in one long word: *Ihavagethome*.

"Sit a while," Jasper says. "Talk."

I pull the chair out farther and lower myself into it, plopping my purse down on the table in front of me.

"What happened in there?" Jasper asks, leaning forward so his chin is balancing on one palm. "You look like you've been through the wringer."

"You could call it that."

"Don't feel like talking?" he asks.

"But I'm guessing you do," I respond, a smile inching over my lips.

Jasper sits back and studies me. "Watch this," he says, and starts waving his hands around, twisting and twirling them like a maniac.

I lift my eyebrows. "Interpretive dance?"

"Magic," Jasper says. "Well, it's not magic, not in the real sense of the word; it's more like a trick of the eye. Like if I wave my hands around a lot"—my eyes follow his flailing hands, and the way his ring twinkles on his middle finger—"you never notice that I stole your wallet."

On the table, my purse is still closed, but my faux leather wallet is lying open beside it, showing my old school ID, with my full name, Calliope Sinclair. The picture was taken before I ever met Indigo, before I knew any of this, and there is some sort of innocence in my eyes that I don't see in the mirror anymore. I'm guarded now—in my eyes, my brain, my heart. "How did you do that?"

"I can't tell you," Jasper says solemnly. "I swore the Magician's Oath."

"The what?"

Jasper sighs. "You don't know anything about magic, do you?" I shake my head. "The Magician's Oath. 'As a magician I promise never to reveal the secret of any illusion to a nonmagician,'" he recites. "Blah blah blah."

"You're a magician? Like, pull a rabbit out of a hat?"

"There's more to it than that," he says, and it sounds like a warning.

"Like sawing women in half and putting them back together?"

"This is serious, Callie," Jasper says, and in his voice there's a hardness I haven't heard before; it's like sitting in the bath for so long you don't notice the water has gone ice cold. Then his face transforms into a smile, and the warmth comes back full force. *Did I just imagine it?* "Can I use your scarf?" Jasper asks.

"Not a chance in hell," I say, but I unwrap the silk material from around my neck anyway. I hand it to him, hoping he'll be careful with it. My dad gave this to my mom before he left, or so Mom said. It's the only thing I have left of him, and truthfully, part of me wants to lock it in a box and preserve it forever, like maybe it contains the parts of my history that I'll never know.

Jasper shows me his thumb, holding it out in a thumbs-up position, and then drapes my white scarf over it. He takes a pin, like one you sew with, out of his pocket. "Do you see this pin?" he asks.

"See these?" I ask, pointing to my eyes. "Eyes. Good for seeing."

He nods, and then he stabs his thumb with the pin, full

force. I gasp, not sure if I'm more upset about his thumb or my scarf. Jasper pulls more pins out of his pocket, and stabs through his thumb a dozen more times. When he's done, there are pins sticking out through his thumb on all sides, like a pincushion.

"What did you do?" I gasp. *And the last remnant of my dad is gone.*

Jasper holds out his thumb, and the scarf is full of holes, just like the story Mom told me about my dad: about how he disappeared when I was a toddler, and how she looked for him for years, but it was like he had never existed. It seemed like his name, and everything else about him, had been *erased*, she told me on one of the rare occasions she talked about him. When Mom eventually gave up, she finally admitted to herself that the truth wasn't that mysterious; Dad just didn't want to be found.

When Jasper pulls my silk scarf off his hand, his thumb is all in one piece, not injured at all. But my scarf didn't fare so well; it is full of holes.

I glance at my holey scarf, and sadness starts to build up in me. *Why is it such a secret? Don't I deserve to know who my father is?* I look up into Jasper's grinning face, as if he's just done the best trick in the world, and my sadness hardens into anger.

"Why did you do that?" I ask icily.

But Jasper just shakes my holey scarf three times and

hands it to me. It is back in one piece; the holes are gone.

"Okay . . . so *how* did you do that?"

"Magician's Oath," he reminds me, as Indigo swings the staff room door open.

The top button of Indigo's shirt is undone, and his tie is skewed across his chest at a strange angle.

"Jasper," Indigo says, walking into the room and plucking a carrot, dotted with pin holes, out of Jasper's sleeve. "If you're done with your parlor tricks, let's get some real work done."

My eyes follow the carrot in Indigo's hand, and then land back on Jasper.

He shrugs and grins. "You didn't think I'd pierce my thumb, did you?"

"And the scarf?" I ask, as he stands up to follow Indigo out of the room.

Jasper turns around and throws a ragged white napkin at me, and it lands on the ground. I can see the green linoleum floor through its holes.

Mom is still sitting in the exact same place at the kitchen table, grading papers, as she was when I left for work this morning. It seems like that's all she does every year in early May. Even though she has three teacher's assistants to help her, she insists on editing her students' final papers herself.

"Hey, Cal," Mom says. "Mind ordering dinner?"

"Mission accepted," I say. "Hand me those menus, will you?"

Without looking up from her grading, Mom pushes the take-out menus toward me with the end of her pen. I notice her pen's all chewed up, like a rabid dog attacked it.

I reach over and grab the red-and-black Japanese food menu out of the stack.

"Noodle bowls okay?" I ask, and she nods, so I hitch my backpack over my shoulder and head upstairs with the menu in my hand. I pull out my phone and dial the number, and it rings several times before a woman answers it.

"*Kon'nichiwa*, Sushi House. What's your order?"

I walk into my bedroom and drop my backpack on the floor. "Delivery please. Two tofu noodle bowls, one vegetable tempura, and a side of cheese wontons," I add, in case Richard gets home in time to join us. Richard loves wontons.

"Forty-five minute," the woman says, and the line goes dead.

I lean out of my bedroom door and grab onto the stairwell's wooden banister. "Forty-five minutes!" I call down to Mom. "Be down soon!"

I hear a mumble in return from Mom, so I know she's deep into her papers.

I unlock the window, open it all the way, and edge my

way out onto the fire escape. When the cool night air hits me, I automatically relax, barely even noticing the cars speeding down Fell Street below me. I gently close the window behind me and lean back against the glass. Above me, the sky is darkening, and I can only see a tiny sliver of moon in the sky. Perfect. Seven o'clock on the dot.

Across the alley to the right, a television plays the evening news out my neighbor's open window, spitting blue light into the dark sky. "It launched from Cape Canaveral at six this morning to a small but eager crowd," the reporter says. I lean forward and peer through the window into my neighbor's kitchen, at the TV sitting on the counter top. The screen shows a picture of a tiny puff of white high up in the sky. "The weather was perfect for launching—"

I hear the creak of a wooden shingle. I get to my feet, wrap my hands tightly around the fire escape, and climb the few remaining steps up to the roof. On the other side, Richard is carefully sitting down on the steeper part of the roof. I duck down and watch him get a good grip on the shingles, trying to figure out what he's doing out here.

When Richard looks like he's not going to plunge to his death, I call out, "What are you watching?"

Richard looks over and grins at me shyly. He points toward the house to the left of ours, where there's a TV playing a baseball game in an empty family room. "My ballgame," he says. "You?"

"The news."

Richard grimaces. "Depressing."

"You're supposed to say 'educational.'"

Richard laughs. "Seventh inning," he nods to the screen. "What's happening over there?"

"Murder, airplane crashes, shark attacks," I count off on my fingers. The news is the same every day; I don't have to watch it anymore to know what happens. "And today, some celebrity probably entered rehab. Shocker."

"Almost as predictable as baseball," he says.

"Nothing's as predictable as a bunch of boys playing with a ball," I say, now standing on the last step of the fire escape to see him better. In the near-dark, he's a silhouette of a man with a fading orange sky behind him. "What are you doing out here?"

"Same thing you're doing," he says. "Rotting my brain."

I turn back to the TV. The news has moved on to a story that Colin would love, about telescopes and other important scientific discoveries. "The objective in a refracting telescope is to bend light, which causes parallel light rays to converge at a focal point," the reporter says. My neighbor walks into her kitchen and starts chopping onions on the counter, briefly blocking my view of the TV.

"Wanna watch with me?" Richard asks. "Close game."

I shake my head. I prefer almost anything to sports. "I think I'll stick with death and destruction."

"Suit yourself," he replies.

My neighbor moves over to the sink, and I can see the TV again. "Finnegan Bishop, known in the hacking community as Bishop Finn, pleaded guilty today after breaking into NASA's databank to name a star after his mother." A picture of a guy with a red beard and large circular glasses appears on the screen. "The situation has weakened NASA's online security system even more, much to the concern of—" The TV goes black, and my neighbor walks out of the kitchen.

"Hey, Richard—" I say, but when I turn, I see that no one's up here with me anymore. I climb to my feet and cross the roof on shaky legs to peer over the edge. From my neighbor's TV, I hear the song "Take Me Out to the Ballgame." I watch the people singing along on the screen, mostly dads and their kids, and I realize that maybe that's what baseball is all about. Is that what Richard was trying to say to me when he asked me to watch baseball with him? The same thing he's been quietly saying with all the magazines he's brought me from the station: that he loves me? Even if it means watching sports, maybe next time I'll accept.

CHAPTER NINE

As Indigo counts down from ten, my eyes keep drifting closed, and I have to pinch my arm again to wake myself up. I know that I shouldn't have stayed up talking to Charlie on the phone past midnight—especially on a Monday—but time flew by with neither of us noticing it. With as long as we've been together, you'd think we have nothing left to say, and sometimes that's true. But usually, we can talk all night without ever getting bored, or in my case, without ever telling the truth.

Since I got so little sleep, my session isn't productive. Sometimes it isn't, Indigo says. Sometimes, when you are distracted, and you dig deep enough into your brain, you find nothing but a series of scattered images. For me, it's just blackness this time, a whole world of it. Nothing to grasp onto: just a bottomless abyss of darkness, accompanied by dizziness and a feeling of suction. Then the image changes, morphing into the silhouette of a small ship in a giant blue sea.

I know I'm not supposed to analyze, but I can't help comparing it to the Russian aircraft carrier. This ship is much smaller, and it has some sort of claw hanging from the back. As far as I can tell, it has nothing to do with the aircraft carrier, but maybe we've moved on to another mission. I'll never know.

When I finally leave the viewing room, I glance toward the staff room, where Indigo has been for over an hour. He was too preoccupied with preparing for his next meeting to wait around until I finished my extensive post-session report. As soon as I finished viewing an hour ago, he rushed out to greet somebody waiting for him in the staff room. So, after I drop off my report in Indigo's office, I join Jasper in the recovery room.

"Up late, Calliope?" Jasper teases as I half collapse onto the other side of the blue velvet couch.

I start to correct him, but I stop myself. My real name, which I usually hate, sounds beautiful on his lips.

"Late enough," I shoot back.

"Why? Dreaming of me?"

"I don't dream," I insist. "And if I did, it wouldn't be about you."

"Everybody dreams."

"I don't." I shift uncomfortably on the couch, throwing a look toward the staff room door with the hope that Indigo will come out and save me from this conversation.

"So then what does it look like to sleep?" Jasper asks. His lips are pressed tightly together, like he's barely containing himself from laughing at me.

"It's like being dead," I shrug. "It's just blackness. I don't know."

"Maybe you're blind in your sleep," he says, scooting closer to me on the couch and wrapping his hands over my eyes so I can't see anything.

"Maybe you have no idea what you're talking about," I snap, but I don't move to remove his hands.

"I dream," Jasper confides, still covering my eyes. "Sometimes I wake up screaming. And maybe I possibly even wake up crying, my pillow soaked through, but I wouldn't tell you that."

"Why not?"

He drops his hands from my eyes and moves back to where he was originally sitting on the couch.

Was he telling the truth? I turn to face him, hoping I can read the answer in his face, but it's blank as a stone. "What do you dream about?"

Jasper shrugs the question off. "We should try to communicate in our dreams," he says, scratching the non-existent dirt out from under his nails with a folded piece of white paper.

"If I did dream, which I don't," I respond, "how would we do that?"

"We each jot down an image we want to implant in the other's dreams before we go to sleep, the weirder the better. Then, when we wake up in the morning, we write our dreams down. Then we read them to each other, and if you hear the image that you implanted, you have to tell the other person."

"Sounds interesting," I say. But do I really want Jasper planting something in my dream? And how do I know if it's really the image he planted, or if he's just tricking me? "How do I know you won't lie?" I ask.

"You don't." Jasper grins. "But I won't either." Then, holding one hand up like a stop sign, he gestures behind his upturned hand toward the staff room door. "Check it out."

From this angle, I can see through the small window in the door, to where Indigo is talking to a pale, skinny guy with black bangs cut straight across his forehead. He's wearing faded jeans with safety pins up the sides, a black T-shirt with the phrase *Save the Planet* plastered across the front, and black combat boots.

"How do you think that guy got past Anthony?" Jasper asks.

"Don't you know who he is?"

Jasper squints at the guy, but no recognition crosses his face. In the staff room, Indigo is talking with his hands, explaining something to the guy, and then he glances out the small window at us. He walks over and pulls down the shade, and their voices drop to a whisper. Game Over.

Jasper looks at me and shakes his head. "Try me."

"Montgomery Cooper Junior," I say. "*The* Montgomery Cooper?"

Jasper looks blank.

"Cooper Mining strike a bell?" I hum a short jingle (da-da-da-da-daaaahhhh!) and recognition registers across Jasper's face.

"The billionaire?" he asks. "I thought he was, like, a hundred years old!"

"You're thinking of Montgomery Senior," I say. "Indigo is talking to Junior. I've heard that his dad was the meanest SOB on earth, and probably the most powerful. He owned half of the real estate in the city before he died last year." I lean toward Jasper. "I heard that Junior inherited all forty billion of it, even though his dad tried to keep it from him."

"Poor guy," Jasper says sarcastically. "And those were the only clothes he could afford?"

"It is kind of sad! His dad actually made a public statement that his son was too incompetent to take over his business." I glance over at the staff office's closed door. "But Junior's pretty cool: he's given half of it away to environmental groups to clean up the mess his dad's mines have left."

"So he's a do-gooder," Jasper shrugs. "He has the money to be one."

"Not everyone with money gives it away," I protest.

Just then, the door to the staff room opens, and the men come out. Up close, I can tell that Junior didn't safety-pin his jeans together himself; they were manufactured that way. Even his black combat boots are polished too brightly to be punk. His whole look screams out that he's trying too hard: anyone could see that just beneath the punk exterior, there's a scared nerd poking his head out. It makes me like him more.

"Then we'll see you tomorrow," Indigo says. He starts to pat Junior on the back, but Junior turns and awkwardly thrusts out his hand, and Indigo ends up patting him on the chest instead. Indigo barely notices, but Junior sees us watching from the couch a few feet away and steps quickly away from Indigo, blushing bright red.

"Can you say awkward?" Jasper whispers. Jasper and I wave, and Junior nods and shoves his hands into his jeans pockets. The safety pins strain with the pressure.

"Callie, Jasper, this is Junior," Indigo says.

"Monty," he says. It comes out squeaky and prepubescent, and although he must be in his late twenties, he sounds like a kid.

I'm sure I see Indigo blush, although it's gone the second I see it. "Junior's—I mean, *Monty's* company was partly responsible for cleaning up after that toxic spill last year."

"There were hundreds of volunteers," Monty responds. "And as Dad always said, I was just another face in the crowd." His shoulders start to slump inward, but he pulls them back and forces a smile onto his face. "Tomorrow, then."

"Tomorrow." Indigo holds his hand out, but Monty just gives him a quick wave as he opens the door and walks out into the hallway.

When the door shuts behind him, Jasper rounds on Indigo. "I thought we didn't do that kind of work," Jasper says. Indigo doesn't say anything, but his lips tighten into firm pale lines.

"What kind of work?" I ask, looking back and forth between them.

"The paying kind," Indigo says.

"The selling-out kind," Jasper retorts.

"His company contracts with the government," Indigo says. "It's not like he's some stranger off the street."

"Still, I didn't come here to—"

"My office, Jasper." Indigo turns on his heel and walks into his office. Jasper rolls his eyes and follows.

"Get over yourself," I hear Indigo say as he shuts his office door. I watch them for a second, trying to make out the angry words flying back and forth through the air. I can't hear them, so, assuming they'll work it out between the two of them, I head out of the office in time to catch the bus to Charlie's house.

When I get off the bus at Charlie's neighborhood, the scent of sulfur is so intense it stings my nose. I don't know how Charlie stands living so close to the salt flats, but I suppose their beauty outweighs the smell, at least on a day like today, when they are glowing bright pink, almost the same color as the hoodie I have on. Mother Nature freaks me out sometimes. Like, where'd she get the idea to put bacteria-creating algae in salt ponds that would make them turn all sorts of neon colors? Seems like something one of the potheads on the Berkeley campus would dream up.

I knock on the front door of Charlie's ranch-style home. "Charlie?" I call, and his mom pulls open the front door. Grace has gray hair, tucked back in a bun, and her skin is rosy, which she claims comes from her diet of brown rice and organic vegetables.

"Hello dear," Grace says as she opens the creaky screen door and pulls me into an embrace. "Any migraines lately?" I shake my head. "I'm so glad," she continues. "Looking for Charlie?"

I nod, untangling myself from her motherly hug.

"Mom?" I hear Charlie's voice call from inside the house. "Who is it?"

"Why don't you come in?" Grace suggests. "Have a cup of tea. I was just on my way out." Grace always has a way of leaving Charlie and me alone just when we need it. She picks up her gray purse and tucks it under one arm, then sidesteps me to get out of the house. I let the screen door close softly behind me. The house smells like chamomile.

"What a nice surprise," Charlie says, wrapping his arms around me so tightly it tunes out the radio voices. In this house, I feel like I go from one hug to another. Not that I'm complaining.

"I thought we could watch the sunset from here today," I say, nestling deeper into his chest.

A scream shatters my ears.

"We can watch it with Colin," Charlie sighs.

"Callie!" Colin says and throws himself into our hug, crushing me between the two of them. "Callie Sandwich," he giggles.

"Hi Colin," I muffle into Charlie's shirt.

"I think we're suffocating her," Charlie says, and gently

pushes Colin back to give me some air.

Colin looks at both of us with his "happy" expression. He's been learning emotions lately. Charlie holds up a picture of a sad face, or a happy face, or an angry face, and Colin has to figure out which emotion it is expressing. Then, he tries to imitate it. Happy. Sad. Bored. Confused. Angry.

Colin is doing his happy face right now, his lips stretching up to his nose in an almost maniacal way. "Did you know that it's just small particles of dust, water, and pollutants that makes the sunset look so colorful?"

"Reflecting the light, right?" I respond, and Colin's grin gets larger. "Are you asking us to watch the sunset with you?" I ask, and he nods.

Soon Charlie, Colin, and I are sitting on the front porch, staring over the salt flats as they turn from a bright pink to a murky red. The wood porch creaks under our weight. With my back leaning against the house, I spread my legs out over Charlie's legs, so I'm half sprawled on him. He lightly rubs my hair with two fingers.

"Did you know that the astronauts used the salt flats' bright colors to help guide the space shuttle back to earth?" Charlie asks Colin.

"Uh-uh." Colin shakes his head.

Charlie has told Colin this a thousand times, but Colin always wants to hear the story. "The astronauts were lost, just wandering around out there in space, missing home. They had gone too far into space to find their way back," Charlie says. "But then they saw the salt flats, and they said it looked like someone had graffitied the earth to help bring them home."

Colin loves graffiti. Big red names edged in black lettering, yellow stars over highways, murals on the outsides of buildings. Last week Charlie caught him drawing on the outside of the house in marker. He is learning how to spell his name, and it took Charlie over an hour to wash C O L off the front of the house. I can tell Colin's looking for a new place to draw by the way he's scanning every square inch of the sidewalk below us.

"There," Colin says, pointing about a hundred feet down the sidewalk. He grabs a purple stick of chalk from the box on the stairs. "Prepare for light speed," Colin says, and starts spinning his arms around in circles like he's revving up. "One hundred thousand . . . one hundred and fifty thousand . . . one hundred and eighty-six thousand, two hundred and eighty-two miles per second," he yells. "Light speed, go!" Colin runs off, arms whirling like an airplane, leaving Charlie and me alone. I snuggle up next to Charlie, and we watch Colin together until he plops down on the sidewalk a few houses down.

"Thanks for being so nice to Colin," Charlie says, and then we are kissing. Kissing Charlie is like swimming in a warm ocean. It gently carries you along until you've completely given up control, and you're floating, mindless, gazing at the sky.

His arms are around me, and as he pulls me onto his lap. I wrap my legs around his and lean all of my weight onto him. He puts one hand behind him for balance, and he holds me up, like he always does.

A hand tugs on my hair, pulling my head backward, and my lips disconnect from Charlie's. "Ouch," I yelp.

"I've gotta show you something," Colin says, and grabs my hand, dragging me off Charlie's lap and across the porch to the front door. Charlie follows a few feet behind us, sporting the "apologetic" look he's been trying so hard to teach Colin.

Colin drags me through the house and out into the back patio in the lush green backyard. My nose stings of salt, but I don't mind the smell of salt here, because it mixes with the scents of mint and basil, sage and rosemary. In her overflowing flowerbeds, Grace grows medicinal herbs. It looks like they are all in flower now, which to Grace means she's left them too long, and they've "gone to seed." I think they're beautiful.

"This is base," Colin says, leaning down and smacking the concrete patio with one hand. "One . . . two . . . three . . . you're it!" he yells and runs back into the house. "CALLIE!" Colin screams from inside the house. "Come find me!"

I smile at Charlie. "I'll be right back."

Colin's not in the living room, or the bathroom, or the den. He's not in his bedroom, or the kitchen, or Grace's room. "Colin!" I call, getting nothing but silence in return. He must be in Charlie's room. Charlie lives in the basement downstairs. Grace works two jobs, so Charlie takes care of Colin when he's not at school or working, and his bedroom is the only place he gets peace. Even I rarely go down there, since we usually hang out at my house, and even when I'm here, we're usually upstairs with Colin, since Colin's not allowed in Charlie's room. But this time Colin's broken that rule, so I open the door to the basement and head down the stairs, calling Colin's name.

In Charlie's bedroom, I flip on the lights, and the stereotypical boy's room springs to life: dirty laundry on the floor, plates of half-eaten food tilting off the desk, blue plaid comforter hanging off the bed. Colin is hiding under the bed, his eyes poking out from behind the blue comforter. But I don't go to Colin right away, because hanging from every wall are framed photographs. *Of me.*

In one, my hair is over my face so only one eye peeks out. I'm leaning against a eucalyptus tree in the Panhandle, wearing a brown cable-knit sweater that blends into the knotty wood. When did he take that?

In another I am sitting in my bedroom window. It's night, and the only light in the picture is from the lamp behind me. I'm only a silhouette of myself. *I didn't know he was taking pictures of me.*

"You were supposed to find me," Colin whines as he crawls out from under the bed. "You have to say, 'I see you.'"

"I see you," I say softly. I'm staring at a picture of me stepping out of my house, my coffee cup in my hand and my backpack swinging from one shoulder. *How much has he seen?*

"Colin!" Charlie's voice behind me is angry. "This was supposed to be a surprise!"

"I forgot," Colin giggles.

"It was," I say, turning to Charlie, "a surprise." *Although I don't know if it was a good or bad one.*

"This is my exhibit." Charlie sighs as he sweeps an arm around the room. "You weren't supposed to see it until the opening." He walks over and tilts a picture so it sits upright on the wall. "This is my favorite. You're beautiful in every one, but in this one, you just look . . . I don't know. Profound, maybe. Like you're gazing into the past." In this one, I'm standing in Death Row at Charlie's work, looking vacantly at the Execution machine. My black hair is hidden under the pale pink hood of my sweatshirt, and my gray eyes reflect the machine's little hanging man. The lights are winking around me, giving the scene this gritty retro feel, like I'm in an old arcade in Atlantic City or something. "My show is called *Muse*," Charlie says. "As in, you."

I glance over the row of framed pictures, and it feels like every heartbeat is half-love, half-fear.

"You know how I'm planning on majoring in portrait photography?" Charlie continues, "Well, there's no one I'd rather take pictures of than you. I had kind of planned on it being an anniversary present anyway. But I don't have to show them at my exhibit," he adds, "if you're not comfortable with it."

I glance up at Charlie's lip trembling with worry, and I am sure that he doesn't know anything about my job. Charlie is an open book, and in his eyes, there's no suspicion, only a soft adoration that warms me from the inside out. I know I could ask him not to hang the photos, and he wouldn't, but his show is called *Muse*. *I never thought I'd be anyone's muse.*

"I love it," I say.

"You do?" A slow smile spreads over Charlie's face.

"I do," I say, and I mean it. *Charlie loves me, that's all. End of story.*

"Sunset!" Colin shrieks, and sprints upstairs. We have to follow, but we do so slowly, kissing every step of the way.

CHAPTER TEN

I'm late to the office on Wednesday. I go straight to the viewing room, hoping I beat Indigo there, but when I open the door, Indigo is sitting in his leather chair, waiting for me. Standing next to him is Monty, wearing patched-up jeans, black combat boots, and a black leather jacket. He's sporting a baseball cap turned backward, and the little Oakland A's symbol stares at me from the back of the hat.

"You an A's fan?" I ask. I'm surprised; he looks as if a particularly vibrant game of chess would exhaust him.

Monty doesn't respond, he just turns the hat around so it faces me. After the *A*, printed in small black letters, is the word *holes.*

"So no," I say.

Indigo is jotting something down on his notepad, and he barely looks up, so it's just Monty and me staring at each other across the room. "Good guess," Monty replies.

"What'd they ever do to you?" I ask. "Miss catching a baseball in the stands?"

"Something like that," Monty says.

"His dad used to own the team," Indigo clues me in, still not looking up from his paperwork.

"That right?"

Monty nods. "Don't tell me you're a *fan*." He says *fan* in the way I'd imagine him saying A-hole.

"You just heard the extent of my baseball knowledge." I cross the room, throwing a curious glance at Indigo, and then settle down on the couch across from him. On the table in front of me is a stack of blank paper, ready to be filled with my visions.

"Well, personally, I don't give a damn about baseball," Indigo says, still looking at his notepad. "Unless they're moving the ball with their minds."

"That's *literally* the only thing that could make it interesting," I say.

"You said it," Monty agrees. We glance at each other, briefly surprised we agree on something, and share a small smile.

"Callie's our youngest," Indigo says, finally looking up, "and our brightest."

"Callie Sinclair," Monty says. "Graduated high school

early, raised in the city, daughter of famous scientist Allison Sinclair," he taps his bottom lip. "And able to see radiation."

Only a handful of people refer to my mother as famous, and all of them work at either Stanford or NASA. You don't become famous in any other circle for solving a physics equation that's never been solved before. But he certainly doesn't look like anyone I've met at the stuffy holiday parties. "You do your homework," I say.

Monty nods. "Indigo says you're crazy talented."

I'm uncertain which word he's putting more emphasis on, but I decide to go with the compliment. "Depends on who you're talking to," I say. "Some say talent, others say freak." I stare at him, daring him to disagree with me, but he doesn't. Apparently Indigo has told him about our reputation in the CIA.

Indigo looks at me sternly. "Monty's a generous donor to our program," he says.

"Really." I can't stop the disbelieving look that creeps over my face.

"Really," Monty responds. "Much to my father's disappointment."

"He didn't believe in psychic powers?"

Monty grimaces, and an angry look comes into his eyes. "He believed in money."

"And you don't?" I ask.

He hesitates. "I believe in what money can *do*, not what it can buy."

Indigo clears his throat, and we both look over at him. "Anyway. When Monty told me what he needed, I told him I had the perfect person for it."

"Perfect could be overstating it," I respond, a smile creeping across my face. "But only slightly."

Indigo stands up and walks across the room. "I'll have to ask you to wait outside," he says to Monty as he pulls the door open. "We don't allow anyone to watch the session from inside the room. It creates distraction that can result in incomplete information."

"I know. I've dabbled in the psychic arts myself," Monty says.

I raise my eyebrows. "Do say more."

"Indigo knows all about my time in India with my guru." He glances at Indigo, who seems to be trying not to roll his eyes. "Maybe later," Monty adds. "I'll be outside."

He walks out and shuts the viewing room door behind him.

"Do I get to know what's going on here?" I ask, although I already know the answer. All of the psychic viewers are on a need-to-know basis, and we rarely need to know anything.

Indigo returns to his chair and starts fiddling with the buttons on his yellow plaid shirt. "He contracts with a branch of the government that can pay a lot more than the CIA can. I know we usually don't take on outside work, but he pays ten times what the CIA pays, and they're not giving us enough to stay afloat."

I lean forward in my seat and try to catch Indigo's eyes, but he suddenly has several other places to look, and none of them are at me. "What do you mean?" I ask. "What happens if we don't stay afloat?"

Indigo shakes his head. "Closing the doors is always an option. Not to me, but you know what most of the CIA thinks of us. I've always suspected they could pull their funding at any moment, and well, here we are."

"Are they cutting us off?"

"Not completely. But the taxpayers want more transparency, and well, let's just say that's why I negotiated the ability to take on outside clients. For situations like this."

I nod. It's a touchy subject with Indigo. We spend our lives finding reliable information for the CIA, but, according to Indigo, they continue to think of us as quacks, and often threaten to withdraw our funding entirely. Indigo says that's because they can't understand that psychic viewing isn't all that different from seeing or hearing something right in front of you: It's just another sense that we've gotten really good at using. But try telling that to someone sitting behind a desk pushing paper for the government.

"We don't have much of a choice," Indigo continues. "And Junior, I mean, Monty, he's a good guy. Just trying to right his father's wrongs. So focus today."

It's useless to ask Indigo questions at this point, so I just pick up the stack of blank paper and the pen from the coffee table, and then I close my eyes and settle back on the couch. Across from me, I can hear Indigo shift in his leather chair.

As Indigo counts down from ten to one, I imagine myself on a boat in the ocean. His voice is soothing, and I am soon flying through a black abyss, nothing below me or above me.

It's so dark that I wiggle my toes and fingers to make sure they're still there. After a moment, my feet land on something solid and firm, and when I look down, there's red smoke seeping out of the ground.

I study my surroundings to get more clues of my location, and I instantly feel my hand moving across the paper. I keep my eyes closed, focusing only on the dark lines of hills and rocks around me.

Am I in the mountains? I wonder before I can stop myself. I push the analytical thoughts out of my mind and focus purely on what I'm *seeing*, not what I'm *thinking* about what I'm seeing.

Moments later, I can feel my hand drawing circle after circle, one inside the other, like rings of a tree. My muscles start to cramp, and then, as my hand gives out, suction shreds through me.

The next thing I know, I'm opening my eyes. I've drawn a bunch of ragged lines, representing rocks and hills. In the middle of the page is a giant circle, with a dozen smaller circles within it, signifying depth. The smallest circle, the size of my pinky nail, is so full of black that I've ripped through the page with the pen tip.

Indigo leaves the room to let me fill out my report in silence. I'm not sure exactly what I saw in the dark, but it's not important for me to know. I just write down the things I saw and felt, trying to avoid using the words "like" or "as." Even though I've been filling these out for over a year now, it still takes effort to avoid any comparisons to anything else. How do you describe a square with a triangle on it unless you call it a house? Or a box supported by four circles if you don't call it a car?

Indigo knocks on the door and pulls it open at the same time. "Are you ready? Monty's been waiting a while now." I nod. *Ready as I'll ever be.* "Just try to be clear about what you saw."

In the doorway behind Indigo, Monty is crouched down on the floor. He's trying to weave one of his long boot laces through the dozen metal holes, but his fingers are shaking so he keeps missing. We both wait quietly for him to finish.

"It takes a while to look this stylish," Monty brags when he finally looks up. Although his voice is cocky, I can tell that he's nervous about whatever I'm going to say. I don't blame him for being nervous. I'm not sure why he is taking it on himself to right his father's wrongs, like Indigo said, but by the anxious look on Monty's face, I can tell he's afraid that what I saw will be something he doesn't want to hear.

Indigo gestures for Monty to take his leather chair, but he shakes his head.

"You take it, old man," Monty says, and Indigo scowls at him.

Monty comes in and leans over me awkwardly, studying the picture I've drawn. The ragged lines and concentric circles mean nothing to me, but they obviously mean something to Monty. For a brief second, his cheeks rise and wrinkle slightly, two micro-expressions revealing joy.

"Is this everything you saw?" Monty asks.

"I'm not sure what I saw," I admit. I've never had an interaction with a client before, and it feels both strange and satisfying. Strange, because I usually don't know what I'm looking for or why. Satisfying, because even if I haven't found it yet, I think I've made progress, and the pleased look on Monty's face makes me realize I'm helping someone. I always am, I guess, but this time, it's different: this time I can see it.

"Is this a hill?" Monty asks.

I shrug. "I only see it. You analyze it."

Monty studies the black hole I've ripped in the center of the picture, leaning forward so far his shirt brushes my shoulder.

"Is this info helpful?" Indigo asks.

Monty nods. He shoves his hat down onto his head, so low that I can't see his eyes anymore, and then he traces my lines on the paper. He starts with the outside circle and follows it inward until he reaches the dark center, his fingers walking a trail that only he can see. "So this must be it," he mutters, "this must be the leak."

I wonder what it is about Monty that makes him determined to clean up his father's messes. If there is a toxic spill from one of his dad's mines, wouldn't the news know about it? Or is Monty trying to clean up the leak before the media finds out, or before people get hurt? I suddenly want to know that I'm making a difference to people, maybe even saving lives that I usually can't save in my sessions. "Do you think you can contain the radiation?" I ask, knowing it's entirely inappropriate of me. But when have I ever been appropriate?

Indigo looks at me sternly, but Monty just nods.

"I think so." Monty points to a curvy line an inch above

the circle. "If this really is the leak, we might be able to contain it." He zips up his black leather jacket and pulls the collar higher around his neck. "Thanks for your help," he says to Indigo. He nods at him, and Indigo nods back. Then, to my surprise, Monty turns to me and awkwardly sticks out his hand. "And thank you, Callie."

It's weird being thanked for psychic viewing. I'm so used to not knowing what I've found or who the information will affect that I'm not sure what to feel about it. But just not having to hide my talent for once is enough.

I stand up and shake his hand. "Anytime," I say, and I mean it.

CHAPTER ELEVEN

Mom is waiting up for me when I get home. She looks stressed, and I remember the old days, when we used to stay up late together talking about her newest boyfriend or what happened to me at school that day. Now we're both too busy.

I drop my backpack beside the kitchen table. "Richard not home tonight?"

"Another all-nighter at the station. But he dropped this off for me." She holds up the half-empty bottle of red wine. "He's so considerate. Just when I needed it."

"Why? What's wrong?"

Mom shakes her head, and I realize that she confided her worries in Richard this time, not me. It makes me feel somewhere between pleased and replaced. "Just work stuff," she says. "Ruining students' lives. Handing out Fs like candy."

I haven't seen the funny side of her in forever, and it makes me smile.

"I didn't know you had such expensive tastes," I say, pointing to the bottle's label, which proudly portrays the year 2005. I don't know much about wine, but I do know that a bottle over ten years old isn't cheap, and that it usually means something.

"Richard said someone at the fire station gave it to him." She shrugs, and pours herself another glass. "Want some?"

Did my mom just ask me to drink an alcoholic beverage? "Um, okay," I say, opening up the cupboard and getting myself a wine glass. I sit down across the table from her and pour myself a glass.

She puts her hand out when it's halfway full. "A taste, I said."

"You didn't actually say that," I point out.

"This relationship thing," she sighs. "How do you do it?"

"Someone's got to," I say, but then I see the seriousness on her face. "Did something happen with you and Richard? Is this an apology bottle?"

She shakes her head. "I just don't want to screw up again, for both of us."

At first I think she means her and Richard, but then I realize that by *us*, she means her and me. "What did he say?" I ask.

"Nothing important, but my track record isn't good," she says. "I just don't want to fall apart again," she adds, finishing her glass and reaching for the bottle. "Your father . . . he was the only real love I ever had."

I hardly breathe. She's talking about Dad. How many years has it been?

"And when he left without a word, well . . ." She trails off. "He was the type of man who always knew what I was thinking, do you know what I mean?"

I nod, thinking of how Charlie can always guess my mood and settle my nerves with one word.

"You don't need to hear this," she says.

"Yes, I do," I insist. "I want to know who he was, and what he was like, and—"

"I want to answer your questions, Cal," she says, her eyes finally meeting mine. "But I just don't know. I thought we were in love. And he adored you," she adds. I roll my eyes, but she takes my chin lightly in her hand and makes me look at her. "*Adored* you. Like you were the only person on the planet. Even I was jealous." I feel myself blush, and she lets go of my chin. She downs her glass and picks up the empty bottle. "Now give me that glass," she adds. "You shouldn't be drinking anyway."

The office is strangely quiet the next morning, but it's not that peaceful type of silence, the kind you feel you could float away in. It's more of a stewing nervous type of quiet, where you can tell that something went terribly wrong and you are the last person to know about it.

Jasper is sitting at the table in the staff room, drinking coffee from a Styrofoam cup. His face is creased with anger. Across the office, Indigo is perched behind his desk, his phone clamped to his ear. He looks relaxed, and anyone who doesn't know him as well as I do would think he is—but I can tell from the way his mouth is tightened into a thin line that he is barely holding in his anger.

"What happened?" I whisper to Jasper, sitting down beside him at the table.

"Just because I'm new here," Jasper says, "doesn't mean I can't see what's right in front of my face."

"What's in front of your face?"

He looks up at me and back down into his cup of coffee. The overhead lights reflect in the brown liquid. "Never mind."

"Were you fighting with Indigo again?" I ask, but Jasper doesn't answer.

"Ready, Callie?" Indigo asks, popping his head in the doorway. He doesn't even glance in Jasper's direction.

I follow Indigo into the viewing room, glancing back at Jasper. He's glaring at Indigo's back, but when he notices me watching him, he winks. I can't help smiling.

"Let's get started," Indigo says, shutting the door of the viewing room and sinking into the chair. I can tell by his voice that he's still irritated with Jasper.

"What's going on between you two?" I ask, sitting on the couch across from Indigo.

Indigo shakes his head. "I run this place. All opinions are welcome, but that doesn't mean I'm going to take them. Do you know what I mean?"

I shake my head, and he sighs.

"Jasper doesn't like us working for Monty. He thinks it compromises our security to view for private companies, even if they do contract with the government. I'm not sure I disagree with him, but I also know that if we don't make more money, we'll have to close the doors."

"It's not like Monty's hurting anyone," I point out. "If he's willing to pay to clean up his dad's messes, and he has the resources to do it, why shouldn't we help him?"

"I feel the same way." Indigo smiles grimly. "I get Jasper's point, I really do. Monty's still private industry, even if he's trying to do good. But our relationship with Monty is especially important right now, since we need more money to keep our office open," he says, and then he hesitates. "I'm sorry. I shouldn't be talking about this with you." He leans back in his chair and taps his pen three times against the palm of his other hand. "Why don't we get started?"

"Okay." I sit back and close my eyes. "But you can talk to me anytime, you know."

"I know," Indigo says, and even through my shut eyes I

know he's smiling. "Ten . . . nine . . . eight . . ."

At first, my mind flits from thought to thought, unable to focus on anything specific, but then I just listen to the numbers, and I'm in before Indigo gets to one.

Immediately everything starts spinning, and it's hard to focus my eyes with my feet constantly swapping places with my head. The suction yanking my body downward is stronger now than it was in my last vision. Dizziness is coming on fast, and I know I won't be able to hang on long, so I quickly try to take in what I can.

I'm perched on a big piece of metal with two wings. I focus on the object I'm standing on, and I notice that there's something etched into the metal between my feet.

"What do you see?" Indigo asks above my vision.

"I'm standing on a metal beam, and there's something written on it, but it's too dark to see much," I say.

"Can you tell me more?" Indigo asks.

The spinning slows to a crawl, and I more clearly see the etching beneath my feet. I'm pretty sure it's the infinity sign logo I saw on the building, where that person was trapped under the red smoke. I force myself to stop analyzing and focus on what I'm actually seeing. Below me, beyond vast amounts of blackness, there's a spot of color in the distance.

"What do you see now?" Indigo asks me, but I can't speak or look away from the blue and green patch of color.

As it revolves slowly in one direction, becoming a colorful, rotating ball in the blackness, I realize where I am, and a thrill jolts through me.

"I'm above Earth," I say aloud. I can hardly believe it. I've heard it's possible, but I've never been out this far, and I'm nearly trembling with excitement.

"How far above?" Indigo asks casually.

I try to keep my voice steady. "I think I'm on a satellite," I say. *In frickin' outer space.*

"Go closer," he instructs.

I gladly swoop closer to the earth, marveling as I coast through the thick whiteness of a cloud, and then pass through it into the clear sky. The ocean spreads out in blue waves as far as I can see, but then below me, in the middle of all that blue, there's an explosion.

A giant wall of water rises up, and starts to roll across the ocean. I can't tell how big the wave is until I see the tiny tip of land protruding into the sea, and on it, the little boy I've seen before. He's standing in the center of a group of people, and they are all looking up at the wave with terrified faces. The boy cries out one sheer, desperate wail, and then he's cut off abruptly as the wall of water crashes over them.

In the blink of an eye, everything is gone. The boy, the people around him, the piece of land jutting out into the sea. Washed away.

CHAPTER TWELVE

I walk out of the building and cut across the quad, dodging the college students' Frisbees. Even though it's been a few hours, I'm still turning over the four events that I carefully detailed in my post-session report. First, I was standing on the satellite etched with what I think was the infinity logo, and then I saw the explosion in the ocean, and the tidal wave that resulted from it, and then all those people being washed away. But what caused the explosion?

The little boy's cry shatters through me again, and the wretched sound of it makes me desperate to make sure the boy is somewhere else when this tidal wave happens, somewhere safe. But I'm not sure what I can do. The only thing

I know is that the logo I saw on the building surrounded by red smoke may be the same logo as on the satellite. If Indigo knew I was analyzing this, he'd be upset with me, but I can't stop thinking about it, and now I'm determined to find out if I'm remembering accurately where I've seen the logo before.

During our after-session, when I told Indigo about the satellite I was standing on, an image flashed through my mind. It was from when I was on the highway headed to Charlie's house yesterday. I glanced out the bus window, and I saw a group of warehouses to the north of the salt flats—in the dangerous part of town that Charlie has warned me never to go—and I think I saw what looked like an infinity sign on the top of one of the buildings. I'm not sure, because the image was gone almost as quickly as it came, but it's enough for me to go on.

I glance both ways before slicing through a residential alley toward the Berkeley train station. In my mind, I keep trying to remember the exact symbol I saw from the bus window, but I can't quite pin it down.

I'm walking through the alley, surveying the windows stuffed with Bob Marley posters and neon beer signs, when a car with four guys in it starts trailing me. I've never had a problem in this neighborhood before, so at first I think they're just students returning home, but on closer look I can tell that they are drunk frat boys. I pick up the pace, but the car keeps getting closer, so I turn out of the alley and out onto the street.

The street is small, with pastel pink houses that look like old people should be swinging on wooden porch swings, but there's nobody on the porches, or anywhere in sight. The car pulls up alongside me, and a guy leans out the passenger side window. He's wearing a collared shirt and a baseball cap with *SIGMA CHI* written across it—the name of one of the wildest fraternities on campus. He's smoking a cigarette, the smoke so thick it tickles my throat, and from inside the car, I hear the other guys whooping and whistling at me.

"Hey sexy. You want a ride?" he slurs.

"Like I want a root canal," I say, keeping my eyes straight ahead. My heart is pounding, and my hands are getting sticky with sweat, but I try not to show it.

"C'mon, baby, don't be like that," the guy says, and the driver slows the car down so that the wheels are rolling beside my moving feet.

"Go away," I say, my heart pounding faster.

Then the guy pushes the passenger door opens a few inches and sticks his arm through the gap. "I won't let you miss the biggest kegger of the year," he says, and I feel his moist fingers skim my arm. "Whether you like it or—" The metal door suddenly slams back onto his arm. "Ow!" he yells. The guy yanks his arm back inside, and I quickly

125

move away from the car. "Bitch," he curses as he slams the door and speeds away.

I stare after him, unsure what just happened, but then I see Jasper sitting on his motorcycle at the end of the street.

I can bend metal within a hundred feet, I remember Jasper saying.

"Want a ride home?" Jasper asks when I get close to him.

"That was you?" I ask, and he nods. "Indigo would kill you if he knew."

He shrugs. "Then don't tell him."

I watch sunlight twinkle off the bike's chrome mirrors, trying to decide what to say. "Thanks for that," I finally say.

"For what?"

"The whole knight-in-shining-armor thing."

"I left my armor at home," he says. "So, are you getting on?"

"On your donor-cycle?" I ask. Mom says that the most likely way to end up paralyzed is to ride on a motorcycle. I suddenly wonder if she's ever ridden one, or she just learned that from a scholarly article about the top ten most likely ways for her daughter to die.

"I'll go slow," Jasper promises. "And it's a half hour until the next train to the city."

"I'm not going to the city."

"Very mysterious," Jasper says, and nods appreciatively. "Now you get this flirting thing."

"I'm not flirting," I protest. "But I *am* glad you showed up. How'd you know where to find me?"

"I know things." Jasper climbs off his motorcycle and kicks the kickstand. He leans against his bike and crosses his arms over his chest. "So where are you going anyway?"

"If I tell you, you can't tell Indigo."

"I'm in." Jasper unlocks a plastic box behind the seat and takes out a black helmet. "Wear this," he says. Before I can say no, the helmet is on my head. It feels too loose on my skull, and it flops back and forth as Jasper tightens the buckle under my chin.

"Just this once," I say as I get on the bike. My body rocks when Jasper gets on in front of me, and the revving engine sends buzzing through my head.

"Go on," he says, turning around so he can see me. "You were saying?"

It's hard not to touch him sitting so closely on the bike. My inner thighs are pressed against his butt, and as much as I try to lean back, I'm still almost on top of him. "I saw a symbol in my session today," I say, feeling heat rising in my cheeks. "I think I know where I've seen it before, but I want to make sure."

"Why?" he asks.

How do I explain that the terror I saw in the kid's eyes will haunt me eternally if I don't do everything I can to stop this from happening? "There was this little boy . . . ,"

I start, and then shake my head. "I saw him get killed. And I don't know, it just affected me in a deep way, you know what I mean?"

Jasper nods, and I realize that he is one of the only people in the world who *could* know what I mean.

"I only have one lead," I continue. "Do you know where the salt flats are?"

Jasper turns back around and revs the engine. "Hold on," he says, and I clamp my legs tighter around the bike. He glances back at me. "Hold on to *me*."

When I wrap my arms around him, I want to pinch my skin to convince myself I'm not dreaming. *This is really happening.* I'm trying not to move my hands at all, so I just freeze, my arms cramping around his waist.

The ride is exhilarating. It flashes by like a vision: bridge, water, building, street, building, hill, all of it accompanied by sweating nerves, so that my hands are sticky and cold.

"Are you having fun?" he yells over the roar of the engine.

"Not a bit," I call into his back, but I am. I'm thrilled by every minute of it, when I'm not thinking about my guts being splayed across the pavement.

As Jasper zooms up the steep ramp to the highway, I imagine Charlie seeing me right now, and I duck my head into Jasper's back. I know I could explain this to Charlie— I missed the train and needed a ride, this is the Bernsteins' nephew who just moved to town—but it feels like I'm cheating on Charlie, when nothing has happened at all, and probably never will. But part of me wishes it would, and that's the part that ducks and hides against Jasper's back.

Thirty thrilling minutes later, the smell of salt hits my nose at the same moment I see the infinity symbol from the highway. "Take this exit," I yell at Jasper. He doesn't hear me, so I tap him on the shoulder and point to the right, and he flies across three lanes and onto the exit. We coast down the ramp to a stop sign. If we turn right, we head into Charlie's neighborhood, where mothers like Grace are working two jobs to make enough money to send their kids to private schools in the city, and still getting home in time to bake whole wheat cookies and put them to bed.

I've never turned left.

"Left," I say.

Jasper turns onto the bumpy road that leads to the salt flats, and we're suddenly in the part of town that looks like someone is going to be killed, and soon. Along the torn-up street are several run-down warehouses, a vacated gas station with the G missing in the neon GAS sign, and a square block of concrete that looks like someone had the intention to build something but ran out of money. At the end of the road, the bright pink salt flats shimmer in the afternoon sun.

"Remind me never to turn left," I mutter.

"It looks like the place where dreams go to die," Jasper says.

Near the end of the row of warehouses, closest to the barbed wire fence closing the salt flats off from the road, is a giant redbrick warehouse. There's a chain lock hanging from the front door, and the windows are so grimy I can't see in, but more importantly, across the top floor of the warehouse is the logo I was looking for: the infinity sign made of two interlocking earths.

I point up at the symbol. "That's the logo I saw," I say. It's strange seeing something in real life that I saw in a session. It's like looking at a photograph that I haven't seen for years: it's the same place, but somehow it's also totally different.

"And in such a romantic location," Jasper says, driving right up onto the sidewalk. The motorcycle jumps under my butt as it crosses over the curb, and I clamp my legs down around the bike rather than cling to Jasper again.

"Do you see the name of a company anywhere?" I ask.

"Nope."

"Go around the side, please."

Jasper revs the engine, and the roar echoes off the warehouse, sending shivers down my arms.

"Maybe quietly?"

Jasper laughs at me, but he drives the bike slowly around the rest of the warehouse.

"I don't see a company name," I say, after searching every outside wall. "*Someone* must own it."

"Can't we google this?" Jasper complains. "We have this thing called the internet. Ever heard of it? We use it to look up things."

"Thanks for the tip," I say sarcastically. I reach into my back pocket and pull out my phone. "Can you stop here?"

Jasper stops the bike but leaves the engine running. "Why don't you want me to tell Indigo about this?" His hands are still wrapped tightly around the gas, ready to bolt away at any minute. I don't blame him: this place is as attractive as a slaughterhouse.

"You know the rules. No taking work outside of work. But I had to see this in person."

"We came, we saw," Jasper says. "Can we go now?"

"Just a sec." I climb off the motorcycle. Stepping back a few feet, I angle my phone up so I can take a shot of the logo. "Okay, we can go."

I climb back onto the motorcycle and wrap my arms around Jasper's waist. He revs the engine and does a sharp U-turn back onto the street. As we pull away, I glance back at the warehouse, getting farther away by the second. I can still see the explosion of red smoke from my vision, which I'm growing increasingly sure will happen here sometime in the future. But what is this place? And why do I feel so driven to see it?

CHAPTER THIRTEEN

The sun is hovering on the horizon as I run across Fell Street, barely dodging a speeding car, and leap up onto the curb of the Panhandle. I can't seem to pay attention tonight: my body is still reeling from my magnetic attraction to Jasper. Holding on to his waist on the back of his motorcycle, I felt like quicksand was drawing me deeper and deeper into him. It wasn't a warm, joyful feeling, like it is with Charlie, more like an intense desire to be with him, split into equal parts exciting and frightening.

Across the Panhandle, Charlie's already here, kicking up leaves under our favorite tree, his hair sticking up in every direction. Adorable.

Charlie looks up and grins his goofy grin at me. He holds out his hand, and when I take it, he says, "Carousel horse."

"Oh," the word slips out as if buried beneath a rug. "Um . . . ." I look up at the tree, trying to think of an answer to our daily game. "Eucalyptus tree."

He looks at me strangely. "Okay," he says slowly, as if I've recently acquired brain damage. "You okay?"

"There's just a lot on my mind." *Like the wall of water I saw crush those people, but I don't know when or why, and a million other things I can't tell you, and will never be able to tell you.* But a little voice says deep inside me, *but I can tell Jasper.*

"Well, if you want to talk . . . ," Charlie says, smiling like a puppy just patted on the head. I know in that moment that finding out about my attraction to Jasper would crush him beyond repair, and my chest aches just thinking about it. I smash the leaves beneath my feet, listening to the *crunch-crunch-crunch* of their cracking skins.

"Look, the sun is setting," I say, changing the subject by pointing to the pink clouds hovering above the ocean. That grabs Charlie's attention, and we watch the sun set quickly over the horizon, our hands linked. That's the funny thing about the sunset: it only takes two minutes to go down. It seems like it's a long process, transitioning from day to night, but the truth is, in less than one hundred twenty seconds it goes from being here, lighting up our world, to being completely gone, darkness.

"Where's Colin tonight?" I ask, after the sun slips behind the sea, and the night comes plunging in.

"He's home with Mom. She's been working a lot, and I can tell he's been missing her," Charlie responds. "And I've been so busy lately between school, work, and taking care of Colin that I've barely had time to get ready," he adds, peering at me in the fading light.

I look at him blankly. "For what?"

"For Saturday," he says. "My photo show, remember?"

It's just the biggest thing that's ever happened to Charlie, and I'm so consumed with Jasper and my frightening visions that I can't seem to remember. "Of course I remember," I say. "Time is just going by so fast I can't seem to keep my head screwed on. But I promise I'll be there. I wouldn't miss it for anything."

We lean against our tree, the one with the skewed branch and a perfect sitting spot. I let my head drop back against the bark that I cut our initials into almost three years ago: C + C. Then Charlie kisses me, a deep kiss that tingles down to my toes.

"I love you, too," I murmur against his lips.

He smiles. "You read my mind."

On the street, a car honks at us as it drives by. We quickly pull away from each other, embarrassed about the whole world watching us kiss.

"I'll see you Saturday night," I say, kicking the tip of his tennis shoe with mine. "At your show."

"Two p.m. Noodles first," he reminds me.

"You and me," I say, crooking my pinky finger out toward him. He wraps his pinkie around mine and kisses it.

"Forever," he says, letting go of our pinkies and smiling at me. "You'll be my lucky charm."

Some lucky charm, I think as I turn and walk away across the Panhandle. "Charlie!" I call after him. Tell him you love him. Tell him that these have been the best three years of your life. Tell him a eucalyptus tree doesn't begin to describe it.

Charlie turns around, and his beautiful face shines with anticipation. I see the slight upturn of his mouth, his copper eyes fringed with long black lashes. But then I remember the dizzying blue of Jasper's eyes, and the way I can't stop myself from falling into them.

"Never mind," I say. He nods and walks away.

Through my bedroom's open window, the traffic blaring by on the street below drowns out the buzz of the ten o'clock news. It's so loud tonight that I can't hear any of the words from my neighbor's TV, so I just lie in my bed and try to think about Charlie, but my mind keeps straying back to Jasper. How exhilarated I felt as we drove to the warehouse, my arms tight around his waist. How he said *Calliope* in a way that made me love my own strange name. His fearlessness about standing up for what he believes in, even to Indigo.

The door opens and Mom peeks her head into my room. Her glasses are askew on her face, and there's a stray hair sticking out of her normally smooth bun. "Can I come in?" she asks, and I nod.

"Will you close the window?" I ask.

"Noisy, isn't it?" She lets herself in and closes my window, then sits on the end of my bed. I scoot my feet up so she has enough room on the mattress. "What are you doing?" Mom asks.

"Plotting the end of the world."

"As usual." She bares her teeth in a nervous smile, which she always does when she's uncomfortable. "Are you okay with this?" she finally asks.

"With what?" I ask, shifting to prop a pillow behind my back.

"With Richard and me moving so fast," Mom says. "I know I've put you through a lot with dating all these years, but I really think this is the one—"

"I know," I say. "I do too."

Mom grins and relaxes a little, and I can tell how much she wanted this to go well. "I think he might . . . you know."

I won't admit that I squeal, but my voice does something

that's a close relation to it. "Really?"

"He keeps hinting about it," Mom says, lowering her voice to a whisper, "and I saw a ring box in the nightstand."

"Oh, Mom, I'm so excited for you."

"Don't get excited yet," she says, crossing her fingers. "I could be wrong. But think, Cal: someone *normal* for a change."

Normal. Mom doesn't know it, but Richard is the only thing normal in her life. "Right, normal," I say, crossing my fingers too.

"And the only man who can find my keys when I lose them," Mom says, kissing me on the forehead. "Good night, sweetie," she says, and then she leans down and wraps me in a hug. It feels good to have her arms around me but also just plain weird. I mean, Mom loves me, don't get me wrong, but we're not the kind of family that hugs and kisses. We're the kind that feels an *I love you* should only be reserved for rare, life-threatening situations.

"Good night," I mumble, my face squished awkwardly against her shoulder bone.

Mom lets go, and even though I'm the definition of a nonhugger, I miss the warmth of her arms. "Sleep well," she says, walking out of my bedroom and shutting the door softly behind her. As I listen to her footsteps fading down the hallway, I glance down at my still crossed fingers and smile.

When the door to her bedroom shuts, I realize my knees are still bent to give her room on the bed, as if she's going to return for another hug. I straighten my legs, and then scoot down deeper into the bed and pull the covers up to my chin.

Think about Charlie, I tell myself, but then I am remembering the discussion Jasper and I had a few days ago, about willing ourselves into each other's dreams by implanting an image into the other's mind before bed. *Maybe it's not too late to try it.*

I pull myself out of bed and hurry over to my desk. Yanking open the top drawer, I take out a pen and a scrap of paper. *Make it as weird as possible. Then, when he tells me what he saw, I'll know for sure that I've planted an image into his dream.*

A flamingo, I write down, and then, to be more specific, *on the moon.*

After folding up the piece of paper, I put it back in the drawer and try to shut it, but the drawer catches on something. I yank out a flyer that's stuck in the back and uncrumple it. It's for the Academy of Sciences museum in Golden Gate Park, promoting their new *Satellites* exhibit. The flyer has one dirty, ragged edge from using it to pick the dirt out from under my nails at the diner the other day.

On the front of the flyer, there's a picture of a large metal satellite. I turn it over, and on the back, there's a list of sponsors for the exhibit. There must be a hundred of them, including everyone from Coca-Cola to Boeing airplanes. But at the bottom of the list, almost torn off by the split in the paper, is the logo that looks like an infinity sign, made of two interlocking earths.

CHAPTER FOURTEEN

I'm standing in the kitchen in that wavering, half-asleep type of way I get at eight in the morning, making coffee with one hand and trying—and failing—to pour creamer into my mug with the other (how hard can it be?), when Mom comes into the kitchen in a maroon cashmere pantsuit, phone in hand. Creamer pools on the counter beneath my mug.

"Morning," I say as I swivel to pour some coffee into her chipped Stanford mug. At the same time, Mom quickly wipes up the creamer under my mug. We move like that: in the spaces between each other. Richard says that we know each other so well our movements fit together.

"Where's Richard?" I ask, yawning. I couldn't sleep last

night after finding the logo on the museum's flyer. I was awake until after midnight, wondering what company it is and why I've seen their logo on both the redbrick warehouse and the satellite, and now, on the list of museum sponsors. I tried googling "infinity sign logo, two earths" and other similar terms, but nothing useful popped up.

Sometime shortly past midnight, I heard Mom giggling, and I was grateful for the distraction. I finally forced myself to get back in bed, and as I drifted off to sleep, it occurred to me that I had thought I knew everything about my mom, but her *giggling* was something totally new: this was my mom in love.

"Richard had an early call at the firehouse," Mom says, pouring some honey into my coffee mug. Without even tasting it, I know it's just the way I like it.

"Do you ever worry about him?" I ask.

"All the time," she says, and takes a long sip. "Constantly. But he knows what he's doing."

I remember the radiation I saw in my vision, and the way the man's body was trapped under the red smoke. Did that man know what he was doing, too?

"Some things aren't worth worrying about," Mom continues, trying to convince herself, and then she abruptly moves to pour herself more coffee, although she's only drunk a sip. "I forgot to ask you: Would you mind if I brought Richard to Charlie's show tomorrow night?"

I'm rendered speechless for a moment, because it's like the hug from last night all over again. I mean, Mom wasn't the kind of parent who came to my elementary school plays—and how could I blame her? If she can't find her keys in time to make it to her morning class, I can't expect her to keep up with someone else's life. But I could get used to this new mom. This new mom in love who will come to my boyfriend's first ever photography show in some obscure art gallery all the way on the other side of town just because she knows it means a lot to me.

"He'd love that," I say.

Her face brightens. "Great."

"Just don't be surprised at the topic," I add.

"What's the topic?" she asks.

"You'll see," I say mysteriously. I grab a granola bar out of the pantry and drain the last drops of coffee. With Mom still staring curiously at me, I cross the living room and shut the door behind me.

Jasper is holding court in the staff room when I arrive, doing magic tricks for the only two adult viewers I know. "It's better that you don't know too many people, for your own safety," Indigo told me on my first day of work. "We're taking a risk employing someone underage, and the more distant you are from the other viewers, the more normal we can keep your life." I wonder if the adults have coffee dates and tea parties, but I'm guessing with the secret nature of the work we do, they don't know each other too well either.

I move closer to Jasper, standing between Martina, the German psychic with the thick accent, and Pat, who, with his military haircut, always looks like he's fighting Nazis or doing something equally heroic.

"What's this kid's story?" Pat whispers to Martina, and I shift slightly closer to Martina, hoping she doesn't notice my sudden interest in being near her.

"I heard Indigo brought him in from New York," Martina whispers back.

Pat sounds impressed. "The New York office?"

She nods. "For some special ability."

"I hope this isn't it," Pat says, and they both snicker.

This time, I clap extra hard for Jasper when he finishes his magic trick.

After a few minutes, Pat and Martina leave, heading for their sessions.

"Wanna see another magic trick?" Jasper asks me, and I nod. Isn't that what people do when they're like seven years old? But right at the beginning of the trick I can tell that this is different. It's really complex, and it doesn't involve cards or pulling a quarter out from behind your ear. He actually makes a coffee cup *disappear*.

Like, gone. *Poof!* It makes me feel unsettled, like when I was in a small earthquake as a kid, and the ground shifted and buckled under my feet. The sidewalk literally *lifted up* into the air. It gave me this feeling that hasn't really gone away to this day, like everything we think is solid can just crack and change beneath our feet. It's that feeling of knowing what my world was, and then suddenly, it's changed into something utterly unrecognizable. The solid facts of my life—just gone.

Jasper's trick makes me feel like that. Or maybe *he* does.

"Where'd you learn to do magic tricks?" I ask.

He shrugs. "Long story."

"Ah, the Magician's Oath," I tease, and he smiles this time.

We try his disappearing act with a printer, then a bunch of paper files, even a whole computer.

"Will you make that disappear?" I ask. "What about that? And that?"

By the time we've worked our way across the staff room to the viewing room, we are laughing around each other like old friends. Indigo must notice the change in us, too, because he glances up from a pile of sealed envelopes on the desk in his office and smiles at us. Then, with his phone in one hand and a business card in the other, he shuts his office door. To anyone but Indigo, I think briefly, we must look like two normal teenagers, talking and flirting. *Flirting.* I wince at the word. *I shouldn't be flirting with anyone but Charlie.*

Jasper must notice my sudden change in mood, because he opens the viewing room door and gestures for me to go in first. "I'll monitor," he says.

"And I'll try not to laugh at your 'serious' voice." I duck under his arm and enter the pale gray room, and everything changes. My body instantly goes into automatic pilot, sitting on the couch and letting my mind float. Jasper perches on the leather chair and holds up a sealed envelope, and I nod and lean back on the couch.

"See you on the other side," Jasper says.

I focus on the sealed envelope as I open the suitcase in my mind and pack all of my worries into it. In goes the radiation at the warehouse, and the infinity logo, and the deadly wall of water. In goes my fear that Charlie will forget me in New York, and my nervousness about Mom somehow screwing it up with Richard, and my fear that I'm starting to fall for Jasper. Then I slam the suitcase shut and lock it.

I let myself relax, picturing my thin body on a boat in the middle of the ocean. I slowly hoist myself into the water, and then, as the cool ocean envelops me, let my mind clear, welcoming in a white space that fills me, suspends me in the water, hovering ten feet above the ocean floor.

The first thing I see when I get into my vision is a box

with red smoke emanating from it. As the box begins to move, my hands start moving across the paper too, mirroring what I'm seeing in my mind.

"Callie?" I hear a voice above the scene. It's calm, and my breath slows down a little. "What do you see?"

"I see a moving box," I say, spitting out my impressions as I see them, and I hear Jasper making a note on a piece of paper. I focus on the vision in my mind, and the image of wheels comes to me, turning over and over on concrete, and then I realize what it is. "It's a truck," I say. I continue watching, suddenly seeing how the lines connect to one another. "On a highway," I add.

"What's the truck carrying?" Jasper asks.

With my eyes still closed, I focus on the red smoke beaming from inside the truck, and a shiver crawls across my arms. "Something radioactive."

"Go closer," Jasper suggests.

I zoom closer to the truck and dread rushes through me, making the hair stand up on my arms. On the upper part of the windshield, there's the infinity symbol logo.

"Do you get a sense of the location?" Jasper asks.

I focus on the infinity logo, but everything begins to get hazy. Around me, the surrounding land starts to fade from view, as if somebody is erasing it from the outside in. "Something weird is happening," I say aloud.

"What's going on, Callie? What do you mean by weird?"

Jasper asks, but by the time he finishes the sentence, the entire image has been erased.

I sputter back to the surface with my hands sweating and heart racing. I've never seen anything be *erased* in a vision, and everything about it creeps me out. After not finding anything unusual at the warehouse, I had started to think that maybe I was jumping to conclusions about this company somehow being involved in the little boy's death. But in over a year of doing this, I've never seen anything like this. If somebody purposefully kept me from seeing the location of that truck, there's got to be something they are protecting. Now I'm more determined than ever to find out what company that logo belongs to.

"Welcome back," Jasper says calmly.

"I saw the logo again," I say.

"So?"

Why does it matter so much to me? I know that Indigo would tell me to just pass the intel on to the professionals, and he'd be right. But then I hear the little boy's haunting cry in my mind, and picture his sweet, terrified face—and something in me rebels against what I'm *supposed* to do. I know that if I just blindly pass on information and hope someone stops it from happening, it could fall between the cracks. The terrified little boy could fall between the cracks. Rage rises up in me at the thought of him dying when I maybe could have done something about it, like alert those people that the tidal wave will be hitting at that location, at a specific time in the future. But when and where? "We have to find out what that company is," I insist.

Jasper leans back and laces his fingers behind his head. "Did you forget the whole 'we are just eyes' thing? We report the information, we don't solve the problem."

Jasper's apathy toward the situation makes me feel like I'm going to burst. It's like I've been calmly doing what I was *supposed* to do for so long, and all that tension, that inability to do anything in the real world, has built up inside of me. "And maybe that's not good enough anymore," I whisper. "Maybe I saw a little boy killed by a tidal wave while I was standing on a satellite with this logo on it." I gaze at Jasper, my eyes a red-hot flame. "And maybe this same logo is on a nearby warehouse, and also on a truck carrying radiation," I add. "And maybe I don't know how they connect, but I know they connect somehow." I tear my eyes away from his as I climb to my feet, already packing my backpack. "We have to figure out what that company is."

Jasper doesn't move. "Why don't we just view it?"

"Because both times I've tried to focus on the logo, everything gets hazy—or erased. It's like I'm being blocked from finding out anything more. And the internet hasn't been helpful at all."

"So what do you want to do?" Jasper asks.

I tell him about the flyer I found in my desk last night with the logo on it.

"It was a pamphlet for some new exhibit at the museum," I explain.

"So we go there and ask what?"

"If that company sponsored the exhibit," I say. "Maybe the museum can tell us who it is."

CHAPTER FIFTEEN

After a train ride from Berkeley and a bus ride across the city—and an hour of Jasper wishing his bike wasn't in the shop—we're finally walking across Golden Gate Park toward the Academy of Sciences. The smell of pizza from a nearby food truck is washing over us, and Jasper obviously can't focus on anything else.

"I'm thinking a slice of pepperoni," he says. "What about you?"

"Seriously? It's ten a.m."

"So?"

I shake my head. "Maybe after."

"I'll hold you to that," Jasper says, but I don't even look at him: my attention is focused on the science museum a hundred yards in front of us. It's a huge building, housing both an aquarium and a giant exhibit hall, all topped by a roof made of live plants. People are streaming in and out of the front doors, under a huge sign announcing a new exhibit about the power of satellites.

As we walk toward the giant front doors, our hands brush, shooting guilt through me. Great. Apparently now I feel guilty just hanging out with him. I know we're not doing anything wrong, but it feels like I'm cheating on Charlie. It's hard to describe, but it's like, when Jasper's nearby, my entire being is magnetically pulled toward his. No matter how hard I try, I can't seem to stop flirting with him. Even when my mind says no, my body says yes.

This is work, I tell myself, and I instantly wonder if the logo is the only reason I've insisted we come here. Or did I also want an excuse to spend more time with Jasper?

In the museum's grand lobby, there are dozens of little kids skirting in and out of exhibitions with *San Francisco Public Elementary* balloons pinned to their T-shirts.

"That's where we need to go," I say, pointing past the kids and a mean-looking security guard to the small sign above the entrance that says Staff Offices, Second Floor. I take out my wallet and start to walk toward the ticket booth, but Jasper flashes a membership card at the guard.

Now that's *interesting*. "Nerdy much?" I say.

"It's my favorite place in the city," Jasper admits, and

I can tell he's embarrassed. Truthfully, I'm surprised. I would have thought Jasper's favorite place would be a hipster café in the Tenderloin, not a telescope in a science museum. "It's the first place I visited when I moved here." He blushes. "It's definitely kind of nerdy."

"I like nerds," I say, stepping onto the escalator. He gets on at the same time, and we stand awkwardly on the same step until we reach the second floor.

When we get off the escalator, we are smack in the middle of the satellite exhibit. It's apparently brought in hundreds of schoolchildren for its last week, and they are all either waiting in line to see the satellites or daring each other to touch something with the sign Do Not Touch.

"Over there," Jasper says, pointing at the small sign for Staff Offices on the other side of the second floor. We're crossing the exhibit as quickly as possible when, inches from my ear, a teacher blows a whistle. My eardrum rings as hundreds of kids jump out of line to gather around a museum staff member wearing a T-shirt with the words *Science Is Cool*. Unfortunately, she is standing right beside the teacher, and we are quickly hemmed in by the approaching children.

"Nice shirt," one of the kids snickers from beside Jasper. "Science is *not* cool."

"Gather round," the staff member says in a squeaky voice. She points across the room at a satellite that looks like a shiny silver dragonfly. "That is a satellite," she adds.

"There are over thirty-five thousand up in the sky right now." She points to a map of the earth, and above it, in the atmosphere, there are thousands of tiny red dots. "Most are between one hundred and four hundred miles above Earth."

"Are they dangerous?" a little girl asks.

She shakes her head. "Not at all. But they are crucial for all of our communication needs, including most of our cell phone and internet connections," she says. "They even connect us to the Facebook," she adds in a serious tone, and the kids snicker. "You can go closer," she says, "it doesn't bite."

As the kids move in closer to see the satellite, we manage to duck out of the crowd without stepping on anyone's tiny little feet.

"Those kids'll eat you alive," Jasper says.

"They couldn't take me down," I say, stopping in front of an open doorway labeled Funding Office. At the desk, a woman sits in front of a sign that says, Ask Me About Our Donation Program.

"Hi," I say. "Actually, I *am* here to ask you about your donation program."

The woman looks up at me with a blank stare, so I point to the sign. She just keeps staring at me vacantly, as if she's never read the sign herself.

"Okay, well," I continue, and Jasper snorts out a laugh behind me. "I'm doing a school report on donors to museums, and I'm trying to find out about one specific donor."

"For which exhibit?" the woman asks.

"Satellites." I take the flyer out of my backpack and place it on her desk. "This logo." I point to the infinity symbol. "What's that company?"

She studies the flyer. "I don't know offhand," she says. "Let me check." She turns to her computer and types rapidly on the keyboard. "Coca-Cola, NASA, Google . . . Here it is. EarthScape Incorporated."

"EarthScape," I repeat. An environmental company? Landscapers? Neither sounds like a company that would have a warehouse in a seedy part of town, but at least I have a name now. "Thanks for the info."

"Glad I could help," she says. She turns back to her paperwork, and we walk out of the office into the room of shouting kids.

"Pizza time?" Jasper asks.

"Uh-huh," I respond, as I pull out my phone and type *EarthScape* into the search browser. The bar scrolls for several seconds, and then tells me that I'm not connected to the internet.

"There's no reception in here," Jasper says.

"Thanks, genius," I say. "Then let's go." I pocket my phone and head toward the escalator. "And we'll get that pizza of yours, too."

We grab two slices of pizza—one cheese, one pepperoni—and sit on a bench beside a small lake to eat, amusing ourselves by watching a bunch of miniature boats buzz their way through the water. To my surprise, it turns out that the best pizza in the city is a deliciously greasy slice off a ratty food truck in Golden Gate Park.

"Are you *sure* you've never heard of EarthScape?" I ask Jasper again, and he nods. I've googled it a bunch of times in the last ten minutes, but I keep being directed to a US government website. "The only thing I can find out for sure is that it works for the government."

Jasper puts his index finger in the air, gesturing for me to wait until he finishes eating. I scarf down the rest of my slice and wipe off the grease running down my chin. "Sounds like a mapping company or something," Jasper mumbles through his last bite. He balls up his paper plate and tosses it in the nearest wire trash can, the one that says Landfill on it.

"Like Google Earth?" I ask, throwing my plate in the other trash can, labeled Reincarnation. Sometimes San Francisco amazes me.

"Maybe," Jasper says thoughtfully.

I shove my phone in my pocket. "Well, there's nothing on here. We'll have to find out about it another way."

"Maybe it's just a satellite company," Jasper suggests. "Did you consider that? That maybe it has nothing to do with any of the things you saw in your sessions?"

I sigh. "I considered that."

A man holding a box full of remote control toy sailboats, submarines, and battleships stops in front of us. On the front of the box he's written BOAT RENTAL: $10.

"Two for one," the man says.

"No thanks," I say immediately, but Jasper's already dug ten dollars out of his pocket.

"Sure," Jasper says, handing the guy the money. I frown at Jasper, and he says, "We can search for it more later. You've gotta learn to relax."

"Fair enough." I put out my hand. "Give me the damn boat."

We get up and join the small crowd of miniature boat owners gathered on the bank, each one focused intensely on his tiny ship cruising through the water. "Just watch me," I say, "I'll relax better than you ever could."

"Not as good as him," Jasper says, tilting his head toward a stout man with large glasses, driving his remote control like a steering wheel. The man presses a red button on the remote, and there's a soft *pop*. Smoke rises from a pirate ship and another boat, a few feet across the water, sinks.

"This stuff is serious." I put the sail up on my green sailboat and place it in the water beside Jasper's black battleship.

"Uh-oh," Jasper whispers, glancing sideways at a man launching a mini submarine into the lake. We watch it slide into the water and disappear below the surface, only its tiny periscope showing.

"He's after us," I whisper.

"Good thing there's two of us," he says.

Jasper and I are soon zooming our boats around each other's, laughing half in embarrassment and half in joy. In less than five minutes, my boat crashes into his, and they teeter together for a second before falling over onto their sides.

"Abandon ship!" I say. "Abandon ship!"

"Never," Jasper says. "A captain goes down with his ship. I took an oath and shall not break it." He mock salutes.

"You and your oaths," I say.

Jasper just gives me a look that says, *Yeah . . . and?*

I reach down into the water to grab our boats, but my sneaker catches on the concrete lip of the lake and suddenly I'm flailing my arms to gain my balance. I manage to spin so that my back is to the water just as Jasper grabs me and pulls. I stumble off the concrete lip and pitch forward.

My lips almost land on his.

Energy shoots through my body, making me shiver from my toes to the tip of my skull, and my lips, an inch from his, ache to kiss him. For one brief second we're completely alone; it's just Jasper and me in the park, our bodies humming together.

I pull away first, and then instantly wonder if he

would've pulled away if I hadn't. "I should get home," I mumble.

Jasper glances down at our little boats lying on their sides in the water. "We're officially shipwrecked," he says, pulling them out of the lake.

"Totally *Titanic*," I agree.

He hands our boats back to the rental man, and then turns back to me. He tries to grab my hand, but I pull away.

"We suck at this anyway," he says.

I pretend he's talking about the boats. With Jasper, I'm getting good at pretending.

CHAPTER SIXTEEN

The front door swings open just as I put my key in the lock, and I nearly jump out of my skin. Standing in the doorway is Richard, as dressed up as he ever gets, in khakis and a button-down shirt. Beside him, Mom is actually wearing high heels and her contacts instead of glasses, or at least I hope she's wearing her contacts. She'll be tripping over her own feet all night if not.

"Hey Cal, wanna come to dinner with us?" Mom asks, grabbing her red leather purse from a hook by the front door.

I shake my head. "Have fun, you crazy kids."

Richard opens the door for Mom, and she waves at me

as she steps out into the street. I watch them walk up the hill until they are out of sight, and then I run upstairs to my room and turn my computer on.

I yank off my jeans and pull on my coziest sweats, watching my computer screen change from a black square to a picture of Charlie and me. Mom took this picture on our one-year anniversary, months before I ever had to lie to Charlie about anything. I can hardly remember those times, when honesty seemed as normal as breathing, and telling Charlie everything I was feeling and thinking was a natural end to my day.

I miss it.

I sit down at my computer and click on the internet tab. As soon as the browser pops up, I type *EarthScape Inc.* into the search bar.

Wikipedia facts about the art of landscaping come up first, and then a term called "Earth scraping," which seems to be some sort of mining. I scroll down the list, much farther down than I did on my phone in the park, and I click on what seems like a hundred different hyperlinks before I get to a page with any information on EarthScape.

According to this website, which only contains a homepage, EarthScape Inc. is a company that specializes in rare earth metals. There's no info on the corporate offices, just a front page with pictures of brightly colored stones and a description of rare earth metals.

Rare earth metals are a series of chemical elements found in the Earth's crust that are vital to many modern technologies, including consumer electronics, computers and networks, communications, health care, national defense, and many others. However, it is the very scarcity of the rare earth metals that led to the term "rare earth," and it is their scarcity that makes them valuable.

I click on the word *valuable*, and it says that some rare earth metals are worth billions of dollars because of their use in electronics and military weapons.

I scan the top of the page for an *About Us* or a *Contact* link, but there's not even a menu. I pull up a new search browser and type in *EarthScape, owner*, but nothing useful comes up. I'm just routed back to the US government website. At least now I know it's the same company. I try searching for *EarthScape CEO*, *EarthScape founder*, and *EarthScape headquarters*, but still, no luck. I scour the internet for another hour, using every search term I can think of, but it's useless. Whoever owns EarthScape doesn't want to be found.

"Callie."

A whisper breaks me out of my heavy slumber. I drag my face off the pillow and see Mom through my black curtain of hair. She's sitting on the end of my bed, shaking me lightly.

"I'm awake, I'm awake," I mumble, sitting up.

"He did it," Mom whispers, and holds out her hand so I can see her ring finger. There's a gold band embedded with a small, glittering diamond.

"Wow," I breathe, pulling my knees up to give her more room on my bed. "How'd he do it?"

"You're not going to believe this," Mom says. She's practically glowing; I could find my way in a dark room using only her grin. "He took me to the fire station to meet his buddies first—"

"Are the hot firemen rumors true?"

"Totally," she says. "And then he brought me up to the roof of the station, and there was a heart made out of lit candles, and he got down on one knee . . ." She tears up.

"And?"

"And I blurted out, 'Do you think this is a fire hazard?'"

"No!"

She nods, embarrassed. "He blew out all the candles just to make me feel better. And then he popped the question."

"No way." I suddenly wish she wasn't sitting all the way at the end of my bed. This feels like a hug moment.

"Seriously, Callie, he is the most romantic man I've ever met," Mom says.

My stomach does a little flip-flop like it does at the end

of romantic comedies, and I smile at Mom. She deserves this happiness. "So when's the wedding?"

"We're thinking of eloping. No big fancy wedding at our age," she says. "Maybe in Hawaii. You'd come too, of course."

"You *do* need a witness."

"So, brunch?" she asks, scooting a bit closer to me. "Do you wanna go celebrate?"

"Of course." I can think of nothing better than celebrating my mom's engagement to Richard. "I'll just throw on some clothes," I say, but then there's a ding from my bedside table. Indigo's text is short and to the point: **Look 4 car.**

"I have to babysit," I say sadly, placing my phone back on the nightstand, face down. "The Bernsteins say it's an emergency."

Mom looks disappointed. "Well, okay, maybe another time then." She stands up. "But I'll see you tonight, at Charlie's show?" I nod. Mom kisses me on the top of my head and then walks out of the room, her hand held up in the air so she can admire her ring. The whole thing feels surreal, in a good way. It's going to take a while to get used to this new Mom.

I climb out of bed and glance out my window, already wondering what could be important enough for Indigo to bring me in on a Saturday. Since he's picking me up, we must be going to the secret bunker or he would tell me to meet him at the office. We only go to the bunker when there is a real emergency, and since every session feels like an emergency, this has to be big. I mean, earth is going to go up in flames sort of big.

Out my window, I watch an unmarked black car pulling slowly up the hill. The windows are darkened, so I can't see who's driving. I'm not even positive that it's the right car: I've only been picked up a couple of times before, and it's always by a different car, but the darkened windows are always the same.

I dig some jeans out of the bottom of my closet, then throw on a tank top and sweater. I grab my backpack and run down the stairs, passing Mom in the kitchen. She's admiring her ring under the kitchen's bright lights.

"We'll celebrate soon," I say, already crossing the living room and pulling open the front door. "Bye!" I glance up and down the street, making sure no one's watching, hitch my backpack over my shoulder, and hurry down to the car.

"Welcome, Jedi," Indigo says when I climb into the backseat. I've never seen Indigo behind the wheel, and I thought somehow his unearthly aura would shine too brightly for him to see or something, but it doesn't. He looks like a normal guy. It hits me, for the first time, that maybe he has a secret identity too. That even though I feel so close to Indigo in the office, he may be a totally different person outside of it. It's a weird, unreal moment for me, like realizing that your elementary school teacher has a first name, that she doesn't always go by Miss Stanley.

"Jed*ess*," I correct.

"How's that sexy mom of yours?" Indigo asks. I always forget that they're the same age, and of course he has a crush on her, even though he's only seen her in person once, at the Stanford spoon-bending party. Mom doesn't remember him, of course. Now, when Mom talks about the most important night of my life, the night I really discovered who I am, the only thing she remembers is how Richard showed up in a fireman's coat. I lucked out, though—she was so obsessed by her first date with Richard that she didn't notice my abrupt interest in a nannying job, or that graduating from high school early was suddenly an offer on the table.

"That sexy, almost *married* mother of mine," I counter, and he grins.

"Henceforth known as 'the one that got away,'" Indigo says.

"Or as 'Mom' to her genetic spawn."

"Lean in," Indigo says, bending over the front seat to reach me. I lean forward, and he wraps a familiar blindfold around my eyes. Everything goes black. I feel the rough material itch against my skin, and wonder again why they can't use silk or satin.

"It itches," I groan.

"This is for your protection," Indigo reminds me.

Everything is for my protection. I'm so tired of hearing about my safety.

The radio is playing from the front of the car. Indigo keeps changing the channels, which is irritating, not only because he only listens to talk radio, but because I get involved in one news report and then it gets cut off, and I get involved in the next, and so on.

"Another shooting at a church today. The shooter says he got his gun from the Lord, and warned us—"

"—Cooper will in question, says the attorney for—"

"—nothing to be alarmed about, scientists say, except for—"

"—toxic spills, making it the most polluted water in the—"

Indigo turns the radio off with a heavy sigh. "All bad news. Like always."

CHAPTER SEVENTEEN

I feel the car pull to a slow stop beneath me. Then the door opens, and the air immediately smells of lemon disinfectant tinged with Clorox. Indigo takes off my blindfold, and I'm back. *The prodigal psychic returns.* The bunker is concrete, with vaulted concrete ceilings and thick concrete walls. I know I'm underground, but I don't know how far, and I never will.

The secret bunker is secret in two ways: First, few people know where it is. Second, it's blocked from most psychic energy, like a giant, warehouse-sized Faraday cage, and it almost guarantees no enemy psychics will be able to break into our minds during our sessions. It was so expensive to build, the whole government shares it: we only get it when the CIA deems our mission important enough to use it for a day or two.

For once, the place is relatively quiet. It looks almost abandoned, so I know there's a lot of work going on. Psychic viewers spying on targets, monitors writing down their impressions, manila envelopes being handed back and forth. Only questions, no answers.

Now that we're out of the car, I see that Indigo's wearing jeans for once, and that his usually tidy blond hair is hanging in stringy rivulets down his back.

At the conference table in the middle of the concrete room, Martina and Pat are waiting for Indigo's instructions. Martina is chewing on a candy bar with what seems like an unnecessary amount of ferocity, and beside her, Pat is sipping his coffee with a look like he's going into battle. I sit down at the table next to Pat.

"What's going on here?" I whisper.

"Better be important," Pat says. "I missed my kid's Little League game for this."

Jasper bursts into the room, followed by Anthony, who is staring at his shiny black shoes. Since Indigo shuts down the whole office while we're here, Anthony becomes our driver. I can only imagine what kind of paperwork Anthony had to sign to be privy to the bunker's location.

"You didn't need to stop me on the side of the road,"

Jasper is complaining as he and Anthony walk in together. "I did get your text; I was just on a joyride at the time. Ever heard of joy?"

"Ever heard of GPS?" Anthony mutters back.

Indigo shoots Jasper an irritated look. "Problems?"

"Nope. I was cruising around when I got your text. I was going to text back, but before I could, this joker shows up, blackened windows and everything," Jasper says, dropping down beside me at the table. "You didn't need to track me. I would've showed up eventually."

"Apparently I did," Indigo says calmly. "There's something happening," he continues, giving Jasper another annoyed look. "Something big. Just heard from one of the suits."

"Which suits?" I ask, knowing Indigo won't answer my question. Across from me, Martina and Pat lean forward in their seats, waiting for his answer. Jasper crosses his arms over his chest and leans his chair back so the chair's front legs don't touch the floor.

"Not that they intend on paying us for our work," Indigo continues, ignoring my question. "At least appropriately." With this, he seems to gather himself together, pulling his hair into a ponytail and smoothing down his jeans. "The suit was from high up, maybe even the Star," he adds.

I'm surprised he told us; we're usually just blind weapons.

"The Star?" Jasper asks.

I always forget that he's new here. "The Pentagon," I say.

"Then why not just call it the Pentagon?" Jasper asks.

"We need to drop all other projects, put all hands on deck for this one," Indigo says. "That means you will be rotating with one another: viewing, monitoring, viewing, monitoring. We can't waste a minute."

"We'll view more than once?" I ask, surprised.

"We'll be taking long breaks between sessions to rest our minds," Indigo says. "I know it's risky, but this is important for our national security." Pat shifts in his seat, and his chair screeches across the tile floor. Indigo glances over at Pat, who stops moving immediately. "I talked to some of the other viewers already," Indigo says, gesturing to several closed viewing room doors around the bunker.

"Viewers we know?" Jasper asks.

Indigo shakes his head. "The CIA sent a team to help. But the less you know of each other, the better," he adds. "Now, what I say doesn't leave this office. Got it?"

We all nod solemnly.

"I have good intel that someone has control of several countries' military-grade lasers," Indigo says. "We're not sure if it's a terrorist act yet, or what locations they are targeting, but combined, these lasers make a nuclear weapon look like child's play."

I feel a bead of sweat gather on my upper lip, and I wipe

it off with the back of my hand.

Indigo shakes a sealed manila envelope in the air. "But we have been given an image of the person who has access to this information."

Jasper's chair legs hit the floor with a loud boom. "What do we know so far?"

"That we will be here until we find out what this person knows," Indigo says, nodding to the envelope. "And that this information is crucial for national security."

"Do we have a name?" I ask.

"I've told you what I can," Indigo says. Conversation closed.

Indigo drops down into the seat beside me at the conference table. On my other side, Martina continues to gnaw at her candy bar. "Any of those left?" I ask.

She nods and points across the room to a bank of candy and soda machines.

"Thanks." I walk over to the candy machine. There's one Kit Kat left, so I dig two quarters out of my pocket and slip them into the slot. The Kit Kat drops to the bottom of the machine and I slam open the slot with a *bang*.

"What did that Kit Kat ever do to you?" Jasper asks, coming up behind me.

"Sorry," I say, loosening my grip on the candy bar. "I'm just nervous." I unwrap the Kit Kat package and hand one half to Jasper.

Back at the conference table, Indigo's still sitting there, his head in his hands, looking more upset than I've ever seen him. I nudge him on the shoulder and he looks up. I hand him my half of the Kit Kat.

"Last one," I say, thinking that he needs it more than I do.

At least until I hear Indigo's instructions. And then I want my chocolate back.

Our instructions are simple:

Find the person whose picture is inside the sealed envelope.
Break into that person's mind.
Force that person to tell us what the lasers' targets are.

I've never done the last one, and truthfully, I'm not sure I'm capable of it. It involves *influencing*, not just watching, and it borders dangerously on mind control.

I've read about mind control, seen all the same movies you have. Where a code word is spoken—*kitten*, for example—and the peaceful soldier becomes a killing machine.

The thing is, this stuff is *real*.

Indigo told me about how it started in World War II. During the Holocaust, there were these evil Nazi doctors, sort of mad-scientist types. They did experiments on the prisoners, really terrible experiments, like torturing someone almost to the point of death and then pulling their eyeballs out to see how they responded.

One of those experiments led to mind control, in which someone was beaten and rewarded over an extensive amount of time, until the Nazis could bury a word, matched with an order, so deeply into the prisoner's psyche that he wouldn't notice it until years later, when that word was spoken aloud. Then to the outside world, it appeared like the person snapped for no reason, but that word had been digging into his mind for years, stressing his brain until the very moment he heard it. It was the straw that broke the camel's back.

In the psychic viewing world, mind control is kind of like that, only you don't just bury a word in a person's mind. You bury *yourself* in their mind, and control them from inside. And hopefully, you don't stress their brain to the point of breaking.

"Just get in and get out," Indigo tells us after we've all come back to the conference table.

"But isn't this dangerous?" I ask. "Isn't this the kind of thing that made Michael—"

Indigo shakes his head. "You'll just be *existing* inside the person, watching out their eyes. It's different than taking over their brain and forcing them to take actions they don't want to," Indigo explains. "Is that clear?"

"As day," I respond, and breathe a sigh of relief. I'm still not sure I'll be useful in this mission, but at least I'm not expected to do something so obviously dangerous to the subject, even if they are involved in some sort of evil plot.

"Jasper and Callie will be working together," Indigo says. I glance over at Jasper, who is still nibbling his half of the Kit Kat bar. "And Pat and Martina," Indigo continues. "I'll be checking in on everyone throughout the day." He claps his hands together. "You know where to go."

"Is there anything special we should look for in our sessions?" Martina asks in her thick German accent, apparently not understanding that Indigo's hand-clap meant "meeting adjourned."

Indigo shakes his head. "Just the usual: Remain open. Do not assume anything. Remember that nothing is as it appears."

The small viewing room is painted a light gray, and the only furniture is a leather chair, a coffee table, and a gray tweed couch. It looks almost exactly like our office. This confirms my theory that creativity is not exactly the CIA's strong suit.

"Nice of you to join me," Jasper says.

"Wouldn't miss it." I settle back against the couch

cushions and try to ignore the annoying sound of Jasper tapping the envelope against the coffee table's edge. I shake my head, hoping to jiggle the distractions out of my mind, but I can't help thinking about how so far I've only played a passive role—watching, not acting, and certainly not influencing. Now I have to: Indigo is counting on us.

"What are you thinking?" Jasper asks.

"Nothing like breaking into a terrorist's mind to start off a day right," I respond.

"Besides a good breakfast," he says.

"Right. Besides proper nutrition."

"Don't worry," Jasper says, sitting up straighter in his chair, "I know what I'm doing."

"Do I look worried?" I ask, and he shakes his head. I'm glad he's by my side. Not that I'd ever tell him that.

I shut my eyes, and then I drop into the deep ocean and, releasing weights from my belt and breath from my lungs, I float down until I'm hovering ten feet above the sea floor.

"What do you see?" Jasper asks, and I think again about how strange it is that it feels as if two minutes have gone by, and it could easily be two hours, if not more.

Focus. I focus on the envelope, and then I'm flying through concrete walls, down a dim hallway, and then, to my fear and surprise, straight into someone's body.

Being in the body of this person is not exactly

175

uncomfortable, it's just a heavy feeling, like lying under a thick comforter, but it's dizzying keeping my view straight while this other person moves around, glancing from one object to the next.

When the person looks down, I can tell it's a woman by her painted fingernails. But my gaze, looking out from the woman's eyes, is blurry. Even if there were a mirror to see my reflection, my vision isn't good enough to do so.

"I can't see much," I say. "There's something wrong with my eyes."

Even though I'm now in her body, I haven't yet accessed her mind. I'm still watching the world, not changing it by manipulating her inner thoughts. There's a huge gap between the two. Being in someone's body is certainly new, but it's not enough. It's like getting into the White House, but being locked out of the Oval Office. I can't actually change anything from here.

Everything's blurry, but I can still see the cardboard boxes stacked on tall shelves around the room, and the high ceiling above me, crisscrossed with metal beams. "I'm in a big room," I say aloud, feeling my fingers move the pen in jolts across the blank paper—a distant feeling. How can I feel her body and my body at the same time?

"Ask her what she's targeting with the lasers," Jasper says.

I try to force myself into her mind by imagining what

she's thinking, but I can't seem to get in. "What are the lasers' targets?" I ask, but the words just echo through her body. "Tell me what the lasers' targets are." But since I'm not in her mind, she can't hear me.

I start to ask again, but then I notice that in front of me, there's a bank of computer screens. Each screen is split into four parts, and in each part is the image of a laser on a different aircraft carrier.

"Tell me where the targets are!" I shout into her mind.

I suddenly feel something cold beneath the woman's fingers.

Her hand is lifting a gun into the air and pointing it at someone.

At that moment, dizziness slams into my brain with an intensity that makes my eyes blur. I try to hold onto the scene, but it gets smaller and smaller as I'm yanked away.

CHAPTER EIGHTEEN

My eyelids pop open. I think a few hours must have passed, but I can't tell what time it is. There are no clocks in this place. It's like the mall, where they want you to get lost for hours at a time, only here you get lost in your own head.

I pull out my phone, and I'm surprised that it's just eleven a.m. I'm supposed to meet Charlie at our noodle shop at two, and then help him hang his show. I should call him to warn him I might be running late, so I speed dial his number, but there's no sound when I put the phone to my ear.

"The walls cut the signal off," Jasper says.

I frown at him. "But what if I have to make a call?"

He shrugs. "You don't."

I'll be there in time, I tell myself. *It's only eleven.*

"You ready? It's my turn," Jasper says.

We switch places: me on the chair holding the envelope, Jasper reclining on the couch, his pen poised over a stack of blank paper. He literally creases his brow in concentration. It's adorable—I didn't know that was actually a thing and not just an expression. As he falls deeper into the vision, his brow loosens and his muscles get more relaxed until he's nearly limp, except for his hand, moving across the page.

"I smell something burning," Jasper finally says, after an hour or so has passed.

"Are there any clues to your location?"

"There are several screens showing different images," Jasper says. "But they're kind of the same too."

"What are the images?" I ask.

Jasper watches for a while. For him it may seem like thirty seconds or five hours, but I think it's actually a little over an hour before he speaks again. "They're all lasers."

He stays in the vision for another hour or so, but he can't see anything more. When he finally opens his eyes, he looks disappointed. "So much for focus," he says.

"Ah, the difficulties of psychic teens," I joke, but he doesn't look amused.

"It's not funny, Callie."

"I know it's not," I say in a softer voice. "It *is* hard, isn't it?"

Jasper nods. "Never knowing if something is real or not. Not trusting your own mind."

"Does anybody?" I ask, the thought just occurring to me.

"I don't know," Jasper says. He shifts on the couch so he's facing me straight on. "Do you ever wish you were born . . . normal?"

I briefly close my eyes, the viewing room disappears into darkness, and for a second I can be normal: I don't have to see these terrible things happen around the world and be unable to do anything about them; I don't have to have visions that forecast people's deaths; and I don't have to lie to everyone I love to protect them from criminals who would kill for the secrets I have in my mind. But then I open my eyes, and it all comes rushing back in. "Sometimes," I say slowly.

"Only sometimes?" He looks at me skeptically.

I pick up the pen and start doodling a tic-tac-toe board on a blank piece of paper.

"Probably more than sometimes," I say. I draw an X on the board. "A lot of times I just want to be like everyone else, you know?"

"I know . . . ," Jasper says. He takes a deep breath. "Like, get married and have kids and live in a house in the suburbs surrounded by a picket fence with a little yappy dog."

"That's not normal." I say. "That's like . . . dreamland. Normal is a divorced family, two bitter kids, and a dog dying of cancer in the backyard."

"Don't make fun of me," Jasper says.

"I'm not," I insist. "I'm making fun of *me*." I draw an O on the paper, followed by the last X.

I win against myself. And I lose, at the same time.

"The day before my parents died," Jasper says, "I envisioned them at their funerals. And then, for years, as I got bounced around foster homes, I wondered if I could have stopped it. If I'd told them what I saw, I mean."

Wow. Wasn't expecting that type of sharing from Jasper.

I open my mouth to respond and then realize I don't know what I'm going to say, but I'm saved by Indigo popping in. "Lunch," he says, handing us each a paper bag.

We tear into the bags and pull out identical roast beef sandwiches and chips. Jasper lifts his eyebrows, but I shake my head at him. I can't remind Indigo I don't eat meat, because he'd feel like he had to arrange another lunch for me, and he has enough on his plate.

"Thanks," I say, as Indigo closes the door.

While Jasper eats his sandwich, I peel the roast beef off mine and drop it in the trash.

"Hey, I would've eaten that!" Jasper says.

"Sorry." I crumple up a few pieces of blank paper and drop them over the meat.

"Good tomato and lettuce sandwich?" Jasper teases when I bite into the dry pieces of bread.

"Better than dining on the tears of dead animals."

Indigo opens the door again. "Your next session starts in an hour," he says. "Take some time and relax."

"And do what?" I ask.

Indigo shrugs. "Talk." He grabs the manila envelope from the table and shuts the door.

You know when people tell you to talk, and suddenly nothing seems important enough to say? There's a long silence, and I almost forget that we *were* talking before Indigo entered with the sandwiches. I turn over the paper and start doodling again. Jasper blows into his paper bag so that it looks like a balloon, then smashes it between both hands. It explodes with a loud *POP*. Could he be any more of a boy?

"Hey, Calliope. What are you thinking about?" Jasper suddenly says. It strikes me that maybe the reason I let Jasper call me my real name is because he's the only person that knows both sides of me. As if I'm usually two people, and I can finally just be one.

"Seriously. What are you thinking about?" Jasper sings in a loud, off-key voice.

"Um . . . about whether I made a wrong turn and this is actually the tryouts for glee club?"

"Very funny," he says. He stands up and leans against the wall near me. "So . . . when was your first time?"

In any other reality, like the one Charlie and my mom

inhabit, I'd be blushing and crossing my legs. But in this one, the one Jasper and I live in, he is just asking when I first started viewing. Not that it's any less personal. But I like how he says it so naturally, as if it's almost normal.

I draw a hangman's noose on a piece of blank paper. "If I tell you, you have to promise you won't sing again."

Jasper crosses his heart. "Promise made," he says, and then he balls the paper bag up and tosses it in the trash. "No more singing."

"When I was a little kid," I say, cringing at the memory, "I imagined that our cat had been torn to pieces by our neighbor's dog. I saw it right before I fell asleep, so I thought it was a dream." I draw four lines below the noose and then five more.

"But then I found the dead cat, and it was so awful. Its head was torn right off its body." I write HANGMAN below the nine lines. "I never wanted to see anything so awful again, so I learned to block it all out. . . . But then Indigo found me."

"And?"

"And he taught me that this curse could be a gift," I say. "I could do something really meaningful with my life. Help people. And make my migraines go away, all at the same time."

"Indigo's good like that," Jasper says, and then adds, "Two words."

I nod.

"A," Jasper says, and I shake my head. "B."

"You're terrible at this." I draw the head and neck attached to the noose. "Pick three letters."

"S, T, U."

I write down *T _ _ S SU_ _ S*

"This sucks," he says.

"Getting better," I say, filling in the rest of the phrase.

"It wouldn't suck so much if you didn't trash your roast beef." Jasper grabs my chips off the table and throws them at me. I catch the bag of chips with one hand and chuck one of the plastic utensils back at him with the other. "Who eats sandwiches with a fork?" he asks.

"You mean a spork," I point out.

"Behold the great plastic bender," Jasper says. He holds his spork between his thumb and index finger, and slowly bends it.

"More like the great bullshitter," I say, putting my plastic spork on the table. "No one can bend plastic."

"True," Jasper says, "but they didn't give us real sporks."

I pick my spork up and snap it in half. "There, spork bending achieved."

Jasper studies me a moment. "You *can* bend metal, can't you?"

I shake my head. "It just happened once, and I didn't know what I was doing, or how I did it."

"But you can see electromagnetic radiation, like dirty bombs and stuff?" he asks.

I nod. "But not just weapons. Lots of things have radiation in them. There's radiation in all kinds of metals, used to build all sorts of things, like, um, computers and TVs, and cell phones too." I take my phone out of my pocket and put it on the table. "But some people say these waves cause brain tumors and other health problems."

Jasper pulls his phone out of his pocket too, and places it beside mine. "I'm not scared," he says.

"You don't seem scared of anything."

Jasper shrugs. "When you live in foster homes, you get used to being scared. It's not that I don't get scared anymore; it's that I know how to walk right into it. Refuse to be afraid."

Refuse to be afraid. If my mom would let me have a tattoo, I'd have that tattooed on my wrist. "When was your first?" I ask him.

"When I was a kid, I was on my own a lot," he says. "But even when I was alone, I felt like there was something bigger out there. Like I was in the presence of something larger. And one day I had a vision." He grabs a piece of paper and pulls it toward him. "It just appeared in front of me, like a mirage. At first I thought I was imagining it, but I could feel it and touch it. Like it was already real. I was standing on this bare piece of land, and I suddenly saw a settlement, for people like us."

"People like us?"

"Psychics. Fortune-tellers, people with the powers of sight. I knew I had to build it, and someday I will." He reaches for the pen in my hand, but his fingers bypass the pen and skim my wrist. "Maybe you'll help me?"

His fingers are now touching the soft skin around my wrist. Everything in me gets loose and tense at once, and a hot liquid rolls around my stomach.

Jasper knows me, I realize. The deep, secretive part of me. The *whole* me. And Charlie never will.

Indigo knocks on the door and opens it at the same time. "Now was that so painful?" he asks.

"No," Jasper says, quickly pulling his hand away from my wrist.

"Yes," I say, and put my hands in my lap.

Indigo hands Jasper the envelope for our next session. "Don't get used to viewing more than once a day, guys. This is a special circumstance."

We both nod, and Indigo shuts the door.

Jasper and I switch places again, and I lie back on the cozy couch cushions. "I wonder if it's the same envelope?" I ask.

"We'll find out," Jasper says.

I close my eyes and picture what's inside the envelope. My muscles slowly relax, and I feel that twitch in my legs that I sometimes feel when I am falling asleep, and then I'm in the woman's body again.

It's less of a shock this time, now that I know what to expect. Her skin is heavy, like a wet overcoat, but not uncomfortable.

"Ask her what the targets are," Jasper says over my vision.

"What are the lasers' targets?" I ask, but she doesn't answer. At the same time, I feel the cold gun in her hand again. I look down at the gun, and then I follow it to where it is pointing. A few feet away, a man is backed up against the computer screens, his hands held up in surrender. His sweating face is almost as red as his beard and his circular glasses magnify his terrified eyes like the end of two microscopes.

"What are the targets?" I yell into the woman's mind.

Bang! I feel the gun jerk in my hand, and the man slumps to the ground. Before I can figure out what happened, the man is lying on the floor, blood dripping out of a hole in his black sweater. Then the legs beneath me collapse, like someone hit the woman behind the knees.

As we fall face-first to the concrete floor, I hear footsteps behind me, and they sound so close that I should be able to reach out and grab the other person's ankles and yank them to the ground. But no, this is someone else's space, someone else's reality. *It's not really happening to me*, I remind myself. *I'm seeing out of another person's eyes. But whose?*

That's the last thing I think before the woman's face hits the concrete floor, and everything goes black.

I jolt out of my vision. Across from me, Jasper is leaning forward in his chair, a concerned look on his face. "It's been over three hours," he says. "What happened?"

"I think I'm gonna stay in my *own* mind for a while." I push the paper across the table to him. As I point at my drawing of the man being shot, I remember the news report I saw on my neighbor's TV about the hacker who broke into NASA to name a star after his mother. He had a red beard too, and those large circular glasses. "It was that hacker," I tell Jasper, "You know? Star guy?" Before I can stop myself, I start trembling. "I've seen people killed before, but I guess I've never *recognized* the person. It makes me feel like I know him or something. It just . . . makes it real."

Jasper puts the envelope on the table and comes over to sit beside me on the couch. "Are you sure?"

I nod. Jasper puts one arm around me, and I let go of myself enough to lean my head against his shoulder. We're probably breaking some rules, but it feels so good not to be alone in this, to talk to someone my age who really understands.

"What can I do?" he asks.

"I don't know." I shake my head, and my lips graze his collarbone, and then he's kissing me.

Jasper's kiss is nothing like Charlie's. It's not drenched in sweetness, in the taste of forever. It's passionate, a fire raging through my belly sort of passion, and I feel like I'm flying through the sky, my arms wrapped around him. Soon his hands are in my hair, and my body is pressed against his until we can't get any closer, and I find I wouldn't be able to pull away even if I wanted to—and I know I *should* want to, but in this moment, the truth is, I don't. His skin is so warm against mine, and I feel my body trembling in his strong grasp. *I'm not alone anymore.*

Then I see my phone on the table, still searching for a connection. The time is blinking on the screen: 5:45 p.m.

Charlie. His opening.

Dread floods into me with such force it makes me cringe. I drop my arms from around Jasper, my cheeks bursting with shame, and he goes still beside me.

"What's going on?" he asks.

I can barely hear him. My thoughts are roaring against my ears. I can't miss Charlie's show. I promised I'd be there.

I dash out of the viewing room and look wildly around the concrete bunker until I spot Indigo in the corner, near Pat and Martina's viewing room. I race over to him. "Can I leave?" I ask. "I have somewhere I need to be."

"Calm down," Indigo says gently, placing his hand on my shoulder. "You know your responsibilities here, Callie. You can't just leave."

"But this is an emergency!"

Indigo studies my face for what seems like hours, and then he glances down at my trembling hands. "Okay," he finally says. "You've probably overtaxed your mind by now anyway. But Jasper's going to have to take you; I can't have Anthony gone that long. I'll pick you up at eight sharp tomorrow morning."

"Thanks," I call over my shoulder as I dash back into the viewing room. Jasper is now standing up beside the chair, his motorcycle helmet swinging from his hand.

"Can you drop me off at an art gallery in the city?" I ask.

Jasper shrugs. "If Indigo's okay with it."

"He is," I say, pulling on Jasper's hand. "Come on. Hurry up."

We race across the bunker to where Anthony is waiting for us. He leads us down the underground garage to an ugly minivan with blackened windows. Jasper and I get into the backseat and Anthony blindfolds both of us. "I'll drop you off at Jasper's bike," he says.

After a few minutes of riding in tense silence, the minivan stops, and Anthony opens the back door. He unties my blindfold and I blink into the early evening sun. I untie Jasper's blindfold, and we climb out of the minivan onto the steep hillside. Leaning against a wall of rock is Jasper's motorcycle.

"No public transportation for us this time," Jasper says.

"As if there's any out here," I respond.

As far as I can tell, we're somewhere in Mill Valley, the very beautiful and very wealthy suburb across the Golden Gate Bridge from San Francisco. It's also very rural, which I usually think is a welcome change from the craziness of the city. But not now.

"Think you can make it from here?" Anthony asks.

Jasper nods, so Anthony climbs back into the mini-van and drives away. Jasper quickly pulls the motorcycle upright and secures the helmet on my head.

"I'll take the shortcut," he says, jumping onto his bike and revving the engine. "All private land so it takes half as long."

"Thanks." I climb on behind Jasper and wrap my arms around him.

We speed through Mill Valley, the green hills rising on both sides of us. Charlie's show must be starting now. I missed meeting him at our favorite noodle place, but as long as I'm at the show, it surely won't matter, will it?

We crest down the hill, and as the cool wind blows against my sweating skin, I suddenly hear a clunking sound. The bike jerks beneath us.

"What is that?" I ask, as Jasper slowly rolls to a stop on the side of a hill.

"I don't know," Jasper says. He turns the key several times, but it won't start. "I think we're out of gas."

My stomach plummets down the hill. "Please be kidding."

Jasper shakes his head. "I've reminded myself to fill up like fifty times. These things can go forever."

I stare past Jasper at the tiny view of the city. High rises climb up the hillsides, and somewhere, among all those buildings, Charlie's show is starting.

I pull out my phone and press the on button, but the phone is dead. Roaming all those hours at the bunker must have worn out the battery. "Can I use your phone?" I ask Jasper. I try to slow my heartbeat, but its quick pitter-patter in my chest must be loud enough for Jasper to hear.

He digs in his pockets. "I think I left mine at the bunker."

"What are we going to do?" I ask, my voice rising in hysteria.

"I think we passed a gas station a mile or so back," Jasper says.

The next four hours are a painful blur. We walk to the gas station, but no one is there, so we have to wait for someone to get back. When they do arrive, I use their phone to call a taxi, but the taxi takes over an hour to get there. And when it does, Jasper insists on using it to go back to his motorcycle and fill it up with gas, which actually is necessary since neither of us has anywhere near enough cash to take a taxi back to the city.

By that time, the show has been over for a couple of hours.

In the city, Jasper's motorcycle zips through the streets, passing where I was supposed to meet Charlie for lunch. Our noodle shop is closed, the cheap wooden stools turned upside down on the tables, a Chinese sign hanging in the window advertising this week's rooftop party.

We roar down Fillmore Street, past the cutesy art shops and boutique coffee houses. Jasper flips on his turn signal at the last minute and pulls up to the art gallery with a *screech*. I hop off the bike before it has fully stopped and rush to the window, hoping against hope that for some reason, Charlie's still here.

The gallery is empty. I press myself against the huge glass front window and look inside at all of those pictures of me, hanging side by side. Many of them are hanging at a slightly crooked angle, as if they were hung up in a hurry. Maybe because he was waiting for me.

I press my palms against the window, mouthing *I'm sorry* so Jasper doesn't hear me crying.

CHAPTER NINETEEN

*I open the front door a few inches and slip into my dark house as quietly
as I can, but it doesn't help.* Mom is waiting in the living room,
the white leather couch creased under her slim figure.

"We waited for you at the gallery," she says. "Why didn't
you answer our calls?"

I've never been grounded, or in trouble. My mom has
never been the type to stay home and watch me to make
sure I've eaten my dinner or brushed my teeth or lived
out my week-long grounding sentence. And it's not like
she can take TV from me. All the same, the shame creeps
in. *How could I do that to Charlie? Will he ever forgive me?* When
I glance at my mom, she's looking at me as if she's barely

hiding her disappointment.

"My phone died," I respond. "Sorry."

"Where were you tonight?"

I wish again that it wasn't so dangerous to tell Mom the truth. *But if I did, and anyone found out, they could torture her to find out what I know,* I remind myself. The thought of Mom being hurt because of me is enough to keep my mouth closed.

"I was so worried about you," Mom continues. "I called the Bernsteins."

I swallow the hot stone in my throat. I've never actually called the Branch 13 help line Indigo had me give my mom in case she ever had any questions about my "government internship," and now I'm wishing I had. I don't even know who answers those calls, and I seriously doubt Indigo would stop running Branch 13 to take house calls. "What did they say?" I ask nervously.

"Mr. Bernstein's very nice," she says slowly, tapping her upper lip with her index finger. "But strange."

"What do you mean by 'strange'?"

"I asked if you were watching Emma tonight, and at first it was like he didn't know what I was talking about," Mom says.

Uh-oh.

"But then I said 'Callie Sinclair? The girl who nannies for you?'" Mom continues, "and then Mr. Bernstein said

195

he was sorry they had to keep you late babysitting and that you probably hadn't had a chance to call."

The knot loosens in my throat. "Sorry," I say, and I remind myself to find out who takes those calls, and thank them for covering for me.

"Mr. Bernstein said his nephew would bring you home," Mom says. "Is that the same boy you had lunch with a while ago?"

I nod. "We've become friends."

"I don't like you being out with a college boy," Mom says. "Does he know how young you are?"

"He's seventeen, too," I say defensively.

"I still don't like it," Mom replies.

I drop down onto the couch beside Mom. "It was just a ride home, Mom. It's not like we were making out or something." *Just kissing while I stood up my boyfriend.*

"Let up on her, sweetie," Richard says, leaning into the living room from the kitchen, his hands covered in soapy bubbles. "Remember being that age?"

"Maybe." Mom growls good-naturedly, but I still wonder if I'm going to be grounded. "Fine," she says. "I'll let up on you. But next time, *call.*" She stands up and rubs her eyes. I didn't realize how tired she looked. "Help Richard with the dishes," she adds.

I nod. I can handle dishwashing as punishment.

"And call Charlie," she says as she walks up the stairs.

"I've never seen a kid so brokenhearted."

Charlie was brokenhearted because of *me*. "Yes, Mom," I say. As I walk into the kitchen, each step feels heavier, as if sadness is creeping through my muscles like black ink. In the kitchen, I pull out my phone, and plug it into the charger. The screen instantly blinks on, showing several missed calls from my mom, and then it quickly fills with text messages from Charlie.

He waited for me at the noodle shop for two hours. He was late hanging his show, and people arrived before he was finished. Only ten people came, including my mom and Richard. He texted me from the bathroom during the show, and afterward, he waited for me until the gallery owner kicked him out.

I imagine Charlie, so proud of his photos, sitting alone in the gallery after everyone left. I picture the lights being turned off, and Charlie by himself in the dark room, waiting for me to show up. I imagine everyone asking about me, and Charlie saying, "She'll be here soon," and the look of devastation on Charlie's face as hour after hour went by, with no call, no text, no nothing. And me, miles away, kissing Jasper. How could I do that to Charlie?

"Some help over here?" Richard says from the sink.

I glance up at Richard. "One sec, sorry."

He nods, and I quickly text Charlie: **I'm sooo sorry.** I press Send, and then I wait thirty seconds, but there's no response. "Just one more sec," I say to Richard. "Gotta call Charlie." I dial Charlie's number, but the phone rings and rings until his voicemail picks up.

"You've reached me. If you know who *me* is, you've dialed the right number," Charlie's voice on the message says.

After the beep, I say, "I'm so sorry, Charlie. Something came up that I couldn't get out of. Call me back," I start to push the End button, but then I bring it back to my ear. "Love you," I add, and hang up quickly. I put my phone down and then move over to the sink beside Richard.

"Hey kiddo," Richard says, handing me a foamy plate. "You okay?"

"I guess." I take the plate and wash it off in the sink while he scrubs another one. "But Charlie's not. And Mom was pretty mad."

"Your mom was just worried," he says. "To her, not calling is the same thing as you being dead on the side of the road." He shakes his head and chuckles. "That woman's got an imagination. Good when doing astrophysics for NASA, bad for late teenage daughters."

I nod. "You pretty much nailed it." He hands me a coffee cup. "Do you think Charlie will forgive me?"

"I don't see why not," he says. "You just missed his show. It's not like you cheated on him or something."

My silence must say more than I meant to give away,

because when I put my hand out for another dish, he washes the soap off himself.

"Go to sleep, kiddo," he says. "I'll finish these."

I open up my email account as soon as I climb into bed, but I'm not sure what to say. I wouldn't be resorting to email if he had answered my texts or phone call. It takes me five times to get the wording perfect.

Please call me. I'm so sorry. I was stuck at work and my phone died, I type, most of which is true. **I thought about you all night,** which is not completely true, but I did think about him once, before Jasper's and my conversation. And our kiss. **Love, Callie.** I hit Send.

I lie in bed wide-awake, waiting for the *ding* to alert me that Charlie's written back, but it never comes. I listen to Richard patter down the hallway to Mom's room, open her bedroom door, and close it behind him.

A few seconds later, I hear Mom's electric toothbrush buzzing through the wall, and I wonder if they realize that I can hear everything when they're in Mom's bathroom.

"Are you okay?" Richard asks her. His voice is slightly dampened by the thin wall between our two rooms, but not by much.

"It was like Callie didn't care," Mom says. But I do care, too much actually. One of the problems with not letting anyone in is that people you love think you aren't feeling anything, when you're actually feeling so intensely you've just pressed the mute button to survive it.

"She does care," Richard says. "You're reading too much into this."

I turn over in bed so I'm staring at the wall. I spread my fingers and push my hands against the wall, like I'm holding it up with my own strength.

"I'm just worried," Mom says.

I bury myself deeper into the covers, having heard all of Mom's worries before. But then, through the bathroom wall, I hear Richard say, "Maybe it's time—"

The roar of the hairdryer covers whatever he says next, and I guess whatever she says back, too. It goes off right as Richard says, "Just talk to her about it."

"She'll tell me when she's ready." I hear Mom walk out of the bathroom and shut the door behind her.

My mind races round and round, chasing its own tail. *Ready to tell her what? Could Mom know who I work for?* I grip the metal sides of my bed frame, refusing to allow that thought to go on one second more. Not only would Mom know I've been lying, it could make her a target. *It's not possible*, I decide, forcing the horrible thought out of my mind. Even though I couldn't tell Charlie the truth either, I wish I could talk to him. Just hearing his voice would make me feel better.

I dig my phone out of my back pocket and text Charlie again: **R u home?**

After several minutes pass and there's no answer, possible answers start gnawing at me. I imagine Charlie hanging out with another girl, laughing and talking and . . . kissing? Fear strums through me, making my whole body vibrate, while above me, the stars on my ceiling twinkle something fierce. *Why are my stickers twinkling like real stars? And why do they look so close?*

It takes me a second to realize I'm floating *above* my bed.

I've never tried astral projection before. I've heard about it, sure. But it's totally different from what I do every day. I usually think intensely about a target, and then my mind allows me to see the target, and sometimes even imagine myself into the scene—but this is taking my actual *spirit body* to a physical location. Most people call it an out-of-body experience because that's exactly what it is: a real experience out of your body.

"Just because you can travel out of your mind doesn't mean you can travel out of your body," Indigo said when I asked him about it, and he should know. Indigo has wandered all over the world, looking in people's windows, finding out government secrets that even closed doors can't shut out. But I've never done this before, mostly because Indigo said I should never use my powers to spy on someone I love.

"It will destroy you," he warned me time and time again. But this time I can't stop myself. I don't know if it's because I missed Charlie's show and I'm afraid he's never going to forgive me, or because I kissed Jasper and I am weighed down with guilt, or because I watched a guy not much older than me die earlier today and I haven't even had a chance to figure out what I feel about it—but the next thing I know, I'm guiding myself further into it.

Lie down and relax fully. Picture yourself somewhere else. I tighten all the muscles in my body at once, and then release. There's this disassociated feeling that washes over my body and mind, but instead of it being frightening, like I thought it would be, it's really nice. Like detaching from the heavy weight of my body, and lifting into the air, beating heart first.

Below me, there's a long silver cord trailing between my ghost body and my real body. *Now think of where you want to go,* I instruct myself. *I want to go to Charlie's house.*

I watch the silver cord stretch through the ceiling, and soon I'm floating above the house, and then above the neighborhood, and then the cord is trailing across the city in a string so thin it's almost transparent. I move toward Charlie's house. Beneath me, the train whizzes by, or rather, I'm whizzing by, and then it's several trains I'm seeing, block after block, all blending into each other.

Does Charlie like someone else? Have I been so busy

with work and Jasper that he's found someone else, someone who has more time for him?

I cross the city in under twenty seconds, but strangely, nothing ever gets blurry. It's crystal clear from the roof of my house to his doorstep.

I float through the open window in the living room, but to my surprise, he isn't home. I don't have to descend to his basement to figure that out. There's something missing, something decidedly Charlie, and the house feels like a floating object without an axis. Inside, Colin is asleep in bed, and Grace is checking something on her phone, but otherwise, the house is empty.

For some reason, the dark beckoning of the lighthouse pulls me forward. *Our place.* I move toward it, more quickly now, watching the ocean waves pound the shore below me. Seconds later, when I reach the lighthouse, I can instantly feel Charlie's presence, and my heart relaxes.

Charlie's solid form takes shape in the darkness, and his hair blows in the heavy ocean breeze. Watching him, I realize that he never needs to know about Jasper. I'll apologize for missing his show, he'll forgive me, and we'll go on like we did before. Maybe I'll even move to New York with him.

But then, from behind him, another figure emerges, blending the one dark shape into two. This one has long hair that snaps in the wind, and a lean bare belly. *The girl from the pier.* My heart sinks. *What is she doing here?*

My stomach clenches; I'm uncertain what to do next. Below me, Amber moves toward Charlie and places her hand on his neck. She runs her fingers up his smooth skin, and then her fingers are in his hair. Charlie dips his head forward and looks at her, and even I can see the desire in his eyes.

As Charlie leans toward her, I try to push my thought into his mind. *YOU DON'T WANT TO KISS HER*, I think with all of my force. I know I'm crossing a line by attempting to get inside his head, but I don't care.

Below me, Amber presses up against him, and two things seem to happen at once: Charlie's phone rings, and he abruptly jerks his head back.

Charlie pulls the phone out of his pocket and puts it to his ear.

"Soon, Mom," he says. "Just hanging with Amber. I'll be home soon." Charlie shoves the phone deep in his pocket, and I can't decide which happened first: the phone ringing, which made Charlie pull away from the kiss, or Charlie pulling away from the kiss, and then the phone ringing? Was the kiss averted because of the phone call, or because I forced my thoughts into his mind?

Before I can stop it, the silver cord zips through the air, yanking me across the city, through the roof of my house, and back into my belly button. I emerge back in my body, gasping, and feel the strangeness of my fingers, the fleshy skin over my bones. I rub my hands over my face, over the physical contours of my nose and mouth. What was she doing there with Charlie? *Is he cheating on me?* I know I'm a hypocrite for even worrying about it, but I can't help it.

I bury my head under my pillow, willing the image of Charlie and Amber, and of what they were doing together out of my mind. I slowly count down from ten to one, relaxing more fully with each number.

Eventually, I sleep.

CHAPTER TWENTY

As I crawl out of bed the next morning, I'm still wondering if Charlie pulled away from Amber's kiss because the phone rang or because I convinced him not to kiss her. If it's the latter, then I *influenced* him, but when I replay the scene in my head, I'm almost positive that the phone rang first, which just means that his mom called at exactly the right time.

Even though I know it was wrong to spy on Charlie, and even worse to kiss Jasper, I'm still upset that he took Amber to our special place and almost kissed her. He wanted to kiss her, and I want to know why, but I can't ask him—there's no way to explain what I saw. A normal person couldn't have seen them together at the top of the lighthouse. From up there, you can see someone coming for blocks, and he would have heard me on the stairs anyway.

I get out of bed and grab my jeans, which are bunched in a pile on the floor. It's not fair of me to be mad at Charlie, but I can't help it. I yank the jeans on and pull a sweatshirt over my head, then I shove my feet into my sneakers. The laces are knotted. Figures.

From my nightstand, I pick up my phone, meaning to text Charlie, but find myself shoving it back in my pocket. I need to see him today, but Indigo said he'd pick me up at eight, so I'll just go to the Musée Méchanique after work and surprise him. And that way, if I lose my nerve, I won't be letting him down again.

I grab my backpack and follow the smell of coffee to the kitchen.

"Have you heard from Charlie?" Mom asks when I walk into the kitchen.

I shake my head. "Nope. He won't even return my calls."

"It's not your fault you had to work," she says. She grabs a granola bar and places it in front of me on the counter. I shove it in my backpack.

"I should've known the Bernsteins would be out later than they said," I respond.

"Well, I'm glad you have a good work ethic," Mom says. She hands me a to-go cup of coffee.

I take a sip and smile. It's hard to stay so grumpy when I've got sweet, creamy coffee like this. "I got it from you, Mom."

"What did you get from your mother?" Richard asks, coming into the kitchen. He throws his big arms around Mom and plants a slobbery kiss on her cheek.

"Work ethic," I say.

"Are you talking about the letter?" Richard asks Mom.

She shakes her head, and then turns to me. "I wasn't snooping around your room or anything, I promise," she says. "I just needed a pen, and I opened your desk drawer and saw your letter from NYU."

Relief pours through me; so that's what they were talking about last night. "And you figured I'd tell you when I was ready?"

She nods. "You guessed it."

"Well, I'm ready. I got into NYU, but I'm not going," I say. "I want to keep nannying, at least for a while, and get some college credits before I do something big like move across the country."

"What about Charlie?" Mom asks.

"Can you imagine me following a guy somewhere?" I ask.

She shakes her head. "Of course not. But—"

"Did I tell you congratulations on your engagement yet?" I ask Richard, eager to end the NYU conversation.

He shakes his head. "You've been a little busy."

"Congratulations," I say. "Welcome to our crazy life."

"Glad to be here," he says. He pours himself a cup of coffee. "You work it out with Charlie?"

I shake my head, mentally replaying Charlie and Amber's almost-kiss. "Still waiting for him to call me back."

"He'll come around," Richard says.

"I hope so." I put a lid on my to-go cup and throw my backpack over my shoulder. As I head out to Indigo's waiting car, I realize I'm fine with Mom knowing about NYU. I can't go anyway, not with my Branch 13 work. And besides, Charlie might want to be in New York with Amber, not me.

"Callie? You okay?" Indigo asks me from across the bunker's viewing room.

"Just dandy," I reply. As far as I can tell, Indigo doesn't seem upset about pretending to be Mr. Bernstein, so it probably wasn't him on the phone to begin with. *Dodged a bullet there.* I'm relieved, because my brain can't handle worrying about anything else right now, not after betraying Charlie by kissing Jasper, and Charlie almost betraying me by kissing Amber. I'm already so distracted today by the thought of Amber worming her way into Charlie's heart that I've barely heard Indigo guiding me off my mental boat into the water, taking me further into my vision. Keeping my eyes closed and my head firmly against the couch cushion, I add, "Fine and dandy."

"Then we'll start when you say you're ready," Indigo says.

"I'm ready," I insist, although I'm not sure that I am. I may have dodged a bullet with Indigo, but I'm still distracted by Charlie's almost-kiss, and I'm also trying not to focus on the fact that Indigo is monitoring me today instead of Jasper. Maybe after our movie-worthy kiss, Jasper didn't want to be partners anymore? A knot forms in my throat. Or maybe he regrets ever being attracted to me in the first place? I know I shouldn't care about Jasper, not with all that's going on with Charlie, but is it possible to be equally attracted to two people?

"Okay," Indigo says, "then focus this time."

I lean back, pack my worries into a suitcase, and drift deep into the ocean in my mind, listening to Indigo's voice counting down to one.

"Ten . . . nine . . . eight . . ."

This is the part I like best: the letting go. The moment when nothing seems to matter, when the world rushes away from me like the drawing of a tide. When even the thought of losing Charlie to a blue-eyed blonde doesn't bother me.

"Seven . . . six . . . five . . ."

I get very relaxed, my body releasing its grip on the world. My mind is still awake, but pleasantly unconcerned, and my body has given in to what it knows will happen. I almost forget Amber's name. And her tiny T-shirt.

"Four . . . three . . . two . . ."

My mind lets go of Amber and Charlie, and what they may have done together, and my thoughts break apart, scattering into the dust cloud of my mind.

"One."

And then the dust lifts and flies away, and I'm left with a wide open space, a plain to play on, to receive colors and images. Like an empty field, or a blank canvas. Waiting for what's to come.

As always, an image comes to me, and this time, I'm looking down on a building on the edge of a large field of snow.

The scene is frozen, as if I am seeing outside of time, or looking at an ink drawing of something that happened long ago. It's more like studying a picture than being in a moment. This is very common in the remote viewing world, as it happens more often than true bi-location, where I am two places at once.

"I'm floating above a building," I say aloud.

"Focus," Indigo says, so I do. Time passes, and nothing happens, no movement. Sketching as I would from a photograph, I draw every detail I can see of the building's roof and the field of snow below.

"Can you tell the time or location?" Indigo asks.

I study the image below me, and try to feel my way into it, but I just get that crawling-skin sensation. "There's snow on the ground," I say, but I don't say, "it looks like winter," even though I'm sure Indigo is thinking it too.

I hear Indigo write something on his notepad. "Can you see into the building?" he asks.

I focus on the roof, and suddenly a scream tears through my ears. It grows louder and louder until it vibrates through my bones, making my teeth chatter. It's so haunting that I am caught up in it, and it takes me several minutes to realize why all of the hairs on my neck are standing on end: the scream sounds *familiar*.

Someone I know is being tortured. The thought pops into my head, and once it's in there, I can't shake it out. I zoom toward the building, needing to get inside, to find out who is screaming, and why. But before I can dive into the building, an inky blackness bleeds in from all directions, erasing my view of the scene.

As soon as I come to, I tell Indigo what I saw and heard, and how a strange blackness stopped me from seeing into the building. I want to include every detail in my post-session report, but Indigo suggests I include the scream, but not the *familiarity* of the screaming because it's clearly analysis. This familiarity would make the entire report an AOL, and if it's deemed by the CIA to be so, it would discount potentially important information from the entire mission, like the snow around the building.

"But why do you think it sounded familiar?" I ask Indigo. "Off the record, of course."

"Most likely your mind heard a scream and associated it with the person you are most afraid of getting hurt," Indigo says. "Did it sound like your mom? Your boyfriend?"

I shake my head. "I don't know. It didn't sound like either of them, but . . . I'm not sure. It was like hearing something for the first time that you've heard many times. Am I making sense?"

Indigo smiles. "No. But you often don't."

"True," I say, and I'm glad at least one of us still has a sense of humor. "But what about the darkness? Why can't I see into the building?"

"I've been thinking about that," Indigo says. "And it seems to me that the building must have psychic protection."

"And by that, you mean—"

"I mean that a psychic is mentally blocking off the building's interior," Indigo says. "It's unusual, but not impossible. Some big corporations even hire psychics to protect their secrets from enemy psychics."

"Then why doesn't the CIA hire psychics to protect their classified files?"

"How do you know they don't?" Indigo asks, and I shrug. "Besides, a lot of government officials don't believe in psychic energy, which is why we're constantly on the verge of losing our funding." He studies my half-finished drawing from the session. "Also, it's very expensive to hire a psychic to do this," he says, looking up again. "The psychic has to be focused on one specific location twenty-four hours a day, which is both psychically exhausting and physically impossible for one person to do."

I look down at my sketch of the building on the edge of the snowy field. Half of the drawing is missing due to the inky blackness that bled in from all sides. "But if I can't see through it, what do I do?"

"You need to stay away from it for a while. In the meantime, I'll put the other viewers on it," Indigo says, and I must look upset, because he adds, "Callie, if that building is being protected, and psychics are watching, they'll know you have tried to break in. It could be dangerous for you."

"What do you mean by dangerous?"

"Whoever is watching the building knew you were there if they blacked over the scene. They're expecting you to come back, and if you do, they could enter your mind, since they already know when and where your mind will be open," Indigo says. He's keeping his voice calm, but he's nervously bending an edge of the envelope. "And if the building is being watched by more than one psychic, the stress they could put on your mind could push you over the edge. They could break you."

"Like what happened to Michael?"

He nods. "So I do not want you viewing the building until we know it's safe for you."

"But—"

"I'm serious, Callie. Do you want to end up like him, locked up in an insane asylum?"

I shake my head.

"Why don't you write your report," Indigo continues, "and then we'll go get something from the snack machine for lunch."

I nod in agreement, and when Indigo leaves the room with the envelope in hand, I'm already half a page in. It's difficult to write the truth while also leaving out specific details, but when I'm done, I think I've done a pretty good job of it. Telling the truth but not the whole truth is what I do in my daily life, anyway.

I sign and date the bottom of the report, and then I stand up and open the door. It misses hitting Indigo by just a few inches.

"I was wondering what took you so long," he teases.

"Perfection takes time," I respond, handing him the report.

He takes the report and pushes the door open the rest of the way. "Ladies first," he says.

"That would be me." I step out into the bunker and blink rapidly in the bright fluorescent lights.

"My treat," Indigo says when we get to the snack machines. He pulls dollar bills out of his pocket and feeds them into the machine. "I wasn't prepared enough today to get sandwiches. Not after such a long night."

For some reason, it didn't even occur to me that after I left for Charlie's show, some of the other viewers stayed and continued their sessions. "What did you find out last night?" I ask, not expecting an answer. Surprisingly, Indigo gives me one.

"The good news is that we found some useful intel about the person we were looking for," Indigo says. He presses B2 for a peanut butter and jelly sandwich and pulls it out when it drops. "But now we are searching for their location."

"Hence the building in the snow."

"Hence that," Indigo says, handing me the sandwich. "You're too young to say hence."

"You're too old to know what young people say."

We walk across the bunker to the conference table, where Pat is slouched in his seat, dunking a candy bar in a cup of coffee. Indigo pulls out a chair for me and I lower myself into it and take a big bite of my peanut butter and jelly sandwich.

"Pat and Jasper were here all last night viewing," Indigo tells me. "They got most of what we needed." He looks at Pat across the table appreciatively. "I told you both to stay home today and get some rest. I don't want anyone going . . ." Indigo rolls his finger around his ear.

"I'm an insomniac," Pat says. "This is better than lying at home, praying for sleep." He dunks his candy bar in his coffee again. "I can be Callie's monitor today if you're busy."

"Or you can have Anthony take you home before you push your mind over the edge," Indigo says sternly.

"So Jasper's at home today?" I interrupt.

"Yep. Apparently he's smarter than this one here." He gestures to Pat. "Disappointed?"

I shake my head. It's better that Jasper's not here today. I wasn't looking forward to the whole awkward post-kiss conversation.

Pat sighs and gets up from the table, stuffing the rest of the candy bar in his mouth. He leaves his half-empty coffee cup on the table. "Crappy coffee anyway," he says as he walks toward the end of the bunker, where Anthony is waiting for him in front of the underground garage.

"Told you you shouldn't have come today," Anthony says when Pat reaches him. "Indigo don't play around." He looks across the room at Indigo. "Do you, boss?"

Indigo shakes his head and chuckles under his breath.

"Why don't you head home too, Anthony, after dropping Pat off? I'll take Callie home."

"Yes, boss," Anthony says. He opens the garage door and they head out.

I stand up and stuff the rest of my sandwich into my mouth.

"Still hungry?" Indigo asks, and I shake my head. "Then let's go back to work," he says, placing his hand on my shoulder. "Unless you're *babysitting* today."

My heart plummets to my feet, and the dread of Indigo knowing I've lied to him—after all he's done for me—pins me to the floor. "I'm sorry," I say, the words muffled through a mouthful of peanut butter. "More sworry than I can sway."

"You have your reasons," Indigo responds. "But I'd like you to enlighten me as to what they are."

I swallow hard and force myself to look into Indigo's disappointed eyes, but it's painful, like staring at the sun. "You said yourself that if anyone I love knows about my job, they could get killed. You said that 'loving people is a liability, a weapon to be used against you.' After all that, do you think I could ask my mom to sign her death certificate?"

"But the form just said you were a government intern, so she wouldn't have—"

"Known? Right. My mom is a MENSA certified genius.

Do you really think she wouldn't have dug until she found out the truth?"

Indigo taps his finger against his lips. "Still, you've put me in a very tricky position."

I stare at him, unable to form any of the words I want to say. At this moment, I want to remind him that I'll be eighteen in less than six months; that I've seen more in my mind than most fifty-year-olds, so I shouldn't need my mother's permission, and that Mom's signature on the form is *real*, even if she doesn't know why she signed it, but I don't. I just cringe silently and watch Indigo make his decision.

"I've never been much of a pencil pusher," Indigo finally says. "Let's get back to the real work of saving the world." He cuffs me on the shoulder, and we walk together across the bunker and into the viewing room.

Indigo and I work for a couple of hours, but we're careful to avoid viewing the building, in case enemy psychics might be expecting me. Usually it's not a problem, because enemy viewers wouldn't even know where to look, but now that they do, I'm more at risk.

Finally Indigo insists that my mind has had enough for one day, and that we've found everything there is to find in this mission, whatever that means. "Back to the regular office on Tuesday," he says.

"Why Tuesday?"

"I'll be out of town tomorrow, just for the day," Indigo says. "You've worked hard all weekend; take the day off."

We walk through the concrete bunker to Indigo's car, where he wraps the blindfold around my eyes and helps me into the car. He shuts the door behind me and gets in the driver's seat. "You'll be home in no time," Indigo says from the front seat.

"I'm not going home," I respond. "Will you take me to Pier Forty-Five instead?"

"Sure," Indigo responds. "Why?"

I sigh. "There's something I have to do."

It's a normal Sunday on Pier 45, which means that half the tourists in San Francisco have flooded onto the docks to eat expensive fried seafood and gawk at the barking sea lions. I hate crowds, I always have—but I'm almost glad for today's masses. With the amount of fussing children and bellowing tourists, I can blend in and feel invisible, which buys me time to think, and maybe even muster up some courage to confront Charlie. I'm not even irritated when I'm jostled by elbows and overstuffed camera cases as I make my way to the museum; being pushed and shoved fits how I feel inside today.

When I'm about twenty feet away, Laughing Sal chuckles that creepy animatron laugh from the museum's open doorway. *Har har har.* I swerve around the crowd, shielding my eyes from the setting sun glinting off the museum's metal siding and walk around the side of the building. Pennies clink as people drop them into the machines. Now halfway around the museum, I see the back entrance, where Charlie sneaks me in after hours on nights that he has to work late.

Someone is lingering by the back door, waiting to be let in. I squint into the sun, and make out Amber's slim figure. With her tousled blond hair and T-shirt tied in a knot above her belly button, she looks just like the boyfriend thief she is.

I duck behind the building, realizing that Amber is wearing the same outfit today that she was last night at the lighthouse. As unlikely as it is that Grace would let him get away with it, the thought of Amber spending the night with Charlie still freezes the blood in my veins. I flatten myself against the metal siding and tip my head out to watch Amber flicking the dead ends of her hair with a painted fingernail.

"Charlie," Amber says, drumming on the door with her nails. *Tap tap tap.* "It's me."

A cold feeling settles in my gut as the door opens and Charlie pops his head out. After looking both ways, Amber sneaks into the museum and I'm left alone outside, the hot metal siding burning my skin. I stare at the back entrance for a minute, and then I walk away, the seals barking a sorrowful good-bye as I head toward home.

"The Embarcadero," the bus driver says over the bus's intercom a few minutes later. People around me gather their things as the bus slows to a stop. The doors open, and a man stumbles onto the bus smelling like liquor. He has so much facial hair I can hardly see his skin, and his clothes are torn at the elbows and knees.

"A great flood will come so suddenly," the man mumbles as he walks down the aisle. I duck down in my seat, praying he won't sit in the empty seat beside me. He passes my row and continues down the bus, getting off at the back exit before the doors close. "One shall not have place or land to attach," he slurs as he half falls onto the sidewalk.

There seem to be more crazy people on the streets than ever lately, I think, watching him stumble away. It makes me wonder if we're coming up to another end-of-the-world date. It happens every few years: some ancient prophet claims to have figured out the exact day the world ends, and the crazies come out en masse. The doomers head for the hills, the Mayan calendars are pulled out and studied, and everyone goes completely crazy, as far as I'm concerned. But I haven't heard anything about that lately.

When the bus starts moving again, I notice that while I've been thinking about the end of the world, I've also been sketching idly on the window. I've redrawn the sketches from my session, and the building stares back at me from the windowpane. But this time, the building in the snow—and the screaming from inside of it—have caught me with their teeth, and won't let me go.

Leave work at work, I remember Indigo saying. *It's the only way to stay sane.* I wipe the window with my open palm, and then lean back and pull my hood down over my eyes.

I half doze the rest of the trip, and the bus is pulling up to the Panhandle stop when my phone vibrates in my jeans, waking me up. I dig it out of my pocket and read the text: **Meet up later? 8pm lighthouse?**

Wondering what I'm going to say to him, I swallow hard and write back: **C u there.**

CHAPTER TWENTY-ONE

I get off the bus at the lighthouse later, after a dinner of falafel and french fries. Stepping into the cool sea air, I feel relief flood through me. It always makes me feel better to be here. Even though the vile memory of Amber running her hands through Charlie's hair still haunts me, the lighthouse is the only place that I feel truly safe, like no one could find me here.

When I get to the top of the lighthouse, Charlie's already here, but he's not alone. Colin is building a Lego tower across from where Charlie is standing, staring out to sea. I wish Charlie hadn't brought Colin. Even though he's playing by himself twenty feet away, I know that he'll be listening. He can't build a high enough Lego tower to seclude himself from this mess.

Charlie doesn't turn around when I approach, and I can feel the awkwardness stretch between us as palpable as the thin silver cord from last night. "Charlie?" I say, and he turns around and looks at me. He doesn't respond, and I realize that both of us are waiting for the other one to speak first. I take a few tentative steps toward him. "I'm sorry I wasn't at your show," I say, and I mean it.

A few silent seconds tick by. Charlie's ruddy faced, like he's been running, or crying. The wind blows his hair into his eyes, and I try to think of what else to say, but nothing comes to me.

"Where were you?" he finally asks, brushing his floppy brown hair out of his copper eyes. "You promised you'd be there. You know how much it meant to me."

What can I say? That I was working on a top secret government assignment? Or that I was kissing my coworker? "I lost track of time," I say softly.

Charlie crosses his arms protectively across his chest. Around us, the wind picks up, rattling the iron lighthouse railings. "Lost track of time?" he asks, shaking his head. "You didn't even call me last night to say where you were."

"I'm sorry," I say. "My phone died."

Charlie bites his lip and looks down at his sneakers. "I was waiting at the noodle shop for over two hours. I was late hanging my photos for the show, so I wasn't ready when the few people who bothered to come did arrive. And I was worried about you all night, and when you didn't respond to any of my texts—"

"I'm sorry," I say again.

"And during the show," Charlie continues, "I kept telling people you'd be there, that you'd never miss something that important to me—" His voice cracks. "So you just lost track of time? Or is it something else, Callie? Or *someone* else?"

I'm not the only one who's thought about straying.

I suddenly need to turn this around, to get this heavy weight off me. I look into the night closing in around the lighthouse, remembering how I floated out there and watched Amber rubbing her hands through Charlie's hair.

"And what about you?" I ask before I can stop myself. "Did Amber like the lighthouse?"

The color drains from Charlie's face. "How did you know that?"

I should stop, but I'm too angry. "You might as well have kissed her. You wanted to."

"Have you been following me?" Charlie asks, his shocked expression turning slowly to anger. I shake my head, but he obviously doesn't believe me. "I have never been anything other than honest with you," he says. "I love you, you know that." Tears are squeezing out of the sides of his eyes, and he hastily brushes them away. I haven't seen Charlie this sad since his father died. I should stop him, take this guilt off him, but I don't. I should say: *You didn't kiss Amber, and I did kiss Jasper, so this is all on me*—but I don't do that either.

"Then what were you doing with her?" I say instead.

"Amber and I were just talking about you, okay?" Charlie says. He chews on the soft skin on the tip of his thumb, his eyes cast down toward the waves hitting the rocks below. "And you followed me, to make sure I wasn't cheating on you?" he asks. "Why, Callie? What have I ever done wrong?"

I grab one of the railings and it stops rattling. "I wasn't following you, not really," I say lamely.

He glares at me. "Yes, you were."

Neither of us notices Colin coming up behind us, but suddenly he's pulling on Charlie's sleeve, whining about his broken Lego tower.

"Not now, Colin," Charlie says.

"But—"

"Not now." I've never heard Charlie talk to Colin like that before.

"We're having big kid time," I say gently. *Which we'll probably never do again.* Colin gets it. He nods and walks back to his broken Lego tower.

"You just have to believe me," I beg. "There are things I can't tell you—"

"But I'm your boyfriend!" Charlie yells, and the sound

bounces around us in the lighthouse, spreading out into the ocean air. "Or is there something you haven't told me about that, either?"

"What do you mean?"

"I was hoping you'd be the one to tell me. You at least owe me that." Charlie shakes his head angrily. Colin glances up from his Lego tower and then quickly averts his eyes. I guess he's learned to read angry faces.

"I saw you with that guy," Charlie continues. "I wasn't sure it was you at first. You hate motorcycles."

It hits me like a punch in the gut. Charlie saw Jasper and me together? How much did he see?

"I was in the back of the art gallery after the show, cleaning up," Charlie says, "and I saw you outside the window. I was so relieved to see you there. You looked so sad for missing my show; I just wanted to make you feel better. I started to run out to make sure you were okay . . . But then he came up from behind, and hugged you, and—" Charlie's voice cracks, and he stops midsentence. "Did you . . ." He looks out at the ocean.

I stuff my hands in my pockets. He didn't ask the question, but he deserves an answer. "Yes, I kissed him." I take a tentative step toward Charlie. "But there's nothing between us."

"Right." Charlie is backing up, as if he's afraid of his own anger . . . or of me.

"I don't know if I can believe you anymore," he says. "I don't even know who you are."

"Yes, you do," I plead. "You know me better than anyone else." *Even Jasper.* "You know that I hate mayonnaise, and that I wore my shoes on the wrong feet when I was little, just for attention. And you know that I have nightmares that I missed my algebra test or that I'm naked in front of the whole school, and covered in warts. You know me!"

"The girl I knew didn't lie, or spy on me," Charlie says bitterly, "or accuse me of cheating—which I would never do. I loved you!"

Loved? Why did he use the past tense?

I reach out and try to touch him, but he pulls away and walks toward the stairs. "I'm out of here."

"Wait!" I say, and I can tell it's the anxiety in my voice that makes him stop walking. *Can I tell him who I really am?*

I cross the few feet between us and place my hand on his shoulder. Charlie doesn't turn around, but I can tell he's listening. *If I don't tell him, I'll lose him forever.* "That guy, he works with me," I say. I feel Charlie's shoulders rise and fall. "And I didn't follow you," I add.

"What do you mean?" Charlie asks, turning around.

"We're both psy—" I stop myself. If Charlie knows about my visions, he could be tortured to find out what I know. I can't let him get hurt—or possibly even killed—because of

229

me, even if I have to lose him. My throat closes up so I can barely speak. "Psyched to be nannies," I finish.

"And that's your excuse for cheating on me?" Charlie shakes my hand off and stalks over to Colin. He quickly gathers up the Legos. "Maybe this won't work," Charlie says, grabbing Colin by the hand. "Maybe motorcycle guy would be cool with being lied to, but I'm not." He storms out, hitting the giant bell with his shoulder as he passes. Colin glances back at the bell in awe as its *dong dong dong* echoes over the ocean.

I sink down into a crouch. I should have known this would happen eventually. I pound my fists on the floor and think about texting Charlie, yelling my love for him from the tower, setting the lighthouse on fire so he comes back to save me. But I don't do any of it. Instead, I just sob until I feel as empty as a roll of used toilet paper. Then I fold into myself, exhausted, and think of Jasper.

"Psychics can't co-exist with normal people," I remember him saying. "We can't protect them from our minds—from what we know. And people think, strangely, that their minds are locked spaces that no one can get into. They think their thoughts are *private*," he said. "We ruin that."

Maybe Jasper's right. Maybe I ruin everything, and I just can't help it. Maybe I'll end up as one of those old psychics with a crystal ball in a dark room, charging five dollars to read someone's palm. Maybe I'll never be loved again. Who could love a mental case who breaks into other people's minds? I curl into a ball on the floor, my head tucked into my chest. I should probably be locked up before I hurt someone else. I'm a freak, after all. And that's all I'll ever be.

CHAPTER TWENTY-TWO

My house is empty, so I go straight upstairs, climb into bed, and pull the covers over my head. It's stuffy beneath the thick comforter, and as I suck in the thick air, I allow myself to feel the full weight of what I've lost. All of these years with Charlie, gone. All we've built, gone. For what?

"Stop feeling sorry for yourself," I mutter, and I force myself to climb out of bed and sit at my desk. My head is buzzing with ways to win Charlie back, and I keep coming around to telling him the truth. Although that wouldn't make up for kissing Jasper, Charlie would at least understand that I haven't been following him (not in person, anyway), and why I've been so distant lately. It would also explain why I was hanging out with Jasper in the first place, even if it didn't make up for the kiss.

I get a pen and paper out of my desk, and jot down all the reasons I should tell Charlie the truth about my psychic abilities, and then list all of the reasons I shouldn't.

Pros	Cons
—He'll know all of me	—He'll be in danger
—He'll forgive me. Maybe?	—He'll think I'm crazy
—We'll share the secret that I'm psychic	—We'll never share anything again
—He'll understand why I kept it secret	—He'll hate me for lying to him

I scan my list, hoping it will give me the answer I can't figure out myself, but it doesn't. I crumple it up and toss it in the wastebasket.

It's self-deceptive, anyway. It assumes that, if I tell Charlie the truth, he'll believe me.

Downstairs, I hear Mom open the front door. I can tell she's trying to be quiet, but she's wearing high heels again, so there's a tip-tap every time she takes a step. As usual, a second, chunkier pair of footsteps follows immediately behind hers. The front door bangs shut, immediately followed by a slurred "Shhh!" from my mom.

"We should still have a small reception here, I think,"

Mom whispers in such a loud voice that I know she must be drunk, or well on her way there. "Your crew can come, and Callie can bring Charlie."

"Maybe we can pay Charlie to photograph the wedding," Richard says. "His photos were beautiful. It's a shame Callie didn't see them."

"She had to work," Mom says. The couch squeaks under someone's weight, and then there are two hollow clunks as Mom takes each high heel off and drops it on the floor.

There's another squeak as Richard sits down beside her. "She does seem very devoted to her nannying job."

"She does," Mom says. "But do you think that maybe she *does* want to go to NYU? She doesn't seem that excited about going to State. I can't tell, with Charlie going to New York and all . . ."

"She doesn't seem thrilled about State, no. More like resigned to it," Richard says.

"I can't tell either way. You'd think I'd know my own daughter better than that. But Callie, she holds her cards close."

"Like someone else I know," Richard says, and I hear him kiss her.

Mom giggles, and I cover my head with my pillow. People shouldn't have to hear their parents date. It's embarrassing. They're old, which makes it even more humiliating when they act like kids. And if they're being the kids, do we have to be the grown-ups?

"You know all of my cards," Mom says.

"And I like all of them," Richard responds, and then the couch squeaks again, but this time, I have a pretty good idea why.

I put my pen and pad of paper in the top drawer of my desk and get back into bed, pulling the comforter over my head. I remember how Charlie and I used to make out on that couch before Mom got home from work, and how, when I was around him, I never felt alone. Before I can stop myself, I grab my phone and text Charlie.

Goodnite, I write.

I don't hear back.

I'm lying in bed for a while, trying to make myself sleep, when I hear a squeaking sound on the roof. It's faint, and it could be the wind, but I hitch open the window and climb out onto the fire escape anyway. Two stories below, I can see the thin, dark line of the Panhandle, blanketed in by moving headlights, and to my right, my next door neighbor's window is closed and her television is off.

I climb up the fire escape and look to the left. On the other side of the roof, Richard is perched on the edge, watching baseball through the window below. "Hey," I say.

"Hey, kiddo."

"Mind if I join you?" I ask.

Richard grins. "I'd be thrilled." He moves over so there's room for me to sit beside him. "What's going on? You don't usually watch sports."

I look at my legs dangling over the edge of the roof. "Charlie and I . . . we broke up today."

"Does your mom know?"

"Not yet. She's always liked Charlie," I explain, "and it's my fault. I kind of . . . screwed up." *In several ways*, I add silently.

Richard pats my shoulder. "Everyone screws up, Cal. Just tell him you're sorry."

"I've tried."

"Try harder," he says, and then he points to the neighbor's television. "Look, the pitcher just threw the first pitch."

"Okay," I say, grateful for the distraction. "So tell me how this goes. One guy throws a ball to another, right? And then they run in circles?"

Richard laughs. "Something like that." He looks down at the cars below. "Your mom brought up something today."

"Hmm?"

"You don't sound excited to go to SF State. Wherever you go is fine with your mom, you know. Even if you have to move across the country." He pauses, as if he's waiting for me to jump in and say something. "So are you sure that's what you really want?" he asks.

I think about what my life in New York could be, if I didn't work for Branch 13. If I was a normal girl with a normal life. I imagine going to coffee shops and the theater and out to parties, and having nothing to hide. It sounds nice and easy. But without spending my days viewing, it also sounds hollow. "Yes, State is where I need to go," I finally say.

Richard looks at me strangely. "Well, okay. But if you're worried about leaving your mom, don't be. I'll take good care of her."

"I know," I say, and then I break eye contact with him and nod to the screen. "So this is where they run in circles?"

Richard nods. "Yep." He pauses. "Charlie will forgive you for whatever you've done, you know that?"

I look at him, embarrassed that there are tears in my eyes. "Not this time."

We lapse into silence as we watch the game together, and it turns out that baseball really is about men throwing a ball around and running in circles, but it's also about the person sitting beside you.

CHAPTER TWENTY-THREE

I'm sound asleep when I hear a knock on my bedroom door. I open one eye and peek out the window at the sun just tipping its head over the horizon.

"Come in?" It's more of a question than an invitation.

Mom opens the door and peeks her head in. "Sorry to wake you."

"Why wouldn't I be awake at this time?" I say sleepily. Mom looks like she's going to back out of my room, so I sit up and say, "No, no, it's okay. What's going on?"

"Why didn't you tell me about Charlie?" Mom asks. She sits on the end of my bed, and I scoot my legs up to give her room.

I run my hands through the thick tangle of hair that's hanging over my eye. "It just happened last night," I say. "And I was going to tell you, I just . . . well . . ."

"Just what?"

"I thought you'd be disappointed in me," I admit. "I mean, we broke up because he saw me with . . ." I pause, wondering how to explain who Jasper is without giving too much away. "Someone else," I finally say.

"The Bernsteins' nephew?" Mom asks, and a hint of a smile tugs at her lips.

"Yeah. Him."

"You don't have to tie yourself down so young," Mom says. "You're not even eighteen yet."

"But you like Charlie."

"I do," Mom says. "Because he's good to you. But you know, I never got as serious as you and Charlie, not until I met your father, and I was almost forty."

"So I'm doomed to be single until then?" I ask, only half joking.

"It's not like I didn't have boyfriends," Mom replies. "Just none as serious as Charlie." She reaches out and puts a hand on my arm. "Charlie loves you, Cal, but four years is a long time, for both of you."

I picture the NYU acceptance letter in my desk, and I wish I could tell her how much I want to go to New York, but that my life, my work, is centered here. "He'll come back in the summers," I say.

"And if he doesn't?"

I shrug. "I guess it doesn't matter now anyway." I hope I sound a lot more confident than I feel, because right now, something inside of me is splitting open. "Charlie doesn't love me anymore."

"I'm betting that he does," Mom says.

I shake my head.

"How can you be so sure?"

I glance at Mom, trying to judge if I should ask her the question tugging at my brain, and decide that I have nothing to lose. "If Dad came back one day, after hurting you so badly, would you take him back?"

"Not anymore," Mom says. "But I would have for a long time after he left." She pulls her knees up to her chest, like a little girl, and wraps her arms around them. "But no matter what, I'd want you to know him. He was just like you."

My throat swells with a mix of pride and anger. "What do you mean?"

"He was gutsy and brave," Mom says. "And wise." She hugs her arms harder around her knees, so she's a tightly wound ball. "I know I don't talk about him enough," she admits. "But when he left . . . it's still painful."

"All these years later?"

"When someone betrays you, someone you love, and you don't know why—" she stops herself. "But I'm supposed to be making you feel better. Sorry." She gives me a weak smile. "I don't have class 'til two. You wanna join us for brunch?"

I shake my head. I don't feel like going to brunch with Mom and Richard; I feel like staying here and finding out more about my dad. But I know it's not worth asking Mom about him again; when she's made up her mind, I won't get anything more out of her. "I think I'll get some more sleep."

Mom pats the covers over my knees. "Good idea." She gets up and leaves my room, shutting the door quietly behind her.

I allow myself to stay in bed for a while, trying to shake off my bad mood, but it doesn't help. I grab my phone off the nightstand and start surfing the web, clicking on random articles and letting them distract me. Web surfing always helps my mood, and it makes me wonder how anybody ever lived without the internet. I mean, how did they find out information, or more importantly, distract themselves from the uncomfortable thoughts in their heads?

On the tiny screen, alongside the random articles about fashion and pictures of kittens is an advertisement for a new industry that's looking for "skilled and dedicated employees." To me, it sounds more like underpaid and overused workers, but since I'm trying to distract myself, I click on the link anyway. A picture of a grayish-silver stone pops up, with a short description beneath it.

Thulium is a rare earth metal, found in the
Earth's crust. Thulium is now being used in X-ray
machines, superconductors, and military grade
lasers across the world. Because of its rarity and
the small amount of Thulium suppliers, it sells
for a high price. But some eco-doomers claim the
metal is too dangerous for civilian use.

I open a new page and search the term *thulium*, and a
hundred companies pop up, and, as Grace would say, they
are all devoted to stealing precious minerals from Mother
Earth. It seems as if everyone from research enthusiasts to
third-world-country dictators to American corporations is
searching for this metal, but no one except for a handful of
environmentalists, or eco-doomers, as these websites are
calling them, thinks the metal is dangerous.

I click on the phrase *eco-doomers*, and it takes me to an
end-of-the-world website. The white letters in all caps
scream something about Nostradamus and how an asteroid will end the world. I'm rolling my eyes at the ridiculous
number of conspiracy theorists in this country when
there's a *ding*. I click on Mail and there, along with spam
emails, is a message from Charlie. With bated breath, I
open it. If this was on the doomer website, it would say *MY
HEART DROPS*.

I need a break from our relationship. Please don't contact me.

Regards, Charlie

Every other thought in my mind disappears when I see the word *Regards*. For the last three years we've been together, Charlie has always signed his emails, *Devotedly,* C. Plus, I know what "taking a break" means. It's just a less painful way of saying "break up."

So it's really over.

With my heart in my mouth, I click reply, and type in the only thing I can think of: OK. Then my stomach ties in such tight knots I can hardly breathe.

With tears pricking the corners of my eyes, I stare at the picture of Charlie and me on the tiny screen. We have our arms around each other, our hands tucked in the other's back pockets, as if this fragile thing we called *us* would never end. I click the X on the upper right side of the screen, and my internet browser shuts down, taking Charlie's email with it, but leaving this picture of what we used to be suspended across the small screen.

I grab a pillow and pitch it across the room, but it doesn't make me feel better. I understand now that *heartache* is not just an expression; the left side of my chest, above my heart, actually hurts. Even massaging the pain with my fingers doesn't help.

I collapse back in bed and stare at the ceiling, imagining myself in twenty years, all alone and surrounded by a dozen cats—or like Mom, trying to start over again at her age.

Although never getting out of bed sounds good, I also don't want to be alone, especially not today. I know I shouldn't do it, but I call Jasper.

Jasper drives up to my house in a neon yellow Mustang. As it rolls to a stop on the curb, the paint is so bright I almost have to shield my eyes to see him through the window. He's drumming his fingers on the glossy leather wheel, and when he sees me, he kicks open the passenger door from the inside.

"Howdy," he says.

I'm shocked by his casual attitude. Somehow I thought he would be nervous the first time he saw me after our kiss, like everything had changed between us, but he doesn't seem awkward at all. In fact, he's acting like our kiss never happened. *I can play that game too*, I decide, climbing into the car and shutting the door behind me.

"Awkward much?" he asks, and I'm immediately irritated that he finds me so easy to read.

"Frustrating much?"

"Always." He smiles and presses on the gas. He must have the other foot on the brake because the wheels squeal beneath the car.

"Whose car is this?"

Jasper shrugs. "I'll return it."

I know Jasper's a bit of a wild card, but stealing a car? If Charlie hadn't just broken up with me, I wouldn't even get in, but I would give anything to escape my tortured mind right now. "You didn't really steal this, did you?" I ask.

"No. Just taking a friend up on a favor," he says. "Let's call it payback."

I shake my head at him in disapproval, but I'm still glad he's here. I lean back into the bucket seat, and my feet lift off the floor like a little kid's.

"So what's up?" he asks.

"I don't want to talk about it."

"Fair enough," Jasper says, and slams his foot down on the gas again. We jolt ahead, and I try to buckle my seat belt, but it won't latch. I dig into the latch with my nail, pull out a fake gold necklace, and then plug in the seatbelt. When I look up again, Jasper's wearing a black blindfold over his eyes.

"Tell me you can see out of that thing."

"What would be the fun of that?" he asks. He swerves the car back and forth, almost hitting parked cars in the empty street.

"Tell me you can see through that blindfold!" I yell at him.

"Of course I can." He turns to me and pulls the blindfold up onto his forehead. "Well, my eyes can't . . ." I shoot him an angry look. ". . . but that's never stopped me before. I may not be Indigo's favorite, but he keeps me around for *some* reason." Jasper pulls the blindfold back down, floors the gas, and the car shoots forward.

I grab onto the door handle and yell, "Slow down!" But as I do, I realize that even though this is incredibly dumb and Jasper's just showing off, there's something alluring about it. The wildness, maybe. Or the fact that he doesn't worry about letting his mind go—that he isn't afraid to trust the things he sees in his own mind. I'm the opposite: I keep my mind on a tight rope, scared of what I might see.

"We're passing a red car," Jasper says, and I nearly jump out of my skin as a maroon monstrosity almost takes off our side mirror. I stare in the rearview mirror as the red car turns onto another street.

"Callie?" Jasper pesters, "was it red?"

Now it's my turn to reassure Jasper, like he does me, that what I am seeing in my mind's eye is correct: that I'm not crazy, but some brand of special that can see without eyes.

"It was blue," I state angrily, hoping that, for once, our minds are wrong. If Jasper doesn't know the color of the car, then it's possible that Charlie didn't really break up with me. *It's possible that I imagined it*, I tell myself, *it's possible the car really was blue.*

Jasper can tell I've gone somewhere else. He pulls the car over, yanks off his blindfold, and glares at me, as if I was the one doing something incredibly stupid.

"Have a little fun, Callie," he says, holding the blindfold out to me.

I slap the blindfold away. "Fun? You could've gotten us killed!"

"Killed?" Jasper looks puzzled by the concept. He clicks the electric locks open and closed, open and closed. *Click click click click.* "I saw everything perfectly. Twenty-twenty, as they say." He stares at me, willing me to understand him. "You can't see things as they happen?"

"With my eyes closed?" I shake my head. "Can you?"

"Clear as day," Jasper says, and stuffs the blindfold into his pocket. "You don't get a turn driving the car, then."

"Fine." I roll my eyes, but I'm secretly relieved that I won't have to look like a coward when I refuse to play his dangerous game.

"Hey, I didn't mean anything by it," Jasper says, laying his hand on top of mine. I hadn't noticed I was gripping the side of the seat so hard my knuckles had turned white, and I force my hand to relax. "There's a lot I can't do," Jasper adds, giving me a shy smile. "Like bend metal from over a hundred feet, for one. Or astral project, for two."

I slip my hand out from under his. "Have you ever tried to do it?" I ask. "Astral project on purpose? I mean, other than the night that your parents . . . um . . ."

"Died?" He shakes his head. I notice he's starting to pick at the skin around his fingernails. "Never. But that time, I almost didn't make it back. You can get stuck out there, you know."

"Out where?"

He lifts his eyebrows. "On the astral plane. Kind of . . . nowhere."

I'm surprised he's confiding so much in me, but I guess I've been confiding in him a lot lately too. "What happened?" I ask, hoping he keeps talking, rather than giving me his usual shrug.

Jasper stares out the windshield, and at first I think he's not going to answer. "I was the first one to the crash, and my parents were trapped beneath the car," he says slowly. "I couldn't have saved them anyway, since no one can bend metal during an astral projection," he adds, "but I couldn't accept that. I kept trying and trying, and I stayed out there so long that my cord almost broke."

"And if it had?"

"No one knows exactly what would happen," Jasper responds. "But I probably would have lost my mind, and then you never would have had the pleasure of my company." He grins at me, and then, without looking, he floors the gas. The Mustang roars onto the street, straight toward an oncoming car. The other car squeals on its brakes, and, as Jasper slams on the brakes, ricocheting me against the seat belt, my scream is drowned out by Jasper's.

The sound briefly jolts me back to what I heard in my vision of the blacked-over building, and then I'm back in the car, gripping the dashboard with both hands.

"Oh my god," I murmur, watching the other car speed away in the rearview mirror.

Jasper safely maneuvers the car to the curb, and we sit there numbly with cars passing us, the body of the yellow Mustang shuddering with each passing car.

"You okay?" Jasper asks. He's leaning back against his seat, breathing hard. He's not wearing his seat belt; it's a wonder he didn't go through the windshield.

"Uh-huh," I say, but the sound of Jasper's scream is pounding angrily through my temples. I'm sure that was the scream I heard in my vision, before the inky darkness covered everything. Could that have been Jasper screaming? I remember the horribly raw sound of it, and recalling how it sounded like someone was being tortured sends chills down my back.

I watch the cars rushing past my window. I can't tell Jasper about the scream, because if that is his future, telling him could greatly change his choices, and therefore, all of his future events. I'd tell Indigo, but he's forbidden me to look into the building again, in case it's being protected by psychics. I thread the necklace from my seatbelt between my fingers, not sure what I'm going to do. It's dangerous for me, sure, but what if Jasper is being tortured in there? Shouldn't I find out? I wrap the necklace around my thumb. And if I do, should I tell Indigo when he gets back into town tomorrow, and hope he helps me, and that I don't get in too much trouble for going directly against his orders? Or should I just drop by the office today to view the building without telling him?

I glance over at Jasper as he carefully maneuvers the car back onto the street. *That's too risky.* What if Indigo finds out I viewed behind his back, directly against his wishes? But Indigo's out of town for the day. Besides, what if Jasper is in trouble?

Forget about it. I rub my shoulder where the seatbelt gave me a carpet burn, trying to focus on my stinging skin to force the sound of Jasper's screaming out of my head, but it just grows louder, until it's pounding across my temples.

"You're looking a little green," Jasper says, taking a right turn at a ridiculously slow speed.

"Just need some air," I say, and roll down the window. I lean my head out, hoping for the wind to take the sound away, but the wind just pounds the scream deeper into my mind, until I'm sure it won't go away unless I know whom that scream belongs to.

Just forget it, I try to convince myself again, but I keep hearing it, like a song on repeat. I have to know who was screaming inside that building, and there's only one way to find out.

"Take me to the office," I say. "There's something I have to see."

CHAPTER TWENTY-FOUR

As usual, Anthony is sitting at the front desk, his feet up against the
metal detector and his head tilted back in an open-mouthed snore.

"Hangover much?" I ask.

Anthony jerks awake, rubbing a string of drool from his
bottom lip. "Uh-huh," he grunts, and flips on the metal
detector.

I hoist my backpack onto the moving conveyer belt, and
Jasper drops his wallet and phone onto it as well. "Could
you let us into the office?" I ask.

"Maybe. If you tell me what you're doing here," Anthony
says, watching my backpack go through.

"Secret project," I say, and put my finger to my lips.
"Mum's the word."

Anthony looks up at me with a wicked smile on his face. "And what do I get if I don't tell anyone?"

That stumps me. What could Anthony want? I scan my memory, finally latching onto his comment last week about being on a Harley on the open road with me. "You love motorcycles, right?" I ask.

Anthony smiles. "You remembered."

"Then you can take my bike for a spin sometime," Jasper says. I give him a look that I hope says "thank you."

Anthony's eyes light up, and then dim. "This isn't anything dangerous?" he asks.

"Not at all," I promise.

Anthony smiles in relief, and then he zips his lips closed with his thumb and forefinger. "And hope to die," he says.

Jasper and I walk through the metal detector, grab our stuff off the conveyer belt, and follow Anthony into the elevator. Anthony turns to push the button, and Jasper sticks his tongue out at me. I stick my tongue out back.

When we get to the second floor, Anthony takes out his large ring of keys. "Make this quick," he says. "I'm leaving in a few."

"Thanks," I say, and Anthony nods and gets back into the elevator.

As soon as we shut the office door, Jasper turns to face me. "What's going on?" he demands.

"I have to view something I saw at the bunker," I explain. "And I need the sealed envelope I was viewing with."

Jasper blocks me as I try to move past him. "So we're here because the envelope's here?" he asks.

"I'm hoping Indigo brought his paperwork back when he cleared the bunker," I say. "That's all I can tell you."

Jasper stares at me for a second, and then he nods. "I like a good mystery."

While Jasper goes into the viewing room, I stop by Indigo's office to look for the envelope. I pick through the Outgoing Sessions file, hoping Indigo returned the envelope after he closed down the bunker last night. Luckily, he did, and I'm soon pulling out the envelope with the slightly bent edge.

As I walk out of Indigo's office and cross the recovery room, my mind is still whirling with doubt. If Indigo finds out I went behind his back, he'll be livid—and I'll feel terrible. There's also the chance that enemy psychics could see me viewing the building again, and try to break into my mind. But if I don't find out if that's Jasper's scream I heard, I might be putting his life in danger, because who knows when that vision may come true.

By the time I enter the viewing room, I know that keeping Jasper safe is the only thing that matters.

"What did you see at the bunker yesterday?" Jasper asks.

"Will you just trust me?" I drop down on the couch with a blank stack of paper, a pen, and the envelope. Jasper crouches impatiently in the leather chair across from me, his gaze focused on the envelope in my hand.

"I'm not sure if this is a good idea," he says.

"But I need this," I say, waving the envelope. "It's not like I'm taking it anywhere."

"Okay," Jasper says hesitantly, and although he usually likes breaking the rules, this may be going too far, even for him. "Let's do it."

Ignoring the doubt in his voice, I lean back on the couch, the soft pillows molding around my back. I hand him the envelope, and then Jasper starts to count down from ten, his voice soothing me into my vision. I breathe deeply and imagine getting off the boat into the water. I slowly release all of the weights, letting them drift to the bottom of the sea, and then I picture the building in my mind.

"What are you looking at?" Jasper asks in a calm voice, and I turn my head and look down at the building on the edge of the snowy field. It's whirling past me so quickly my mind can hardly catch it.

"Slow it down," I whisper to myself, and the world slows to a standstill.

This time, there's nothing there to stop me. I nervously look around for enemy psychics—although I'm not sure what they'd look like if I found them—and then I easily swoop into the building. I float down to the floor of what looks like the main office, landing in front of a bank of computer screens. Beside me, a man types on a keyboard, his round glasses slightly skewed above his red beard. On the screens are dozens of pictures of large, military-looking ships.

Then everything speeds up; time courses past me like water through a sieve.

As soon as it stops, I immediately feel a heavy weight come down over me. I nervously lick my lips. I want to leave this place. There's something very wrong here.

The man is now standing with his back against the computer screens, his hands in the air. Then, from behind me, I hear a *bang*, and I turn to see a bullet flying toward him, spiraling like a football. Inch by inch, the air slowly sucks away from it, and it seems to take forever to get to him. When the bullet finally strikes his body, I hear someone scream.

A jolt races through my muscles, and my whole body tenses up. With my fists clenched at my sides, I flip toward the sound. The first thing I see is a gun, but its floating in air; there's just a blank space where a person should be.

And beyond that, I see something even more terrifying—I see me, across the room, blood streaming down the side of my head.

I'm the one screaming.

The air is cool as I shove the doors open and shuffle blindly onto the quad. Behind me, I hear Jasper calling my name, but it just makes me move faster. I don't want to try to explain what I saw in there. My mind churns the same questions over and over: What was I doing in that building? And why was my head bloody?

Across the quad, combat boots appear in the grass, and I look up to see Monty Cooper walking toward me. He's wearing his safety-pin riddled jeans with a T-shirt that says *Clean Land, Clean Water*, and a black leather armband of a snake eating its tail. We both stop when we see each other.

"What are you doing here?" I blurt out.

"Leave your manners at home today?" Monty says.

"On the train, I think."

"Well, as hard as it may be to believe, I actually teach a class here." Monty tries to run his hand through his hair, but his bangs just move as one solid piece and then pop back into place.

"A class on how to be an environmentally-conscious punk?"

"Very funny. Intro to mining," Monty says. "It's just a lecture, really, one I usually give at Stanford."

"How very fancy of you," I respond, a smile playing on my lips.

"That's me. Fancy Monty," he says. "I'm sure it has nothing to do with my name being on the building." He rolls his eyes toward the science building. There's a plaque on the front door with the name COOPER etched into it.

I'm unsure how to respond. "They're probably all here to see your lecture," I finally say, gesturing to the students in every window.

"Yeah. They're all camped out to hear my lecture tomorrow," Monty replies. A smile briefly flashes across his face, making his pale skin and awkwardly stiff haircut look almost cute.

"You should smile more," I say.

"As soon as world poverty comes to an end," he responds. "Or man walks on the moon." He presses his index finger against his lips. "Wait, that already happened."

"Calliope," Jasper calls. He comes up behind me, stopping short when he sees me standing with Monty. "Hi?" Jasper says hesitantly.

Monty nods at Jasper, and then looks at me and winks. "I'll leave you to whatever *this* is," he says. Then he turns and walks toward the science building, but on the edge of the quad, he stops, turns around, and looks at the envelope in Jasper's hand. I didn't even notice Jasper was carrying it. "Jasper," Monty says, his smile vaguely unnerving. He pushes his armband higher up on his arm, and then he turns and disappears into the building.

I turn on Jasper. "Why did you take it? What if Indigo realizes it's missing?"

"I didn't mean to," Jasper says, holding it up. "I just raced out after you and . . ."

"Well, we can't get back in to put it back," I say. "Anthony already left for the night."

"I'll return it tomorrow. Nobody's gonna miss it," Jasper says, and I reluctantly agree. Indigo won't even be back in the office until tomorrow morning, and there's no reason he would use an already completed envelope anyway. "Now, what happened in there?" Jasper asks. I try to turn away, but he gently lays his hand on my arm. "Tell me," he says.

"I saw myself in a strange building," I say. "It was awful."

"What happened?"

"I was screaming," I say slowly. "And I was hurt, pretty badly, I think."

Jasper looks concerned. "Is that why you bolted out of the office?"

"Sorry I ran. It just freaked me out," I say. "I've never seen myself in a vision before."

"Could you tell when it happens?"

"I have no idea. I mean, I looked pretty similar to how I do now, so it must be soon, right?"

Jasper shakes his head. "Although we see other people's future selves clearly, our view of ourselves is skewed. We always associate ourselves with how we look now," he says. "You could be fifty when this happens. Or even eighty."

"That's so not helpful," I say. "And how do you know this?"

"We did a lot of this kind of work at the New York office," Jasper says. "That's how I realized how goofy I look."

I roll my eyes. "Be serious."

"Seriously?" Jasper says. "I guess it's our minds protecting us from ourselves." He nods up toward the windows of the science building, where several students are staring at us. "Let's get out of here. Away from these nosy kids."

I snort out a laugh. "You sound like a cartoon villain."

"Har har har." Jasper weaves his arm through mine, and we start walking across the quad. "Besides, I don't see why you're so freaked out. If your vision is true, just stay away from that building," he says. "Then it can't happen to you."

"Brilliant plan, genius," I respond. "If I knew where the building was."

"Did you see any clues of its location?" he asks.

"There was a field of snow," I say, stepping off the grass into the parking lot. "So avoid wintery places for a while?"

Jasper and I cross the parking lot and stop in front of the Mustang. "I'd say so," he says, and opens the door for me. "Or we can go and look for your inner demons. Blindfold optional."

I shake my head. "Sounds fun, but I have to pass," I say. "I prefer to face my inner demons at home."

•　　　•　　　•

Charlie is sitting on the front steps when Jasper and I pull up. I open the car door and jump out before it comes to a full stop, my mouth falling open in surprise. Charlie stands up, and he's obviously just come from work since he's wearing a *Musée Méchanique* T-shirt with his name tag on it.

"Hi," I say.

Charlie looks at me, and then over at Jasper, who is pulling the car to the curb beside me. To my horror, Jasper gets out of the car and approaches Charlie.

"I assume this is Charlie," Jasper says, glancing at Charlie's nametag with a sly grin on his face. "Nice of you to announce who you are to everyone."

"Why is he here?" Charlie asks me.

"Well, he . . . um . . ."

Charlie's face gets really red. "*This* is the guy you chose over me?"

I'm not sure if I'm more afraid that I'm going to cry or that Charlie is.

"Did you *choose* me?" Jasper asks, his gaze firmly settling on me. "Are we dating?"

I'm so embarrassed I can barely speak. "I'm sorry," I say, addressing Charlie first. "I didn't choose Jasper over you, I just . . . um . . ." I bite my lip and look at Jasper. "No, we're not dating."

I glance over at Charlie, whose fists are balled by his side. He looks like he's going to punch Jasper.

"So why are you here?" Jasper asks Charlie.

"Shut up, Jasper," I say.

Charlie ignores him and stares directly at me. "I regretted that email as soon as I sent it, so I came over to see if we could maybe work this out," he says, "but now I see that we can't." He glares at Jasper for a long, awkward moment. Jasper just gazes back apathetically, and then Charlie storms off.

"Wait!" I call after him, but Charlie disappears over the hill.

"So we're a thing?" Jasper asks me. I can't tell if he's making fun of me or not, but I don't have the energy to figure it out.

"Just go home, Jasper," I say as I climb up the stairs to the front door. "I need to be alone right now."

"But what about your . . . you know?" he asks, stopping himself before he says the word *vision* aloud. "Don't you want to talk about it?"

"No," I respond.

Jasper looks like he wants to say something back, but he just climbs into the Mustang and drives away. I unlock the door and enter the house, and then I shut the door softly and lean back against it. My phone vibrates in my pocket. I pull it out and look at it, hoping it's Charlie, but it's Jasper.

U ok? the text says.

Ok, I write back.

I pocket my phone and take a deep breath, and then I cross the empty living room in three steps and pop into the kitchen. My mom is sitting alone at the kitchen table, and I'm relieved to see her by herself for once. After that horrible image of me bleeding in that building, and then the disappointment written across Charlie's face when he saw me with Jasper, I could use some Mom time.

"Hey Cal," Mom says, glancing up from her work. "You should teach my students to write."

I sit down at the table and look at the paper in front of her, which is filled with red slashes and phrases like "Remember commas!"

"Or at least punctuate," I say. It actually makes me glad I went to Bloody Hell. Even though it was an altogether boring experience, at least I learned my grammar.

"I saw the Bernsteins' nephew gave you a ride home from work," she says. "What's his name again?"

"Jasper."

"Right, Jasper," she says. "And Charlie was waiting for you."

"Yeah, it was bad."

"Bad?"

"Worse than bad. Like, gut-wrenchingly terrible." I sit down at the table and drop my backpack by my feet. "You ever do something you wish you could take back?"

Mom shifts her eyes away. "Once," she says, her voice

distant. "But sometimes we do things because we have to, not because we want to."

"But I wanted to kiss Jasper," I argue. "It's just . . . I want to be with Charlie more."

"I know what you mean," Mom says, and it really sounds like she does. But before I can ask what she means, she adds, "And work? It's good, I hope?"

I nod, but the hair prickles at the back of my neck. I wish I could get Indigo's opinion on what I saw, but I can't ask for his help without admitting that I broke into the office, stole the envelope, and viewed the building against his wishes.

"Work's fine," I finally respond, trying to remember what I last told her about my fictional job. "Where's Richard?"

"Pulling an all-nighter at the station," she says. "They're doing some training tonight."

Mom starts to describe Richard's annual training exercises, but my mind drifts as I flash back to my vision again. Shivers creep up my neck, and I realize that all of the hairs on my arms are standing up.

"You okay, honey?"

I snap back to the conversation with Mom. "I guess so," I respond, trying to pick the right words out of my scrambled thoughts. "I was just thinking about Jasper. We have sort of a . . . connection." It feels good to be confiding in Mom about something, even though I can only tell her part of the story. "He's different than Charlie. He's kind of—"

Mom's phone rings, and she points to it and raises her eyebrows, asking me if I mind if she gets it. I shake my head, and she picks it up.

"Hiya," she says. I instantly know it's Richard by the way she coos into the phone. I've experienced this enough times to know it could be a while, so I get up and pour myself a cup of coffee. I add a heavy dose of creamer and honey, and watch them swirl around before disappearing into the coffee.

At the table, Mom cups her hand over the phone and mouths "just a second" at me.

"I'd love to," Mom says as I lower myself back into the seat across from her. "But I have a lunch meeting tomorrow." She taps her pen against her grade book, where I see she's drawn a series of boxes. The tapping is my cue to continue the drawing. She knows I can never resist this game we've been playing since I was little. I take the pen from her and draw a line coming out of the last box.

"How late are you working tonight?" she asks into the phone, and her smile tells me he'll be home soon.

In my pocket, my phone *bings*. I wrestle it out and glance at the text. Jasper again.

Re: envelope. I'll return tomorrow. No worries, the text says, and ends with a smiley-face emoticon.

I write *gotta get this* on the edge of Mom's grade book, and Mom cups her hand over the phone again and mouths, "The nephew?"

I nod and head up the stairs, thinking about how strange Jasper acted today, first picking me up in that expensive car, then pretending our kiss didn't happen, then accidently taking the envelope from the office. But then again, Jasper is confusing sometimes.

As soon as I get to my room, I type **You better** into my phone, and then I strip off my clothes and pull on my pajamas.

I'm more ready than ever to climb into bed and sleep my thoughts away, but I end up just lying in bed, staring at the ceiling, watching the image of me in the building replay again and again like a terrifying GIF. I turn over in bed and force the image out of my mind, but the only other thing I can think about is that Jasper needs to return the envelope before Indigo finds out it's missing. I try to clamp down the nervous fluttering in my chest. Indigo would kill me for going behind his back if he knew.

I pull the covers over my head and stare at the light leaking through the material.

Go to sleep, I beg my mind, *I'll think about it tomorrow.*

CHAPTER TWENTY-FIVE

I immediately know that Indigo and Jasper have been dueling this morning because the energy in the office is like a harsh wind blew over the landscape of chairs and printers, computers and telephones, knocking out everything. All power. And everything is silent in their furious wake.

I find Jasper and Indigo in the room behind Indigo's office, which contains only the Faraday cage and a small chair and table. Indigo is sitting on a chair outside the cage, the Outgoing Sessions folder open beside him. Since Indigo smiles at me when I walk in, I assume Jasper found a way to put the envelope back in the Ongoing Sessions folder without him noticing.

Perched on the metal bench inside the cage, Jasper is filling up page after page with obscure sketches, and then taping the pages together to make a long landscape of jagged drawings. The hastily taped paper now stretches over ten feet long, and shows a type of primitive story—an army base of some kind, maybe, or a warehouse?

Psychic battles have been going on for thousands of years. Native American shamans used to battle among the tribes, knocking things over with a point of their fingers, changing the weight of objects using just their minds. This isn't new: it isn't even particularly creative. It's just a twisted type of machismo, where one person gets to win while the other has to lose. And it doesn't help that psychic battles cross the line between playing and working. The competition of which psychic can find the best information first is intoxicating, making the battles feel like play, but the fact that we usually do it in order to solve difficult problems for the government makes it the most serious work imaginable.

Jasper is talking now, short stuttered words and barely comprehensible sentences. "Someone's on the ground," he says, his hand flying over the paper. "And he's bleeding . . ."

He rips himself out of the trance, sweating and panting. He stabs his finger onto his drawing of a man lying on the ground, and there's a look of triumph on his face as he asks Indigo, "Did you catch that?"

I look at Jasper, but I don't think he's even noticed me standing outside the cage yet, my fingers wrapped like tinsel around the bars.

"Very good," Indigo says. His voice is calm, almost cold. "But I can do better." He flicks his finger to suggest that Jasper move off the bench. "Try to keep up."

As Indigo climbs past him into the cage, Jasper moves out of it in short, jerky movements, and I can tell his mind is still in his vision. I know the feeling.

When Indigo dips in, it's like a storm gathering. His hands flicker above the paper, like bits of lightning waiting to strike. He doesn't speak, but his lips move. He gets there quicker than others; he's had years of practice.

"I'm in," he says, and he sounds victorious. "The air is thin here. I'm looking down on the clouds."

In a psychic battle, both people must view the same scene to see who gathers the most information, so Indigo's viewing the same moment as Jasper, but from outer space. *Show-off.*

I grip the cage and lean in farther so as not to miss anything. Except for these battles and occasional monitoring, it's rare to see another viewer at work. We're all left alone in our own heads, wondering if we are doing it right, and if anyone's doing it any different, or any better. "We all have our own process," Indigo told me when I first started working here. "The important thing is to give into it.

That's the secret of shamans for thousands of years. Don't doubt. Just do."

Indigo is speaking now, so fast it's almost in tongues. "There are screens. I can't see much else, but . . . wait. I see a gun firing . . ." Indigo is sketching rough lines across the paper, but his hand seems disconnected from his body. His lips are clenched so tightly I'm afraid he's not going to breathe, so I hold my breath with him.

"It can't be," Indigo says, and a tear rolls down his cheek. I tighten my hands around the cage and shake it.

"Wake him!" I hiss at Jasper. "He's too deep."

But Jasper is already moving, opening the cage and shaking Indigo by the shoulders. "Indigo, come back to us," he's saying.

"Come back, Indigo," I say.

"Indigo, can you hear me?" Jasper shouts.

For a few seconds, tears streak down Indigo's face, but then he snaps out of it. He jerks his head up, his eyes clear, and he laughs weakly. "I think I've found something."

He immediately gets out of the cage, and barely looking in my direction, glances at his watch. "We'll pick this up tomorrow," he says. "There's something I have to find out." He picks up his briefcase, shoves the Outgoing Session folder in it, and dashes out of the office.

"That was weird," I comment.

Jasper shrugs. "Indigo's weird."

When we hear Indigo's old Volvo clunk to a start, Jasper and I both walk into the recovery room. He collapses onto the couch.

I sink down onto the couch beside him. "Did you put it back?"

"Of course. He didn't even notice," Jasper says, smiling triumphantly. "I *am* a magician, you know."

I'm so happy Indigo didn't find out that we borrowed the envelope that I'm almost giddy. "As long as you use your magic for good, I'm fine with that."

"Wanna go to lunch to celebrate?" Jasper asks. "That battle took it out of me."

I know I shouldn't keep spending time with Jasper outside of work and I'm still upset over the breakup with Charlie, but I'm starving. It couldn't hurt just to eat with him, could it?

"What about veggie burgers?" I ask, climbing to my feet. I put out my hand and pull Jasper up.

"They're something seriously wrong with putting those two words together."

We leave the office and take the elevator down, arguing about the benefits and drawbacks of tofu bacon. "It's more humane," I tell him.

"Not for the tofu," Jasper says. He follows me off the elevator across the lobby. "It has to suffer the indignity of pretending to be what it's not."

Jasper nods to Anthony, who is sitting at the front desk, his feet kicked up against the back of the metal detector as usual.

"Yo," Anthony says. "Bike keys?"

Jasper growls and throws the keys to Anthony, who catches them midair. "North side of the parking lot," Jasper says. "And fill it up."

Anthony nods, and zips his lips closed. "Still sealed."

Jasper just rolls his eyes and pulls the front door open. "What were we saying?"

"Cruelty to animals."

"Oh yeah. I want my bacon to oink before I eat it."

I shake my head, feigning anger. I don't get to choose what other people eat, and I'm fine with that. But if you could hear the thoughts of animals, would you eat them?

"This is my treat," Jasper says, but then he stops in the open doorway and pats his back pocket. "Forgot my wallet. Be right back."

"I'll be here," I say, and step out into the quad. Directly across the lawn, Monty is coming out of the science building. I barely recognize him. He's wearing dark pants with no holes or safety pins and a khaki suit jacket. He's even carrying a briefcase in one hand, and a clipboard with a neat stack of papers in the other.

"So you *do* clean up well," I murmur. But despite his cleaned-up appearance, Monty looks uncomfortable in his skin. He keeps tugging at the bottom of his jacket, and then he has to push up his sleeves, which are so long they hang down to his knuckles. He stops briefly in a crowd of students to straighten the papers in his clipboard, and then rebutton his khaki jacket, and then to readjust his briefcase on his shoulder.

Then, just as Monty walks straight into a boisterous game of Frisbee, one of the papers slips out of his clipboard and flies across the quad. He chases it down and stomps it into the grass with his boots. I burst out laughing.

"I think it's dead," I call out to him.

Monty glances up and spots me across the quad. Snatching the paper off the ground with a scowl, he heads toward me. "Twice in two days," Monty says when he's a few feet away. "How'd I get so lucky?"

"You did have a morning lecture," I reply. "How'd it go?"

"I think they're gonna take my name off the building."

"You didn't call the A's a-holes again, did you?"

"Not yet." He looks at the ground. "But I think they were expecting someone like Dad," he says softly. "And instead, they got *me*."

"Hey, you're not so bad."

There's a moment of awkward silence. "I hate these clothes," Monty finally says, and starts to unbutton his khaki suit jacket.

"Is this part of your lecture?" I joke, and he scowls.

"Hey, at least you got to wear the boots." Monty pulls the coat off and shoves it into his briefcase.

"That's gonna get—" I start to say *wrinkled*, but the words freeze in my mouth when I see his T-shirt. It's ripped across one faded black shoulder, above a picture of two interlocking earths. On the upper right corner is a sewn-in symbol of the infinity logo.

Monty sees me staring, and glances down at the rip on his shoulder. "Cheap material," he says. "They all ripped during the cleanup."

"Cleanup?"

"The toxic spill," he says. "EarthScape gave these out to the volunteers."

"Then EarthScape should have spent more on them," I say slowly.

"We can't waste money on clothes, not when the Red Cross depends on us. We didn't make many anyway; we try to remain anonymous. Just give some assistance to the people doing the real work."

I stare at him. "Do you mean like behind every success-ful man is a hard-working woman?"

Monty smiles. "You ask a lot of questions."

Jasper taps me on the shoulder, and I jump an inch in the air. "Geez! Can't you walk like a normal human?"

Jasper shrugs, and I glance back at Monty, expecting him to say hi to Jasper, but he ignores him completely. I can't blame him: it's not like Jasper's anger about Indigo selling our gifts out to the highest bidder isn't obvious.

"Hi, Junior," Jasper says.

"What's your name again?" Monty responds, and then he turns back to me. Now that Jasper's here, Monty's tone changes abruptly from informative to bragging. "We just sent up a cutting-edge satellite that picks up seismic activity before it happens," Monty says proudly. "In twenty-four hours, we can get our supplies to anywhere in the world from our warehouse."

The words echo in my brain like someone yelling into a cave: Satellite. Warehouse. EarthScape. The pieces start falling into place. The satellite I've been seeing in my sessions picks up on natural disasters before they happen, which means it would pick up on the tidal wave that kills the little boy, and send supplies on emergency vehicles from the EarthScape warehouse. It all makes sense.

"The news said the military sent that up," Jasper says from beside me.

Monty nods. "That's the point of being anonymous."

The bell in the Berkeley clock tower starts to chime. Monty shoves his clipboard into his briefcase beside his coat, and the leather briefcase bulges at the seams. "That's my cue," he says, and then glances at me. "Let's go for three days in a row next time."

As Monty walks away, something funny starts tickling at

the edge of my mind. The satellite that picks up on seismic activity and sends a signal to the warehouse makes sense, but it doesn't answer what EarthScape has to do with rare earth metals, like the internet said, or why the truck was carrying radioactive materials. Or stranger still, why the EarthScape warehouse looks closed down if it's an active emergency supply warehouse.

"C'mon," I say to Jasper, starting to follow Monty across the quad. "Let's find out where he's going."

"Why?" Jasper asks as he hurries to catch up to me. "He's probably just late for lunch."

"Maybe," I respond. "But something's off."

"But what about *our* lunch?"

"I can meet you at the restaurant," I say, and he huffs.

"Fine. I'm coming."

We trail Monty across the Berkeley campus, staying at least a hundred feet behind him the whole time. Monty keeps his eyes on his feet, only looking up a few times to glance anxiously at his phone.

"Can we turn around now?" Jasper asks, and I shake my head. "What are you looking for, anyway?"

"I don't know," I say. "I just have a weird feeling. But feel free to turn around anytime."

Jasper doesn't turn around, even though we practically have to run to keep up with Monty, and we're out of breath by the time we get to the other side of campus. But when Monty turns onto a little street lined with Painted Ladies—Victorian-style houses painted with cheerful pastel colors that are famous in the Bay Area—we continue to follow him, staying as far back as possible.

"I'm hungry," Jasper complains.

"Just a few more minutes," I say quietly.

When we get to the main drag through campus, Monty goes into a coffee shop. Through the tall glass windows, I see him approach the counter and talk to a pretty barista. Her big fluttering eyelashes tell me that she knows exactly who he is—and how much he's worth.

"Look." I nudge Jasper and point to Monty.

"She's definitely not into him for his personality," Jasper says.

Monty buys a coffee at the counter, and then walks over to the condiment table and grabs a napkin. He puts his briefcase on a booth beside the condiment table, right beside a piece of paper someone must have left behind.

"Can we go get that burger now?" Jasper asks.

"Veggie burger," I reply. "And no, not yet."

At the booth, Monty opens his briefcase, but instead of reaching into it, he looks around the room, and then he glances at the piece of paper that was left on the table. He takes a pen out of his briefcase and copies down whatever is on the paper onto a napkin. He folds the napkin and puts it in his pocket, and then he scribbles something on the piece of paper. Then he shuts the briefcase, picks it up, and goes back up to the counter to talk to the sexy barista.

"What's he doing?" Jasper asks.

"That's exactly what I was wondering."

"I know! She's way out of his league."

I roll my eyes. "Focus, Jasper, focus."

At the counter, the barista calls out an order, and a woman, her frizzy brown hair sticking out under a wide-brimmed black hat, picks up her to-go cup. With her back to the window, the woman stops at the condiment table to put something in her coffee, and then she walks past the booth. Without stopping, she picks up the piece of paper Monty just wrote on and returns to the condiment table. From behind, I see her fold it in half and place it in the pocket of her ridiculously large black overcoat.

"It can't be," I mumble.

"What?" Jasper asks.

The woman lingers at the condiment table just a second longer than most people would, not long enough for someone to notice who wasn't paying close attention, and then she grabs a lid and seals her coffee closed. She yanks her black hat down lower on her head, and, staring at her feet, turns around. My heart stops in my chest.

It's my mom.

"Good score, Monty," Jasper says.

I turn on him. "What?"

"What?" Jasper looks confused. "She's hot."

"That's my mom," I say.

He stares at me open-mouthed. "Sorry about the hot statement. And the good score comment."

In the café, Mom doesn't glance at Monty as she walks past him, or as she opens the door and steps onto Telegraph Avenue. She doesn't look back as she throws her coffee in the nearest trash can and raises her hand to hail a taxi. Within seconds, one stops in front of her. She climbs in and slams the door behind her, and the taxi takes off.

I stare at the cab's taillights as it flies through a yellow light and disappears over the hill, my mind spinning with questions.

Could Mom know about my job? Is that why she's meeting with Monty? But I'm almost positive Mom doesn't know about my job. If she did, she would have confronted me about it. Plus, why would Monty tell her about my true identity? He has nothing to gain from breaking my secret, especially after I helped him. So, putting that aside, there's only one reason she could have met Monty today: for work. Monty said that he lectures at Stanford occasionally, in the science department, and she runs the science department. He even knows about her "famous" math equation incident. . . . But if they're working together, she would have met with him there—and she wouldn't have been in disguise in her black hat and overcoat.

"Do you think they're dating?" Jasper asks.

I shake my head so hard it almost spins off my neck. "She's almost married."

"That's never stopped anyone before." Jasper laughs. "Why don't you just ask her?"

"Because, first of all, she's *not* having an affair with Monty. But this means she might know the truth about me." I take a deep breath. "What am I supposed to ask her? Mom, do you know that I'm a psychic spy and have been lying to you for years?"

"I'd go with the affair," he says.

"I'm going home to talk to her," I say, "before I lose my nerve."

CHAPTER TWENTY-SIX

It's only been an hour since I left Berkeley, but Mom's already on her way out. She's wearing sweats and sneakers, and her hair is back in a ponytail. She looks totally different than she did when she was meeting Monty at the café.

"Hey Cal," Mom says. "I'm heading to the store." She grabs the empty honey jar out of the pantry. "Want anything?" she says, as she drops the empty jar into her recyclable grocery bag.

I stare at her. What do I even say? Do you know about my work with a secret psychic spy agency? "Um . . . milk?"

Mom looks at me strangely. "We have milk." She opens the fridge and nods to the two pints of milk lined up on the shelf.

"I meant *creamer. Coffee creamer.*"

Mom shuts the fridge. "Right." She hitches her grocery bag onto one shoulder. "Hey, how was work?"

"Okay," I say. I can't accuse her of anything, or she'll know I was there. And what excuse would I have for being in Berkeley when I was supposed to be nannying for the Bernsteins?

"Your day was just okay?" she asks.

"Well, good." Behind me, the radio sputters National Public Radio, as usual. It gives me an idea of how to bring up what happened today. *Thank you, talk radio.*

"My day was very good, actually," I continue. "Mr. Bernstein was home from work today, so he took me and Emma to the Berkeley Art Museum. It was really cool. Have you been there yet?"

"I never go to Berkeley, you know that," Mom says. "I haven't been in . . . well, years."

Why is she lying to me? I take a deep breath and try again, going for a more direct approach this time. "I thought I saw you at a café in Berkeley this morning, when we stopped to buy a hot cocoa for Emma."

"Not possible," Mom says. "I was at Stanford all morning. It must have been someone else."

I'm dumbfounded. Somehow I thought we were close enough for her to tell me what's on her mind, but I guess not.

I turn it over in my head. If Mom was meeting Monty to talk about something to do with teaching at Stanford, she wouldn't lie to me about being in Berkeley today, so that seems to leave only one option I can think of, and Mom finding out that I'm lying to her makes my heart sink to my toes.

Behind me, Richard walks into the kitchen, and I jump at the sound of his footsteps. "Hey kiddo," he says.

"Hi Richard," I say weakly.

"You okay?" he asks.

I nod.

"I'm going to the store, honey." Mom says. "Want anything?"

Richard walks over and wraps his arms around her. "Jell-O," he says. "My weakness. And you." He shifts around her so he's giving her a hug from behind. "How was work, Callie?"

"Good! Mr. Bernstein took me and Emma to the Berkeley Art Museum today."

"That sounds great, Cal," he responds.

"He's a scientist," I continue. "And the whole way there, he kept talking about that guy that just shot a satellite into space. It's pretty cool. Monty something. Have you heard of him?" I ask, staring straight at Mom.

"I'm not sure," Richard says.

"No," Mom says.

Mom just traded notes with Monty and she's never heard of him? What's going on?

"I'm heading upstairs," I say. "Enjoy your Jell-O."

"Will do," Richard says.

I walk upstairs and pause in front of my bedroom door, listening to Mom leave the house. Richard starts the coffee pot, which means he'll be down there awhile, so I continue walking down the hallway until I get to Mom's room. Her door is open. In front of her dressing table, her work jacket is hanging off the back of her chair, and her heels are lined up below it.

I glance down the stairwell to make sure Richard's not coming up, and then out the window to be sure Mom didn't forget something and is coming back up to the house to get it. Once I'm sure, I quickly search the pockets of her jacket, but there's nothing in there except a hair band with a single strand of black hair dangling from it. I slip my hand inside the jacket and run it across the silk lining. When my fingers stumble across the inside pocket, I unzip it and take out the folded piece of paper.

I unfold it, and on the paper is a long series of numbers in Mom's handwriting.

At the bottom of the page, under the numbers, is a phrase in a different handwriting: *Operation Firepoker*.

I instantly know that I can't ask Mom about the paper. She'll know that I snuck into her room and looked through her private things. Besides, I already poked around once today, and she denied even knowing Monty or going to Berkeley, so she's obviously hiding something from me. I know it's none of my business, but there's something weird going on here, something that Mom feels strongly enough to lie to me about.

I hear Richard wash off his coffee cup in the kitchen sink; he'll probably head upstairs soon. I pull a Sharpie out of my backpack and then push up my sleeve and copy the numbers onto my arm.

"Want a cup of coffee while the pot's still warm?" Richard calls up to me.

"No thanks," I yell, and then I fold the piece of paper and quickly shove it back into her jacket's inner pocket.

I hurry to my bedroom and lock the door, and then I sit down at my computer and click on my browser. When the search bar appears, I type in the numbers written across my arm. The first several search results are random groups of numbers, including the number of insects in the Amazon, the highest amount of jellybeans ever put in a jar, and the number of hair follicles on a human head.

I scroll through all of these listings, and countless more pages of links, until I find a link with the list of numbers in the same order as on my arm. I click on it, and it redirects me to another site, which redirects me to another, until it

285

looks like I'm inside someone's database. It's like I hacked into someplace without even meaning to.

"Access Denied," it says across the screen.

I click on a hyperlink, and it says, in tiny letters:

Classified. Property of the US Government.

What the hell is going on? What kind of information could Mom have that is property of the government, and that Monty needs to know? I pry my phone out of my pocket and text Jasper.

Got your bike back from Anthony? I press Send, and then I go back to the browser, and type in *Operation Firepoker*.

A bunch of listings come up, mostly to do with operations on people who have been stabbed through the leg with a poker. To my surprise, I already know what to do if someone gets stabbed, thanks to Indigo's after work training sessions. I scan the information anyway, reminding myself that to stop the bleeding, I have to wrap a tourniquet tightly around the wound to cinch off the blood flow, using anything but parachute cord—until I come across an interesting article on a government conspiracy website. The first couple of lines say:

Operation Firepoker was a government operation
focused on locating materials for use in military
weapons. It is highly classified, and it appears

that all possible leads to this operation have been eliminated.

Eliminated. Shivers tremble through my body. I scan the rest of the article, but that's the only mention of Operation Firepoker. What could this have to do with my mom, or even Monty?

My phone vibrates in my hand, and I jump halfway off my chair.

Yep, w/ full tank, Jasper's text says. **Everything okay?**

No, I write. I press Send, and then pause before texting: **Can you come pick me up?**

I hear the rattling of Jasper's motorcycle on my fourth attempt to scrub the numbers off my arm. I've already taken a picture of my arm for when I scrubbed it completely off, but it turned out that permanent marker is called that for a reason. I towel my arm off, push my sleeve back down, and dash downstairs. Mom's coming in the doorway with an armful of groceries.

"Be back soon," I call behind me.

Out of my peripheral vision, I see Mom watching me climb onto the back of Jasper's motorcycle and wrap my arms around him. Jasper hands me his helmet, waits until I've strapped it on, and then squeezes the gas lever.

"Thanks for coming," I say, when my mom's worried face fades into the distance. "Can we go somewhere private? I need to view something, and I don't want to risk going back to the office."

Jasper nods and turns onto Fell Street, heading east toward Berkeley. I squeeze my legs around the motorcycle's shiny black body, thinking about what Mom's string of numbers refers to, and why Mom has information that's valuable enough to deny the public access to it. I grip onto Jasper's waist as he turns a sharp corner, and the smell of salt water washes over me. What did Mom get herself into, and what does it have to do with Monty Cooper? I know I shouldn't view again without Indigo's permission, but if Mom is involved in something dangerous—where all the leads have been *eliminated*—and she thinks it's worth lying to me about, shouldn't I find out what it is?

"What's going on?" Jasper yells back to me as we pass the giant sculpture of Cupid's arrow in Rincon Park.

"You know that paper Monty wrote on?" I ask, and he nods. "I found it, and there were some numbers . . . and I googled them, and I sort of ended up on a private database," I say. Then the ground falls away beneath us, and I hold my breath as we drive over the Bay Bridge. Hundreds of feet below, waves crash against the black lava rocks, spitting white foam into the air.

"So what does it mean?" Jasper yells.

"I'll tell you when we get there," I yell back. But truthfully, I'm not sure what it means. I just know that this feels like a deep secret I'm uncovering, and if there's one thing I understand, it's how dangerous secrets can be.

CHAPTER TWENTY-SEVEN

Jasper's apartment takes up an entire floor of a building, and it has windows overlooking Telegraph Avenue. It's super spacious, especially since the only pieces of furniture in the huge living room are a black leather couch, a mini-fridge, and a giant flat screen with an Xbox.

"Do you work the same job I do?" I ask.

"Rent control," he says. "Took the lease over from a friend."

"Lucky you." I sit down on the couch and glance at his selection of Xbox games spread all over the floor, most of which are all violent shoot-'em-up games. "Can we start?" I ask anxiously.

"Give me a second." Jasper turns down the lights, picks up the games off the floor, and grabs us sodas from the mini-fridge. He drops onto the couch beside me and hands me a soda. It's so sweet it makes my teeth hurt.

"So what are these numbers we're viewing?" Jasper asks.

I push up my sleeve to show Jasper my arm. "I found them in my mom's room. It's what she exchanged with Monty," I say. "And he wrote down Operation Firepoker. Heard of it?"

Jasper shakes his head. "Why don't you just ask your mom about it?"

"I tried," I say, "but she lied. She claimed she didn't know Monty and hadn't been to Berkeley in years."

Jasper whistles under his breath. "Now it's time for other methods? Like breaking into her mind?"

"I don't want to, but I'm worried that she's gotten herself into something dangerous."

"Your mom sounds like a real rebel."

I shake my head. "Not at all. More like a real flake. A lovable flake," I add.

Jasper nods in understanding, and hands me a pen and a piece of paper. "When I was working in New York, I had to break into people's minds all the time," he says. "I used to imagine their breath first. I'd listen to it until I found a gap in it, you know, like a thinking gap, of sorts, and then . . ." He looks up. "What? It's not like I've ever done this to *you*."

"You better not have."

He rolls his eyes. "Trying to help here."

"Don't look at me like that. You *did* suggest planting images into each other's dreams."

Jasper raises his eyebrows. "And did you do it?"

"Maybe. Did you?"

"Maybe." Jasper gestures for me to close my eyes, but I keep them open. Something about Jasper brings out my stubborn side. "So like I was saying, once you find the gap between your mom's breaths, push into it until you get into her mind."

"Easy as pie," I say sarcastically, but I shut my eyes anyway, trying to ignore the fact that I promised Indigo I'd never do this to anyone I love.

This is different, I tell myself.

I shove away my doubt, and settle deeper into the couch, taking a few deep breaths myself. Then I focus on Mom. I imagine the sound of her breath, the in and out of air through her lungs, the rise and fall of her chest. It takes a little while, but eventually, whatever part of my brain is psychic somehow transitions from just imagining her breaths to actually observing her breathing. It feels like I'm inside her breath. I sit this way for some time, just letting the rhythm of her inhales and exhales become a part of me.

After a while, I start to see what Jasper means. There's

sometimes a small gap between the inhale and exhale, like the slit in a barely open window. I let a few more breaths go by, and then I seize my chance.

I push. I push and push and push . . .

. . . but no matter how hard I push up against Mom's mind, I can't get in.

"Damn it!" I curse, opening my eyes. I'm not sure how much time has gone by, but the room is considerably darker. Jasper's gotten more comfy on the couch.

He shrugs. "So try another way," he says.

I take a deep breath and attempt to relax. I shouldn't have expected it to work on my first try anyway. "Okay. I'll try focusing on these numbers, as if they were in a sealed envelope." I lean back on the couch and close my eyes. "I'm ready whenever you are."

"Ready," he says.

I don't imagine getting off a boat into the sea. Instead I focus on the numbers on my arm while he talks me into the vision.

"These numbers signify something in the real world," Jasper says calmly. "Just follow them until you find out what."

It happens quickly.

I'm on a ship, my head beside a cylindrical beam of light.

I plunge my fingers in, and they melt and streak away from me. A feeling of both searing heat and bitter cold washes over me. I jerk my hand out, and my arm goes back to normal. Amazing.

"Focus on the numbers," Jasper guides me.

Where are the numbers? They're not here, so I force myself to turn away from the light and follow it off the ship, out into the sky. It parts around me as I whiz past the clouds, past an airplane, past a flock of birds, until I join dozens of other light beams in the sky.

"Wow," I hear myself say.

As I move across the sky, my body spreads across the length of the beams. I can see a million of me, as if I'm looking into an infinity mirror, like I'm everywhere and nowhere at the same time.

"Calliope," I hear Jasper call, but it's so distant from these beautiful lights that I'm flying through space with that I turn away from it. When I do, though, I remember Indigo's warning about getting too far in. He warned me about this: full body bi-location, or, as he called it, perfect site integration.

"There are some visions that take you too far out of your mind," Indigo said. "Don't let yourself get stuck out there." And now, staring at the dazzling beam of light, I know that it's happening to me: I am going out of my mind. But still, even though I know I need to pull out of the vision, the lights are so beautiful I can't look away.

"What's your location?" Jasper asks.

I look around, and there are countless satellites moving like a swarm of metal dragonflies around me. The light beams slowly filter through them, slowly coming closer together until they are almost parallel, and then they meet at a large satellite with a logo etched into it.

"I'm at the EarthScape satellite," I say.

"What are you doing there?"

"I don't know," I respond, and then I start to get sucked into a metal tube that is attached to the satellite. It looks just like the telescope in the science museum, but a lot bigger. "I think I'm entering a telescope," I say, and I'm swirling around inside with all the light beams. They slowly merge into one . . . and I'm shot out as a single, blindingly bright laser beam.

"Callie!" Jasper yells.

My eyes pop back open. Jasper's on the couch next to me, closer than before. He's turned the lights back on, but even so, it's impossibly dark in the apartment compared to all that light I was just in. All that light that I just *was*.

"I was in outer space," I say. "There were these laser beams, and they were meeting at a satellite, and there's a telescope attached, and they make this bright white beam—"

"Slow down," Jasper says, and waits while I bring my breathing back to normal. "Maybe we should stop."

"No! I have to go back in!" I insist, but Jasper's already

standing up, turning on the lights, and picking up a video game off the floor. "Listen to me." I get up from the couch and stop him from sliding the game into the console.

Jasper turns and looks at me, and his eyes are wary. "You can't go back in," he says. "I saw that look. You were . . . gone."

"There's something going on. Remember the tidal wave I saw, the one that killed that kid?" I ask, and he nods. "This has something to do with it."

"But a laser beam can't cause a tidal wave," Jasper says.

"I know." I'm stumped. Jasper turns away from me and pokes the power button on the TV remote. Techno music pumps through the speakers, and a shooter in camo clothing is pointing a gun directly at me. "Just help me go in one more time," I insist.

"Fine." He puts the TV on mute. "But I'm pulling you out after a couple of minutes. Understood?"

I nod. Jasper dims the lights, and then follows me back to the couch. "Count me in," I say.

"One minute. That's all you get." When I close my eyes, he's still looking warily at me. "Ten . . . nine . . . eight . . ."

At six, I get off the boat into the ocean; at three, I settle a few feet from the ocean floor; and by one, I'm inside the powerful laser beam.

"Wow," I say.

"What's wow?" Jasper asks. "What's going on?"

I am shooting across the blackness of space, and even though I'm going the speed of light, my movement feels slow and deliberate. I get farther out, until I see what I'm shooting toward: a large black rock hurtling through space. As it moves, I see the blurred line of numbers trailing behind it.

"Mom's numbers are some sort of trajectory," I exclaim.

"A trajectory of what?" Jasper asks over my vision.

"Of an asteroid," I respond. "A big one." I suddenly feel suction from below me, and the air gets hard to breathe. I try to back up, but I can't, and I—inside of the bright laser beam—collide with the black rock. Pain rockets through me. This must be what it feels like to be crushed alive.

"Calliope, come back," Jasper says.

I feel my mind teetering over the edge as the laser beam pushes the asteroid in a different direction.

"Callie!" he yells.

My nose starts to sting and run. I see the black rock become a ball of fire as it crashes through the atmosphere, passes the clouds, and smacks into the big blue ocean. Where it hits, a wall of water rises up out of the sea.

I quickly scan the surroundings to find out where in the ocean this happens, but the vision starts to tremble and tear apart. Then there are hands on my shoulders, shaking my body back and forth.

"Callie? What did you see?" Jasper's voice snaps me out of it, and I jolt awake, my eyes watering, blood dripping from my nose.

"It's coming," I gasp, "and fast."

When I finally shudder my way completely back to reality, my cramped hand is frozen around the pen. On the paper, I have drawn what looks like a whirlpool with a straw coming out of it. It's strikingly similar to the drawing from my first day with Monty.

I try to unclench my fist, but even though I know I'm safe here, I can't seem to unlock my fingers from around the pen. Jasper puts his hand around mine, and folds each finger back until the pen drops out of my hand.

"Better?" he asks in the gentlest voice I've ever heard him use.

I nod. Jasper's now sitting so close that my hand brushes his arm, and I feel his arm hair tickle my palm.

"Lean your head forward," Jasper says, and he strips off his blue sweatshirt and holds it against my nose. The blue cotton darkens into purple as blood seeps through the material.

"You don't need to do that," I protest through my blocked-up nose. "You'll ruin your hoodie."

"It's washable," he says.

When I feel the blood flow lower to a trickle, I take the hoodie off my face. Jasper turns it inside out and balls it up in both hands, while I scrub any possible blood off my face with my sleeve.

"So what did you see?" Jasper asks me.

I tell him how I saw a bunch of lasers combine at the EarthScape satellite, where they funneled into a telescope that was attached to it and became a super laser, and then how that bright laser beam pushed an asteroid toward Earth. His mouth drops open when I explain how I saw it land in the sea, and the tidal wave that rose out of it, and eventually, how it kills those people, including the little boy.

"What do you think we should we do?" Jasper asks.

"Besides alert the media, who would never believe the story of a psychic seeing a coming asteroid?" I say, shaking my head. "I'll tell Indigo all of it. He'll contact the people he reports to, whoever they are."

Jasper's face is angry when he looks at me. "You know what that means."

I stand up and walk to the window. I'm well aware that telling Indigo about the numbers might reveal the whole story: Jasper and me breaking into the office, stealing the sealed envelope, following Monty, finding the asteroid trajectory numbers that my mom must have stolen from NASA, viewing outside of work to find out what the numbers meant. It might mean losing my job and making Jasper lose his, or worse. "I do," I say sadly.

"But I was involved too," Jasper says. "It's not just you that's going to get in trouble."

"I know. But it's my responsibility to tell him."

"Are you going to tell him everything?" Jasper asks.

"If I have to," I say, but I know I'm lying. I know that I'll do everything in my power not to tell Indigo that my mom was involved. Although I still don't understand why she would steal asteroid trajectory codes from NASA, or why Monty would want them, I know she must have a good reason. Maybe he's blackmailing her? But with what? Jasper turns away, muttering "Fine" under his breath.

"Fine," I say back. I'm dreading telling Indigo—breaking his trust in me, probably losing this job that means the whole world to me, and maybe unintentionally bringing harm to my mom—but from what I've seen in my visions, the tidal wave, if it's the same one, is deadly.

But it may also be preventable.

I look out the window at the darkening sky, and I'm glad, for once, that I live in a place where I can't see stars. What else would I see coming toward Earth?

When I get home from Jasper's apartment, Mom isn't there, and she isn't answering her phone, either. I'm secretly relieved. Even though I know I should try to talk to her right away, I'm not sure what I'd say. Hi, Mom. Are you committing treason by sharing state secrets, which is punishable by death? Oh, and I only know this because I'm a psychic spy? Even if she believed me, she would probably just deny it, like she denied meeting Monty or going to Berkeley.

In the kitchen, Richard is sitting at the table, drinking his nightly cup of decaf coffee. I throw my backpack on the kitchen floor and slump down in the seat across from him.

"Hiya, kiddo," he says, and pushes his coffee across the table to me.

I smile gratefully and take a sip. "Yum. Cold decaf," I say. "Where's Mom?"

Richard stands up and puts the coffee in the microwave. "End-of-semester faculty meeting she forgot about."

I nod, realizing that I don't believe her anymore. But I also don't believe that she knew anything about the destruction this asteroid could cause. She's not a killer. There has to be a good reason for her to give the asteroid trajectory numbers to Monty. But what? And what would he want with them? "Have you noticed anything strange about Mom lately?" I ask Richard.

"She's been pretty wound up, sort of on edge," Richard says, handing me the now-warm coffee. "But she always is during finals. Why do you ask?"

"She just seems . . . different. Like she's hiding something." I don't know why I'm saying any of this, but I guess

I just need someone to commiserate with.

"She's been a bit more worried about you lately, I know," Richard says. He sits down across from me again. "And not just her dreams about losing you with her keys again. Like waking up in the middle of the night declaring you can no longer do the dishes because you might cut your hand off in the garbage disposal."

"You're kidding."

"Unfortunately, I'm not."

"And to think that all of this time I've been at risk for hand mutilation," I say. "Well, that's what I must have noticed." I stand and pick up my backpack, sure I'm not going to learn anything new about Mom from Richard. If she actually stole state secrets, she wouldn't tell anyone anyway. "Bedtime for Bonzo."

"You've barely had a sip of your decaf," Richard says.

I pick up the cup and take a long gulp. "Mmm. All the flavor, none of the punch." I head up the stairs, cup in hand. "Night."

"Night, kiddo."

CHAPTER TWENTY-EIGHT

In the morning, everyone's gone when I wake up, and we're out of coffee. I've got a few minutes to spare before I catch the bus, so I hustle out of the house and stop by the American Dream Diner on the way to work. Even though it makes me sad I'm not meeting Charlie here, the coffee is good, and Sylvester always cheers me up.

"Hiya, girl," Sylvester says as I walk in, the bell jingling behind me. He's not wearing an apron today, and as he gets to his feet behind the counter, I see the bright colors of the Ugandan flag on his T-shirt.

"Hey Sylvester," I say, walking up to the counter. "Rockin' the homeland today?"

"American diner, Ugandan heart," he says. "Miss the bus?"

"Not yet." I shake my head. "Just a coffee to go."

"Eat something," he says. "I'll make it real quick. I don't want your mama saying I don't feed you."

"Okay." I smile. "I'll have a breakfast bagel, no meat, no egg, just cheese."

"So a cheese sandwich," Sylvester says. "Coming right up." He walks into the kitchen, propping the door open so I can see him. "Where's Charlie boy?" he asks.

I pull out a stool and sit at the counter. "We kind of broke up."

Sylvester presses a spatula onto the cheese bagel on the skillet. "You've been together too long for that," he says, leaning his head back to see me. "I had a bet you two were gonna get married."

"Me too," I sigh. "You win or lose the bet?"

"Lost. Leroy said the world would end first, though, so I didn't totally lose."

"Where's Leroy been, anyway?"

"Called me from Mexico last week, talking loony, as usual," Sylvester says, pouring a cup of coffee in a to-go mug. "Something about a great flood coming so suddenly—"

"One shall not have place or land to attach," I interrupt, recognizing the line the crazy guy on the bus said.

Sylvester raises his eyebrows as he dishes the cheesy

bagel into a white paper bag. "How did you know that?" he asks. "Been talking to Leroy lately?"

I shake my head. "I've heard it around," I respond, remembering how both the homeless man at the pier and the crazy guy on the bus were ranting about a flood coming. "All the crazies are saying the same thing," I add.

"They always do."

I put a five-dollar bill on the counter. "Thanks for the coffee," I call behind me, as I open the door and walk out.

"A great flood shall come so suddenly, one shall not have place or land to attach," I say aloud. The bus pulls up at the end of the street, and I jog toward the stop, my coffee spilling over my hand. The bus driver sees me and waits until I get on the bus and sit down, breathing hard.

I pull out my phone and type in the lines, and a quote from Nostradamus, the ancient psychic, comes up. There are several theories on what Nostradamus meant, but everyone agrees that the other two lines in the prophecy, including something about a guy named Jason and a specific mountain, refers to a great flood happening when an asteroid hits the ocean.

A flood that destroys most of Greece.

Even though I stopped by the diner, I still beat Indigo to the office today. It's never happened before. He's usually waiting in the staff room, a cup of coffee in his hand, or he's pacing the recovery room floor, or setting up the viewing room with pen, a stack of blank paper, and a new envelope. Never to waste a minute. But today, I'm the one pacing the recovery room floor. I've already laid out the paper and pen in the viewing room and dimmed the lights. I've also drunk the coffee Sylvester made for me, eaten the lukewarm cheesy bagel, and then made myself more coffee. I'm about to give up on Indigo when he hustles in, his hair popping out of his ponytail and his tie skewed across his white work shirt.

"I can't talk about it, not yet," Indigo says before I can ask him anything. I follow him into the viewing room. "The info's under lock and key at the CIA, and I don't have permission to talk to anyone until they give the go-ahead."

"What are you talking about?" I ask.

He shakes his head. "Can't tell you. Like I said lock and key." I start to protest, but he adds, "I haven't got a lot of time today, so let's get to work."

"But I have something important—"

"It can wait," he says.

Normally I would fight him on it, but since what I'm about to tell him could ruin our relationship forever, as well as make both me and Jasper lose our jobs, and if I'm not careful, expose my mom as a traitor, I am eager to put it off. Besides, I tell myself, who knows what I could find out in this upcoming session?

We take our places in the viewing room—me on the couch, him in the chair—and I promise myself that I'll tell him everything after our session.

"Focus, Callie," I hear Indigo say, his voice impatient.

The first thing I see when I get into my vision is the man lying facedown on a pile of broken glass, in the shade of a large building. He's wearing a black hoodie, the hood pulled over his head. Above him, the air is thick with red smoke. I get a nervous, gnawing feeling in my stomach, like I haven't eaten in days. There's something about him, something I can't put my finger on. I want him to move, to show me he's still alive, but except for his right arm twitching, he's completely still. Then slowly, his right arm moves to one side of his body, and then his left arm, getting ready to push himself up. On his left hand, I see the star-shaped tattoo.

"What are you seeing?" Indigo asks over my vision.

I focus on the man as he pushes himself onto his knees under the layer of red smoke, and then raises his face to the sky. His hood falls back, revealing his face, and my throat feels like it's being squeezed by a giant fist.

It's Charlie's who's trapped under the radiation.

It can't be him! My mind screams over and over. *Charlie doesn't have a tattoo.*

But it *is* him. It's his copper eyes staring up at the building above him, and his lips mouthing words I can't hear. At this moment, all I know is that I have to stop this from happening to Charlie before it happens, although I don't know where, and I don't know when.

"What are you doing?" Indigo asks.

Behind my closed eyelids I see Charlie again. He's fighting to get to his feet, red smoke pressing in all around him.

"I just saw Charlie—" I start, but then I hear another voice, one I've never heard in this office before.

"Calm down, Mr. Starr," the voice says.

I open my eyes, and a few feet from me, Indigo is struggling between two security guards, both wearing T-shirts that say *Shady Hills.*

"I'm not going anywhere," Indigo says, but they're not listening. They move him out of his chair and across the room in one fluid motion.

"What's going on?" I demand.

"Answer the girl!" Indigo says, but his order is met by complete silence. I've never seen Indigo so angry. His face is this crazy pink color and he's spitting out obscene words as the security guards finally lug him out of the viewing room. "That son of a bitch," Indigo shouts as they drag him past the recovery room's pale blue couches. I jump up and stumble out of the viewing room after him, noticing how Indigo's voice is alternating between whiny and deep, like maybe he *is* a little crazy. "*He* did this!"

"Who are you talking about?" I ask, but Indigo can't hear me over his roaring voice.

"Where's Anthony?" Indigo demands. He looks wildly around the room, as if expecting Anthony to jump out and knock the men out at any moment.

"This is above his pay grade," one of the guards says.

"You can't just take him!" I yell. "This can't be legal!"

The guards just sneer at me as they continue to pull Indigo toward the door.

"I'm not the first," Indigo warns, wrenching his body around to stare at me, "and I won't be the last."

One of the guards reaches for the door handle, but it opens before he gets to it. Jasper strolls in, motorcycle helmet hanging from his hand. He stops and stares at Indigo, the two guards, and me. "What going on?"

"Get out of the way, kid," a guard says.

Jasper blocks the doorway leading out to the hall. His arms are crossed and there's an angry scowl on his face. "You're not taking him anywhere."

"Move before you get hurt, Jasper. You can't help me," Indigo says, and then he looks at me. "You have to stop it."

"Stop what?" I ask.

"We are under orders to take him, by force if necessary," a guard says to Jasper, who still hasn't moved. He pushes Jasper from the doorway as the other guard leads a hysterical Indigo out into the hallway.

"Stop Operation Firepoker," Indigo says. He wrenches his neck around to look at me as the guards push him into the elevator and press the *close* button.

"What *is* that?" I ask Indigo as the elevator door closes between us. "What is Operation Firepoker?" I yell through the elevator door.

"Callie, wait!" Jasper says, but I'm already racing to the stairwell and down two flights of stairs. As I run through the lobby, Anthony steps out from behind the front desk, and I run right into him.

"Where are you going?"

"Move," I say, shoving him out of the way. "Please."

I dash outside, and next to the waiting van, Indigo's head is ripped back, and his eyes are wilder than I've ever seen him. He's roaring, his arms spread out like wings, and the two guards grapple to maintain hold of him.

"They need me here!" Indigo yells, squeaking on the word need.

Yes, we do. I need you. I run up to the van just as a guard lowers Indigo's head and shoves him into the backseat. The guard slams the door and turns around to face me.

"Back up," he says. I step forward anyway and yank on the door handle, but it's locked. The guard stares at me in amusement, and then he walks around the van and joins the other guard in the front.

I push my face against the window to try to see Indigo, but the glass is too dark, so I just place my hand against the cold glass as if I could reach him. Then the engine starts, and the van begins to move. Jasper is suddenly beside me, touching my arm gently, guiding me backward with only his fingertips.

"Don't, Callie," Jasper says. "There's nothing you can do."

The van slips out from beneath my palm and drives away, taking Indigo with it. I want to run after it, but I know that Jasper's half-right: there's nothing I can do *right now*.

But I can, and will, find a way to help him. "Indigo is not crazy," I say to Jasper. "Someone made him look that way."

Around us, the students in the quad have dropped their books and Frisbees and are watching us with curious eyes.

"It must be a mistake," Jasper says. "Paperwork or something."

"I don't think so," I respond, trying to ignore their stares. "You didn't hear what Indigo said this morning when he got here. He knew something," I add, turning my back to the students. "And he was in a hurry, like he knew they were coming for him."

"Who would want Indigo locked up?" Jasper asks.

When I think about it, names scroll through my head faster than I can count. There are hundreds of people who could want Indigo locked up. He could be the target of any of the criminals who Branch 13 has managed to stop. The thought makes me shiver.

"At least we know he's somewhere safe," Jasper continues. "If there's a good side to this, it's that Shady Hills is a treatment center, not some criminal's basement."

I reluctantly agree, but I'm still upset that Indigo is being held anywhere against his will. "Let's go to Shady Hills and demand an explanation," I say. "See if we can get him out of there."

"At the risk of sounding insensitive, we have no grounds to stand on: we're not family, and officially, we have no ties to him. As far as we're concerned, we've never met Indigo Starr."

"Maybe I'm his long-lost niece, then," I respond. Jasper starts to argue, but I interrupt. "Are you going to take me there or not?"

"I know you'll go there with or without me," Jasper says, "and I don't want you going to that place alone."

I smile at him gratefully, but the grin quickly fades off my face when I remember how Indigo was forced into the back of the van like an animal. "You get your bike, I'll find out the visiting hours." Jasper nods and jogs off in the direction of the parking lot.

I pull my phone out and search for Shady Hills Treatment Center. On the About page, it says that the visiting hours are between eight and ten every morning, and it's around nine now. "Absolutely no visitors outside of visiting hours," the website says. We can make it if we hurry.

Getting to Shady Hills takes almost thirty minutes, and we wouldn't have made it without Jasper's insane (but not blindfolded) maneuvering through traffic. But since Shady Hills is all the way across the city in the Tenderloin neighborhood, which is scary at the best of times, I'm glad I didn't come alone. The way Jasper is nervously looking around as we drive up, he's probably doubting his decision to drive me here.

"Stop here," I say, and Jasper stops the bike in front of a neon cross that says Jesus Saves. Underneath the cross, there are two dark glass doors with no sign. I glance at the GPS on my phone.

"It says it's here," I say.

"I don't see it—"

"There," I say, pointing to a small sign that says SHTC. "That was on the side of the van. Shady Hills Treatment Center."

"Or Shit Happens Take Cover," Jasper jokes.

I scowl at him. Who can joke at a time like this?

"I'm going in alone," I say. "They might believe I'm Indigo's long-lost niece, but niece *and* nephew, who are almost the same age, but look nothing alike? That's pushing it."

Jasper sighs. "Fine. I'll wait for you out here."

"Just drive around the block a few times," I say. "Don't

sit here like you're waiting to get shot." Jasper nods, and I get off the bike and walk to the door. I don't hear him drive away until the doors are shutting behind me.

Inside, the cold is oppressive. It's a squeaky-clean type of cold, impressed further by the glossy white marble floors. A matching white desk lines the wall opposite the doors in the empty lobby. Behind the desk, a secretary chews on the end of her blue pen, and I can hear the plastic breaking on her upper molars.

"Oh," she mutters when she sees me, and pulls the pen out of her mouth. She lays it beside the neat pile of lined paper on the desk before her, and folds her hand over the pen. "Are you here to see somebody?" she asks brightly.

"Um, I'm here to see my uncle," I say, then clear my throat. "Indigo Starr. Your staff picked him up this morning."

The secretary squints at me suspiciously. I think she's going to ask me to leave, but she doesn't. "Let me look him up for you," she says, typing something on the keyboard. She clicks through computer screens, her finger moving quickly across the mouse. "There were no pick-ups today," she says. "Could he have been picked up yesterday?"

I shake my head. "Your van showed up at his office an hour ago."

She taps her pen against her desk, considers chewing it again, but lies it down. Her expression is puzzled. "We don't have a van. We have a bus." She points outside to the handicapped-accessible bus parked on the street.

Horror washes through me. Oh my god. Where is Indigo? If Shady Hills didn't pick him up, then who did?

"Could your uncle have checked in under a different name?" the secretary asks.

I shake my head. "Thank you," I say, but as I turn to leave, I remember something: Michael lives here. He spends a lot of time with Indigo, and he sometimes still works for us. He might know something about who could have taken Indigo, or even about Operation Firepoker. "Wait," I say, quickly turning around. "Do you know all of the patients in this facility?"

She shakes her head. "I'm new here. Why?"

"My uncle might have checked in under the name Michael. Michael Ferrara." She looks at me strangely, so I add, "That's his legal name. Indigo Starr is just his pen name. He's a writer."

The secretary nods in acceptance, which makes me think that maybe there are a lot of writers locked up in here. She clicks her way through several computer screens, and then she picks up the phone and says: "Guard needed at the front."

A minute later, a uniformed guard leads me through the facility door and down the empty hallway into a large circular room. Here, people in wheelchairs are gathered around the television, moving their mouths with the Dean

Martin song the man is singing on TV, but no sound comes out. A nervous giggle escapes me, but it dies quickly in my throat when I see Michael. He's sitting cross-legged on the floor, a few inches from the TV screen. Under his stringy brown hair and his wandering lazy eye, he's mouthing the words to the song.

"Um, there he is," I say, crouching beside him.

"Michael?" The guard asks. "Is this your niece?"

Michael looks puzzled, but he nods slowly. The guard leaves, and I sit down beside Michael.

"Michael?" I whisper. "It's Callie. I work with Indigo."

He nods again, his eyes still locked on the TV.

"Indigo's missing," I continue. "He's supposed to be here."

A high, wavering voice bursts into song behind us. "Somewhere over the rainbow, bluebirds fly," a woman in a wheelchair sings along with the television. I glance back at her, but she doesn't see me. She sings louder and louder until a guard comes in and wheels her out of the room.

"Indigo is missing," I say to Michael again. "Do you know who could have taken him?"

Michael taps his hands repeatedly on his laceless sneakers. "Is it his turn?" he asks.

"His turn?"

"To go to the place." Michael beats his fingers more

316

rapidly against his shoes, making a clicking sound with his chewed nails.

"What place are you talking about?" I try to calm him down by taking one of his hands, but he just hits them even faster against his sneakers.

"No, no, no, no, no!" Michael wails. I look nervously toward the door, hoping no one comes in to get him now.

"Michael? What place?"

"Get them out!" he shrieks, smacking his forehead with his open palm. "Get them out!"

A guard appears in the doorway and starts moving toward us. Michael's now rocking back and forth, his head in his hands.

"What place?" I repeat.

"Your uncle has had enough," the guard says. He puts his hands on Michael's shoulders and says his name gently. "Michael? Can you hear me?"

"I need to know," I whisper.

"I said, he's had enough!" The guard helps Michael to his feet, and he looks around unsteadily, like he's not sure how he got here.

"Michael. *Please.*"

Michael drops his eyes to the floor, and then he whispers, "The place that smells like salt."

The place that smells like salt? My mind flashes through several images at once: the vision of Charlie trapped under the radiation in the shadow of a large building, the Earth-Scape warehouse by the salt flats, and my head bleeding inside of the building I had trouble seeing into, the one on the edge of a field of white snow. Or, if a flat is being dried for environmental purposes, white *salt*.

"Are you talking about a warehouse near the salt flats?" I ask Michael. The guard is leading Michael away, glaring at me as if insanity must run in the family. "The Earth-Scape warehouse?" I continue, ignoring the guard.

Under the guard's large hands, Michael stops, and his body tremors as if a cold wind blew across him. "That's where they do it," he whispers, and looks up at me. One eye wanders to the right, while the other stares straight at me. "That's where they break you."

I run out of the front doors onto the street, having already tried calling Charlie three times with no answer, to where Jasper is waiting for me. He's acting macho on the back of his motorcycle, but I can tell that the bums glaring at him from under the glowing neon cross are making him nervous.

"I have to warn Charlie," I say, jumping on the back of the bike.

"Your boyfriend?" Jasper asks.

"Ex-boyfriend," I say. "Thanks to you."

"You're welcome," Jasper responds. He squeezes the gas, but then slams to a sudden stop as a car cuts him off, and the loud squeak of the bike's wheels echo across the buildings around us. "Did Indigo tell you something about Charlie?" he asks.

"He's not there."

"What?" Jasper turns around and stares at me.

"Indigo's missing, but I might have an idea of where to find him."

"Where?"

"I'll tell you later," I say. "But first, I need to talk to Charlie. I saw something bad happen to him, and I have to warn him."

"Do you know when or where it happens?"

"I know where, but not when," I say. "But it could happen at any time. The sooner he knows, the safer he'll be."

"Fine," Jasper mutters, turning back around. "Where is this ex-boyfriend of yours?"

"Bleeding Heart Catholic School, four blocks northwest of the Panhandle."

"I'll take you there," Jasper says, maneuvering the bike into the street. "But I think you're making a mistake."

"What's that supposed to mean?"

"It's just . . . you're unusual, Calliope," Jasper says. "In a way no normal boy will ever know."

"Shut up and drive."

As we speed through town, I don't notice the houses or buildings or streets. I just think about Charlie, and how he never asked for any of this, and how, even once he's broken up with me, he's still in danger. Now that I recognize the warehouse by the salt flats, I need to warn him to stay away from that warehouse at all costs, no matter what anyone says to him. I need to convince him to change his future.

CHAPTER TWENTY-NINE

I get a sickening feeling of dread as Jasper drives up the hill toward my old high school. Bloody Hell is a redbrick building overlooking San Francisco Bay. I would consider it a beautiful building if I'd never seen the inside. Lined with ugly orange lockers and smelling of locker room sweat, it looked like how I imagine any other high school in the country would.

"Stop here," I instruct Jasper when we're halfway up the hill.

"Why? Embarrassed by me?"

"Charlie won't listen to me if he sees you," I say.

Jasper shrugs. "Okay. Want me to wait?"

I shake my head, an idea so obvious occurring to me

that I wonder why I didn't think of it before. "No. Go back to the office and see if you can find the name or number of Indigo's CIA contact anywhere. Indigo usually called the contact from his desk," I add, "and I've seen him glance at some sort of card before he called."

"Right," Jasper says. "Like they're going to listen to us."

"They might," I retort. "Indigo said the CIA had some intel under lock and key, so maybe his contact will know where he is, or at least who took him."

"Good idea," Jasper says, and then lays his hand on my arm. "Be safe."

As his motorcycle shoots away, I start the short ascent up the hill toward the school, thinking about what I'm going to tell Charlie when I see him. For Charlie to believe that's he's in danger, I'll have to explain what I'm warning him about, which means telling him the truth about me. The thought is terrifying, and I look down at the sidewalk beneath my feet. But if I'm honest with myself, not only am I afraid that Charlie's going to get hurt, but I have the scary feeling that I'm next.

"I'm not the first," I remember Indigo saying, "and I won't be the last."

Even if Charlie stays away from the warehouse and avoids his fate, what if something happens to me and I haven't told him the whole truth? Charlie will try to find me, which could put him directly in the path of whoever took Indigo. Telling him the truth could save his life, in more ways than one.

As I reach the front steps, the bell rings, a shrill sound that flashes me back to all those mind-numbing years of stuffing my brain with useless knowledge. I quickly duck behind the giant stone column to wait for Charlie. I don't want to explain to any of my old classmates why I'm here.

As the shrill sound fades, students flood out of the school for lunch, their identical maroon uniforms rubbing against one another. I only step out from behind the column when a group of boys comes tearing out the doors, with Charlie trailing behind. His khaki tie brings out his eyes, which are caramel colored today, with flecks of gold.

"Callie." Charlie stops in the doorway, and students continue to push out of the door around him. "What are you doing here?"

"I have something I have to tell you," I say. Around us, the students' pace slows just slightly, but enough that I can tell I'll be gossip for days to come.

"Not sure I want to hear it," he says.

My heart is pounding, pounding, pounding. "It'll just take a minute." *A minute to tell you the biggest secret of my life, a secret I've been keeping from you. But this time, instead of the truth hurting you, it can hopefully save your life.*

"Hey, Charlie, you coming?" A guy yells from behind me.

Charlie stares at me for a moment before yelling back. "I'll catch up with you guys," he calls, and turns to walk back into the school, expecting me to follow. "C'mon," he says. "We can talk at my locker."

I trail Charlie down the hall, my feet having memorized the way years ago. At locker number 153, he drops his backpack with a sigh and leans back against the orange metal, his hands stuffed in his pockets. "What?" he asks.

Down the hall, people are banging their lockers closed, racing to get out of here for the day. Although it was only four months ago, that world already feels years behind me.

"Um . . . I wanted to tell you . . ." I glance down the hall at my old locker, which has already been taken up by another student.

"I've only got a minute," Charlie says, and taking his hands out of his pocket, he raps his knuckles against his locker. On the back of his left hand is a temporary tattoo in the shape of a star.

Charlie notices me staring at it. "What? Not like you care anymore about Colin's birthday party."

I know I have to tell him now, because if Charlie's wearing the star tattoo today, it means this happens to him *soon*. I suck the air through my nostrils, trying to gather up the courage to tell him the truth about me. "You know how I said that I saw you and Amber together at the lighthouse?" I ask.

Charlie nods, and I notice that he's standing a foot away from me, as if I'm contagious with some fatal disease.

"I knew about Amber because . . ." I pause, and then force myself to continue talking. "Because I know things."

Charlie stops rapping on his locker. "You know things?" he repeats.

I scratch my fingernail against the locker next to Charlie's, and feel the paint peel off under my fingernail. "I mean, I'm . . . um . . ." The paint's thick skin pries into my soft flesh. "I'm . . . um . . ."

"What?"

"I'm psychic," I say. It sounds absurd as I'm saying it, and I know it sounds absurd to Charlie, too, because he looks at me like I've just told him the biggest lie in the world. "That's how I knew," I continue, babbling now, "about you and Amber. I wasn't spying on you, not in the traditional way, at least." Charlie is standing incredibly still, so I quickly wrap my arm around his waist and try to pull him closer. "Jasper is a psychic too, and we work together undercover, for the government." Despite Charlie's angry face, I force myself to keep talking. "I came to warn you to stay away from the redbrick warehouse near the salt flats. I saw something terrible happen to you there, sometime in your future. Sometime *soon*. Promise me you won't go there, ever."

Charlie stares at me, his hair falling lightly across his

face. "You expect me to believe that?" he says bitterly, taking my arm firmly off his waist. "You think I'm an idiot?"

I fall back, my body detached from the floor without his waist to steady me. "No, I don't think—"

"I'm just some moron you can lie to?"

This is spinning wildly out of control. He doesn't believe me. This isn't how I pictured this at all. I thought we'd bond over it, maybe share stories about what we thought psychics were, as opposed to what they really are—normal people, like me. And he'd stay away from the warehouse because he knows I'm not crazy, because he knows me well enough to believe what I say. But I forgot about one thing in my equation: reality. Of course Charlie doesn't believe me. He doesn't believe in ghosts or aliens or psychics. He's a pragmatist—and I'm a fool.

"How else would I know about Amber?" I protest, desperately trying to remember why I thought this was a good idea.

"You're expecting me to believe that you followed me *with your mind*?" He shakes his head. "That's rich, Callie."

"But it's true—"

"We've been together for three years!" Charlie continues, as if I hadn't said anything. "I've never given you a reason to distrust me—or to lie to me."

"Please believe me," I beg him.

"Fine," he snaps. "Are you reading my thoughts right

now?" Anger has filled his face, and it looks like it could burst. "What am I thinking?"

"That's not how it works," I say softly. I reach for Charlie again, but he pulls away.

"Then how does it work? Prove it to me!"

"I'm not . . . I'm not sure how much I can tell you, for your own safety."

"That's convenient," he snaps. "And that guy, the one who *kissed* you, he's a psychic too, right?"

I nod frantically.

"Good joke, Callie," he says. "Good bloody joke." He pushes off his locker, his face a mix of anger and hurt. I try to grab his shoulder, but he shakes me off and storms away. His shoes echo down the hallway. I know I could go after him, but what's the point? I can't think of anything I could say that would change his mind about me in this moment.

The linoleum beneath my feet suddenly feels unsteady, and chills course through me. An overwhelming weariness comes over me, making me feel slightly numb. I still have to do *something*. If Charlie won't believe me that he's in danger, who will?

I think of calling Grace, but she's more of a pragmatist than Charlie. She wouldn't understand why I'm begging her to keep Charlie away from the warehouse. "He would never go there anyway," Grace would say, which I'd agree with if I hadn't seen Charlie's future, and if I wasn't trying to prevent it from happening.

My phone vibrates, and I dig it out of my pocket. The screen is lit up with Jasper's text message: **R U coming to the office?**

Yes. Have you found it? I type back.

Not yet.

Keep looking. I'll be there soon. I stuff my phone back in my pocket, feeling relieved.

Indigo's CIA contact—that's who will believe me. I know Indigo well enough to find where he's hiding his information, and once I find it and reach the contact, he'll have the power to help save both Indigo and Charlie.

CHAPTER THIRTY

There's this strange sort of silence at the office that Indigo always covered up with his vibrant energy; it's like the electricity has been shut off. No one is preparing the viewing room with paper and pens or lounging in the recovery room. There's just Jasper sitting at the table in the staff room, picking from a bag of Doritos.

It's only been an hour since I left Bloody Hell, but I'm terrified that I'm going to be too late to help protect Charlie from his terrible fate. I know that I have to find the information about Indigo's CIA contact, and *soon.* If I can't find the contact, I'll have to just call the CIA myself—even though I'm sure they'll just think it's a prank call, since according to Indigo, very few people in the government know about us anyway.

Jasper holds the bag out to me when I rush into the staff room. "You look exhausted," he says. I shake my head at the chips, and Jasper withdraws the Doritos bag. "Suit yourself."

"Did you find Indigo's contact?"

Jasper pops another chip into his mouth. "I looked everywhere. Practically tore apart his desk doing it."

I rush into Indigo's office, dropping my backpack in the corner, and Jasper comes in behind me. Two of Indigo's desk drawers are pulled open, and his bookshelves are slightly messed up, but besides that, the room's in tip-top shape. "You call this torn apart?"

"I put everything back," Jasper says. "Maybe we can help Indigo another way?"

"This isn't just about Indigo anymore." I pull out a drawer and dump it on the ground. "Charlie's going to get hurt too, in some sort of radioactive attack," I continue. "I need to let Indigo's contact know." I pull out another drawer, and another. I know I'm destroying Indigo's desk, but I don't care.

Jasper looks confused. "What are you talking about?"

I'm done with Indigo's desk now so I pick up a book off the bookshelf and start to riffle through it. "This is not the time—"

"You keep saying that!" Jasper glowers down at me.

"Tell me what happened at Shady Hills. You said Indigo wasn't there? Did the guards take him to another facility?"

"It wasn't their van. We don't know who took him."

Jasper freezes, his mouth slightly agape. "How is that possible?"

"I don't know, okay?" It comes out harsher than I meant it to and Jasper spins around and starts pacing. Finally— maybe he's starting to get how serious this is.

I open every book, flip through it, and drop it on the ground, until there's a pile of books at my feet. Then I search the rest of the office. Nothing. Pausing to look around again, I nervously pick at the cuticles of my left hand. Jasper's watching me from the corner. He seems to have calmed down, which is good, because I'm getting more worked up by the minute.

"I saw Michael when I was at Shady Hills," I say.

Jasper comes over and puts his hand over mine to stop my nervous picking. "The crazy guy?"

"He's not crazy. He's—" I try to think of a word for it, and what Michael said about getting them out comes back to me. "Out of his mind. Literally."

I wiggle my hand free of Jasper's and walk out of Indigo's office, Jasper right behind me, and open the door to the staff room. I rifle through the staff room's shelves, check behind the candy machine, and pull everything out of the drawers, but I don't find any information about

Indigo's contact. It's starting to sink in that we might not find a contact at all. I lean up against the candy machine to think a moment.

"Did you ask Michael about Indigo?" Jasper asks. He digs two quarters out of his pocket.

I nod. "Michael told me about this place where Indigo might be. I saw it in a session, but I never knew where it was." Jasper loads both quarters into the candy machine and presses B2. "Now I do. I think he's at that warehouse near the salt flats," I say. "And I think that's where I saw Charlie too."

Jasper reaches through the slot and pulls out the last Kit Kat. He quickly unwraps it and offers one side to me, but I shake my head. "Are you sure?" he asks.

"Totally sure."

Jasper sits down at the table and makes a steeple with his hands, pressing his fingers together until the tips are white. "What are you going to do?" he asks.

"I'm going to call the CIA hotline and warn them that something's going to happen there," I say, "and if they don't believe me, the police. And the FBI. And the goddamn Coast Guard. And then I'm going down there myself." I push off the candy machine and head toward the door.

"They'll never listen to you," Jasper says.

"Maybe not. But it's the only thing I can do."

"But going down there yourself? Sounds dangerous to

me," Jasper says. He stands up. "You don't even know for sure that Indigo's down there. And why don't you just call your ex and warn him?"

"I've already tried," I mutter, as I reach the door.

"Where are you going?"

"I left my phone in Indigo's office," I say. "I'll just call the authorities from the road. Are you coming with me?" I grab the doorknob.

Jasper doesn't respond, but below my palm, I feel the metal lock turn. I jerk the knob, but the door is locked.

I forgot that Jasper has metal bending skills.

"That's not funny," I say, jerking on the doorknob again.

"No, it isn't," Jasper says in a tight voice.

Shaking my head, I try to turn the metal lock in the opposite direction to unlock it, but it won't budge. I'm about to scold Jasper for his childish behavior when I hear a voice in my head.

"You're not calling anybody," the voice says from inside my mind.

"Did you say something?" I turn around to face Jasper, and confusion sweeps over me.

Jasper is standing beside the table, his chair clattering to the floor beside him. He looks rigid, as if someone is bending his body in an uncomfortable way, and his face is cold and far away. "I wish you hadn't said that."

"Hadn't said what?" I can feel the hair starting to stand

up on my arms. There's something terribly wrong here. I step toward him. "What's going on, Jasper?"

"I didn't want to, Callie. He just offered me an apartment, if I would . . . and I've never had a home."

"Jasper, slow down. What are you talking about?"

But now he's blubbering. "I'm in too deep to get us out. I'm sorry."

The next few moments are pure confusion.

Jasper moves across the room to the candy machine, and I'm looking at the candy machine and noticing there are no Kit Kats left, and then I'm on the floor, a chair pulled on top of me, and my mind is racing, thinking about what Jasper meant by being too deep to get us out. Across the staff room, a door opens, and there's somebody coming into the room. I can't turn my head to see who it is, but I see the reflection of a black turtleneck in the candy machine, and then there's a wet cloth pressed against my mouth, and I'm breathing in, and in, and in . . .

CHAPTER THIRTY-ONE

When I open my eyes, I'm in the trunk of a car. I can tell because of the thin strips of light that are flashing through the cracks in the blackness above me. My legs are bent at the knees and pressed against the padded lining, and my neck is bent at a strange angle, so it cramps when I move it.

In the darkness, I remember the lock turning under my hand, and the cloth pressed over my mouth. *Jasper. Why did you do it?* I tilt my neck back and forth, trying to stretch out the searing pain along my shoulder blades. I'm not sure how long I've been in here, but judging by the feeling in my cramped muscles, it's been quite a while.

My legs are pressed against the wheelbase so I can't

stretch them, but my arms are free. I lift them above my head and grasp the roof of the trunk, trying to find a release button, but there's nothing to grab onto. I pound my fists against the trunk, but I know it's hopeless. I can tell that we're driving fast since I can feel the rumbling of the ground below me, and there's no way someone could hear me anyway.

I feel around the edges of the trunk until I find a crack leading to the car's backseat, and when I press my ear against it, there's a voice coming from inside the car. It's muffled, but I can still hear it.

"I'm telling you she won't tell anyone," Jasper says.

There's a second of grumbly silence, and then my ears are blasted by the sound of a drum solo pulsing out of the speakers.

My heart beats blood into my brain so rapidly I can feel it pulsing in my temples. *Slow my heartbeat down. Try to view my location.* I take a deep breath of the stuffy trunk air and try to calm myself down, but I can't stop the pounding behind my eyes, and my heart is racing too fast to get into a calm viewing mode. I suddenly think of Indigo. Did Jasper have something to do with his disappearance, too?

"Let me out!" I scream, and the sound of my voice fills the trunk with my fear. I need to settle down, breathe, and think of a way out of here, but it's so dark I can barely tell if my eyes are open or closed.

Panic rushes over me, and even though I know it's useless, I pound and pound at the trunk until my arms hurt from holding them above me. Then, trapped in the fetal position, I curl my arms tightly into my sides and wait for it to be over.

Sometime later, I hear a popping noise above me and startle awake. I must have fallen asleep from lack of oxygen, because I wake up gasping for air. I can't feel the wheels moving below me anymore, so I know the car has stopped.

Above me, there's a slit between the car and the trunk, where I can feel cool air on my face. I suck it in, filling my lungs until they feel like they could burst. When I've had enough oxygen, I look through the slit, wondering who left the trunk open for me, and if they wanted me to get away, or just give me enough air to keep me alive a little longer. Strangely, nobody is nearby, so I pop my head out farther.

In the fading light behind the car, I see the curved concrete of a loading dock. I push the trunk open slightly, and try to move my body to get out of it, but it's asleep. Tingling rushes through all my limbs at once, making me want to scream. I bite down on my lip and maneuver my leg so it's halfway out of the trunk. As I grip the trunk and pull my belly over it, I smell salt. The EarthScape warehouse is towering over me.

When Jasper and I came here in the bright daylight, the redbrick warehouse looked like an abandoned shell, but now, it's even creepier. There are only a few windows, and those are too grimy to see into. The salt flats, a hundred yards away, are a white sheen under the cloudy afternoon sky.

I slide the rest of my body out of the trunk until my feet touch the pavement. Immediately falling into a crouch to stay low, I scan the loading dock. Jasper is standing on the concrete edge, and across from him, his back to me, is Monty Cooper. The phrase *This Is the Light at the End of the Tunnel* is printed across the back of his turtleneck.

I crouch lower behind the car, my mind spinning. If Monty is blackmailing my mom for NASA secrets, and has also convinced Jasper to bring me to this warehouse, then why? What does he have to gain?

On the loading dock, Jasper and Monty are so involved in their conversation that they don't notice me sneaking around the car.

"Nine-oh-two. Not before, not after," Monty says sharply.

Jasper nervously shifts his weight from foot to foot. "Understood."

Keeping my eyes on the loading dock, I tiptoe around the car and crouch down beside the front wheel. I look down the street to where I can barely see the cars whizzing by on the highway, and then back at the loading dock, which is now empty.

Before I can move, Monty is standing over me. His safety-pinned jeans are stuffed into his combat boots, and he's wearing this silver spiky collar, which seems a little much, even for him. "Going somewhere?" Monty asks, leaning down and grabbing me by the arm.

I shake my head as he pulls me off the pavement. "Just stepping out for a minute."

"That's what I like about you," Monty sneers, "always witty."

I try to yank away from him, but he just grips my arm tighter, his nails digging into my flesh. Against my skin, his fingers are as dainty as a woman's, and his fingernails are painted black.

A cold shiver creeps over my skin when I realize where I've seen those painted fingernails before: when I was looking through the eyes of a killer. Monty's the person who shot the hacker Bishop Finn in my vision. Or he will shoot him, if it hasn't happened yet.

Monty follows my gaze to his black fingernails. "You think I'm too old to go to a rave?"

I shake my head. "Based on the necklace, I'd say too nerdy."

"My bastard father didn't like it either." He rotates his collar around his neck with his thumb and pinkie finger.

"I got it in India, with my—"

"Guru?"

"Don't do that!" Monty snaps. "*Never* interrupt me." He throws an irritated glance toward Jasper, who's standing on the other side of the car. "A little help here?"

As Jasper hurries over, I stare at Monty. His bangs look pasted onto his forehead, and his skin seems paler than when I last saw him, possibly because of the black kohl eyeliner smudged around the rims of his eyes.

"Forget your makeup remover at home?"

"You wouldn't understand," he glowers at me. "It's a rave thing."

"That explains it," I say sarcastically. It actually does explain the eyeliner, but that's about it. There's this hard edge to Monty now that I can't put my finger on. It's like he was only playing with that edge before, but now he's gone off it. Even the vengeful glare in his eyes feels like it comes out of nowhere. But the more I stare at him, the more familiar it is: I've seen him look this way when he was talking about his father. Back then, in the office, it seemed justified; his father was the big bad polluter, and he was just trying to right his dad's wrongs. Or was he? What was he really doing? "You're right," I say slowly. "I *don't* understand."

"Let's just say I'm done playing the nice guy," Monty says.

"You were never that nice," I reply. "So it won't be a huge change." Jasper grabs my free arm, and I kick out at him, but he holds tight. "Let me go!"

My words are met with tense silence as Monty and Jasper lift me onto the loading dock and drag me across it. To the right of the warehouse door, Monty reaches into a hole dug out between two bricks and pulls out a key. He unlocks the door, puts the key back in the hole, and drags me inside. Held prisoner between the two of them, I shuffle down a dark hallway.

"How about you get your hands off me?" I suggest.

"How about you shut your mouth?" Monty responds.

Jasper shoots me a deadly look, but loosens his grip slightly, glancing at Monty to make sure he didn't notice.

As they lead me down several winding aisles, filled with every kind of emergency supply I've ever imagined, I catalog everything in my mind to help me remember how to get out of here: row 9 is full of bottled water, canned goods, and vitamin packets—I force myself to remember; row 10 is devoted to rescue signal devices: smoke bombs, mirrors, and matches; and row 11 is stocked with batteries, flashlights, and cans of gasoline.

"Preparing for the apocalypse?" I ask.

"What about 'shut your mouth' did you not understand?" Monty says.

At the end of the rows of emergency supplies, a white

van is parked in front of a glass-walled office. The security guards who sneered at me as they took Indigo away are peeling a *Shady Hills* decal off the van.

I glare at the guards as I'm dragged past them into the office. Against one wall, there's the bank of computer screens that I saw in my vision. Every screen is split into four frames, and on each one of them is an image of an aircraft carrier, as seen from a satellite. The ships all have the same military-grade laser, and by the chaos onboard all of them, I can tell that each crew is trying to regain control of their laser's direction. From above, the ships look similar, but they have different names on the sides, names such as *Jefferson* and *Imperia Italia* and *Sovetslaya*, each with a different national flag.

In front of the computer screens, Finnegan Bishop, distinguishable by his red beard and circular glasses, is typing commands into a laptop. I recognize him immediately, and I wonder how he went from a hacker breaking into NASA's computer system to name a star after his mom to controlling military-grade lasers in a shady warehouse.

"Finnegan?" I say aloud. He glances over at me quickly, and I can tell how young he is. He can't be much older than me.

"It's Finn," he says before dropping his eyes back to the laptop.

"Zip it, sweetheart," Monty says.

"I don't go for the 'speak when spoken to' command," I shoot back.

Jasper tightens his grip on my wrist. "Shhh."

"Don't shush me," I snap, and Jasper looks away. Across the office, Finn glances at me from his hunched position over his laptop, and there's sweat beading up on his brow. Is he sweating because he knows what those lasers are going to do? Somehow I doubt that he'd murder knowingly. "You do know those lasers are going to kill people, don't you?" I ask Finn.

Finn stares silently at me, the sweat beads rolling down his forehead. For a second, he looks as if he's reconsidering what he's doing, but then he glances at Monty's glowering face, and quickly turns back to the computer.

"What the hell happened to you?" I ask Monty. "Did nobody show up for your lecture?"

"Lots of people showed up. They loved it. They loved *me*," Monty brags.

"Then what? Did they actually take your name off the building?"

"Shut up," Monty growls at me, and then turns to face Finn. "Are you into the system yet?" he asks. "We have less than an hour left!"

"I'm going as fast as I can," Finn says. "But overriding the original programming takes a long time."

"What did I hire you for? Even an ape could do this."

"I said, I am going as fast as I—"

Monty slams his small fist on the table, but it hits the edge and bounces off. He winces, and quickly turns his back so we can't see him inspect the bruise. "Can you read my shirt?" Monty asks, as if that's why he turned his back to us. "Prepare to be flattened."

"Okay . . . ," Finn says slowly.

"*I am the light at the end of the tunnel,*" he says, pointing to the message on the back of his shirt. Monty picks up a tattered leather jacket from a chair and shrugs it on before he flips it back around. "Get it? You're staring at your death, and *I'm* the train!"

"Are you threatening me?" Finn asks.

Monty shakes his head. "But I told you, no mistakes. If we miss it, then all of this was for nothing." He gestures to the bank of screens. On every ship, panicked sailors are inspecting the lasers, trying to figure out how to regain control of the weapons. "And you don't get your money."

"Give me time," Finn says. "I'll make this happen, and we'll both walk away rich."

"Richer," Monty corrects. "Richer than Dad ever was." He glares at Finn. "If you do your job, that is."

"I told you: it's a very complicated program. There's almost fifty lasers," Finn says, "and they all have to hit the refracting telescope and fuse together at the same time, just as the asteroid passes closest to Earth."

"Then why don't we just give up?" Monty asks, and he slides his hand inside his leather jacket. He looks like a fake drug dealer in a B-movie as he moves his hand a couple of inches out of his coat, just enough for us to see that he has a gun. "I'll tell you why." I can't imagine Monty shooting a gun, but his trembling hands and vengeful eyes—and my vision of him shooting Finn—say he's desperate enough to use it. "Because we aren't quitters," he says.

Finn looks as shocked as I am. "You're not going to kill me," he states.

Monty blushes like he's been caught in a lie, and he slides his gun back into his jacket. "And kill off the things I need to know from that big brain of yours? I'm not an idiot."

And neither am I. Because I'm suddenly certain of one very important thing: if I have information that Monty needs to know, he can't kill me either. The only problem is that I have no idea what kind of information that would be.

As I'm scanning my mind for ideas, Monty turns to Jasper. "What is she still doing here?" he asks.

"I can hear you," I say.

Jasper elbows me in the side, hard. "You didn't tell me to leave," Jasper replies.

"No?" Monty rolls his dark-rimmed eyes. "Leave."

Jasper shifts uncomfortably, but he keeps his hand clamped tight around my arm. "Why do we have to take her to the room?"

"What's in the room?" I ask. "Jasper, tell me what's in the room."

"Can't you just lock her up somewhere until this is all over?" Jasper asks Monty.

"You know I would like to; really I would." Monty nervously turns his spiked collar around on his neck. "But she can communicate with her mind," he says. "So we have to lock up her mind, not just her body."

Lock up my mind? My gaze flees to the office's open door. I could make a run for it right now, but I'm not sure if Monty would shoot me in the back or not. He seems nervous about using his gun, but then again, fear makes people do stupid things.

"We don't have time for this," Monty continues. "Just get her out of my sight."

"Yes, sir."

"And don't *sir* me. Sir was my father, not me."

"Yes, friend," Jasper responds.

"Never say that again either."

Jasper nods and leads me away, his hand clamped around one wrist. We walk past the white van, now completely void of the *Shady Hills* decal and toward the aisles of emergency supplies. Without Monty on the other side of me, I could break and run at any second, and I know that Jasper knows it.

"'Yes, *friend?*'" I ask as we get closer to the aisles.

"I didn't say he was mine."

When we step into the closest aisle, I twist under Jasper's arm like I learned in training, and he's forced to let go. I step away from him, my back against a shelf of canned gasoline. "Tell me why I shouldn't kick your ass right now."

"Because I'm taking you to Indigo before we kill him," Jasper says.

"I can find him myself."

"Not in this maze, and not before I call Monty over," Jasper says. "Deal?" He reaches out one hand to me, as if he's going to hold my hand instead of drag me through the warehouse by my wrist.

"Fine," I say, and let Jasper wrap his fingers around my arm. I'm sure that once I get to Indigo, I can get both of us past Jasper and out of this warehouse, maybe even in time to stop Charlie from coming here. "Take me to him. But he'd better be alive. And safe," I add.

"Alive, yes. Safe is questionable." Jasper leads me out of the winding aisles, past the back door, through several rooms, up a flight of stairs, and to an old metal elevator. He presses the button, and the door springs open. I step inside. Jasper follows me in and pushes the button for floor two, and the door closes. As the elevator rises a floor, it makes a high metallic screech that hurts my ears.

"You could've picked a classier place," I say.

"I didn't pick anything," Jasper says. "And if I were you, I'd keep your mouth shut. Monty invested a lot of money in this, and if his plan doesn't work . . ." The doors open with a sharp cracking sound. "None of us goes home alive."

"Do you think he'd really—"

"I've seen inside his brain," Jasper interrupts. "And there's not much wiggle room for sanity."

"You have a lot in common then."

Jasper shrugs. "We're all broken in one way or another." He turns right at an intersection of two hallways. "But unlike you, when I break, there's no one to fix me." He takes a sharp right at the next hallway. "But now I can afford to fix myself."

"So that's what all of this is about? Money?"

"Said like someone who grew up having it," Jasper says. "Now be quiet." We continue winding down the long concrete hallway until we finally reach a wooden door. He's right; I never would have found it myself.

"The room," Jasper says. As he unlocks the door, I imagine the torture chamber I'm about to see. I picture chains and knives and medieval machines, but when Jasper opens the door, it's a completely normal room. It was probably a staff room back when this place was still a salt mining factory; there's even an old soda machine in the corner. Aside from that, there are just a few chairs around a table, like the staff room at our office. It's shockingly normal, except for Indigo, who is sitting in a chair, staring blankly at a soda hanging halfway out of the coils.

"Indigo," I whisper.

"Sorry," Jasper says, and then he shoves me into the room and slams the door behind me. I jump for the door, but I'm too late; he's already locked it.

"Damn it!" I curse. I frantically jiggle the plastic handle—which has apparently been installed specifically for metal benders—but it holds tight. Panic races through me, and my hand trembles on the door handle. *Good plan, Callie. Now you're locked in here too.*

"I have information Monty needs to know," I yell through the door. Jasper doesn't respond, but I'm hoping he will at least deliver the message. If he does, and Monty comes to find out what it is, I might get another chance to get Indigo and me out of this place.

I wait a few more seconds for Jasper to respond, but when I hear the horrid squeak of the elevator, I lean back against the door. Sitting at the table in the corner, Indigo is still staring at the soda machine, his lips moving silently.

"Indigo?" I walk over to him and pull out a chair at the table. "Can you hear me?"

Indigo continues to stare at the machine, but he starts sputtering words out loud. "He's gonna miss another soccer practice," Indigo drones, and then he shakes his head back and forth, and another phrase comes barreling out:

"They all know I'm ready to retire." Indigo slams his head against the soda machine, leaving a moon-shaped streak of perspiration on the glass. "I'm going to be home late again, honey," he says, and then he slams his head once more. I place my hand between his forehead and the glass before he can hurt himself again. When his forehead hits my palm, it's sweaty.

"What's happening to you?" I ask him.

"Get them out," Indigo whispers, and he sounds exactly like Michael did at Shady Hills, when I asked him about Operation Firepoker.

And then a headache hits me, and the force of it snaps my head back on my neck. The pain is worse than anything I've ever felt. I grab my head with both hands and fold myself forward until I'm leaning into the table. I can't hear anything but my moaning and the sound of Indigo's head pounding against the soda machine.

The pain gets steadily worse, and then I start to hear words and phrases. "Gotta get out of here," I hear a woman's voice saying. "It's been days since I've gone grocery shopping." A man's voice chimes in, "So what if I was late for work again?"

There are other people in my head, I realize. I feel the hard wooden tabletop hit my forehead. And not just one person: lots of people.

"Why does it keep making that noise?" a voice in my

mind asks, and then another one says, "I hate the smell of paint." I feel the hard tabletop against my head again. "At least we didn't have to get on that thing," someone else says in my mind, and then several voices start in at once, blending together so that I can't understand any of them.

I force myself to stop hitting my head on the table and look at Indigo. He's still staring at a soda hanging from the machine's coil. Thinking he might be trying to tell me something, I force myself to my feet and walk past him to the vending machine. I grab the side of the machine and shake it, and the soda falls to the slot at the bottom.

"What's going on, Indigo?" I ask, attempting to ignore the voices yelling in my head. "What are you trying to tell me?"

Indigo just stares silently at the machine, so I reach in and grab the soda. I pop it open and pour a few drops into Indigo's mouth, and his eyes clear for a second. It looks like a thick film is lifted off his pupils, and underneath, his eyes are raw and red.

"You have to distract them," Indigo says.

"Who?"

Indigo shakes his head. "I'm not sure who exactly. But we're part of it now."

"Part of what?" I ask, pouring a little more soda into his mouth.

"Operation Firepoker," he says, and then a thick film

covers his eyes and he shrieks. His hands fly to his head, and he leans forward so far that he falls off his chair and collapses to the floor, eyes squeezed tightly shut.

I get down on the floor and shake him. "What is Operation Firepoker?" I ask. "Indigo? Answer me!"

Indigo opens his eyes, but there's nothing there.

CHAPTER THIRTY-TWO

Time passes slowly, and the voices and pounding increase tenfold in my head. I try to wake Indigo with more soda, but when that doesn't work, I drink small sips of it myself, whenever I feel myself drifting away with the pain. I keep hoping to hear Monty's footsteps coming up to find out what I know and give us a chance to escape, but it never happens.

After a while, I hear a voice coming from outside the warehouse, followed by a slamming door. I quickly scan the room and see a tiny, grimy window over the soda machine. I climb up on the counter beside the machine and press my head against the bars until I can see Jasper standing outside.

The warehouse door slams again and Monty steps out into the quickly approaching night. From above, I see that the center of his scalp, where the hair should be growing from, is in the wrong place. He stops, grabs the top of his head, and shifts his whole head of black hair over several inches. First, his bangs tilt absurdly high on his skull, and then he moves them down until they are over his eyebrows.

Jasper jerks his thumb upward. "Up a bit more," he says.

Monty shifts his hair backward, and his wig finally settles in the right place.

"Now *that's* a good look," Jasper says sarcastically.

"You think so?" Monty asks. He turns around and checks himself out in the door's reflection, and then he glances back at Jasper. "Not that I need your help."

"You don't? Great," Jasper says. "Then I've done my job. I'm leaving."

"Good try," Monty says. "But you're not finished. Not even close." He slowly crosses the pavement toward Jasper. "It's time to join the others."

Jasper backs away. "You didn't tell me this was part of the job."

"I don't remember you complaining when you were living in my pad," Monty says, "or driving my car, or that death trap you insisted on buying."

Jasper takes another step backward, toward the street

running parallel to the dry white salt flats. "Look, I hid everything from her, like you asked me to. No thanks to you," he says, shaking his head. "Showing up at the office and buddying up to Indigo like you did." He glares at Monty as he takes another step backward. "But Callie still knows nothing."

"You know better than that," Monty says. He slowly rotates his collar around on his neck with one black-painted fingernail. "She knows about the asteroid, and the telescope, and the lasers." Monty takes the last few steps to reach Jasper and glares down at him. "Without her, billions in thulium will rot on the sea floor. Is that what you want?"

Jasper shakes his head. "But what are you gonna do with her?"

"It's none of your business. You got your money."

"She'll never tell," Jasper protests, but I can tell he's backing down.

"I know she won't," Monty says. "Because once they drive her out of her mind, I'll make sure she ends up in Shady Hills, where no one will ever believe what she says." He claps his hand on Jasper's shoulder, and leads him back toward the warehouse. "You chose the right team."

When they get close to the front door, Jasper stops and looks up at my window. Two stories below, his upturned face is stained with regret. "I would never have helped you if I'd known," he says to Monty, almost too quietly for me to hear.

"Then it's a good thing I didn't tell you," Monty says. He waits for Jasper to pull the door open, and when he does, he kicks his boot against it and blocks the whole doorway so Jasper can't get by. "If the metal gets to earth safely, you can keep the pad. And the car. You'll have so many girls you'll forget all about her."

"I doubt it," Jasper says.

Monty glances at himself in the door and readjusts his wig. "Stop stalling," he says.

"Okay. She does know something," Jasper says, glancing at Monty as he walks past him into the warehouse. "If I were you, I'd find out what it is."

"Thanks for the advice," Monty snarls as he follows him in and shuts the door behind them.

Pounding immediately bursts through my temples again. Without Jasper and Monty to distract me, I can't handle the pain in my head. I grip onto the window bars and grit my teeth as voices break through my mind, hurtling toward me as if a talk radio station is pressed inside my ears.

And then, just as suddenly as it came, the voices disappear from my mind, and the pain is completely gone.

"Callie," I hear Indigo say from across the room. I pull my head away from the bars, jump off the counter, and hurry over to where he's sitting on the floor. He's staring at me with unclouded eyes, so I'm guessing the pain in his head is gone too.

Indigo grabs my hand. "This won't last long. Something's distracting them," he says quickly. "So listen carefully: Operation Firepoker was a government experiment. A group of psychics were hired to find a new type of metal, and figure out its military potential. It led to a new generation of deadly radioactive weapons."

The pounding in my head starts lightly, and Indigo's must too, because his eyes start to zone out. I snap my fingers in front of his face. "Go on!"

"Michael saw too much. He figured out there were billions' worth of this metal on asteroids, and envisioned how to get to it. Once he gave them all they needed, they drove him out of his mind," Indigo says. He lifts his hands to his forehead and massages his temples with his thumbs. "They used you to find where the asteroid will land in the ocean." Indigo rubs his temples harder. "When I figured out what was going on, they took me away. And now they've taken you." His eyes start to roll back in his pasty face. He's getting worse, and quickly. "You've got to find them. Break their concentration," he says, "before they destroy you. And then find Michael—he's the only one who can help you stop Monty's plan."

The pounding breaks through my mind with such intensity it makes me dizzy, and Indigo's thumbs stop moving on his temples. His eyes go as blank as an unpainted canvas.

"Wait," I say to Indigo. "Do you mean crazy Michael?"

"Your only hope is to leave," he mutters. "Get away." Indigo's lips stop moving and he slowly slumps over.

My head is pounding harder with each heartbeat, and voices are streaming in from all sides. What did Indigo mean by leave? We're locked in here, and the window is barred, and too tiny to climb out of anyway. But as I cup my head between my hands and push on both temples, trying to squelch the pain, a thought comes to me: maybe Indigo doesn't mean leave the *room*; maybe he meant that I have to leave my *body*.

It makes a crazy sort of sense: If there are people in my head, I have to astral project in order to get out of my physical body. These psychics, whoever they are, are focusing all of their psychic energy on my physical self, and they are getting into my mind that way. But if I'm not in my body anymore, then my mind is no longer attached to my physical body, and they can't get in. It's a long shot, but worth a try.

Trying to remember how I astral projected when I found Charlie at the lighthouse, I lie down and picture myself floating toward the ceiling, attached to my physical self only by a thin silver cord. I immediately start to feel woozy. My head spins as if I'm seasick, but this sickness is coming from deep down inside my body, at a cellular level.

After a minute or two, I feel a strange disconnection in my body, like two of Colin's Legos taken apart, and then my body cracks out of its casing.

First my feet get sucked up, and then my legs and torso, like mist rising out of the water. My head pulls away from my body last, with the most resistance, and my neck bends backward until the back of my head finally snaps out of my body. My headache goes away instantly, and the voices fade to nothing.

This sudden, hollow feeling, like being ejected from a seat, is completely different from the peaceful feeling I had when I floated up to the ceiling of my bedroom. That was a choice; now I'm forced to flee my body in order to escape the people in my mind.

I float upward, the thin silver cord stretching between my body and me until it snaps tight like a rubber band, and I'm at the end of it. I put my hands out and catch myself before I bump my nose against the ceiling.

Suspended in the air, with my back pressed against the ceiling, I see Indigo from above. His skin is bloodless and pale, and his eyes are staring upward, wide open and vacant like mine. In the air above his body is a silver cord leading to his astral body. I follow the cord straight up through the ceiling and into the sky, passing the stars. Soon I'm flying upward so fast the wind is whooshing in my ears, and I feel the heat from solar flares at my heels. I am part of the night sky: the universe isn't big enough for me.

I sail upward for a long time. I'm not sure how much time passes, but it could be a minute, a week, a year. Light filters away as the darkness gets darker, the space between floating chunks of rock more distant.

I think about my life, about how much my mom loved me, although she made mistakes I'll never understand; about how Charlie picked me out of all the other humans to give his heart to, even if I did screw it up; and about my calling as a psychic spy, and how few people in this world get the chance to do something really meaningful with their lives.

It's like I'm dying, but my life isn't exactly flashing before my eyes. It's more like a catalog of people, their faces rotating before me, and I want to hold onto them so badly, but they're slipping away.

I'm slipping away.

Eons later, I'm surrounded by complete blackness.

But then light again.

And soon, bright pinpricks of light are rushing past me, and in the center of all those silver flares is Indigo.

I can barely see him at first. He is almost translucent, like the fog that comes in over the Bay. He is floating cross-legged among the stars, quickly fading into the blackness behind him. From his spirit body dangles a silver cord, worn down to a thread.

"Indigo," I call out to him. My voice doesn't travel, or maybe it travels too fast to make any sound, because his gaze remains focused downward. Somehow, though, I think he knows I'm here. There's some sort of charged energy between us; it ripples across the air like waves. "Indigo," I call out again, but he doesn't look at me. He just stares down through the stars and the clouds, a frown tugging at his lips.

In this moment, I want to tell him that he's always been there for me, that he's been like the father I never had. I want to tell him that he's the only one who believes in what I'm capable of, even more than I do.

"What are you looking at?" I ask instead.

I float toward him, noticing how my long silver cord, which is much thicker than his, spirals down to earth. Beside mine, Indigo's cord looks like a fragile thread the wind could tear apart at any moment, and I know that the longer these people are in his mind, the more cut off from his body he is going to be. I know I have to find them and kick them out of our heads.

"Hold on," I say as I float sideways toward him. "I'm not going to let you die up here."

Indigo finally looks over at me, and something passes between us. I'm not sure what it is, but when he gazes back at his cord swaying down to Earth, I understand that he's trying to communicate something without words. "Ignore what people say," I remember him telling me during my first training session. "Listen to their bodies speak."

I follow Indigo's gaze down through the sky, past the stars, until I reach the EarthScape satellite floating above the atmosphere. I stare at the satellite as it turns slowly in circles, and then I see the refracting telescope attached to it. *This is where all the lasers come together to make a super laser: a laser that can deflect an asteroid.*

I look up at Indigo, but he's staring past me, toward Earth. I glance back at the satellite and then I follow Indigo's gaze through the ozone layer and the drifting white clouds, and into Shady Hills Treatment Center.

In the circular TV room, thousands of miles below me, my mom is sitting on the floor beside Michael. He's tapping his hands against his shoes and muttering.

"What is my mom doing there?" I say aloud.

"Open your mind," I hear Indigo say, as if he's speaking right into my ear.

I imagine my mind opening like a set of French doors. I feel the breeze come through and lift the dust from all the crevices in my brain. The cool touch of the wind relaxes my mind, and then the drifting light illuminates what I was unwilling to see.

My father.

. . .

If there were a core for an astral body to be shaken to, I would be trembling like a tree limb in a harsh wind right now. Instead, since my body is cut off from me, my mind reacts by racing through everything I know about Michael: how he was a powerful psychic whose his mind was broken years ago, and how he has been in Shady Hills ever since, except when Indigo takes him out for crucial viewing sessions. Then I remember how my mom told me that my father went missing fifteen years ago, and it seemed like all of the public information about him had been *erased*.

Although I don't have a headache anymore, my head pounds with uncertainty, and though there are no voices in my mind, I hear questions racing back and forth: If it's true, then why didn't Indigo tell me? And did my mom always know where he was, and if so, why did she keep him from me?

Below me, in the TV room in Shady Hills, Michael is rocking faster, his hands skipping off the soles of his sneakers. "Need paper," he says to Mom.

"What?" Mom asks.

"PAPER!" he yells.

Two women in wheelchairs glare at him for interrupting their television show, and though he doesn't seem to notice, Mom does. She digs through her purse and pulls out a pen and her grade book. "Okay, I have some here," she says, handing them over.

On the grade book cover, Michael starts sketching something. Below his fingers, machine parts take shape: it looks like some sort of pump, or like the black light in Charlie's bedroom. Then he draws arrows from one part to the next, and when he looks up, it feels as if he can see me.

"What are you drawing?" Mom asks gently.

Michael doesn't respond, but starts drawing faster, with increased intensity. I see a circle emerge from a rectangle, and then he labels the parts with the numbers one through six. I stare at the drawings, willing myself to understand what they are. Eventually they start to blend into a series of steps, like watching the flip-through action in a flip-book.

I realize that when seen individually, it looks like just a tube and a couple of circles, but when looked at step by step, it is an instruction manual for how to break the telescope that's attached to the satellite. "The objective in a refracting telescope is to bend light, which causes parallel light rays to converge at a focal point," I remember the reporter saying when I was watching my neighbor's television from the roof. *The asteroid is the focal point.*

Suddenly, all the pieces fall into place. If I bend the telescope's parts even slightly, the lasers won't come together to make a super laser; they'll shoot harmlessly into space, instead of hitting the focal point, the asteroid.

I look at the steps again and try to memorize them, knowing that I've got to get *inside* the telescope first. But even if my astral body can get inside the telescope, how will I follow the steps without a physical body? Before I even ask myself the question, I already know the answer: metal bending.

My heart sinks. It's impossible to bend metal during an astral projection. To alter physical substances, I have to access my body, but I can't get back into my body because of the people in my mind. If I could only disrupt the people breaking into my head long enough to get back into my body, I could attempt metal bending again. But how would I do that? I don't even know where they are.

"Callie!" a voice calls, and somebody is shaking my shoulders back and forth. "Wake up!"

The re-entry to my body is sudden and hard, like diving into a pool covered with ice.

When I open my eyes, Monty's face is inches from mine. His spiky silver collar brushes my cheek when I try to move my head. "What do you know?"

"Besides that your necklace looks like something out of a freak show?" I ask. "Or that this whole punk thing you have going on isn't hiding the scared nerd underneath?"

"Shut up!" Monty yells, and then he takes a deep breath and lowers his voice. "Just tell me what you know."

I press on my temples, trying to get rid of the headache

and the voices, which have come back with more intensity than before. "I won't tell you anything until you get these people out of my mind," I say through gritted teeth.

"Not going to happen."

"Then you'll never find out what I know."

"Oh, I will," Monty says. He gazes at me for a second, and his angry glare softens. "Do you think I *want* to do this to you? Like my father did to your dad?" He puts his fists together and turns them in opposite directions, like he is snapping a twig. A despondent look crosses his face, and he shakes his head. "I don't."

My father. I know who my father is. I force the thought out of my head, willing myself not to react. *Just focus on getting out of here.*

"But I don't have a choice anymore," Monty continues. Sweat breaks out on his forehead, and as he wipes it away with the back of his fist, I see his hands are trembling. "Not after this." He pulls out his phone and scrolls through a list of news headlines, and then holds it out to me like a kid doing show-and-tell for his class. The headline says: *Real Cooper Will Discovered: Fortune to be Donated to Charity.*

"See, I will get nothing," Monty insists. "He's finally done it."

"Done what?"

"Fully humiliated me." There are tears in his eyes. "Callie, I *need* this." He sits on the floor beside me and pulls his knees up to his chest like a scared kid. "I'm sorry you're caught up in all this. If I could find another way to do it, I would."

His lower lip trembles and pouts out, and his jaw comes up: all classic signs of sadness, the hardest micro expression to fake. I almost feel sorry for him. "It takes money to make money," he adds. "Once it's all gone, I won't have a chance to make it back. I'll be as useless as Dad always said." He shakes his head. "It's all Dad's fault, you see? If he wasn't taking it away, I wouldn't have to do this." Monty climbs to his feet and peers down at me. "I have one more chance to prove to the world that I'm worth something. And when I make billions in thulium from the asteroid, I'll prove to everyone I'm worthy. Better than my father." Monty's eyes narrow to an angry squint. "I'm going to make the bastard sorry he ever put me down."

"But he's dead," I remind him. "He can't hurt you anymore."

"He already has. And as long as his name is on buildings, he used to say, he'll be immortal," Monty says. "And now *I* will be."

My legs feel too weak to get up, and my head is pounding with the echo of voices jabbering inside of it, but I make myself sit up anyway. "You believe in what money can *do*, not buy. Isn't that what you said?" I ask. "At the time, I thought that was an inspiring thing to say."

Monty holds my eyes for a second, then tears his gaze away. "*You* inspired me, not the other way around."

This is seriously the last thing I was expecting to hear. "What?"

"You became what you are despite being the daughter of a famous scientist."

"She's actually not that famous," I counter.

"You told me once that I'm not that bad," Monty continues as if he didn't hear me. He paces across the room, his arms crossed in front of his chest. "And when I thought about it, I realized you were right. I'm not bad at all. I can do this."

"Glad I could help?"

Monty pauses in front of the soda machine, his frown reflecting in the machine's glass. He shifts his wig an inch across his skull and then paces back to me. "Callie, don't you get it? This metal will change the world, and it will be *me,* not my dad, to do it."

"I thought you were all into protecting Mother Earth?"

"I am. I am not digging this out of Mother Earth," he says. "Do you know what this metal can do? Its medical technology can save lives. It can improve how we communicate. It can change the world!" he says. "I'm a frickin' hero for getting it off an asteroid."

I sigh. "Some hero."

"Shut up."

This is how I imagine talking to a brother would be. A demented, definitely insane brother. "You're not a murderer," I say. "I know you're not."

He rolls his eyes at me. "The asteroid is gonna land in the ocean, duh. You told me that." He walks over to Indigo, leans over, and lifts up one eyelid with his index finger.

"Leave him alone."

Monty drops Indigo's eyelid back into place and then glances up at me. "What am I going to do, crush some sharks?"

"For someone who says he's very smart, you're very dense sometimes," I say. "It's going to cause a tidal wave. It's going to kill people."

His eyebrows raise and curve into two small question marks as alarm flees through his eyes.

"People are going to die," I repeat.

His forehead creases into horizontal worry lines, and then he shoves both hands over his ears. "I'm not listening. I'm not listening."

"Monty, please listen to me." I reach toward him, but he shrinks away.

"Nobody touches me," he shrieks. "Not without my permission."

"May I?"

He nods. I place my hand on his left wrist and slowly remove his hand from his ear, and then I take hold of his right wrist. He closes his eyes, as if no one has touched him in years. "Please stop the lasers," I say.

Monty's eyes pop open, and his cheeks flush an angry crimson color. He jerks his hand away. "You're just like everyone else," he says. "You just want to use me for what I can give you. 'Stop the lasers, Monty. Don't hit the asteroid, Monty,' he mimics in a high voice that's supposed to be mine. 'Give me your last chance, Monty. Be better and stronger, Monty.' His voice deepens into his father's voice. 'Don't be weak, Junior!'" He slams his fist against the table, and Indigo's soda falls off and spills at our feet. "But you know what? I have nothing left to give!" Monty laughs weakly. It's a desperate tinkling sound, as if all of the safety pins have popped off his jeans at once and he's splitting apart at the seams.

I put my hand gently on his arm, and he doesn't pull away this time. "Monty. Why are you doing this to us?" He shakes his head. "To me?"

"I don't want to," Monty whines. "I hated it when my dad did this to yours. I thought it was awful seeing your dad crying and drooling, like him." Monty gestures to Indigo. "But what your dad knew made my dad rich. Which if my dad let him go and he told everyone else?"

"But I wouldn't—"

"Shhh." He places his finger against my lips. "I now I see it's necessary if I want to make a difference in this world. You have to crack a few eggs to make a dozen."

"I don't think that's actually an expression."

"It's genius, actually," he continues. "Only smart thing that son of a bitch ever taught me. Murder leaves too many questions unanswered. But nobody gets blamed when someone goes crazy."

Stand up, I command my body. When my muscles and bones obey my orders and lift me to a standing position above the table, I'm relieved I at least have that much of my mind left. "Even if the pressure drives me out of my mind," I say, rocking back and forth unsteadily. "I'll still tell people what I know."

"Nobody believes the crazies," Monty says.

"So you're not just a nerd," I say, pressing my fingernail into my thumb as hard as I can to distract me from the pain in my head. "You're an evil nerd."

"Evil nerds will take over the world," Monty says. He rotates the collar around his neck several times, as if he's winding himself up for battle. "Now, stop distracting me and tell me what you know, and why I should believe you."

I take an unsteady step toward him, but my head pounds so hard I have to stop and lean on the table. "I found the location of the asteroid in the ocean, didn't I?"

Monty studies me for several seconds, and I wonder if he knows how to read micro-expressions. If so, I'm screwed: my face spells out the fact that I know absolutely nothing he needs to know. He taps his bottom lip with his pinkie finger. "If I were psychic, what would I know that I needed to know?"

He briefly looks confused by his own question, but I don't say anything. I just turn my face away from Monty and examine the doorway, trying to figuring out exactly how I'll slip past him before he shuts the door—and whether I can get Indigo out at the same time, or if I'll need to come back for him.

"I don't think you know anything," Monty finally says. "I think you're lying."

"But I do," I reply quickly. If I can just find out what information he still needs to know, and leak a bit of it, he'll need to keep my mind intact to get the rest of the information. But to find out that information, I have to read his mind.

I take a deep breath and slow my heartbeat, and then I focus on Monty's breathing, trying to find a gap to get into his mind. It's difficult to ignore the distracting voices yelling full-force in my head, but I push them aside for a second as I find a gap and force my way in—only to run straight into an invisible barrier. I glance up at him, surprised to see him smirking at me.

"Do you think I'm stupid enough not to have psychic protection?" Monty brags. "I've got your buddy Jasper watching over me. No one can get into this baby." He taps his temple. "Think of it as Jasper's higher-paying job," he adds. "With a half-dozen other mind-breakers backing him up."

So there's seven of them. I squeeze the soft pad of skin between my thumb and index finger until pain jolts through my body, narrowing my focus. *Where could seven enemy psychics be?* Attempting to ignore the chatter that now burns like fire through my brain, I try to recall their comments in my mind from back when I could pick out their individual words, but nothing comes to me.

"Thinking's getting painful for you," Monty says. "That's the stress of your brain breaking down." His lips curve down on the edges, but he abruptly forces his mouth into a cheerless grin. "But the good news is," he says brightly, "it means the fight's almost over."

"But what if I have crucial intel that you never find out?"

"And I never retrieve the thulium from the ocean floor, you mean?" He shakes his head. "Won't happen. But if it did, then your charming mother will go to prison for stealing the NASA codes," he says, "and the information I gave her about your missing father in exchange? It will be for nothing."

So Monty did coerce Mom into giving him that code. "She wouldn't become a traitor to the US for him," I retort.

"No, she wouldn't," Monty says. "Did I forget to mention that your life was part of the bargain too?"

No wonder Mom did it. She works too much, and she doesn't hug, and she loses everything not physically attached to her, but she'll do anything to protect me. Rage fuels every muscle in my body, and I let go of the table and stand firmly before him. "Part of the bargain?" I press forward until my face is inches from his, and he has to back up a step to keep standing. "Will you be able to live with yourself if your actions destroy an entire country?"

"Then EarthScape will be a hero for coming to the rescue," Monty responds. "*I* will be a hero."

My heart sinks to my feet. He's right: the public will honor him for coming to the rescue of the disaster *he* caused.

"Now I'm done wasting time. Tell me what you know."

"I know that you're a pathetic little boy who will never live up to his father."

Monty raises his fist to hit me, anger flashing through his eyes, but then he slowly lowers his hand. "You don't know anything," he says, and forces his clenched fist into his pocket. "And *nobody* will make me into my father."

I glance at him hopefully. Monty knows that what he's doing to me is exactly what his father did to mine. Maybe he'll stop the chain right now, because he knows that somewhere inside his battered exterior is a kind and generous person. "Then don't be him," I say.

"I won't be," he responds. "I will be better than him: Richer. More successful. More admired. My name will grace every building. I will be like a god." Monty glances at the time on his phone. The glowing numbers say 8:50 p.m. "Now, if you'll excuse me, I have to check on my mindbreakers, make sure they're doing their jobs." He smiles.

"And if they are, you might not know who I am the next time we meet. But don't worry; I'll remember you."

Monty walks to the door and unlocks it, and I rush at him with all of my force. Just before I hit him, he whips his gun out of his jacket so that I run straight into the barrel. It knifes into my stomach so hard I almost double over.

"You wouldn't," I say, trying to get my breath back.

Monty takes a step backward, his gun still pressed against my stomach. "No? I've beaten every shooter video game out there. I've been considering taking it up in real life. You know, for the challenge." He backs quickly out of the room and slams the door closed, locking it before I can grab for the handle.

As his footsteps fade away, I jiggle the plastic handle, feeling suddenly dizzy again. I'm distantly aware that my headache has gotten much worse, and the voices are so loud now that I can barely hear myself breathing. Desperately needing air, I climb up on the counter and stare out of the tiny barred window over the soda machine.

It's over, I realize. I'm never going to get out of here.

Outside the window, the sun has set over the salt flats, and the sky is a dark, bruised color over the vacant street. I stare numbly out the window, holding the metal top of the vending machine to steady myself. Under my hand, I feel the hollow vibration of electricity as the night slowly plunges in, leaving me utterly alone.

CHAPTER THIRTY-THREE

Time passes, and when I say time, I mean long sections of it, which could be anything from one minute to three hours. There's no way to count it in here, except by Indigo's breathing, and he'd exhaled eight hundred fifty breaths by the time I lost count. So when I hear something else to count time with, the distant pitter-patter of footsteps, I think I'm imagining it.

I get to my feet from where I've been sitting on the floor beside Indigo, and climb up onto the counter to look out the barred window again. There's a figure at the end of the street, his black hoodie blending into the night sky. He weaves around each of the warehouses, staying close to the abandoned buildings as if he's attempting (and failing) to stay out of sight.

When he rounds the closest building and stops beneath the fading red brick of the EarthScape warehouse, he looks up, and I see that it's Charlie. He's come for me.

You'd think I'd be excited, but I'm not. I'm terrified, because Charlie's life is in danger, and that is more frightening to me than my own. A lump builds in my throat. Why did he come when I told him not to? Or is it *because* I told him not to? But I've seen what happens to Charlie outside this warehouse, and I know I can't let that happen to him.

Clunk! Clunk! Below me, Indigo is gripping his head with both hands and smacking it against the floor. His eyes are still closed, but his lips are moving around the words: "Get them out, get them out, get them out."

I leap off the counter and rip off my sweatshirt, and I swiftly ball it up and put it beneath his head before he can hit it against the floor again.

I climb back onto the counter and look back out the tiny window, hoping that Charlie has changed his mind and left, but now he's standing on his tip-toes peering into one of the dirty windows. I need to make him leave before he gets hurt, but if I yell out to him, Monty will know somebody is here, and Charlie may end up in this room with me. I can't let that happen. The only way I know how to talk to him without speaking aloud is to break into his mind, like I tried to do when I was astral projecting at the lighthouse. Although it's unlikely to work, I have to try.

At that moment, a debilitating pain courses through my head. It feels like a spike is being driven between my eyes and out the back of my skull. The voices are getting louder, and I know I have to get out of my head again, and fast, before I'm in too much pain to break into his mind.

I climb off the counter and lie down on the floor. I let my eyes close, and, doing my best to ignore the throbbing, I focus on sucking breath in and out of my nostrils. My breathing slowly clears my mind until it's a blank white space. Then I focus on getting into his mind through a gap in his breathing. A small space opens between two breaths, and I focus all of my energy on seeing myself as a tiny piece of dust floating through the air and down to Charlie's body . . .

Then I am falling faster and faster . . . I picture myself as a speck of dust floating down his ear canal and into his brain . . .

I try to pick up on his thoughts, but they shoot back and forth more quickly than I can pinpoint . . .

. . . and his mind is about to open up and let me in . . .

And then I'm shooting down a long tunnel and emerging into an open space behind two large, brown lenses. Through Charlie's eyes, I stare at the warehouse's grimy window.

Fighting back the pain in my head, I push my thought into Charlie's mind. "You need to leave," I insist. "It's too dangerous here." At the sound of my voice, Charlie freezes, and then he tilts his head slightly to the right, just like he did when I tried to enter his mind at the lighthouse, when he pulled away from Amber's kiss. I continue talking before he pushes me out. "You don't know this yet, but your life is in danger," I add. "Please believe me."

"Callie?" Charlie whispers aloud. "Is that you?"

"It's me," I say into his mind.

Charlie looks around wildly. "Where are you?"

"I told you the truth earlier," I say. "I'm a psychic."

"I believe you," Charlie says. "It's unbelievable . . . but I believe you. I called you to tell you that, but you didn't answer your phone." He pauses. "It actually explains a lot."

"Like what?"

"I'll tell you later," he says, and pulls the black hood back over his head. "But when your mom and Richard didn't know where you were either, I started to worry. Then I remembered where you told me *not* to go, and here I am."

I want to shout with joy that he finally knows who I really am. It's been torture hiding the truth from him for so long. But no matter how much I want to celebrate that he can now know all of me, his safety is more important. "Well, you need to leave," I say. "Now."

"I'm not leaving," Charlie says. "Not without you."

Through Charlie's eyes, I see that he's staring straight up at my window now, and although I know he can't see me, it still makes me nervous to have him so close to the warehouse, so close to his potentially fatal future. "Just go home," I beg. "It's too dangerous for you here—"

"No," Charlie says, his voice getting louder. "I am not leaving. Just tell me how to get to you."

"Keep your voice down," I hiss. "Leaving is your only choice."

Charlie crosses his arms and grounds his feet hard into the pavement. "I'm staying right here until you tell me how to get inside. You can't pressure me to leave."

I picture Charlie trapped under the radiation, and I know that if he won't leave, then I need to get him inside the warehouse quickly. The longer he's standing out there, the more likely it is that it will happen to him.

"Fine, I'll help you get in," I say. "But move quickly, and don't make any noise."

"How do I get in?"

"Go around the back. Look for the tiny opening in the wall, to the right of the door." I watch the ground moving below Charlie as he quickly walks around the warehouse, and then I'm looking up at the barely noticeable hole between the bricks. "There's a key in there," I continue. "Unlock the back door and go in. But carefully."

Charlie reaches his arm into the tiny gap and pulls out

the key. Then he unlocks the door next to him and sneaks quietly into the warehouse. "Now tell me where you are," he says quietly, "so I can come get you."

"I need you to do something first." I hate to ask anything more of him, but even if Charlie were to get me out of this room my mind would still be invaded by enemy psychics. The only way I can get them out of my mind is to distract their focus away from me. But where could they be? There's another spike of pain through my head, and something the psychics said earlier, back when I could still make out individual voices in my mind, jolts through me. *Why does it keep making that noise?* I remember one person complaining, and the other responding: *At least we didn't have to get on that thing.*

I rub my temples furiously with my thumbs, and the pressure keeps me present enough to think over everything I know. If Monty was going to check on them, like he said, they must be somewhere in the warehouse. And maybe the noise they were hearing was the screeching of the elevator, which could be that 'thing' they didn't have to get on. And if they didn't have to get on the elevator . . .

"They must be on the first floor, near the elevator shaft," I murmur.

"What about the elevator shaft?" Charlie asks. "Is that where you are?" He pauses. "Hey, are you still here?"

"I am, but probably not for long." The voices are coursing

like a flood through my head, and I can tell I'm beginning to break down from the pressure in my mind. I try to grip onto the arms of the chair to steady myself, but I'm too weak. I know that I don't have the strength to take the psychics on right now; in order for me to leave this room with Charlie, I need him to break their concentration first.

I need my mind back.

"What's going on?" he asks.

"This is going to sound crazy," I say, as if Charlie breaking into a warehouse due to my psychic instructions isn't crazy enough. "Some psychics have broken into my mind. My brain is fighting back, but eventually, the stress will wear it out."

"What do you mean?"

"I mean, there's so much pressure in my head right now"—I press my knuckles hard along the base of my skull—"that it will drive me out of my mind," I say. "Told you it would sound loony."

"Totally insane," Charlie says. "So where are they?"

"I think they are on the first floor, somewhere near the elevator shaft."

"What do you need me to do?"

"I need you to distract them somehow, or force them out of the room they're holed up in." I scan my memory of the aisles I mentally cataloged earlier: food, water, flashlights, gas, matches, smoke bombs. *Smoke bombs.* "Remember, do not go outside, no matter what you do, okay? Promise me."

"I promise."

"Okay, then go down aisle ten."

Charlie locates the number 10 sign hanging from the top of the aisle, and takes a sharp left under it. He passes a towering stack of rescue mirrors and stops in front of shelf stacked with thousands of waterproof, light-anywhere matches.

"Grab a book of matches," I say.

"How do you know what I'm seeing?" Charlie asks. "Are you seeing out of my eyes?"

"Yeah, but don't worry; this is the first time I've ever done this."

"Okay," he says nervously. He grabs a pack of matches and then continues down the aisle.

"Now grab a smoke bomb," I continue.

Charlie snatches a tiny smoke bomb, no bigger than a birthday candle, off the shelf. "Are you sure this is going to work?"

"No." My head is pounding so hard, and the voices are so loud, that I'm having trouble staying in Charlie's mind, and I'm starting to feel nauseous. "Charlie, listen carefully. I may not be able to stay in your mind much longer—"

"Why not?"

"I can't explain now. But you need to distract these psychics. They're all focused on getting into my mind, and unless you break their concentration, I won't be here much longer."

"I won't let that happen," Charlie says. "No matter how crazy that sounds." He rolls the small smoke bomb between his thumb and index finger. "Now what do I do with this bad boy?"

"Go to the room near the elevator shaft," I instruct.

I can barely hold on to Charlie's mind as he hurries down the hallway to the elevator shaft. When he gets there, he looks for the closest room, and finds a door right beside it. He puts his ear against the door, and through Charlie, I hear muffled voices mirroring the much louder voices in my own head.

"Now what?" Charlie whispers.

"Light the smoke bomb and roll it under the door, and then get the hell out of there. Hide somewhere until they are gone. But no matter what you do, do not go outside. Understand?"

"Yep. But what about you?"

I can't respond anymore. I slump over in my chair, my head pounding too much to speak. "Do it now," I say with all of the strength I have left.

Charlie pulls one match out of the box and slides it across the strip, and a tiny flame bursts into life. Then he pulls the smoke bomb's wick out so that it's taut, and after yanking his hood down to cover more of his face, he lights the red wick.

When fire flares at the end of the wick, Charlie rolls it under the door and backs up into the hallway. Within seconds, red smoke is leaking out from under the door.

The voices in my mind suddenly fall silent, and all the pain in my head disappears.

Seconds later, the door flies open and several people run out, coughing into the sleeves pressed against their mouths. To avoid them, Charlie ducks behind the open door, so he's stuck between the back of the door and the corner window.

"It smells like paint," he says.

Paint? "Get out of—"

There's a giant *boom* I can feel in the floor beneath me, and from inside Charlie's mind, I see Charlie blown forward, through the window. The glass shatters around him as he crashes through it and hits the sidewalk outside. Through the broken window, red smoke escapes into the night air.

"Charlie!" I shout into his mind, and I know that this is the scene I saw, of Charlie lying facedown in a pile of broken glass, red smoke surrounding him. I breathe several long, shuddery breaths as I wait for him to move. "Get up, Charlie," I urge. "Get up."

He doesn't move at first. But slowly, Charlie pushes himself over with one arm, and climbs to his knees. "Smoke bombs come in colors?" he asks weakly. He gets to his feet, his legs shaking beneath him, and the glass shards fall off him onto the pavement. "Tell me where you are," he says.

"I'm in a room on the second floor, the one with a window facing the salt flats," I say, trying to remember the confusing way Jasper brought me to this room. "Take the stairs to the left of you, then take them to the elevator up to level two. After that, there are three hallways. Take your first right at each one, and you'll end up at a wooden door. That's where I am."

Charlie mumbles under his breath, "I'm coming."

CHAPTER THIRTY-FOUR

Time passes slowly while I wait for Charlie, but since I've pulled out of his mind, my mind is now mine again—the voices are gone and the pounding has stopped. So, despite being stuck in this room, I can relax a little into the peace of having only my own voice in my head.

Less than five minutes have gone by since I got my own mind back when I hear yelling outside the warehouse. A door slams several times, and each time, another set of footsteps echo across the pavement.

"Where do you think you're going?" I hear Monty yell. "It's only nine! I paid you until two minutes *after* nine!"

I climb onto the counter and peer between the bars.

Below me, a group of people I don't recognize are streaming out of the warehouse, still covering their mouths with their shirts. They are headed toward a black SUV with darkened windows parked on the street, and Monty is right behind them. The wind is blowing hard against the building, and Monty leans into it, one hand securely holding his wig on his head.

"I said you have two more minutes of work!" Monty yells.

Without looking back, a tall, balding man unlocks the driver's door of the SUV. "Did you not see the bomb go off?" he asks.

"That wasn't a bomb, fool!" Monty yells. "Look around you; it's just red smoke!"

"I told you it wasn't worth the money," the man says. He shakes his head at the other psychics as they get into the car, and then he climbs into the driver's seat and starts the engine. The others grumble in agreement as they shut their car doors.

"You can't leave!" Monty wails. He runs toward the SUV, but they drive away before he reaches it. "Come back!"

When the car is out of sight, Monty leans over and puts his hands on his knees, and takes several loud, ragged breaths. "Gotta do everything myself," he says. He spits on the pavement, and then stands up. With his black bangs skewed diagonally across his forehead, he walks back into the warehouse.

Two more minutes, Monty said. One hundred twenty more seconds until the super laser fires at the asteroid, and half of Greece gets wiped off the map.

I climb off the counter and crouch down by Indigo's side. "We only have two minutes, Indigo. I need your help." I shake him gently, and a drop of blood lands on the dark bruise that's bloomed across both of his cheeks. I reach up to my forehead, and when I pull my hand away, it's bloody from where I hit my head repeatedly on the floor, trying to force the voices out. "Wake up!" I say, shaking Indigo until his body rattles like a dry stick, but he doesn't open his eyes. He's too far gone.

I have no other choice: Now that I'm back in my body, and my mind is clear, I know I'll have to stop the lasers from merging into a super laser on my own.

I can do this, I tell myself, as I sit cross-legged on the floor beside Indigo. I focus on breathing deeply, trying to get myself into a space calm enough to view the telescope, and hopefully, to bend it. I figure that if I bend it far enough to break it, the lasers won't merge into a super laser, and the asteroid will pass Earth safely.

I count myself down, starting at five, and when I get to one, I imagine myself flying up to the satellite. Sooner than I had hoped, I am soaring above the earth and funneling myself into the attached telescope's metal tube.

The darkness inside the telescope feels smothering, so I try to focus on the steps Michael drew for me, and slowly, the pictures become instructions in my mind. *Twist the metal frame of the large lens until it faces another direction, adjust the lens's new angle, rotate the tube* ... In this complete blackness, I imagine bending the metal gears that I saw in Michael's sketches, feeling their shapes meld in other directions. Once I can fully picture it, I try to recall how I felt on that night a year and a half ago when I accidentally bent the metal spoon, before I ever met Indigo, and it seems like a lifetime since then.

I remember I had just finished finals, so I had all of Christmas break ahead of me. Mom was talking to Charlie about college, and I was holding my coffee spoon after swirling in loads of creamer and honey. I was studying myself in it, how my face contorted in its silver surface, and feeling that day like I could do anything, that there were no limits to my life. It's like the world cracked open and showed me all the pathways I could take to get wherever I wanted.

I remember the intense energy of possibility that trembled through my body, until I felt all shaky and hyped up, and then my upper arms started to tingle. Heat coursed down my arms, through my wrists, into my fingers, and then, without moving my hand, the metal spoon was bending.

I have to do it again.

I funnel all of my thoughts about what my life could be—both normal and exceptional—into the metal gears. I think about going to New York with Charlie, attending college, living a normal life, but also one with a purpose, stopping people like Monty—and my arms slowly grow warm. But then I imagine trying to balance it all, and leaving home, and my doubt weighs on my mind, and my arms get cool again . . .

Focus, Callie, focus! The possibilities funnel through me, burning all of my edges, and although none of the options for my life are exactly *normal*, I'm okay with that, because maybe Mom's right and normal is boring—

—and then my future seems to crack open and show me everything I could do and be, taking my breath away. The swirling mass of emotions slowly becomes an intense tunnel of energy, and I can feel it project out of me and move objects as if I'm bending them with my own hands.

I envision the machine parts in Michael's drawings and let the arrows guide me through the steps. Heat races down my arms, through my wrists, and, as my fingers pulse with heat, my tension is replaced by this unearthly calm—and I can almost hear the screech of metal bending.

I first twist the metal-rimmed lens and bend it forward to change the angle, and then adjust the tube that looks like a black light. Each movement sends heat waves down my arms and through the tips of my fingers. The last three steps—bending the metal frame of the smaller lens, turning it back on itself, and tilting the bigger lens again—are slow going, and I have to keep focused on the feeling that the world has broken open and showed me all of my possible paths.

I imagine that the bending metal is screeching louder and louder, each millimeter twist a nearly blinding noise. In my head, it sounds like two cars slamming into each other, the crushing of steel against steel.

My fingertips feel like they're on fire, and the veins running up the insides of my wrists are pulsing with heat, until I'm sure I'm going to burn alive. . . . But then I feel the heat fading out of my arms, and the screeching winding down to a low whine, until it stops completely.

Moments later, my mind still focused on the broken telescope, I view the laser beams shooting from Earth. They travel across the dark sky for several seconds, until they merge at the satellite. As they funnel into the telescope, I hold my breath, hoping that I bent the metal far enough.

Then, as 9:02 turns into 9:03, the laser beams bounce against the mirrors and shoot off in all different directions into the dark universe, like falling stars.

In that second, I know that somewhere in the distance,

the asteroid is passing Earth and disappearing into the solar system, and across the world, a dark-eyed little boy is still alive. Then my mind lets go, every part of it burned to ash, and I sink into the floor, exhausted.

CHAPTER·THIRTY-FIVE

Heavy. Unbearably heavy.

Who knew skin could be so heavy?

There are weights in each part of my body, disguising themselves as bones. I am pinned to Earth by my body mass. But even though all of my muscles ache from the effort it took to bend the telescope, my head doesn't hurt, and more importantly, it's all *mine.* With my eyes still tightly closed, I start to hear sounds outside of my own head. First there's a loud, repetitive pounding, and then the pounding gives way to a sharp splintering sound.

When I finally wrench my eyes open, it takes inhuman strength, but it's worth it to see Charlie breaking through the door with an ax.

I feel a grin creep over my face. "You found me."

"You're a hard girl to find," he says through the broken slats of wood.

"The worst," I agree.

"I missed you," he says, slamming the ax into the door, "in my head." Charlie slams the ax into the door again, and another piece of wood splinters off. He peeks through the broken slats, and his gaze immediately flicks over to Indigo lying unconscious on the floor. A worried look crosses his face. "Did he hurt you?"

I shake my head. "That's my boss."

"Your boss?" he asks as he chops through the last piece of wood. It clatters to the floor, and Charlie leans down to get through the broken door. "What happened to your head?"

I wipe the blood from my forehead with my sleeve. "I'll tell you everything later," I promise.

Charlie steps through the broken wood slats, and runs across the room to me. He pulls me to my feet and wraps me into the tightest hug I've ever felt, one I had forgotten the exact taste of. I feel myself relaxing, muscle by muscle, because even though I'm still in this room in this horrible warehouse, Charlie's here. He's like a rock that the stream goes around but never pushes over.

"You made it," I whisper.

His hands rub up and down my arms, as if trying to reassure himself that I'm really here. "Was there ever a doubt?"

"No." His breath is warm on the top of my head. I lean my head back so I can look into his eyes. There are tears slipping out of the corners. I kiss each tear off his face, until I reach his lips.

There's nothing in the world like Charlie's kiss.

It's as warm as sunshine, cashmere blankets, and hot vanilla tea, all rolled into one. It's the kiss I live for, and would die for.

"I'm sorry," I say, my lips hovering an inch from his. "That kiss with Jasper, it never meant anything. Honestly. It was always you." Our lips touch again, and I feel sparks down to my toes.

"And I'm sorry too," Charlie says, "about bringing Amber to our place."

"Forgiven," we say at the same time.

Some minutes last hours, or months or years. Our minute lasts decades. The wind whistles through the barred window, carrying with it the smell of salt and the promise that somewhere outside this room, this world is waiting for Charlie and me.

"Let's get you home," he whispers in my ear, and I know at that moment that Charlie *is* home. He always has been.

"Help me get him out of here?" I ask, gesturing toward Indigo.

Charlie nods, already moving over to where Indigo is lying on the floor. He bends down and grabs Indigo's ankles, and I grab his wrists. Between the two of us, we lift him up and half drag him through the broken shards of door. In the hallway, Charlie hoists Indigo up and arranges him around his shoulders in the fireman's carry Richard taught him. "I got him from here," he says.

Charlie slowly follows me to the end of the long, twisted hallway to the elevator. We get in and press the button for the first floor, and the door closes us in.

"I'm not sure if he's still here, but we need to get out of here fast," I whisper, and then I flinch as my words are covered by the deafening squeak of the elevator.

"Whoever you're talking about," Charlie pants, his breath coming fast under Indigo's added weight, "I think they know we're coming."

The elevator stops with a bone-shaking jolt at the first floor. Charlie almost drops Indigo, but he grips Indigo tighter around the knees and widens his stance to keep his balance.

"Let me help."

"Got him," Charlie says. "Just get us out of here."

The doors open, and I peek my head out and look around. "I don't see anyone," I whisper. Charlie nods, readjusts Indigo on his shoulders, and follows me out of the elevator into the last row of supplies. I feel much safer in here than in the exposed warehouse. Even though Monty could be hiding anywhere in these aisles, the tall shelves of emergency supplies make me feel hidden.

"This looks familiar," Charlie says.

We walk through the canned food aisle, and then sneak down the rescue signal device aisle and pop out into the first aid aisle. As hard as we try to be quiet, our shoes keep squeaking across the concrete floor.

"Just a sec," Charlie says. He stops in front of a shelf stocked with oversized bandages, and sorts through the stuff with one hand while balancing Indigo on his shoulders with the other. When he finds a box of extra-large Band-Aids, he slides his finger into the box and pulls out a Wonder Woman bandage. "Hold still," he says, but I shake my head. "Don't tell me you don't like Wonder Woman."

"Who doesn't?" I ask. "But we have to hurry."

"And you have to stop bleeding." Charlie rips the backing off and sticks the bandage onto my forehead.

"Thanks. Seriously." I throw him a quick smile before moving down the aisle.

Charlie drops the bandage backing on the floor, grabs onto Indigo with both hands again, and hurries to keep up with me.

"I'm sorry I didn't believe you about being psychic,"

Charlie whispers. "There's no reason you'd lie to me about something like that."

"It's okay," I whisper back. I peek my head out of the end of the row, nod once, and we scurry across the aisle into the next row of shelves. "It's kind of hard to swallow."

"But I should've listened," he says. "When I told Colin that we fought again because you lied to me, he started peppering me with questions, like *he* was suddenly the expert on lying." He imitates Colin's voice. "'Were Callie's eyebrows raised? Did she touch her nose? Were there wrinkles across her forehead?'" He laughs quietly. "I guess he'd heard a Radioman show about these little expressions that give everything away in, like, less than a second."

"Microexpressions," I say. "In one one-hundred-twenty-fifth of a second."

"Yeah, that's it. And when I answered no to all those questions, he told me you weren't lying."

"And you believed him?"

Charlie peeks out of the second to last row and nods, and we quickly cross the aisle into the last row, which is filled with thousands of gas cans. At the end of the aisle is the back door. "Not at first," Charlie says. "But the more I thought about it, the more I realized that you'd have no reason to lie to me about something like that," he continues. "So I went to your house to apologize, and I found a pros and cons list of whether to tell me the truth. I couldn't believe it, so I googled the Bernsteins in Oakland, and they don't exist, not with a little girl named Emma, anyway."

Charlie turns to look at me, and when he does, he rotates Indigo's body too, and Indigo's foot smacks into a gas can. It falls to the ground, and its loud *thump* echoes through the warehouse. We stop moving immediately, but nobody comes down the aisle to find us. After several seconds, we start walking again, talking more quietly this time.

"So I put the pieces together," Charlie whispers. "End of story: I believe you."

"That means more to me than I can say," I respond. I'd say more but there's this big lump in my throat, like I swallowed my heart.

We reach the back door at the same time. Charlie tugs on the handle, but it doesn't budge. "Locked," he says.

"Then the front door is our only option."

We tiptoe back through the aisles and emerge into the main section of the warehouse. Here, the ceiling rises at least forty feet above us, crisscrossed with metal beams. Scattered across the floor are random boxes of emergency supplies, some dented like they've been kicked in, others cut open and overflowing with canned food.

"That's where we need to go," I whisper, pointing to the far end of the warehouse, where the EXIT sign glows above the front door. Between the front door and where we are, standing just on the edge of the aisles, there's enough room for two city buses, nose to tail. There is no sign of the two guards, and the room's practically empty, except for the white van. It's parked halfway across the space, directly in front of the glass-walled office, where Finn is sitting with his head in his hands.

Charlie hikes Indigo up on his shoulders again and peers across the space. "Should we make a run for it?"

Footsteps pound past us down the next row, and we leap back into the last aisle, grateful that there's a wall of boxes between us. Still, the person can't be more than twenty feet away. I listen to the footsteps getting farther away from us, and Monty pops out at the end of the aisle. He storms across the warehouse, his face steaming red with anger. In the office, Finn springs to his feet.

"Let's go while Monty's distracted," I whisper to Charlie. "But make sure he doesn't see you."

Charlie points at Monty, disbelief crossing his face. "Is that Montgomery Cooper, Junior? The billionaire?"

"The billionaire *psycho*." I glance at Monty as he passes the white van, and then back at Charlie. "Tell you later. Let's just get outta here."

Charlie nods. We step carefully out of the last aisle and tiptoe across the warehouse, every squeak of our feet strumming my nerves with fear. Across the warehouse, Monty reaches the office and steps into the open doorway. Finn, cowering a few feet away, strokes his red beard nervously. Both of them are so focused on each other that they don't notice us inching our way across the warehouse.

"Fifty-three years!" Monty shrieks as he steps through the doorway.

Charlie glances at me, and I point to the white van. "Hide there," I mouth, and he nods. He readjusts Indigo's body on his shoulders, and even though he hasn't said anything, I can tell that he's getting tired. With his back starting to bow from Indigo's weight, Charlie follows me toward the white van.

"If it stays on its current trajectory," Finn responds, "It'll return to earth by then. Otherwise—"

"Tell me you're kidding." Monty punches his left fist into his right palm once, and then again, and again. Each time, the smack of his fist gets louder.

Finn's glasses slip down his nose, and he quickly pushes them back up. "Sorry. I don't know what happened this time. The lasers just didn't merge."

"This time?" Monty spits on the floor. "This was the only time I had!"

Charlie and I duck behind the white van before they see us. We're halfway across the warehouse now, and as long as Monty doesn't turn around, we should be able to get past them and out the front door in less than a minute.

"Like I told you, I don't know why it didn't work," Finn says. He opens the laptop and starts punching buttons on the keyboard. "But the asteroid will be back in only—"

"Fifty-three years," Monty repeats. "When I'm over eighty years old." He kicks the trash can by the office door, and it crashes onto its side and spills out the plastic remains of what looks like several frozen dinners.

Finn picks up a plastic plate and places it back in the trash can. "That was unnecessary," he says.

"Unnecessary?" Monty yells. He storms into the room, pushes Finn out of the way, and shoves the laptop off the table. Finn leaps for it, but the laptop hits the floor with a loud crash. "So is waiting fifty-three more years!"

Finn falls to his knees, picks the laptop up, and cradles it like a baby. Behind his large circular glasses, his eyes gleam with anger. "I'll add this to your bill."

"You want me to pay for your stupid computer?" Monty says. "And who's going to pay for this, now that all of this is useless?" He shoves the table toward Finn, but he rolls out of the way and the table smacks into the floor. "And this?" Monty adds, kicking a chair toward Finn, who leaps to his feet. "And what about this?" Monty shoves the edge of a computer screen toward Finn, and Finn recoils just as it shatters across the floor where he was standing.

Charlie taps my shoulder, and we both duck our heads back behind the van. "Let's go," Charlie says, and he nods to Indigo's unconscious body across his shoulders. "We've gotta get him out of here."

I hold my index finger up. "Just a sec."

We poke our heads out from behind the van again and peer into the destroyed office. Monty is pacing back and forth now, kicking everything in his way. Finn is staring at Monty with pity, as if he's watching a spoiled child's temper tantrum.

"Look, I did everything you asked," Finn says patiently. "If you want to go ahead and destroy everything you have, do it, but I'm leaving." He hugs his laptop close to his chest and tries to step around Monty, but Monty blocks him from leaving the room. Finn steps in the other direction, and so does Monty. "Very funny," Finn says. "Now let me go. I expect that money in my account today."

"I don't owe you anything," Monty growls. He pulls his gun out of his jacket and points it at Finn. Finn immediately throws his hands up and backs up into the room. The laptop clatters to the floor once again.

"Don't do it," Finn says. His voice is steady, but I can tell he's fighting to stay calm. "It won't prove anything."

"What do you know about it?" Monty shouts. "Get back!"

Finn backs up against the computer bank, his hands in the air; and I immediately recognize this moment: I saw this in my vision, when Monty shot Finn. A shiver courses through my body when I see it. It's startling coming face to face with your own precognition: it's like having a déjà vu, but it hasn't happened yet.

"You move when I say you move," Monty continues.

Charlie taps me on the shoulder again, but I glance at him and shake my head.

"I can't leave him here, Charlie. But you should go. Get Indigo to safety."

Charlie crouches down and lays Indigo behind the van. "I was going to say I'll come with you." He stands back up. "I never thought I'd say this, but I wish I still had my ax."

"Me too." I feel blood dribble down my forehead to my cheek, and I wipe it away with the back of my sleeve. "Let's do this." I slip out from behind the van and move silently toward the office, and without looking back, I know that Charlie is right behind me.

"Monty, come on," Finn is saying as we get closer to the open doorway. "Just put the gun down." Monty's only a few feet away from him now.

"I was going to do something big," Monty rants. "This metal . . . it will change the world. And I was going to be on the forefront."

"You're not a failure," Finn says, and then his eyes bulge as he notices us. I put my finger to my lips and he nods slightly.

"But this would have made me a leader," Monty says. "A leader like Dad. But better. *For* something better." He's waving the gun around like he's forgotten it's in his hand.

We are right outside the office now. In the glass, my reflection doesn't look like me at all. The girl in the reflection has blood streaming down her face, but she doesn't look scared; she looks determined. On the other side of the glass, Monty hasn't noticed us yet, and Finn is struggling not to look at us or give us away.

"Run," I whisper to Charlie, who shakes his head. Instead, he grabs my hand and holds it, and we enter the doorway together.

"Finn didn't do anything," I announce. "I bent the telescope."

Monty flips around and glares at me. He points his gun toward us, and there is a huge circle of sweat under his armpit. "Shut up," he says to me, and then he turns back to Finn. "And you—" Monty takes a step toward him, and I push Monty from behind just as Finn sticks his foot out. Monty stumbles and falls forward, his arms spinning and one hand grappling to hold onto his weapon. As he hits the concrete, he tries to catch himself with the hand holding the gun.

BANG!

I scream as Finn collapses to the floor, blood pouring from his shoulder.

Groaning, Monty lifts his head up an inch off the concrete and stares at Finn as if he can't believe what just happened. "Did I . . . ," he stutters. "Did I just do that?"

I move quickly across the office toward Finn. "He'll bleed to death if we don't—"

"Don't move!" Monty orders, swinging the gun my way. I stop and watch Monty climb slowly to his feet.

"Monty," I say. "You have to help him."

"Help him?" Monty asks. "He didn't help *me*." Despite his tough words, Monty looks like the scared kid I first met, the one with the A-holes cap, and I know that he doesn't want to do this. He just wants to be somebody, and he doesn't know how else to do it.

"You can still prove your dad was wrong about you," I say, "if you help him."

Monty's lip trembles. "How?"

"Take that power cord and wrap it around his wound," I say, silently thanking Indigo for his annoying after-work training sessions that I thought were totally useless at the time. "An inch or so above and below," I add. "It should stop the bleeding." Monty hesitantly picks up the power cord and wraps it around Finn's shoulder, even though Finn shrieks in pain every time Monty touches him. "Now tie the ends under his arm," I continue. Monty ties the ends of the cord under Finn's arm, and Finn whimpers.

"I'll call an ambulance," Charlie says, but as he pulls his phone out of his pocket, Monty startles like he's been in a dream. He snaps his gun up toward us again.

"No cops," Monty says. "Put it away. Now."

Charlie slides the phone back into his pocket.

"Who are you?" Monty demands.

"Callie's boyfriend."

"Well, Callie's boyfriend, if you never see my name on a building, you can thank your girlfriend for that."

"But your name *is* on buildings," I insist. "Remember the Cooper Science building?"

"That's my dad!" Monty walks toward the doorway, his gun still pointed at us. "Now I don't want to do this, but you know I can't let you leave." Monty clicks the trigger back, and as calm as I'm trying to be, having a gun pointed at you in real life is totally different than in a vision. In this case, my body takes over before my brain can stop it—my palms start sweating and adrenaline rockets through my muscles—and I have to force myself to pull it together, and quickly.

"You won't kill us," I say slowly. "Because then the police will come looking for us, and eventually, it will lead them to you," I add, trying to sound more confident than I feel. "And you don't deserve to end up in prison, although some therapy would do you a world of good. Now put the gun down."

"I can't." Monty shakes his head back and forth violently. "You've left me no choice," he says. "I was never the best at anything," he adds. "*This* was my gold medal!"

"You're not a killer," I insist, trying to draw his attention away from Charlie. "You don't deserve to go to prison."

"How do you know what I deserve?"

"I don't. But I do know that this isn't who you are," I say. "You're better than this."

Monty steps forward and presses the gun against my chest. His hand is shaking, and the cold barrel trembles against my T-shirt, making my heart pound with fear. "You don't know anything about me." He presses the barrel against my body so hard that it pushes me out of the office and across the warehouse floor. "You don't know what I'm capable of."

"But I do," a voice says from behind us.

Monty stops, and his eyes narrow into a deadly glare. He unconsciously lifts the gun inches away from my chest, and I glance behind me. Jasper is standing in the office doorway, shaking with rage. His fists are clenched by his sides, and his face looks as if the blood has been drawn out of him. *He didn't leave.*

"What are you gonna do, boy?" Monty asks him. "Time to choose: money or—"

Suddenly there's a screech as the right end of a metal beam bends away from the ceiling. Monty looks up, and his eyes widen when he sees the sharp piece of metal dangling above him.

"Not money," Jasper says, and the left end of the metal beam bends with a loud screech, forming a large C-shape.

"You wouldn't—" Monty says, but before he can finish his sentence, the metal beam crashes down on him, trapping him against the floor. He tries to wriggle out from under the curved beam, but one side of it starts wrapping tighter around him. He squirms in the other direction, but the other side wraps around him until he's pinned on both sides, and he can't move. "I gave you everything," Monty shrieks. "You were just a kid on the street until I—"

The metal beam bends over Monty's mouth, and he mumbles angry words beneath it.

Ignoring Monty, Jasper stares across the room at me. "I'm sorry, Callie," Jasper says. "I choose you." Our eyes lock for a long moment, and my heartbeat explodes like fireworks in my chest. It's like the first time we met all over again: with my heart in free-fall, I circle round and round into the blue whirlpool of his eyes. I try to rip my gaze away from his, but it's like we're stuck there, our fates locked together in a passionate, confusing embrace. After several seconds, Jasper walks quickly past me to the front door. He puts his hand on the doorknob, but pauses, still facing the door. "Even if you don't choose me."

He pulls the door open and walks out into the night, and I watch him until the door closes behind him. I don't notice until that second that I'm gripping Charlie's hand so tightly my fingers are cramping up.

I glance at Charlie, and my heart starts to slow its rapid

pounding. Charlie nods at me, and I look back at the closed door, envisioning Jasper still standing there. *Jasper chose me.* He chose to save my life and give up everything Monty had given him. And some part of me knows that that's what love is—the ability to sacrifice yourself for the person you love, even if you don't get love in return—and I wish Jasper didn't feel that way for me. Even though it doesn't change how betrayed I feel by him, there's a softness in my heart that wasn't there a few minutes ago. It reminds me that Jasper was someone I cared about deeply. Sure, he betrayed me in the worst way possible, but then he came back for me. He didn't leave Charlie and me to die. I know, at that moment, I will always love him for that.

"Callie?" I feel someone squeeze my hand, and I tune back into Charlie talking to me. "Should I call the ambulance now?"

I nod. "Tell them there's three pick-ups."

Charlie pulls out his phone and dials 911, and I glance back at the door. There's good in Jasper, I've seen it. Part of me wants to run out there and tell him I forgive him, but the other, stronger part of me is going to stay right here with Charlie. I lock my hand in his, and we walk over to where Monty is trapped under the metal beam.

"An ambulance is coming," I say, glaring down at Monty. "And I'm going to tell them everything. But if you ever tell them that my mom helped you—" I feel Charlie look at me questioningly, but I continue, "I will haunt your dreams for the rest of your life."

Monty mumbles angrily as we turn away.

"Wait," I say, and turn back to Monty. I lean down and carefully straighten his fake black bangs across his forehead. "There. That's better."

Monty mumbles through the metal. I can't make out any exact words, but I imagine they're an equal mix of vengeance and vanity.

Charlie and I walk over to the van, and behind it, Indigo is still lying across the floor, unconscious. Charlie picks him up off the ground and strains to lift him over his shoulders.

"Think he'll wake up soon?" Charlie asks, settling Indigo's weight equally across both shoulders.

"I sure hope so."

"Wait for me," Finn calls from behind us. He stumbles out of the office, one hand pressed against the extension cord wrapped around his shoulder. Charlie and I turn around and wait for him to catch up to us.

"You okay?" I ask Finn.

"Do I look okay?"

Finn's shoulder is dark with blood, but it looks like the bleeding has stopped. Still, when he reaches us, I try to help him by lacing his uninjured arm over my shoulder, but he pushes me away. Then the four of us, bloody, hurt, conscious and unconscious, limp through the warehouse toward the exit.

"Can you really do that?" Charlie asks as we walk slowly across the warehouse. "Haunt dreams?"

"Nah. But he doesn't know that."

Charlie grins at me, and for a moment, everything is okay again.

But then I pull open the front door, and look out into the empty night. I quickly scan the surrounding buildings, looking for any hint of Jasper, but there's no one as far as I can see. He's gone.

I slowly shake my head, and force myself to focus on what Charlie is saying to me.

"I said, do you want me to go after him?" Charlie asks.

I glance out at the salt flats, to where Finn is stumbling off into the night.

"Let him go," I say aloud, and I know I'm not talking about Finn at all: I'm really convincing myself of what I have to do with Jasper.

Charlie and I settle Indigo comfortably against the outside of the warehouse, and then Charlie takes my hand again and squeezes it. I look up, and in Charlie's eyes, there are questions about me and Jasper, and me and him.

"Emergency ax," I say, and he smiles at our familiar game. It's my answer to Charlie's unspoken question about who I choose to love, and he knows it.

"Lit wick," Charlie responds. "With both ends burning."

In the distance, the ambulance's siren breaks through the night. Charlie's arm laces around my waist, and we both look at the salt flats glowing white under the moon, like a fresh field of snow.

"Let's start over," Charlie says. He turns to me and holds out his hand. "Hi, I'm Charlie, and I'm not psychic."

I grin and twist my pinkie finger around his. "Hi, I'm Callie, and I am," I say. "Is that a problem?"

"Not at all," Charlie says, shaking his head. "Not at all."

Charlie kisses me.

It is more than I remembered a kiss could be: it is true, and good, and life-affirming. It is *everything*. Because with Charlie, it's not about flash and glamour, smoke and mirrors, things that look better from the outside than the inside. In other words, we don't have a movie-worthy love scene.

We have *us*, which is better than a movie. Our kiss is real, and rich, and deeper than anything I've ever felt before. And after, both of us breathless with all of life's possibilities, we hold each other as we watch the ambulance race toward us, its red and blue lights painting the salt flats bright colors we've never seen. Then we look into each other's eyes, and I don't hide anything—because now, he can know all of me.

"I missed us," I say, and his lips murmur his agreement.

US. A two-letter word that spells out a whole life.

THREE MONTHS LATER

I'm almost packed for my move to New York when Mom opens my bedroom door and pops her head in. "You almost ready, honey?" she asks.

I nod. Over the past three months, I've packed everything meaningful from here: my computer, my clothes, a few books, a picture of Mom and Richard, and a picture of Michael, the man I'm getting used to thinking of as *Dad*. I wanted to bring a picture of Indigo, but he refused. "You can always come back to visit," he said when I dropped by the office to say good-bye. It's hard for him, though: Indigo's returning to normal more slowly than he had hoped after being cut off from his body for so long. And as supportive as he's trying to be about my move, I can tell he's going to miss me.

"Are you nervous about classes?" Mom asks. She's trying to stall me from zipping my suitcase.

I roll my most faded hoodie into a tight ball and stuff it into the last few available inches of space. "Very," I respond. It's sort of true. Although I'm not very nervous about the few freshman NYU courses I'll be taking next fall, I'm very nervous about my psychic training classes—which are much more strenuous than biology and algebra—of how to bend all types of physical substances with my mind, and how to use mind control to convince people to change their decisions, hopefully for the better. "Finding the bad guys," Indigo used to say during my initial training. At the New York office, the training will continue, but I hear it's harder, and the boss is tougher. But luckily, Charlie will be beside me the whole time. And even Amber, who's starting to become a friend.

I finish stuffing my hoodie into my suitcase and try to zip it, but it just pops right back open. "Let me help," Mom says, sitting on the overstuffed bag and holding the zippers together.

"Maybe I packed a bit too much," I say, but quickly zip the suitcase closed before she can agree with me.

"Did you ever say good-bye to that guy friend of yours?" she asks. Mom's thrilled that I'm back with Charlie. She's reminded me a few times about Mr. Bernstein's nephew, the one with the motorcycle—and I can tell she hopes I have nothing to do with him.

"Haven't seen him," I say, and it's true. I haven't seen Jasper since he saved our lives from Monty. But I got a letter in the mail the other day. It was postmarked from some random city in the Midwest, one that started with a C, like Cincinnati or Cleveland. There wasn't a return address on it, just the picture of a flamingo on the moon and a bubble caption that said, "Wish you were here." I recall the night I planted the flamingo into Jasper's dream, and I remember telling Jasper that I didn't dream, and so sleeping felt like being dead, but that's not true anymore. Now, every time I sleep, I have dreams of Jasper, and in every one of them, I'm painfully alive. Every time I've said *I'm sorry*, and *I loved you, too*. But not everyone you love is a forever. Sometimes you can love someone for a reason, and for a time, and although you never stop loving them, no matter how much they may betray you, you move on, because they aren't the one who makes you into an *us*.

"Make sure to say good-bye to my hubby," Mom says shyly, and I grin at her. Ever since they eloped, Mom has loved calling Richard her hubby.

"Will do," I respond, and Mom reaches over and gives me a hug. I know how rare those are, so I try to soak it up.

"Love you," I say.

"Ditto, kiddo," she responds, the closest words she can find to the word *love*.

I zip my suitcase and drag it downstairs to the living room. Richard is sprawled out on the couch, drinking a soda and watching a baseball game on television. Now that they're married, we don't have to watch our neighbors' TVs from the roof anymore. She gave Richard a television for his wedding present, which I thought was a grand gesture on Mom's part.

In front of the television, sitting cross-legged on the floor, is Michael. He's visiting today from Shady Hills. Although Indigo refuses to say why he hid the truth about Michael from me for so long, he's making up for it by bringing him here once a week to spend time with Mom and me. And Richard doesn't mind having Michael here occasionally. "Someone I can watch the games with," he says.

I've started to get to know Michael, but I know it will take a long time and many hours in front of the television, tapping our shoes and trying to communicate, for us to really understand each other. There's so much I want to know about him, and most of these are things that Mom can never know.

Mom's still in the dark about my psychic abilities, which I know Indigo wouldn't approve of, but it's the only way to assure her safety. Mom doesn't even know that I'm aware she stole government secrets, and luckily, she never has to. Finn had already pleaded guilty for breaking into the NASA website to name a star after his mother, which briefly made the website available to the entire public, so no one knows exactly what information went missing. Besides, it's irrelevant that Mom took the asteroid trajectory information since the asteroid passed safely by the earth. And since Finn plea-bargained down to no jail time by testifying against Monty, who ended up in prison for treason and attempted terrorism, no one has to take the blame. Now Mom's no longer in danger, and I'm going to make sure it stays that way.

A *bing* sounds on my phone, and when I glance at it, it's a text message from Charlie. **r u ready?**

"Time to go," I say. On the floor, Michael just taps his shoes as fast as he can. I smile down at him. After spending the summer with Michael, I know that his tapping means he's feeling emotional, and this time it's about me. And although I'm not ready to call him Dad, at least I know that he never abandoned me. He was just across the city all this time, locked up in Shady Hills.

"Hey kiddo," Richard says, standing up from the couch and pulling me into a giant hug. "I'll miss you."

"Right back at you," I mumble into Richard's broad shoulder. "No good-byes, remember," I add. "I'll call you when I get there."

"Drive safe," Richard says, handing me the car keys, "and keep your eyes on the road." Ever since Richard gave me his old car so that Charlie and I could drive to New York, he feels responsible for my safety, and for once, Mom isn't worried about finding me dead on the road somewhere. When Richard says I'll be okay, she trusts him.

"I'll drive like I already know what's coming," I say, and Michael grins down at the floor. I pull open the front door, and then I pause for a second, looking at the world I love around me, the one that is about to change.

Then I throw my bag over my shoulder, give my mom a good-bye hug, and head out to my future.

On the road, I text Charlie. **See you soon.**

ACKNOWLEDGMENTS

Writing teaches you a lot about life. It teaches you that you can persevere past the hard parts and start over fresh the next day. It teaches you that you can bring forth your best on command, but sometimes your worst sneaks through, and that's okay too. But mostly, it teaches you that you can't do it by yourself.

I didn't do this by myself.

My gratitude goes out to my amazing editors, Katherine Tegen and Katie Bignell, for all their hard work, as well as the rest of my KT Books team: Katie Fitch, Amy Ryan, Kathryn Silsand, Maya Packard, David Klimowicz, Ruiko Tokunaga, Alana Whitman, Rosanne Romanello, and

Lauren Flower. And also Josh Cochran, for my beautiful cover.

I am incredibly grateful to my agent, Jodi Reamer. You are truly a magic maker, and a great inspiration to me. Here's to lots of Disneyland trips in our future!

My writing community has been invaluable to this book—it would literally not exist without them. I especially want to thank Tara Dairman, Jenny Goebel, and Laura Resau. Thanks also to the SCBWI Rocky Mountain division. This is our TRIBE! My special thanks goes to Kami Garcia for all of her support and encouragement. It's meant more to me than I can say.

My teachers deserve thanking too—Simon Fill, for helping me with character, and my earlier teachers who believed in me despite all evidence that they shouldn't: Jewel Speers Brooker, Dick Hallins, Breda Ennis, Pauline Fry, and Mrs. Shindler.

To my readers, thank you! thank you! And to the readers who gave my first book great reviews, please know that I've read them over and over. You gave me hope that I could write a second.

To the Edwards family and the Barnard family, who showed me that in-laws can be a wonderful and fulfilling part of my life. Thank you for being a part of my family and heart.

To Allie, Danny, Fletcher, and Maddie—every day I

find another reason to love you! F&M—I know you will do great things. (An aunt can tell.)

My love and eternal gratitude goes out to my parents, for whom there are not enough words to thank them for all they have done for me. They are truly extraordinary and deserve all the happiness this world has to offer. You did good!

To my husband, Tyler, for helping to write and rewrite the plot of this book numerous times, and keeping me sane more times than that. Thank you for believing in me way beyond the point when I believed in myself. I love you and Alex (and our soon-to-be-born son!) beyond reason. You are truly the home in my heart to which I will always return gratefully and with open arms.

Her Oscar-nominated performance
killing villains on screen did nothing to prepare
her for escaping a madman in real life . . .

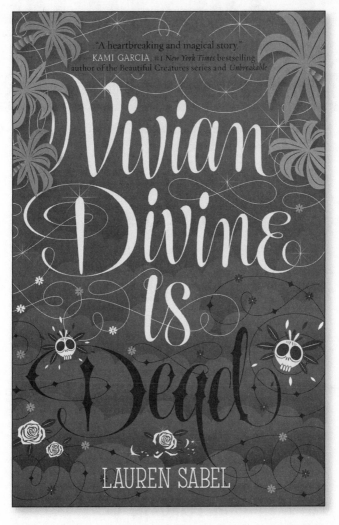

"A heartbreaking and magical story."
KAMI GARCIA #1 *New York Times* bestselling
author of the *Beautiful Creatures* series and *Unbreakable*

Vivian Divine Is Dead

LAUREN SABEL

"An enticing combination love story and murder."
—*Publishers Weekly*